THE
Best
AMERICAN
SHORT STORIES
1952

THE
Best
AMERICAN
SHORT STORIES
1952

and The Yearbook of the American Short Story

Edited by
MARTHA FOLEY
ASSISTED BY JOYCE F. HARTMAN

19   52

HOUGHTON MIFFLIN COMPANY   BOSTON

The Riverside Press Cambridge

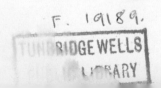

TO
DAVID BURNETT

ACKNOWLEDGMENT

GRATEFUL ACKNOWLEDGMENT for permission to reprint the stories in this volume is made to the following:

To the Editors of *The Atlantic Monthly, Epoch, Furioso, Harper's Bazaar, Harper's Magazine, The Hudson Review,* Little, Brown and Company, *Mademoiselle, New Mexico Quarterly, New-Story, The New Yorker, Northern Review, Prairie Schooner, Today's Woman, Tomorrow, Town and Country,* and *Western Review;* and to Bill Berge, Robert O. Bowen, Kay Boyle, Ray Bradbury, Hortense Calisher, Nancy Cardozo, Nancy G. Chaikin, Ann Chidester, Charles Edward Eaton, George P. Elliott, Elizabeth Enright, Hugh Garner, Martha Gellhorn, Emilie Glen, Nancy Hale, Philip Horton, Susan Kuehn, Bethel Laurence, Frank Rooney, William Saroyan, Stuart Schulberg, Jean Stafford, Wallace Stegner, James Still, Harvey Swados, Mark Van Doren, Daniel Waldron, Christine Weston, and Hisaye Yamamoto.

FOREWORD

A *SHORT STORY* is a story that is not too long." This
definition was lightheartedly agreed upon after a lengthy
discussion some fifteen years ago by a group of eminent writers
and critics, including Sherwood Anderson and Edward J. O'Brien
and has been often quoted. Whimsical though it is, as a definition
it is essentially correct.

Approaching the short story from another angle, that of how to
write it, in a fiction workshop at Columbia University, my students
and I have come up with an appraisal of just what a short story writer
is trying to do. This appraisal, too, is much oversimplified but goes
like this: "Dear Reader," the short story writer is saying, "I want to
tell you about some interesting people I have known; how they became
what they were; what they did; what happened to them when they
did it, and how they felt about what happened to them."

Looking at the stories in this collection in the light of that appraisal,
readers will find, I think, that the writers of 1952 have known an
excitingly wide variety of people. Some, such as the schoolteacher in
Hortense Calisher's "A Wreath for Miss Totten," or the husband and
wife in Philip Horton's "What's In a Corner," or the father and son
in William Saroyan's "Palo," they certainly have met and will recognize. Even the settlers on another planet in Ray Bradbury's fantasy
"The Other Foot" will be recognizable.

The boy in Kay Boyle's "The Lost" or the eccentric skater in
Emilie Glen's "Always Good for a Belly Laugh" probably will be
brand-new to readers while the decaying main character in Nancy
Hale's "Brahmin Beachhead" is likely to have been met before only
by those who know a certain segment of New England society. But
whether the characters in any of the twenty-nine stories in this volume
are familiar or strange, I believe readers are likely to remember them.

And is this all, readers may ask, to these stories — the people in
them? The answer is that every worth-while fiction writer, in taking

the living material he has known, transmutes it into something beyond flesh and blood, imbues it with a fourth-dimensional quality which is known as art.

Illumination of this was magnificently given by William Faulkner in his speech accepting the Nobel Award for Literature which I quoted in the foreword to last year's collection of *The Best American Short Stories* and which can stand many requotings. "I decline to accept the end of man. . . . I believe that man will not merely endure: he will prevail. He is immortal, not because he alone among creatures has an inexhaustible voice but because he has a soul, a spirit capable of compassion and sacrifice and endurance. The poet's, the writer's, duty is to write about these things. It is his privilege to help man endure by lifting his heart, by reminding him of the courage and honor and hope and pride and compassion and pity and sacrifice which have been the glory of his past. The poet's voice need not be merely the record of man, it can be one of the props, the pillars to help him endure and prevail."

"Not merely a record" — these are words which should help readers become aware of the difference between the kind of writing that is found in the daily newspaper reports, feature articles in magazines and in non-fiction books, valuable although many of these may be, and the kind of writing found in good fiction. It is this "not merely a record" which I hope you will find in this collection.

There are few war stories. Comparatively few were published during the past year. Important war stories have a way of being written during times of peace. In spite of the number of war stories which appeared shortly after the close of the Second World War, it is likely that most of the significant stories of that conflict still are to be written. It was many years after the end of the First World War before such books as *All Quiet on the Western Front* and *Farewell to Arms* appeared.

Wordsworth described poetry as "emotion recollected in tranquillity." This seems equally true of fiction. Writers who have lived through the Second World War and the Korean outbreak need time for distillation of their reaction to the impact of such events.

This year again a great many stories either about children, or about adult's from a child's point of view, have been published in the magazines. Tennessee Williams, speaking to one of my classes at Columbia, said he believed all fiction writing stemmed out of a writer's childhood, that he knew it to be true in his own case. Whether this is generally true I am not sure although it can be said definitely that most new young writers first write about children. We are seeing emerge, as we have for several years now, an entire new generation of authors and so we have many stories about children.

With so many magazines, both "little" and popular, devoting a majority of their pages to articles, it is sad to have to note the passing of a magazine like *Tomorrow* which published so many excellent short stories. At the same time, it is good to see that *New-Story*, edited by Americans, printed in English and published in Paris, and devoted entirely to short stories, has thus far been able to maintain high standards.

Harper's Magazine this year has been especially outstanding for the distinguished short stories it has published. And *The New Yorker*, often accused of a "typed" story does not receive quite its due from some critics. Fifty-two weeks a year, *The New Yorker* publishes serious fiction of much wider range and scope than most magazines.

Mademoiselle and *Harper's Bazaar*, as usual, have printed fiction of a very high standard. It has been said in a previous foreword that it is a pity men miss so much reading pleasure because, of course, they do not see the fashion magazines.

Twelve of the stories in this anthology are from the "little magazines." I believe that one of the real values to the general reader of a collection such as this is that it provides him with access to the stories in these magazines which have limited circulations and do not appear on his newsstand. Long before Ernest Hemingway had his first short story published in the *Double Dealer* in New Orleans, the little magazines were the birthplace of most important new writing in this country.

In spite of the trend toward non-fiction in many magazines, more short stories of literary merit have been published this year than for many years previously. Ninety-three short stories by Americans appear on the Roll of Honor in the back of the book. All are worthy of being reprinted. The list of distinctive short stories, also in the back of the book is the longest in many years. Nineteen-fifty-two's is a rich literary harvest.

Joyce Hartman's assistance again has been of great value to me this year. I wish to thank her publicly here.

I close with my annual tribute to one of the greatest friends American literature ever had, the late Edward J. O'Brien, the founder and editor for twenty-six years of *The Best American Short Stories*.

MARTHA FOLEY

New York City

CONTENTS

Contents

Contents

THE
Best
AMERICAN
SHORT STORIES
1952

(From Furioso)
Winner of the Knopf-Furioso
Fiction Contest for 1951

THAT LOVELY GREEN BOAT

BY BILL BERGE

*S*HE WAS a duckboat, you know, like the kind you've seen and hungered after in the catalogues you look through during winter nights when the river's frozen hard and black like granite, and the wind is moaning to come in, and the train whistles are howling like souls come out of Chippahanock Cemetery. Only in the catalogue, her lightness and smoothness don't show, and you can't feel her turn in her own length or guess how fast she'll go upstream against an east wind and the waves chopping at her.

She was made of thin lath, her bow decked over, and she was painted light green — the color of maple leaves in early spring, and varnished with clear varnish and sanded and varnished and sanded again, and worked on with steel wool until the bottom was as smooth as the granite ice in winter that froze without wind. She was swift and light, like a kingfisher, and she seemed blonde in her greenness.

She would have been perfect for a light motor if the back end had been built up stronger, but we didn't have a motor. But she rowed well, and nothing could touch her. And she looked blonde in her greenness.

We would come down to her by the river early in the morning — the three of us, Carl, his sister, Helen, and me — and she would be waiting for us there on the sand that had been left by the June rise of the river, and her greenness and the dry gold sand and Helen's hair all seemed blonde and light and lovely at once.

Helen and Carl and I would come down to the river early in the morning and find it smooth, without a ripple, save where a snag divided the surface or a whiff of wind ruffled it like a ribbon; and we would get in the boat and row out on the dark glass, heading downstream with the sun behind us, for the Mississippi flows from east to west there.

We would anchor her on the sandbar that ran down the middle of the river, lining her bow on the trees that stood a breath above the far bend to make sure she was over the center, and then we would get out of the boat in water only up to our knees, and walking toward shore, steadily go deeper until the water was over our heads and as deep as anyone could want.

We wore suits that summer, though it was early in the morning, for Carl was sixteen, and I was fourteen, and Helen was just fourteen, and she didn't have just nipples any more like a boy, but soft round swellings the shape of lemons or young pears. And I wished I was her brother instead of Carl so that her Uncle John would be my uncle too, and then I could stay there on the river all year around, fishing and swimming and skating, and rowing her in the green duck boat.

Then, while we were swimming, the river would begin to break up like a girl's skin that gets wet and cold and then wrinkles; but you would never see it doing this, but all at once you would look up and see that the mirror was shattered and shrivelled the way you find it at noon or any other time of the day; and you would feel just under your skin the peacefulness gone out of the river; and you would know the river's night was over and that it was time for breakfast.

Aunt Jane Springer would have a pile of pancakes as big as plates waiting for us, and after breakfast we would run the trotlines and pull up the fish traps that were longer than a man is tall, and the length of a man's arm across, shaped in a cylinder of strong wire with an entrance like a cone that a fish could come in by but never leave again.

And then, if Carl didn't start working in the garage, making something like bird houses or broom holders or anything you could make in the winter when it was too cold to go outside, or if he didn't have chores to do, the three of us would cross to the island and hunt for coon tracks, or stalk the big blue herons, or shoot crows or swim off the bank. It was deep along the shore of the island, so deep in places that you could not touch bottom when you dived — even by holding a rock in your hands when you went down; and you would come up, sometimes, with your chest feeling crushed and then about to explode and then crushed again; and once my nose bled and I could not go down again all day.

But sometimes, when Carl stayed behind, Helen and I would cross the island and lie on the bank on the channel side and watch for the towboats pushing their barges up or down the river, and if the *Mark Twain* or the *Lone Star* came along, we waved, because their crews always waved back. Sometimes we saw diesels, but we always felt sad about the diesels — both of us — because they were so small and blunt and ugly and work-a-day, and never so nice as the stern-wheelers.

At night, the three of us slept on the sleeping porch — Carl on my left and Helen on my right, if I was lying on my back. Carl always fell asleep immediately, like a stone dropping into the river, but Helen and I would light the lamp between our cots and read until midnight. Sometimes Carl was troubled and talked in his sleep, and once he got up and walked completely around his bed talking in his sleep, and then lay down again without waking up. Helen and I would ask him questions and he would answer the sound of our words but not the sense, saying, "Got to tie up the boat. That lovely green boat's going to float away. Got to tie up the boat."

Things would happen to me at night that summer, and in the morning I would wake and find them and think I had some awful disease until finally I was so worried about other people catching it from me that I told Carl about it, but he said it was regular and natural enough. And he took me out in the green duck boat and talked to me and connected it up with other things I already knew; and then he gave me makings and we smoked and just drifted.

Every day was maple-green and gold and lovely that summer.

II

One day in August as Helen and I sat resting after a swim off the dock, the water drying on us leaving our skins wrinkled as though with age, one of those high-priced, syrup-colored, inboard motorboats came barrelling down the river, passed us, and then made a wide sweeping turn just inside the sandbar, and came back upstream.

"My, that's a fine boat," Helen said.

"Yes, it is," I said.

The motor cut out just then, and the boat coasted over before the dock like a fat mallard hen floating half asleep with the current, but coming upstream and being braked by the current so it could land with just a little bump at the far end of the dock. A brown-haired boy about as old as Carl held the boat to the dock and in a voice just a cut above normal talking said, "Do you want a ride?"

He said it in the way a man with five dollars offers to loan you a dollar just to show you he's got money and can afford to borrow out.

"No, thanks," I said. "We got boats of our own."

"I see you have," he said, as though I had been trying to explain to him an arithmetic problem he had solved the year before. "You got a motor for that green boat?"

"Don't want a motor," I said. "Rowing, she stays on the water. With a motor, she'd fly."

"Do *you* want a ride?" he said again, nodding his head toward Helen.

"I told you once —"

"I don't mean you, I mean your sister."

"He's not my brother," Helen said. She didn't even look at me when she spoke.

"Do you want a ride?" the boy said again

"No, she doesn't want a ride," I said.

"Yes, I'd like a ride," Helen said, as though she had just been awakened for breakfast.

"Wait a minute, Helen, you don't even know his —"

But she was running down the dock to stop suddenly by the boat and put her hand out, touching and petting the syrup-colored deck as though it was a horse's neck. "Yes, I'd like a ride," she said again, and she stepped down into the boat and settled on the leather seat like a great blue heron feeling for land under her when she's coming in to land big and awkward against a rough skipping wind.

The stranger gunned the motor and they cut away from the dock and up the river. I watched the boat go flying up the river and then go out of sight around the point. And I watched after it was gone until I couldn't hear the motor any more — as if I could watch instead of hear its sound — and I knew they must be up near Andalusia by then.

I sat on the dock and splashed my feet in the water and got cold and shivered and wrote my initials in the oil scum on the barrels that hold up the platform of the dock, and then wrote Helen's initials and then scratched them out and got up and ran and dived off the dock and hit the water wrong so that I was hurt where a boy hurts the worst and felt sick as though I had swallowed too much river water, and then came back to the dock swimming on my back, and crawled up on the platform and banged my shin and lay down on my back with my knees up, watching the sky and the trees change suddenly from blue and green-gold to red to hot white and then to October dun — all in a minute.

Helen was late for supper — so late Aunt Jane Springer got mad and told us to go ahead and eat without Helen, and asked herself out loud where Helen could have gone — clear up to the Rock Point dam, certainly not much farther. And then, as we were sitting down, we heard the motor faintly like a fly buzzing outside the screen door, and then it commenced to get louder and pretty soon it sounded like a nighthawk coming out of a dive, and we knew that the stranger had cut his motor and was coasting upstream to the dock. Then the motor gunned up again and in a few seconds it began to die away up the river. Helen came in then with her cheeks showing red even under her sunburn, and she was pretty and breathless and a little nervous and she asked Aunt Jane's pardon for being late. She would have been pretty any other day but this — her hair the color of dry gold sand and her skin blushing red under the color of wet gold sand — but I didn't even look at her.

But by bedtime, I could forgive her, and after we had undressed on the dark porch, standing with our backs to each other — Carl was already in bed — I said to her, "Do you want to read tonight?"

"Not especially," she said.

"You can read the book I got," I said.

"I don't want to read it."

"I'm almost done with it, anyway," I said. "You can go ahead and read it."

"But I don't want to read it."

"Oh, go ahead," I said. "I can finish it after you're done."

"But I don't even want to start it," she said.

"All right then," I said.

"And please turn out the light," she said. "I can't sleep with the light in my eyes."

The next morning, Carl and I ran the trot lines by ourselves; Helen stayed on the dock. She hadn't even gone swimming with us before breakfast, but had slept right up until breakfast. I rowed while Carl caught the floats and ran us down along the lines rebaiting the empty hooks and taking off the fish we had caught. As we were running the third line, we heard the sound of a motor and we saw the stranger sweep around a half-turn and coast up to the dock. Helen got in the boat, and they went ripping away.

"Handsome boat," Carl said.

"Yes, I guess it is," I said.

She hadn't even told us his name.

Carl and I went hunting for crows on the island with his twenty-two rifle, but we didn't get a thing except a rain crow I shot. The crows stayed on the island nights, and at dawn they flew eastward over the trees cawing a racket, and then turned south to the mainland to hunt out cornfields. Not getting any crows made Carl mad, and my shooting the rain crow made him madder.

"What did you shoot that for?" he said.

"It's a crow, isn't it?" I said.

"Heck, you know better than that. It's a yellow-billed cuckoo. What did you shoot it for?"

"It's a rain crow," I said again. I didn't know why I had shot it. We had just been walking along and when I heard it calling, in a tone like it was pleased with itself, "Tyok, tyok, tyok," I just up and banged away at it.

"It's a rain crow but it ain't a black crow. What's the matter — you color-blind or something?"

We walked over to where it had fallen and we found it was still alive. The shot had gone through its chest without killing it. Its chest pumped up and down squirting out blood with each pump, and it didn't make a sound but looked up at me with the eye in the left side of its head. I wished it had died right away.

"Get a stick and kill it," Carl said.

"You kill it," I said.

"It's not my bird," he said. "You started the job, now finish it."

I turned and began to walk back toward the river, and Carl shouted after me, "I'll be damned if I'll finish it for you."

"Hold your horses," I said. "I'm just going to look for a rock."

"The heck you are." He knew there weren't any rocks on this side of the island where the banks are cut out so high above the river.

"The heck I'm not." I broke a stick from a dead branch and went back and stood over the bird and held my breath and counted three and smashed it. Carl had started toward the boat when I had gone back to the bird. I caught up with him at the boat.

"It's bad luck to kill a rain crow," he said quietly, as though telling me a secret I hadn't heard.

"You got holes in your head," I said.

"What you so mad about?"

"I'm not mad!"

"If you weren't mad, you wouldn't shout so telling me you weren't."

"Oh, go to." I untied the line and threw it over the bow of the boat.

"You shot your luck," Carl said. "Going to rain like hell."

"Go to hell."

"Like a cow pissing off a flat rock," Carl said. He took out his makings and gave me a paper and passed me the sack of tobacco. "Trouble is, I'll be in the same rain you are."

I rolled the tobacco in the paper, wet the edge, and wiped it down. Carl struck a wooden match and held it toward me. I puffed on the cigarette. "Do you want to row or should I?"

"You can row," Carl said.

At supper, all Helen could talk about was Richard Wellman and his motorboat and her rides with him up and down the river. She was just brimming full of Richard Wellman, like low-cut banks in a spring rise. His grandfather had been a contractor; no, he had not lost anything in the depression; yes, he was in love with his grandson; certainly, he was going to send Richard to college; sure, he was the one who bought Richard the boat; also, he had set up Richard's father in business; oh, it was a wonderful summer camp he was building above Andalusia — it even had an electric pump so they could have a toilet in the house. She just splashed and flooded and ripped with Richard Wellman.

I excused myself early and went down to the dock and got the double-ended Mississippi fish boat and rowed over to the island. The sun was just going down and the horizon was all fire halfway up the sky so I knew it wouldn't rain the next day. But I went back into the woods and found the rain crow and buried it anyway.

By the time I got back to the boat, the river was dark and there were no lights on shore yet. I rowed for where I thought the dock should be, and when I came close to shore, I heard Carl's voice — not shouting, but talking low as though speaking to a man next to him — "Pull on your right oar a wee bit. There's a little less current tonight. Steady. That's it."

It was an awful quiet night and his voice carried as over a telephone wire. He took the bow line and tied it to a ring.

"Did you bury it?"

"Yes," I said.

"That was a good idea."

"Sky was red tonight."

"I know," he said. "Maybe burying it will keep the rain away."

"I hope so."

We went behind the garage and Carl gave me makings and we rolled cigarettes and had a long smoke.

"I think I know why you're mad," he said.

"I'm not mad," I said, this time quietly.

"Well, then, I know why you would be if you were mad," he said.
"Does it show?" I said.
"Not much," he said. "Not so's you'd notice it."
"I buried it," I said.
"Yes, you did."
"I killed it and buried it."
"I know you did."
The cigarette was sending me off the ground and then bringing me back and then sending me off again. I was inhaling.
"But don't worry," he said. "Have you noticed the river?"
"What about it?"
"Have you noticed it?" he said.
"Not especially," I said.
"Look at that maple sapling standing in the water. See the marks?"
"She's dropping, that's all."
"Yes, she's dropping, and that's enough."
He handed me more makings, and just then it came to me and I laughed so hard I blew the tobacco off the paper. The river was down six inches at the very least.

III

The next morning, Richard Wellman came down the river and offered us rides on his surf board. He had it strapped on the deck, of all places. He didn't give a tinker's dam about the finish.

Carl told him not to go below the docks, and he asked why, but Carl just said not to go below the dock or nobody there would ride. Richard said he wouldn't, so we all took rides, but Helen took the most of all. She hated to give up the board, and anybody with half an eye could see Richard had just made the offer to Carl and me to be polite. He and Helen took turns riding the board and steering the boat.

When Helen rode the board, she screamed and yelled all the time she was whipping back and forth behind the boat; and sometimes she would stand on one leg and hold on with one arm, or else she would try other tricks you might see in the movies and she would get flipped off. But she always came back for more. She was as golden brown and wild as a hawk.

After dinner, Richard came back towing one of those tin, non-sinkable rowboats behind him. He told us what we already knew — that it had airtight compartments and so on, and then he asked us

to race. We lined up his boat and our two and I said he could have
first choice, but Helen jumped up —

"I want the duckboat. I want to race too, and I want the duckboat.

"Sure," Richard said. "Then I'll take my own boat."

You could tell he had not been on the river much because he preferred every kind of boat to the double-ended fishing boat, and plainly,
he did not know how well balanced they were for all their size, nor
how light and swift they were for all their clumsy looks, nor how
little water they drew for all their depth of side, nor even how practical
they were for running trotlines or setting nets or fish traps. He preferred the tin boats because their lines were more nearly like those
of his motorboat, but they were not easy rowing; and his only right
choice had been when he preferred the duckboat to the double-ender.
And then his choice had come from its having lines like those of a
speedboat.

We were to row up to the point and back, Carl giving the word go,
and deciding the winner. When Carl said go, I started out slow and
watched Richard over my shoulder. He was rowing fast and had got
a good lead from the start, but his tin boat was awkward and he was
rowing with his arms instead of his back. Being half a head taller
than me wouldn't help him if he did that, so I set my back into it
with long easy pulls.

Helen was leading in the duckboat, and I could tell he was letting
her lead because he was sure I had the wrong boat to win by, and
that he could keep ahead of me and still let her win. I was just behind
him when he turned at the point. Helen was already started downstream, and she was laughing so hard she could barely row. She
couldn't see how Richard was sweating at the turn nor how he chopped
with his right oar, turning toward the bank.

I turned out into the stream, and current out from the point helped
swing my bow around and I started down even with Richard. He
saw I was getting more current than he was, and he tried to correct
it but it was no use. I was using my back and he was using his arms.

Halfway to the dock, I caught up with Helen, and then thinking
of how much she liked to win, I dropped in just behind her. She
wasn't laughing any more, but rowing hard. She reached the dock
half a length ahead of me, and then we just sat there waiting for
Richard.

"It was a good race," I said.

"Uh-huh."

"But he doesn't know his boats."

"He's got a motorboat," she said.

"But I beat him rowing."

"I've got eyes," she said.

"Did you want him to win?"

"It was a race. I wanted to win."

"Well, you won."

"I suppose you let me win," she said, mocking me with the tone of her voice. She looked at me for a minute with her mouth open. "Darn you. Darn you if you did."

Richard stayed to supper and met Aunt Jane and Uncle John Springer. He even started calling them Aunt Jane and Uncle John right away, and nobody seemed to mind. I felt uncomfortable enough to be sitting on tacks, and I was glad when Carl said that one of the trotlines was gone and that he and I should go look for it.

"Either she's loose or the float got busted and sank."

"If it's loose, it should be snagged somewhere downstream," I said. For floats, we used gallon glass jugs, and if one of them broke, there was usually no finding the line.

"Well, let's commence to begin to start," he said. "I'll take the fish boat and look over toward the island."

"I doubt that it would have gotten over there," I said.

"There was a south wind today," he said.

"But it wouldn't blow far dragging line."

"It might have snagged on the bar," he said. "The river's awful low on the bar."

We worked our way down the river slowly, searching the low places, Carl over by the bar and I over by the shore. We had been out about half an hour when Helen and Richard went spinning by us in his tin boat. They hailed us, and we hailed back, but I didn't pay any more attention to them, although I did notice they landed quite a way down and went in among the maples.

But I was really surprised when a while later I looked up once and saw their boat just ahead of me. I tied on to her and took out the makings Carl had given me and had a smoke. I looked over to where Carl was working along the bar, and he waved his arm and started rowing back upstream. "It must have busted and sank," he said just loud enough to hear. "Going back up?"

"In a minute," I said, and I blew a puff of smoke for him to see.

"O-kay," he said. "I'll see you."

Just as I flipped the butt into the river, Helen came out of the maple grove walking fast, her head down. She didn't see me until she got right up to their boat, and then she sort of jumped and said, "Oh." She looked back once at the maple grove, and then she said, "Just what do you think you're doing here?" Her face was red under the suntan.

"I just stopped for a smoke."

"Oh? Where's your cigarette?"

"I just now flipped it away."

"Yes you did."

"I can't show you the butt, but I can let you see the makings if you want to."

"You haven't got them. You're just spying around."

"Here they are."

"Well, why don't you roll me one?"

"You're awful jumpy tonight."

"Am I? I hadn't noticed."

"What's the matter?" I said.

"Nothing. Nothing's the matter."

"Where's Richard?"

"Back there," she said, waving her cigarette at the maple grove.

"Did he do anything to you?"

"Who, Richard? No, of course not."

"Well, if he did —"

"But he didn't," she said.

"You kind of like him, don't you."

"What if I did?"

"Do you like him enough — Never mind. Here's a light. Catch it."

"What were you saying?" she said.

"Me? Oh, nothing. Do you want to ride up with me?"

"I'm waiting for Richard."

"But I can take you up as well as not."

"No," she said, "I'm waiting for Richard."

"All right." I threw her the sack of makings. "Cast me off and I'll get out of here."

She untied my line and threw it over the bow.

"See you at the house," I said.

"Rob —"

"Yes?" She hadn't called me Rob in a long time.

"Rob — you won't say anything. About this?"

"About what? About something I never saw? You got holes in your head."

As I rowed home, my back pointed upstream, I saw the sun hover on the horizon like a hawk just before it drops. The sun was just one great big red ball, but there was no redness outside of it; the sky was white all around it. Then it dropped slowly, keeping its color all inside itself, leaving the sky white around it — but not with the white of clouds.

When I reached the landing, Carl was waiting for me.

"You took a long time," he said. "What were you doing?"

"Just looking."

"See anything?"

"The sun. Just the sun, that's all," I said. "Did you see it?"

"Yes."

"Maybe not for two days," I said.

"Maybe not. Maybe not tomorrow, maybe not even the day after," he said. "But then — like a cow off a flat rock."

"Burying doesn't do any good, I guess."

"No," he said, "I guess it doesn't."

IV

A west wind came up and wakened me about midnight. It howled up the river, and then slowly began to swing up from the south, and then shifted back again, trying to collect every cloud in five states. It would be angling across the river by morning probably, and settling down for a good blow.

Helen woke up and asked what was all the noise, and when I said that it was the wind, she just rolled over muttering, "Awful lot of racket."

Even Carl was troubled in his sleep, and once or twice he said, "Got to tie up the boat. That lovely green boat's going to float away. Got to tie up the boat."

Richard came bouncing down the river late in the afternoon as the three of us were standing on the dock looking at the river. Carl and I had gone out in the morning and had taken in the trotlines and had pulled both boats up on shore, and we were surprised to see Richard out, though it looked like a lot of fun bouncing over the waves like that.

"You better get your boat out of the water," I said as he tied up at the dock. He had been able to land downstream because the wind was so strong.

"It's a lot more fun like this," he said.

"So is jumping off a moving train," Carl said.

"Is everything all right?" Richard said to Helen.

"Sure," she said. "Why not?"

"Good. I came down to see — just to make sure. And to take you for a ride."

"She doesn't want to go for a ride in this," I said.

"Yes, I do," Helen said.

"You've got holes in your head if you go out in this." It was growing as dark as evening; I couldn't even see the trees on which we lined up the bar.

"But you like to go out in storms yourself," she said. "Remember when Mr. McCormick let you and Carl sail his boat last summer and then took it away from you because you always sailed at night or out in a storm? Well, I like it too."

"But not today," I said. "And you're not going out either — is she, Carl?"

"You listen to what he says," Carl said.

"Don't call Carl in to this," she said, and she climbed down into the boat. "Hurry up and cast off, Richard." Richard gunned the motor and the boat slid away from the dock and began to pick up speed. "You're just jealous, that's all," she shouted back to us. Big drops of rain began to fall then, but we could hear her laughter even above their splash.

"Look out for the bar!" I shouted. "Stay away from the sandbar! The river's low!" But they were too far away now to hear me above the wind and the rain.

"Don't worry," Carl said, "she can line the bar."

"Oh, yeah! Look!" I pointed downstream to where the darkness had hidden the trees at the bend.

"Damn! Goddam! And all the water's rough water now. Nobody can see a bar by ripples or drift now."

The rain began to come down heavy — like a cow off a flat rock — and Helen and Richard swung downstream hugging the island bank. If praying could raise water, the river would have come up a foot just then.

"They're all right if they keep close to the island for the length of the bar," Carl said.

As they passed us on the far side of the river, I shouted again, "Stay clear of the bar!"

As though to hear me better, Helen stood up in the boat holding on to the windshield, and just then Richard whipped the boat toward the center of the river, smacking the white-capped waves, and flipped Helen out. Helen had barely hit the water when the boat struck the bar and ripped out her bottom with a sound like more thunder. Carl and I were already running to the fish boat.

I got in and set the oars while he untied her and shoved her out. I pulled straight for Helen, thinking the wind would offset the current, but there was more wind than I had expected and Carl had to correct me: "Left oar, left oar."

I braced my feet and stiffened my legs, reaching and pulling with my back. As we came near Helen, Carl shouted, "Swing her, swing her," and I pushed the right against pulling the left, the boat shivered and paused for an instant, and Carl reached out and dragged Helen into the boat.

"Go for Richard," he said while Helen's legs were still in the water. Helen choked and spat the water out of her throat.

"Richard?" she said.

"We're coming to him," Carl said.

I was too winded to talk. I glanced over my shoulder once to locate the motorboat. It was beginning to settle and I couldn't see why until I thought that the speed of the boat must have carried it past the bar and into deeper water, or else the waves had knocked it off — or maybe both.

My right oar struck the bar and Carl jumped out. The water was only at his waist when he reached the motorboat, but Richard — knocked out against the wheel — was already settling up to his neck. The bow of the boat was sinking first, the stern still caught on a high place on the bar. Carl lifted Richard out of the motorboat, floated him to the bow of the rowboat, and then, ducking under him, lifted him into the rowboat.

"Get in the stern," Carl said to Helen. "We want some weight in back. Slide over, Rob."

We each took an oar and pulled for shore, Carl counting, "One . . . two . . . three . . . One. . . ."

As the boat struck beach, Carl and I grabbed Richard and ran for the house. Uncle John came down the yard to help us. Aunt Jane swung the door open.

"I've already called the doctor," she said. She swung the door closed, turned toward the cot where Richard now lay, then swung around again. "What in heaven's name is Helen doing?"

I looked toward the river. Helen, in the green duckboat, was pulling for the wreck. She was already almost halfway there.

"She's going to haul in the wreck," I said. "She'll pull the back end out of that boat."

I didn't stop for Carl but ran out the door and down to the double-ender. Helen had reached the wreck by the time I was launched, but I knew it would take her some time to tie on to it. I looked around once to set my course, and then didn't look again, but pulled and pulled and pulled. Then I heard the crack of parting wood and I turned just in time to see the duckboat scoot suddenly forward, Helen's legs kicking up in the air, and then begin to settle stern first. When I reached her, she was standing on the bar.

"You goddamned fool," I said.

I took both oars from the duckboat and jammed their handles first into a high part of the bar and tied the motorboat and the duckboat to them. The oar blades were chipped and broken. She must have set both blades into the sandbar to use the oars as levers.

"If they stay, they stay," I said. "If they don't, they don't. Now get in."

On the island, a tree fell with a rush of breaking limbs ending in a sudden boom. I was too tired to row fast, but I used the wind as much as I could, and we went at a pretty good clip. At the shore, we dragged the boat up on the bank and went up to the house. The doctor's Ford V-8 stood in the driveway.

"Everything will be all right," he was saying as we opened the screen door.

V

Helen and I both woke to the sound of wings beating against the screens. It was earlier than we usually got up, but Carl was already gone. We looked around the porch to locate the sound. The sky was not even gray yet; light kind of oozed through the clouds, seeming like wet and pulpy rotten wood.

The wings fluttered again and I looked up to the ceiling. Two bats, one inside the porch and one outside, kept flying toward each other, hitting the screen, and then flying off. It was as though they were trying to kiss through the screen.

"I thought bats never hit things," I said.

"Try and catch it," Helen said.

The bat inside the porch whacked against the screen and glided off onto Helen's bed. I jerked the blanket over it and then reached under and caught it with my hand.

"Put it outside," Helen said.

"Oh, no. Bats are lovely birds. Feel how soft she is."

"Keep it away. I don't want it in my hair."

"It won't get in your hair if I hold it. Here, touch it."

She reached out one finger in a scared way as though hunting for a set mouse trap in the dark. Then, when she touched it and felt how soft and silky was its fur, she petted it with her whole hand.

"It is lovely," she said. "But bats aren't birds. They're mammals the same as people."

"We ought to keep him," I said. "Or her, which ever it is."

"What would you feed him?" Helen said.

"I don't know, but we could find out."

"No, you better let him go."

"Why? Wouldn't you like to be able to take her out of her cage and pet her every so often? You just said she was lovely."

"No, it would die," she said.

"Do you think it would?"

"I'm sure of it. All wild things are like that. Remember that little rabbit Carl caught in his box trap last summer? We fed it everything but it wouldn't eat, and it died."

"Coons don't."

"But you have to keep them chained," she said. "And once they get loose, they go hiking off to the nearest river or woods."

"Yes, I guess they do."

"Wait till I get dressed and we'll put it outside."

I put the bat under a blanket and tucked the blanket edges under the mattress, and then I began to dress. I was watching Helen dress, and she watched me, and neither of us said a thing. Her breasts were shaped more like lemons than young pears. They looked soft and tender and shy like wild flowers that die quickly when you close them in your hand. But I wanted to touch them just as you always want to pick the flowers.

When we had finished dressing, we both smiled, and I felt my face go red as I saw hers go red.

"Let's put the bat out," she said.

I took the bat from under the blanket and we went outside. Neither one of us wanted to let it go. Helen kept stroking it. Its fur was lovely, soft, and dark.

Carl came toward us from the dock. "What you got there?"

"A bat," Helen said. "It was on the porch."

"So that's what it was. I got up before light this morning, and when I opened the door, I knew something came in. It brushed my shoulder, but I thought it was a bird."

"Isn't it lovely?" Helen said.

"What are you going to do with her?" Carl said.

"Let him go," Helen said.

"When?"

"Right now," I said. "I'm going to let her go right now." I threw the bat into the air. It flew around crazily for a minute, and then winged away toward the trees by the river. We watched it until it disappeared, and still we looked after it. The second bat came from around the house and shuttled back and forth, but going always toward the river and the trees. Then it too disappeared.

Finally, Helen turned and said, "The boats?"

"The motorboat's there," Carl said, "but it isn't worth a tinker's dam now."

"And the duckboat?" I asked, though somehow I had already guessed what he would say.

"Gone," he said. "That lovely green boat has floated away."

(From Western Review)

THE OTHER RIVER

BY ROBERT O. BOWEN

*I*N *THE BEGINNING* he thought it was that dream that used to come to him, rather the thing that had so often awakened him cold and beyond trembling beside Pat in bed and left him to fear the night out wondering whether it was a dream or whether the horrible almost-forgotten-memory quality of it meant that it had been real once.

He always had the same feeling about the thing. He had killed someone somewhere in a close dark place and hidden the body, a long time ago, and it was someone whom he knew only obliquely, not part of any regular crowd he'd ever been with anywhere. Only he'd been so many places drifting around all his life. The war, the Pacific, and moving around the country before he got married last year and started back to college. It could even have been when he was a boy. That was possible; it had always seemed like a very old memory when it seemed like a memory at all.

He always felt that he would know the place if he saw it, that some secret part of him would then let out the whole thing, the one whom he had killed — it must have been strangled, he was almost sure of that — the time and even the why of it. It had not been an ordinary killing, like in combat, of that he was certain. There was some special and terrible guilt to it.

Sometimes he wasn't sure it was in the past. Then it was worse because he felt that it might be a prophecy. He believed in second-sight, had to, he had felt it before, overseas, known irrationally many times where a Jap was. It had never been understandable though, and often when he'd felt most certain, it had been wrong.

When he began to awaken this time, all of these mingled in his not yet conscious knowing of what was happening, the almost-memory, the foreknowledge, the dream, and the fear — the dark, deep, lasting fear.

Through a swirling mist he saw the shadowed girders of a steel bridge around him and a river far below with the moonlight shimmering on the water as far as the dark hills that rolled back from the bank. I'm dreaming this, he thought, trying to rationalize it away. This mustn't happen again — yet.

I'll wake up and touch Pat and she'll mumble and tell me to go back to sleep. This is one of the nights that I need her to hold me and tell me that I'm all right. He tried harder to rouse himself from the dullness, and then he felt the very real cold on his arms and chest and his bare feet treading the concrete walk. He knew vaguely and terribly that it was not a dream and that when he awoke more fully the walls of the bedroom would not be around him. Then he entered the lane in the darkness beyond the bridge.

It's the time, he thought, the time's wrong. This isn't me. This can't be happening to me. It's somebody else. I go to the University and live in the apartment that we painted with cream walls and white woodwork . . . a long time ago. His body continued to move forward without volition. He felt the legs drag and heard the feet swish on the sandy path beside the curving blacktop road. Then there were cinders and he stopped because they ground into the tender soles of his feet. It was like a jungle night in the Philippines. But it couldn't be that because that had been already — before. He shuddered in the dark beneath the trees that overhung the path and tried to draw together the broken threads of the patchwork that was himself.

There were no names or faces, only the certain knowledge that he couldn't go back to where he had come from, which had been. . . . He delved in his mind for something, anything to cling to, and suddenly things were there in his head, clear and bright like figures spotted by a searchlight. A memory, a certain memory.

He had pitched headlong down an embankment and felt the rocks and roots on the slope tear at him, and at the bottom he had launched himself doglike into the brush and under the trees. There was an animal awareness of the solid growth about him and the shelter from the bright moon and the silence of the dew-wet leaves; it was not thought but a blood-felt knowledge more real than any thought. He crouched on a knob of land at the edge of the wood, and it was there he first noticed the long heavy knife in his right fist. He sniffed it and slid it forward into a narrow shaft of moonlight, looking along the blade for the dark stain he did not see but knew that he had smelled.

He grunted and the savageness of the animal sound stirred something within him that was almost dead. But he did not start. His hand probed behind his back and jammed the blade firmly beneath the waistband of his trousers. Then he was moving again down the incline in the shadows, the leaves rustling beneath him in the dark.

There it stopped, a fragment of experience complete in every detail — but suspended in a void, related to nothing. The void was *now*. The experience was *then*. He groped trembling to support himself against the trees beside the path, and the trees were of *now*, dim, shapeless, dull as his own tired body. But they were real, there was no doubt there. He clung to a rough trunk with both hands and strained to catch more fragments of *then*, to assemble, to bring order. And the next chip of memory came more swiftly. It was no more than a chip though, a shard from some unrecognizable whole.

He had hurtled down through the dark air turning slowly, his head indrawn and spine arched for the shock of striking he knew not what. And now, not remembering but reliving, he struck again the water that slammed into his back and shoulders and wrenched him into the swimming blackness.

The gap this time was short. By seconds he was knowing more and more like a man groping upward from an anesthetic sleep. He moved his hands from the tree and stood hypnotized by the terrible clarity of the *then* that swept across his mind.

They were after him in the dark hills that shouldered the river behind him, and he swam without lifting his arms clear of the surface to avoid the splash of his hands. He smelled the swamp-life of the water that gurgled secretly about his face as he forged ahead into the moonlight far out from the bank. He felt the wetness and the surging pull of the current, and he looked back toward the shore. A hundred yards, and he was tired already. And the far bank lay almost samile across the stream that he knew was brown even now beneath the silver light that flowed across it. He smelled the brownness cf it and felt it close in over him, and at first he let himself drop slowly through it. Then he was fighting to reach the air again. He pulled in long clutching strokes against the solid depth overhead, and he felt his thighs strain against the cloth of his trousers.

The water had trapped him almost without his knowledge, as though he had been another person lost in another darkness of this same river and had not seen himself slip silently beneath the surface.

This was to die. He savoured it calmly, as he would study a picture

that did not touch on him. And yet there was a reality here that he
had never felt in any art.

No!

He gulped the air he fought to keep his head in and felt the dead
weight of the shirt on his arms. Then he went down again reaching
for the knife that wasn't there to cut the shirt free with, tearing at
the wet tautness across his shoulders with his hands, struggling upward again. And then free, swimming slower and slower with his
arms, his legs dragging. His face settled lower and he saw the banks
equidistant now — both too far to reach. For no reason his lips
moved and he heard his own hoarse whisper.

"Go out clean."

He slipped his wedding band free and, treading water, flung it
far out in the clear streak of moonlight. The ripple it left was gone
almost as it struck and his left hand felt strangely lighter. Then
there was only light and shadow and smell and wetness — and the
terrible waste of himself. He would go now and the world would
live without him. And this would be a thing that he would never
remember, never look back on or ponder over. He would sink and
he could see already his body rolled on the mudflats swollen with the
river. He could feel the deadness of it, the same as the deadness of
any corpse, any other dead animal he had ever seen, the unpurposed,
chance-flung form, the matted hair.

It was to die, the thing that he had always known, had skirted
through shell fire and in a hundred other crashing places where there
had not been time to think. At first the water was a thin flickering
film across his eyes, then murky, then a strangling mass.

The arms that were dead and the legs that dragged the trousers
stirred again, and his last thought was a longing to see the very end,
to be able to remember the flicker of the spark that came when the
light that had burned in him flared out.

Then that picture too was gone like the others, leaving no frame
behind to place it in time, in past or future.

He began walking again along the real cinder path that hurt his
feet. The flesh of his face sagged with the weariness in him and he
felt that he would have pitched forward but that to fall would have
been a greater effort than to stay erect. Then I'm not dead, he thought.
I'm here. Where? It was a long time ago and I can't go back to
before, to Pat and the people who wore neckties and talked about
poetry and Picasso.

I'm cold. I'm waking up.

The thoughts came with a labored slowness, piled like brick on brick to build a wall that he could lean against. He saw that he had reached the foot of a hill and that the road wound upward. On his left a few lights shone yellowly through the trees. Nigger shacks, he thought. Down here by the river, they'd be nigger shacks. In the sky above the crest of the hill he saw a glow that marked the town he had left so long ago. There was an unknown reason that the town wouldn't want him now, and that reason was cold and wet like the air he felt against his skin.

His vague shuffling forward stopped and he looked down at the man that was himself to see if looking would tell who he was or when it had been that he had gone where. I'm still scrawny, he thought. I'm like me, anyway. The hair on his chest showed like a splotch of shadow and the undershirt hung tattered and stained from one shoulder. His feet jutted stark and white from the bottoms of the muddied trousers onto the cinders. He ran his fingers across his features, probling as though to recognize by touch what he could not by thought. I'm cold, he thought again, and he moved forward along the path.

At the sound of footsteps, he looked ahead on the path and saw a man turn from a side road and walk toward him. He slipped in the shadows and waited until he saw that it was a Negro. Then he lurched back onto the path and heard himself plead almost in a whisper.

"What year is this?"

The voice was his own but it belonged to a time so far in the past that he couldn't believe that he had been the child who used it. The Negro crouched, circling him, his hands out from his sides like a bird. He felt the impact of the white staring eyes and saw the moonlight flash on the dark face as the Negro backed into the road. Then there was only the pattering slap of feet on the pavement to tell which way the figure had gone.

I'm not a dead thing from the river, he thought. It was the thing I did and now the curse is on me and the mark shows so that even at night they run away.

He began to walk stolidly along the path again and at the corner he turned left down the side road away from the blacktop that led up the hill to the town. He had no direction, but as though he knew exactly where he was going he stumbled across the fields turning neither right nor left for the tall weeds and scattered rubbish. Tonelessly, like a man so sick that he feels but no longer reacts, he approached the cracked light that split from the windows and single tall door of the sagging, paintless, frame house. He climbed the steps that had no railing to hang to and knocked at the door.

Inside the voices stopped, and the light struck his eyes when the door opened. He saw two black girls and four men laughing around a mason jar of clear liquor on a red table.

"What the hell that?" the fat Negro said.

Then the girl on his lap began to call in a shrill outraged voice. "You George! Big George, come back heah!"

The one called George stooped into the room from a hall behind the table. His eyes fell on the doorway and his hamlike fists unfolded slowly. He ran a finger as thick as a garden hose along the scar on his cheek and his tongue rubbered out across his lips before he spoke.

"Where he come from?"

"Don' know," the girl in the green silk said. "Just opened the door and he there."

Then he said the only thing that was in his mind, the thing that he had come here to say.

"I'm cold. Can I come in out of the cold?"

The voice was still the child's voice. It broke the silence in the room and the talk started again like jays in the brush when a man passes. The tough black hand was gentle on his shoulder, but he felt himself being steered down the steps again to the yard and heard the deep voice saying, "Look here, white boy, this here's a tough place. You don't want to come here. Why these the toughest people in this whole country."

"I'm cold."

"Where you from, white boy?"

He shook his head. But he was waking faster now and he knew that soon remembering would be part of him again.

"Where you from? You looks in a bad way. Now why don' you let me call you a taxi or somethin' like that? Huh?"

"No."

He was sure that would be wrong. There was no money, and the apartment with the desk and notebooks would be empty now and thick with dust the way it had been when Pat found it with him that day when the sun was shining. Oh Jesus God, he prayed silently, bring back the sun. But he knew there was no Jesus God.

"I'm cold." He looked towards the road that was a tunnel of darkness running backward to where he had been. "I was in the river."

"You best go up with the white folks. Don' you belong someplace?"

"I'm from the University."

It pushed into his mind and he said it as he might have said, "I'm twenty-six years old," or "I was a soldier." He followed the thoughts no further because they had no meaning. He could if he tried remember his name, but he knew that whatever he had done had taken from him the right to use the name — so he didn't try.

"You best do like I say," the voice urged. "Better just go up with the white folks at the University. They take care o' you fine."

"No. The white people don't want me now."

He knew for no reason at all that the words were absolutely true and as irrevocable as the names written on the white wooden crosses after a landing. He started towards the road and he was colder and the weariness was coming stronger now. His hurts were stiffening. He had not felt that until now, and now he knew without looking that his whole body was mauled. He didn't bother to even lift his hand to explore the wound that he felt throbbing over his right ear.

The one called George caught up with him as he climbed the gulley to the shoulder of the road, and he stopped, looking up into the broad face with the eyes and teeth that shone in the moonlight.

"You hurt anywhere?"

The warm hand touched his shoulder again as though to catch him if he fell — or when he fell.

"No. I'm cold. That's all."

He shivered now and he was beginning to think ahead to the time when the sun would rise. If he was alive he would have to have food and he couldn't work without clothes and shoes. And he had no papers. No name.

"I just can't let you in that place." The black hands gestured helplessly. "I just can't do that."

He waited, looking at the maroon stripes in the shirt stretched across the thick barrel of the Negro's chest on a level with his own eyes.

"Them people over there. . . . You know how that kind of place is like. Whyn't you let me get you a taxi? Huh?"

"I'm all right," he said, and all the sadness of going alone down the lonesome cold road was in his voice. He patted the heavy muscled arm clumsily. "You've been very kind to me."

And when he had taken a step back onto the road he wondered why there were no tears.

The lights swept around the corner shooting towards him, and he stopped, rocking slightly with his feet spread. He waited because he knew that they had come for him and that they would put him where the other people would be safe. The Negro was beside him again with the familiar arm about his shoulders, and six white men broke from the car like cockroaches from a dirty cupboard. They all spoke at once but out of the staccato babble he understood only the one standing in the headlight beams with the shiny pistol in his hand.

"He ain't got no knife, has he?"

"No sir. He all right. Don' know what's goin' on with him. Just come to the door and say he's cold." The soft burr of the voice blended into the night and the white faces surged forward around him.

He held out the thin arms with the hands knuckles up and close together. And he waited grayly for the metallic click of links across the wrists that would be the sign of the end of many things and the beginning of nothing.

"All right." There was a firmness in his tone that had not been there before.

He saw the man with the mustache directly before him turn away ashamed and muttering. Then the policeman pushed his hands down gently, not looking at them.

"There's nothin' wrong," the policeman said. "We're just here to help you out a bit." He waited to see if the words were understood before he went on. "Is your name Clayton?"

He nodded while he went through the shadows and mist in his mind to check the name against his own.

"Yes," he croaked, and then he cleared his throat. "I'm Clayton. Bill Clayton." He paused to let the name adjust itself to the thing that was him. "It was all a long time ago." He felt like a man who had stepped out of a front-line foxhole directly onto the calm known streets of his home town.

In the car he felt the animal warmth of the men on both sides of him and saw the neon silence of the main street when they topped the hill. So he was going back to something. To Pat? But he couldn't think of her because to think was to hope.

The man on the left cleared his throat. "You was a guerrilla a long time, wasn't you, Clayton? In the Philippines, huh?"

He thought aloud, not trying any longer to sift the words before he uttered them. "Yes . . . yes, I was. It was a long time ago. I was with the guys. Markland and Lemanski and Sergeant Jack."

"Your wife told us about it." The speaker hunched forward and asked in an eager familiarity. "Three years, wasn't it? I bet you killed a heap of them Jap bastards, huh?"

The slowness of his mind didn't hurt so deeply now because he knew that it was fatigue and not the lapse of time he always feared.

"Yeah, it was three years."

Not three years to when I was with Pat, he thought. They mean in the islands with the gang. The gang understood about things. But why should these people ask about. . . .

The car stopped and he saw the glare of the bus station and the men piling out on the sidewalk, saying "Good night" to the policemen and staring at him with a primitive curiosity in the bright light. That passed, and he was alone in the front seat with the officer who neither stared nor implied more than the words that he spoke.

"You want to go back where the party was, Clayton? I think your wife is still there."

"All right."

Now he remembered Pat and the apartment almost totally. There was a strangeness though about the time. It still seemed in the distant past.

"Did it happen tonight?" he said.

"Yeah, about eight o'clock." The car slowed on a side street. "This is the place. No lights. I guess they're all asleep."

He could remember boarding the bus with Pat, wearing his tan gabardine suit. These must be the trousers, he thought, but he didn't look at them.

The car swung back through town towards the apartment that he was not yet sure was there. Now he could talk again while they drove, talk and thank the officer for taking him home and hear the answer to the question that he had been afraid to ask before.

"No, nobody was hurt." The officer studied his face in the dim light. "Least they didn't report nothin'."

The car stopped in front of the only house on the avenue with lighted windows. It was the apartment, the same cardboard venetian blinds that sagged in the middle — the way Pat had said they would.

"Clayton," the officer stammered. "I know . . . I mean we see the guys that came back." Then the voice got firmer. "It's not up to me to tell you, but I hope you'll never touch another drop as long as you live."

He helped Bill out of the car and across the walk to the door. Pat was thanking the officer who was saying from the porch, "No ma'm, everything's just fine." Then the door was closed and he was with the wife in the apartment that he had thought might have been only a memory.

He stood on the floor that they had waxed together and saw their puppy cowering in the corner, and then he smelled the river smell again and knew that that part of it at least had been real. He let

Pat wrap his robe around him and lead him to the big stuffed chair. She brought hot coffee and he felt the life flow through him from it. There was nothing to say. He sat huddled in the shame of his presence, knowing that he had no right to speak to her at all. And she faced him from the sofa opposite with the hurt of trying to understand that he had seen so often in her eyes.

"Larry wasn't hurt bad," she said.

She sounded glad, and he looked up, not comprehending, but knowing that somehow she was trying to reassure him of something.

"He told the doctor that he fell on a bottle. It wasn't . . ."

He felt the hot coffee on his knee and looked down stupidly at the cup it poured from. Then she was on the arm of his chair, one hand around his steadying the cup, the other pressing his head to her.

There had been a knife. That part of it was real too. That and. . . .

"Bill, everything's going to come out all right." She stroked his temples. "Bill."

He knew then that it had all been real, the knife, the blood, the river. And he knew better than he had ever known anything in his life that the whole dream had always been real too. He might walk and breathe with Pat within these plastered walls for a time, but for him other realities would make these walls like mist and he would be again strangling in the realness of the other river, the other jungle while this hulk of him would linger for a span in a world he would never know again the way Pat knew it.

Her arm tightened around his shoulders, and he felt the mothering warmth of her and knew terribly that he could not stay close to her for long. Not if he had been insane enough to stab . . . And why? Why did it happen that of all men she had married one whose mind was like an ancient engine, breaking down on any road, rolling backward? A mind existing in a constant dread that the order about it would topple because nothing maintained it but the fragile thread of man's reason.

It should have ended at the river, he thought. After the last sight of the bright moon he should have let the dark water slip over him. Then it would have been simple, like the putting out of a light. But it had not ended. He had struggled even after consciousness was gone.

"We had to tell the police you had a knife. Don't you see, Bill? We looked along the railroad embankment for you." She stopped again and caught his chin in her hands. "Don't you feel better now that you know the worst of it can be patched up?"

He breathed heavily. Know the worst of it, he thought. How can I know I didn't meet somebody in the bush and leave him . . . How can I know anything when I come by *that* so easy?

"Bill."

"Sure," he said. "Sure. I'll be all right."

She passed him a cigarette and his hand trembled so that she had to take it back and light it for him.

"I thought all this was gone," he said. "I thought nothing like this would ever come back again."

He saw the river in the spiral of smoke that drifted up before him, the long serene length of it stretching silently for miles until it swung around the turn far down between the brooding banks.

She helped him run water in the tub, and he let himself sink down in the warm lather that would take away the river smell. He would throw the trousers and rag of an undershirt in the trashcan when he had toweled down. That much of it could be put away. But when the sun came up there would still be Larry with the wound that he had made in Larry's apartment, and the others at the party, Blacky and Jean and Sid Johnson who all walked the same broad concrete paths across the campus that he did and sat in the same lecture halls with open notebooks before them.

In the bedroom he stopped before the dresser and looked at the electric alarm clock that was never wrong. It told him that the hour was two and that eight o'clock had been only six hours away. He sank down on the bed and let his arms go around her and his head lie on the hollow of her shoulder where it belonged.

"Bill. I love you."

She held him tighter and he felt the hopelessness seep deeper in him with the wetness of her tears on his face. He kissed her clumsily.

"I love you too," he whispered. "But it's not enough. Look at what I do to you. To everybody."

He listened to her breathing in the dark for a long time before she spoke again.

"I love you, Bill, and I'll stay with you. You're better now. You've been working too hard. Only Bill . . ."

He heard the sob start deep in her chest and he groped to soothe her with his hands, to comfort her until it passed.

"Please," she said, "please don't ever drink again. That's the only thing that makes it come back. Please."

They lay silently together. Then the tiredness was stronger than him and he knew nothing until the warmth of her was gone and he felt his head alone on the pillow.

"Pat."

His hand swept towards her in the darkness, and as it touched her hair on the other pillow he knew suddenly the whole world he had lost, knew all that she could never mean to him and that he could never tell her. He knew that he had to keep her from ever knowing he was still alone and that she couldn't help him back.

Then he felt her arms about him and for a moment there was the sure safe feeling that came with them. And knowing that sanctuary again, he wondered at it as he always had. Her embrace made him feel safer than any foxhole or concrete wall. It went beyond all reason. In her arms he knew that not even death could hurt him — though it took him. But she could never hold him long, only long enough for him to draw a few quiet breaths, and after those all the safeness was lost again.

He kissed her and got up to cross the room in the darkness and light the lamp on the dresser.

"What is it?"

At the stifled fear in her voice he stepped back to kneel beside the bed, nuzzling her hair.

"I have to set the clock."

"But . . ."

"I have a Shakespeare class at nine."

"You should sleep tomorrow."

"No." He was very tired now, he could feel his eyes closing against his will. But he was sure of something again and he held it tight in his mind. "It's only one class and I ought to go."

He went over and picked up his yellow plastic clock from the dresser.

"I think it'll be good for me to stick to the schedule." He turned back to her and nodded and then waited for her nod to agree with his.

There was doubt around the corners of her mouth.

"I have to keep on going," he said casually.

She nodded all right.

He set the clock and withdrew the plunger that would set the routine again. Then he snapped the light off and stood running the fingers of his right hand across the empty place the gold band had left on the other. In a little while he slipped beneath the covers and lay flat on his back, staring into the darkness overhead and feeling the night press in around him.

He would get used to it in time, he thought. He had gotten used to a lot of other things. He guessed that in this world and this time a man has to make a lot of changes and that some men, like himself, lose their elasticity, and then something happens to them. They can't change themselves any longer. Like a rubber band, he thought. You can stretch it just so many times and then it's no good.

At least he knew now who it was he had killed in the dream. There wouldn't be any more questions about that to bother him.

(*From Tomorrow*)

THE LOST

BY KAY BOYLE

THE WAR had scarcely come to a close when an America Relief Team drove up in jeeps through the little hills of Bavaria toward a property which had been, in former times, a baronial farmer's demesne. The place was set back off the country road, a good ten kilometers from any village, and the tree-bordered lane which led to the vast manor house, and its barns and stables and dependent buildings had long since become a cattle-and-wagon road, deeply rutted in the mud of springtime, and encumbered with stones. The heavy iron gates hung, as derelict as unhinged shutters, from the scarred blocks of granite which had stood for generations at the entrance to the drive. There were wild birds flickering through the branches of the trees, but no other sign of life; and even before the Americans had mounted the cathedral-like steps, and opened the massive door of the stone-winged house, they felt the chill of winter and silence and death that stood like a presence in its feudal halls.

The place had served as a Selection Camp from 1938 to 1945, so that any vestiges of personal effects or of individual life had been eradicated a long time before. But the official records of those who had passed through it, on their way to forced labor or to extermination, were found, neatly and alphabetically filed, in the bookshelves of what had once been the ancestral library. Attached to these records were the photographs, each with a number stencilled across the base of it, and each reproducing the grief and the exhaustion of one human being's unforgettable face — photographs of men with rumpled shirt collars and ties either missing or askew, taken full face as well as in profile, in order that the full measure of their anguish might be known; and photographs of women, some wearing blouses caught by antique brooches at their necks, and others in variously patterned aprons, as if they had come from their kitchens or their housework to this place, without having had the time to do their hair. It was the eyes of these men and women, who were there no longer, which looked now at the Americans, and beyond them, upon some indescribable vista of hopelessness and pain.

But when the Americans came, the nature of the place was altered. It became a Children's Center, and children who had journeyed from factory to factory throughout the war, or drifted from home to temporary home, were brought here from wherever they were found, brought singly, or in couples, or in groups. If they had wandered so long that they could no longer remember their people's names, new names were given them, and they were given Displaced Persons' cards, these children from Poland, or Holland, or Czechoslovakia, or Hungary. They were known as Unaccompanied Children, and they were given clothes to wear, and food to eat, and the outline of a plausible future at last. The Americans set up slides and swings on the grass of the lawn that lay between the stables and the manor house, and they made a sandpile for them, and then began the long and painful probing of their memories.

It was these slides and swings which the three boys saw first when they rode up on the American Army truck one morning — the wooden slides with the dew of the spring night still beading them, and the empty swings swaying gently on their ropes in the clear morning air. The soldier at the wheel brought the truck to a halt at the curve of the drive, and the three boys who had ridden in front with him waited a moment, looking out through the window and the windshield, reluctant, it seemed, to leave the Army vehicle and commit themselves to a civilian site and setting, for this was a part of life of which they knew nothing at all. Then the boy sitting next to the door pushed it open and jumped down — a tall, dark-haired boy of fifteen or sixteen maybe — and the other two followed, jumping clear of the step and down onto the gravel drive.

The tall one wore a faded khaki battle jacket, with the length of the sleeves turned back in cuffs, and a strip of German parachute silk, mottled green and tan, and as soft as the wings of a moth, knotted around his long curved neck. The jacket was buckled in tight where the waist of a man was intended to be, but the boy had no hips to hold it up, so it hung down long on the shabby G.I. trousers which had been cut down to his size. The two other boys were younger; they were twelve or fourteen, maybe, but they too were dressed like deserters from the ranks of the same army. They wore khaki, machine-

made sweaters over their G.I. shirts, and their khaki trousers were
thrust inside the mudcaked boots of the U.S. Infantry.

"Thanks for the lift," said the tall boy, speaking as good American
as you might hear at home. He stood looking up with a kind of
deference at the soldier sitting behind the wheel of the truck, and the
soldier looked down at the three of them, and fumbled a package of
chewing gum out of one pocket of his khaki pants.

"You guys like a stick of gum?" he said, and each of them reached
casually up, and took a stick from the package he held.

And then the soldier slammed the truck door closed, and he started
the motor, and the three boys stood there, chewing fiercely, the bits
of tinfoil and the colored paper lying on the driveway under their
feet, as they watched the truck back up and go. They had met for
the first time the night before, and even when the truck was gone,
they did not look into one another's faces for any of the answers that
might be given, each in his own fashion seeking to dissemble his
timidity. The tall one, his shoulders slouched in the battle jacket,
put his hands into his trouser pockets, and his dark, grave eyes looked
across the lawn toward the slides and the swings, and the thickly
leafed branches of the trees. The boy who was second in size had a
square, tawny-colored face, with a short nose and a humorous mouth,
and he stopped at once and picked up a pebble from the driveway, and
sent it skimming toward the sandpile where it hit hard against the
side of a child's wooden bucket that had been forgotten in the dark,
damp sand. The youngest boy's hair was of the texture and color of
a pony's shaggy, chestnut hide, his skin was delicate and white, and
he had a shy, quiet look of expectancy, of hope even, in his wide,
auburn eyes.

"I bet a nickel that's the kitchen over there," he said in a high,
bright voice, and he jerked his chin toward the right wing of the house.

"You hurtin' for chow already?" said the second boy. His accent
might have come straight from Brooklyn, except that it had come from
somewhere else before that, and, as he spoke, he folded his arms
upon his breast, and spat casually across the drive.

The tall boy looked back from the trembling leaves in the strong,
ancient branches, his eyes sober, his head hanging heavy on his soiled
slender neck.

"Let's go on up and sign ourselves in," he said, the drawl of his
voice having come, it seemed, from a Southern state. "That's what
we come here for," he said.

He led the way up the worn stone steps, and through the panelled door that stood open, having summoned courage, now that there was no other choice before them, to face this that was not an army deal. The youngest boy, his back and shoulders straight, and his hands in his trouser pockets, followed behind him, but the second boy lingered on the driveway, skimming stones across the grass. Because it was early still, there was no murmur of life in the house, and after they had come into the flagstoned hall, the tall boy moved on tiptoe toward the flight of stairs. But, at the foot of it, he stopped, and he jerked the battle jacket he wore up to where his waist should be, and tried to peg it on his hipbones. Then he lifted his thin, big-knuckled hands, and he smoothed back his lank black locks of hair.

"Hey, I smell chow," the other boy whispered behind him, but he did as the tall boy did, and sat down upon the first step of the stairs.

"Where'd you pick up you' outfit?" the tall boy asked, speaking quietly.

"Anzio," said the youngest boy, looking up into his face. "My mom and dad, they was bumped off when we bombed the town. I joined up with the Fourth Rangers and done the whole campaign with them," he said.

"My buddy's a mechanic, he's an ignition expert. I been suhvicing cars with him since 1944," said the tall boy, the words spoken soft and low. "He done tried every way there was to take me back, but they just couldn't see it," he said. He was leaning forward, his elbows on his knees, his long hands dangling. "We wanted to do it legitimate. When they Z.I.'d him last week, he tole me to come straight off down here and see what they could do."

And now the second boy came slowly up the outside steps, and crossed the threshold in hostility, wanting none of what might be offered here.

"Why the hell don't we make a break and run for it?" he said, stopping before the two others on the stairs. He stood there, recalcitrant, resentful, the lids narrowed on his opaque, black eyes, speaking savagely to them through his teeth. "You guys too yellow?" he said.

"Breakin' out won't get us nowhere," said the tall boy quietly.

"It'll get us the hell out of this here kid joint," said the second one. He fumbled a half-empty pack of Lucky Strikes from his trouser pockets, and put a cigarette on his lip. "Christ knows I didn't ask to come here," his Brooklyn accent said.

"None of us done asked," said the tall boy, and the smallest boy raised his head, and looked toward the end of the hallway.

"I bet a nickel it's ham and eggs," he said.

Because he was standing facing the stairs, it was the second boy who saw her first. It was only when the hot sullenness in his eyes had shifted to alarm, and, with the cigarette on his lip still, he had spoken the words of blasphemy under his breath, and turned, and gone out the door again, that the two others knew someone was there. She was big, and grayhaired, and matronly, and she held a flowered cotton dressing gown around her as she looked down from the landing at them through the steelrimmed spectacles that rode her nose.

"Hello," she said. The two boys had got to their feet, and they stood looking up at her.

"Hello," the tall one and the small one said.

"You men come up to the bathroom and wash your hands," the grayhaired woman said to them. "I'll get some clothes on, and then we'll have breakfast with the rest"; and it might have been mother or aunt, who was saying these things to them, except that neither mother nor aunt, nor the prototype of these, had meaning for them. It was not these names, these words in any tongue, that could stir the memory of anything they knew.

"Maybe you been expecting us, ma'am," the tall boy said.

"We're G.I. mascots from Bremerhaven," said the small boy, saying it with pride.

"You bet," the woman said. She did not say "so you're two more the M.P.s got when you were trying to slip onto the transport," although it may have come into her head. She did not put any of the questions to them until breakfast had been eaten, with the hundred-odd others, at the long tables in the dining hall. Then she took them away, a hand laid on each shoulder, into a room that was furnished with wicker armchairs, with flowered chintz cushions tied in the seats, and she took her place behind a paper-encumbered desk, and she looked at the two boys through the steelrimmed spectacles on her nose. "Sit down, men," she said, and she watched them sit down on the cushions of the wicker chairs. "If it's easier for you to speak German, we can talk German together," she said.

"I been speaking American three-year now," said the tall boy. "I learn German working in a munition factory. I done near forget every word of it I knew."

"And before that?" asked the woman, but she still did not write anything down.

"Czech," the tall boy said.

The woman did not seem to hear his answer, for she went on speaking of other things, as if saying these things to herself, speaking of countries and peoples the boys had perhaps known once but which they scarcely remembered, and in whose present and future they no longer had a part.

"It's like a big puzzle, or like the pieces of a big vase somebody dropped and broke here, right on the ground in Europe," she was saying, "and the pieces are jumbled together, and maybe we'll never get it straight, because a lot of the pieces are lost. We're trying to find them and put them together. That's what we're trying to do here, and we're doing it slowly, and maybe we're not even doing it very well," she said, and the sunlight from the window glinted on her glasses as she talked. "Maybe the G.I.s you were with made you promises about going to the States," she went on saying, and the two boys sitting in the wicker armchairs seemed to come alive now as they listened to her, but to the tall boy at least she was neither woman nor American, perhaps not human being even, but a voice — disembodied, quiet, direct — which might be coming now to the words they had been waiting to hear her say. "And probably when the G.I.s made you those promises they thought they would be able to keep them," she said. "I've talked to some of these men, I've had letters from them, and I know they believed they would be able to keep the promises. But there were other kinds, too. There were some kinds who didn't care what happened to you men afterward. I've known that kind, too. They wanted you to learn how to drink and smoke and gamble and shoot crap and use the kind of language they used —"

"I begin shooting crap in Naples," the small boy said in his high, eager voice. "I clean up seven bucks the first night there."

"Look, kid," the woman said abruptly, "if Italy's your country, perhaps you ought to pack up and go back there. You think it over. Perhaps that's where it's right for you to be."

He was sitting upright on the edge of the wicker chair, the khaki shirt open at his neck, the shaggy pony's chestnut hair growing long at his temples and behind his ears, the cut-down G.I. trousers bagging at his knees. He faced the woman for one more untroubled instant, and then the brightness perished in his flesh, and he looked down in grief at the mudcaked boots of the U.S. Infantry.

"I ain't no Eyetie no more," he said, and he did not raise his eyes to look at her because of the tears that were standing in them. "I'm American. I wanna go home where my outfit's gone," he said.

"Wait," said the woman quietly. "What would happen to you over there? We're an organization, and we make our list of candidates for emigration, and then the American Consul decides. We got thirty-five over last year, sent to adoption centers. But there's one thing we can't do much about changing — if you have anyone left to go back to in your own country, then we've agreed we'll send all you men back," she said.

"But if you ain't got nobody left where you come from?" the tall boy said, leaning forward from his chair.

"How do you know you haven't anyone left?" said the woman.

"My folks was hung in Noverzcimki in '42, when the Germans come in," he said.

"What proof have you got of that?" asked the woman.

"I done saw it," the tall boy said, and as the sunlight struck the woman's glasses, she swiftly lifted her hand, as if warding off a blow.

It was after that that she took out the forms and arranged them on the table, holding the fountain pen in readiness above them as she spoke.

"Tell me your name," she said to the tall boy, not looking at his face.

"Janos — it used to be Janos when I was a kid," he said. "But in the army they called me Johnny Madden." He leaned a little further forward, his thin shoulders hunched, his dark, anxious eyes fixed on her. "He wrote you a letter about me. He wrote it last week. Did you get it yet?" he said.

"Yes — a letter. I got a letter from a man named Madden," said the woman, her fountain pen still moving across the paper. "He's on his way back to Chattanooga. He's got a partnership in a garage."

"Partnership with his brother-in-law," the tall boy said, shifting further forward in his intensity. "Sergeant Charlie Madden. He want me to try to get over legitimate. That's why he tole me to come down here."

"Yes," said the woman again. She stopped writing now, and her middleaged hands straightened the papers on her desk. "He's colored, isn't he?" she said, and now the gray eyes, that might have been aunt's or mother's eyes behind the spectacles, lost their anonymity, and they looked at him in inexpressible kindliness.

"That's right," said the tall boy. "His wife, she done pass on back in '43, and he ain't got no one left to care for. He's an ignition expert, and I learn how to suhvice cars with him. He's got fifteen hundred dollars put in the bank, so he's able to pay for me to come."

"Yes," said the woman. "He wrote me that." She sat there silent, musing a moment, while the tall boy leaned forward from the chair,

his eyes asking the question of her even before the words were spoken
out.

"Do you think I got a chance of getting over there, ma'am?" he said.

"We can only recommend," the woman said quietly at last. "We
don't have any final say." When she was done with the forms, she
told them that they could go; they could go to the foreman in the
workshop and find out what there was to do, and in the afternoon
they would be processed by the Supply and Medical Corps. "You'll
get on to the ropes," she said, and they stood before her, the tall one
and the short one, incongruously matched. "The third man who
came with you, the one who went out to take a walk," she said, "you
tell him he needs a license to go fishing. That's what most of them
start in doing when they're uneasy here. And he didn't get any
breakfast. Tell him we mess at twelve o'clock," she said.

But all day the others did not see the third boy. Wherever he was,
he did not come in at the sound of the messhall bell at noontime, and
he was not in the empty classrooms or in the workshops, or the dormi-
tories, and he was not outside with the children who played underneath the trees. The boy from Anzio swung on the bars with the others
in the afternoon, and had the third boy been there, he could have
been seen at a glance, for he would have stood out as a stranger among
them, perhaps lingering, handsome and sullen and contemptuous, on
the outskirts of their activity. Janos went seeking him through the
buildings, through the barns and stables, and down the fields that lay
behind the house. As he walked, he unknotted the parachute silk
from around his neck in the heat, and he fanned it at the thin young
wasps which swam about his head. In the gully below, where it
seemed to him that water must pass, he could see an area of pine trees
stretched in an isthmus of shadow in the pale, shining sea of grass
and flowering bush. And there, at the end of the path, where the
full stream poured musically from the trees, he found the third boy
sitting, his back in the khaki shirt turned against the fields and against
the house, as if against the sight and sound of all humanity.

"If you just goes up there and tells her your name and everything,
then you got a chance," Janos said to him at once. "You got the
same chance as Anzio and me." The boy was sitting on the bank,
with the khaki sweater pulled off and lying, beside the cast-off combat
boots, upon the trampled grass. He had rolled the legs of his G.I.
trousers up, and his strong bare legs were hanging in the stream.
"She fills out the papers that you got to have, and if they finds out for

sure that you got nobody of you' folks left back where you come from, then you has a chance," said Janos. He stood, tall and stoop-shouldered, beside the other boy, watching the water flow swiftly over his naked feet, and mount high upon his muscular brown calves.

"Nuts," said the Brooklyn accent on this alien air, and the boy moved one foot slowly back and forth in the running water of the stream. The side of his face looked golden in the sunlight, and the dark hair lay thick and glossily dressed upon his shapely head. "I got the whole thing lined up. Have a butt," he said, and he took the crumpled paper of Lucky Strikes from his pocket, and held it out towards Janos. "I been looking around. It couldn't be sweeter," the boy said. Janos took a cigarette from the boy's hand, and he straightened it carefully in his fingers. Then the boy brought a silver lighter out of his pocket, and flicked it with his thumb, and Janos leaned to light his cigarette at the puny flame which the boy held shielded in the cup of his smooth hand. "I been contacting people in the area. Natives," the boy said, and he lit his own cigarette. As he drew the first breath of it in, he snapped the lighter closed again. "I got a deal on if you wanta come in on it. I got it fixed up with a Kraut down the road," he said.

"What kind of a deal?" asked Janos.

And now he sat down on the grass of the stream bank, folding his long legs awkwardly, as a young horse will, and settling down in the shimmering tide of sun.

"I'm going over the hill tonight," said the other boy. "All the good guys that come here, they don't stay. I got that straight from the Krauts," he said. He leaned back on his elbows, his eyes half closed against the smoke of the cigarette hanging on his lip. "All this here kid stuff. Don't let them give you the run-around," he said. "Swings, slides, sandpiles, and standing in line for a bowl of Grape Nuts. I'm through with that kind of crap. I'm fourteen. I got tired of hanging my stocking up for Christmas about ten years ago."

"You going back where you come from?" Janos said.

He sat smoking the cigarette, his shoulders hunched, his long legs drawn up, and his thin arms clasped around them, looking away across the flowing stream.

"Do I look like a dope?" the other boy said, and he gave a jerk of laughter. "I come from Poland once, but that don't mean I'm going back there. I been two and a half years with the Army, and I got my campaign ribbons, and my overseas service stripes, and I know my way around this little continent." The smoke from his mouth drifted lazily across the sunlit air, and his feet hung in the clear cool water still. "I'm going where things is easier. I'm going where all my friends is doing business now," he said.

"The sergeant I was with," Janos began saying after a moment, "he comes from Tennessee. We been working together since '44. When I get over there, I can start right in working with him again."

"Sure. You bet," said the other boy in irony.

"So I'll stick around here until the papers comes through," said Janos.

"You must be kidding, bud," the other boy said. "I saw action with three different outfits," he said then, and the sound of derision was gone from his voice as he turned his mutinous eyes on Janos's face. "I done everything that every son-of-a-bitch in the army ever done. I done peter parade, and had my broads, and wrote my own Saturday-night passes out, and, sure, they was all going to take me home with them, the whole God-damn Army was going to see to it possonnaly that I got Z.I.'d when the rest of them was! Sure, all you had to do was to go to Bremerhaven when they went, and walk up the gangplank with them, and nobody'd ever stop you, nobody'd ever have a word to say. Nobody except the M.P.s, the God-damn bastards," he said, and he lay there, looking back at the water again, and calling them the several names. "I got three times to Bremerhaven," he went on saying after that, "but I didn't get no further. The first time it was the colonel who had the uniform issued me in '44 who was going to see that I got shipped back when the others went. Except he forgot to fix the M.P.'s, just a little detail like that he forgot!" he said in high, fierce irony. "Sure, they'll wave to you from the deck when the troop ship pulls out, and when they get home they'll send you a post card of the Statue of Liberty! Up in Bremerhaven, they'll tell you just how it can be done, and the brass hats gives you advice for free. Run along to one of these God-damn kid centers, where they'll fix your immigration papers up! Hell, I ain't asking no favors of nobody! I been two and a half years in the American Army. I'm no emigrant," he said, and he shot the butt of his cigarette away.

Janos sat smoking a little while in silence, watching the water stream quickly, melodiously, past.

"That sergeant I was talking about, Sergeant Charlie Madden," he said after another moment, "he used to tell me a lot of things. He used to tell me how they first started measuring the days and nights," he said.

"You can't measure days and nights," said the other boy, but now the scorn was gone, and his voice seemed inexplicably filled with sorrow.

"Sure; way back in the time of emperors, they started in measuring the days and nights," said Janos. "They started in measuring them by letting water fall. They done took two jars, and when the sun come up in the morning, they let the water start dripping from one jar into the other, and when the last drop fell, the sun was already setting, and that was the end of the day. And to measure the nights, they let the water drip back into the jar it come from first," he went on saying, his legs drawn up and clasped in his arms still, his sober eyes looking at the trees. "And the drops of the water falling for a thousand years was like the ticking of a clock. Charlie Madden said for a thousand years they measured up the nights and days that way."

"Christ, I need a drink," said the other boy, and he sat up abruptly. "Listen, kid, if I let you in on this deal, we could make a break together," he said. He took his feet out of the stream, and he spread his toes in the warmth of the sun, and the beads of water ran off his smooth brown legs and feet and glistened on the grass. "This Kraut down the road, he's doing business with the Army — a nice little racket in jewels and schnapps. There're a lot of big shots in the country around here, and they don't want to contact the army direct, so this Kraut, he picks up their family jewels and their cases of schnapps, and he does it for them. The Army truck, it comes down from Frankfurt at night, maybe two-three times in the week it comes, with a load of coffee and cocoa they lifted out of the commissary depot stock."

Janos drew in the last deep breath of smoke from his cigarette, and then he threw the end of it away, and his long fingers reached out and pulled at a stalk of grass which grew tall beside the stream.

"And then what are you aiming to do?" he said, and he put the fresh, bleached end of the blade of grass between his teeth.

"I'm going to hop that Army truck back to Frankfurt, maybe tonight, maybe tomorrow night. The Kraut down the road's fixing it up for me," the other boy said.

"And what'll you do once you git to Frankfurt?" asked Janos, chewing slowly at the end of grass.

"The truck drops you off at Rhine-Main," the other boy said quickly. "By that time it's maybe three-four in the morning, and the M.P.s is groggy, and you slip in when they're loading the transat plane. The next stop's Gander, and then New York." He smiled with one side of his humorous mouth at Janos. "Do you get it?" he said.

That night was the first night Janos wrote to Charlie Madden. He wrote him to his home address in Chattanooga, sitting there in the chintz-bedecked, lamplit room where the grayhaired woman had put the questions to them in the day. She had drawn up a wicker chair on the other side of the table from him now, and the lamplight fell on the paper she had given him, and on the knitting in her hands, as she helped him with the words he couldn't spell.

"I just wanted to let Charlie Madden know what the score is," Janos said when he had written the first lines out, and he waited, as if there were some answer to be given.

"Nobody knows the score," said the woman, knitting. "It's like life," she said, as mother or aunt might have said it to him. "You have to wait and see." Mother or aunt, she thought as she knitted knowing the look of her own face in the glass; knowing it was neither mother nor aunt that any of them wanted, but the other things they had learned how to pronounce the names of — the name of a game of cards, or of a regiment whose insignia they had worn two years now, or the name of a city they had never known; or else the smell of a special beverage, or even the smell of car grease, or the turning motor of an army car. "The other one, the one who went out for a walk this morning," she said, saying it casually, her needles knitting still.

"He's a little doubtful about coming inside and signing up," said Janos, speaking slowly, softly, his eyes fixed on the words he had written carefully out.

"Sometimes they'll stay out for a week, and then they'll come in," the woman said. "You tell him the food is good. You tell him we're not M.P.s." Or aunts or mothers either, she did not say, still knitting. "You tell him we leave you free."

"Yes, ma'am," said Janos, but it might have been he had not been listening to her. "Please, how does you spell 'ignition'?" he said.

But the other boy didn't leave on the truck that night, and he didn't go the next night. He had settled himself in the hayloft above the empty stables, and only Janos knew that he was there. The second night he said he was getting a bottle of schnapps from the German farmer in exchange for two packs of cigarettes, and Janos said he would carry food out from the mess hall to him. So that was the way it began. All day the boy from Anzio played with the other children on the swings and slides, or else he worked in the classroom, or he went to the vegetable garden with the others and helped pull the radishes and the new lettuce out. He did not wear the cut-down G.I. clothes any more, but boy's short trousers, as the others did, and he did not speak of his outfit any longer. And Janos did what Charlie Madden had taught him to do in the shed behind the house where the driveway came to an end — all day he cleaned the carburetors, and checked the ignition, and overhauled the motors, of the American Relief Team's cars. But when it grew dark, he went out the back door with his head down, and he passed the shed with the cars standing in it, and he went on toward the stable underneath the trees. He wore his battle jacket still, for they did not have the other things to fit him, and inside his jacket he carried the bread and the cheese and whatever else he had slipped from the messhall tables after the evening meal was done. Once inside the stable door, he crossed in the darkness to the thick-runged ladder, and he felt with one hand for the polished wood, and closed his fingers on it, and then he began to climb.

But on the third night, the boy in the loft was still drinking water. For half a carton of cigarettes, he said, the farmer had given the bottle of schnapps to an American Army colonel instead of to him, and he lay cursing the farmer. But on the fourth night he had the bottle. He lay stretched in the farthest corner on the hay, with the square of a window standing open in the boards above him, and the stars shining clearly in it, and Janos could hear his voice speaking out across the hay-sweet dark.

"My God-damn lighter's gone dry as a witch's tit," the boy said, and Janos could hear the rasp of the lighter's stone in his hand. "I got to get me to a P.X. and get me some lighter fluid. I got to find me an American shoe-repair and get some soles put on my shoes. I walked through 'em today, but I got the schnapps," he said. When he sat up in the hay, his head and his neck and his shoulders in the G.I. sweater showed dark against the starry square of night. "Have a swig, kid," he said, and the bottle was more than half empty then when Janos drank from it. He had to tip his head far back, and hold the bottle tilted before the sharp hot trickle of liquid ran into his throat. "I got to get me to a man's-size town where there's a P.X. quick," the boy was saying in the darkness. "I bet I got two weeks' ration of butts coming due."

"Maybe when you hits Frankfurt," Janos said, and he wiped his mouth off, and stood the bottle up carefully in the hay, and now, without warning, the other boy began to laugh. He lay laughing beyond Janos in the darkness, shaking with laughter, as if something had come loose inside him, and was rattling around hard inside his belly and his chest.

"In that hick town?" he said, and he lay there swearing at the name of Frankfurt, and laughing in dry, hard jerks of sound.

"I got hole of a piece of sausage for you tonight," Janos said when the laughing had stopped a little. He had undone the buttons of his battle jacket, and now he laid the bread and the cheese and the sausage on the hay.

"For Christ's sake, pass me the bottle," the other boy said, and when Janos had found it in the darkness, he passed it to the unseen, outstretched hand.

"My buddy, that sergeant I was telling you about, he could tell you the names of all the stars there is," he said, and he sat looking at the stars in the open bluish square of night. "They might be one place in winter, and another place in the summertime," said Janos, "but he'd call them for you. We was in three countries together, and the same stars was usually there."

There was a lingering suck of air as the other boy lowered the bottle from his mouth.

"Oh, Christ," he said, his voice sounding thick and strange and far. "I'm thinking of the brass, the God-damn brass," he said. "I'm thinking how everything they got — chow, or cartons of butts, or pieces of hide — was always bigger and better than what we got." And then he began to laugh again, and he lay there, shaking as he jerked the laughter out. "Have a drink," he said, handing the bottle across the hay-whispering, hay-fragrant dark.

Janos closed his fingers around the bottle's neck, and then he drank, and with the second long swallow of the liquor, the promise made was no longer a thing that lay, heavy with longing, in his blood. It had come alive now, and he no longer doubted as he handed the bottle back across the hay.

"I know if I just sticks around here, and works, and waits," he began saying, and then he stopped it to say something else. "He taught me how to write in the two years we been together. I wrote him every night since I been here," he said.

"You listen, kid," said the other boy after he had drunk again. "The cards is stacked against us. We ain't got a chance, not you and me. Frankfurt," he said, in the same far thick voice, "I'm through with Frankfurt. I heard the air strip at Rhine-Main wasn't so good, so I changed the plans I had. I go down to the Kraut's place this morning, and he tells me the M.P.s got the guys that was in the setup with him, and they puts them in the clink. Bust up a nice little racket because they wasn't getting a big enough slice of it themselves. To hell with Frankfurt. I'm going to work a bigger area, like Munich, or Berlin," he said. He lifted the bottle of schnapps and drank again, and the stars stood sharper and brighter in the open window above his head. After a moment, he lowered the bottle from his mouth. "You got dependents anywheres?" he said.

"I ain't got nobody," said Janos. "That's why I know it's going to be all right, and I won't have to be going back home again."

"My old lady, she must've been fixing chow," the other boy said, his voice muffled now, as if he were holding the laughter in. "Because when I come home from school, there was her arm sticking out the end where the kitchen used to be. A direct hit. Pretty neat for '41," he said. "I couldn't get over the gold bracelet that was hanging on her arm still. Funny as hell how the bracelet wasn't twisted or nothing —"

"Maybe gold don't twist," said Janos.

"Maybe it don't at that," the other said across the hay.

That was the last time Janos ever saw him. When he climbed the rungs of the ladder the next evening, the boy was gone, and there was only the empty bottle lying in the hay. But because nobody else had known that he was there, no one else knew that he had gone, and the children stood in line for meals, or swung on the swings, or filed into the classrooms, and even the official memory of him was lost in the endless shuffling of children, effaced by the endlessly changing faces and names and histories. Once the grayhaired woman had said to Janos: "That other one, the one who went out to take a walk, you tell him we're having fried chicken this evening," and then the sound of her voice had perished of itself, as if knowing it had come beyond this, and there was nothing left that any living woman might find to say.

Twice in the next month the repatriation trucks came in through the heavy iron gates, and the children left, twenty or thirty at a time, carrying their string-tied bundles in their hands. As the trucks moved off down the driveway, the children sang in high clear voices of hope, returning now to places and people they did not remember ever having seen; perhaps to people who had been mother or father once, and to countries called France, and Holland, and Poland, and Czechoslovakia, and Hungary. And after a while the boy from Anzio left too, and the afternoon he left, the woman of the American team came down to the shed and looked through her steelrimmed spectacles at Janos working on the Army car.

"He had a grandfather in Naples," she said, and she sat down, in her rose-colored sweater and her old gray skirt, on an empty case marked "Tomato Juice" that stood against the side wall of the shed. "And that grandfather never stopped looking for him, he never stopped giving his name and his description to every G.I. he met." Janos was on his knees by the car, smearing the grease on the wheel nuts with his long thin hands. "And now he's on his way back," she said, "and he'll grow up in Italy where he belongs. I wish you were all as easy as that. Your papers, Janos," she said, and for a moment she did not say any more. She sat pressing the gray stuff of her skirt out under her square, strong palms, and she did not look at Janos. "They've checked back on the records, and the Consul says it's official enough that your people were killed. There's nobody of your family left," she said, but it did not seem easy for her to say.

Janos did not move at once; he crouched by the car a little longer, his shoulders hunched, scarcely daring to hear this thing that she had said. And then he undid himself slowly, the long legs straightening joint by joint, the long bent torso coming erect, until he stood up in the shadow of the shed, wiping the car grease from his hands.

"So I can write Charlie Madden it's all right about my coming over?" he said, and he felt his own mouth shaking as he smiled.

"Well, that's what I wanted to talk to you about," the woman said. She sat there below him on the upturned box, carefully and steadily smoothing the stuff of her gray skirt out. "Over there, back home, in the States, it isn't the same as here about a lot of things —"

"Why, sure, ma'am, I knows that," Janos said, and then the fear closed on his heart again. "If I ain't got nobody left, then I'm all right, ain't I?" he said. "If my folks was all killed off, then I'm eligible to go?"

"Well, Charlie Madden," she said, beginning again, "he's colored. Maybe in a combat outfit you didn't hear much talk about men being colored or men being white, or maybe you didn't pay much attention to it if you did. But over there, back home, in the States, there's the color question."

"There's what?" said Janos.

"There's the color question," she said in a dogged, quiet voice, and she did not lift her head to look at him. "There's the question about people being colored or people being white," she said. "In some parts of the country at home, they don't live in the same part of town that white people live. And they don't always go to the same schools, or to the same doctors when they're sick." Janos stood there listening to the words she said, and, as he listened, the woman again ceased being woman, ceased being human being even, and it was merely a voice in the shed that spoke quietly and bitterly of the separate lives that must be lived by people of different colors, as she had on that first day spoken of the hopes that might never come to anything at all. The voice was troubled as it searched logic or history for justification of the nearly incredible story it told. "I cannot explain to you why it is like this, but it *is* like this," it said, the voice faltering in the telling. "So if you did get to the States, there wouldn't be any way for you to live with Charlie Madden. The Consul's office has talked it over with me, and we thought we'd put it up to you. If we put your name on our list, and if you were cleared for emigration, then it would be better if you went to another family, a white family. We'd explain to them about Charlie Madden, and all he'd done for you over here," she said, "and he could come and see you, and you'd still be able to be friends" — and then the voice came to an end, and there was silence in the shed. The grayhaired, bespectacled woman sat on the wooden box against the wall and looked down at the backs of her hands, and the boy in his khaki clothes stood motionless between her and the dismantled car, seeming not even to breathe.

"I got all Charlie Madden's letters," he said then. "He don't make no mention of anything like that at all."

"The adoption committee might find somebody for you who had a garage himself," said the woman.

"Yes, ma'am," said Janos. "O.K., ma'am," he said.

He did not make the decision at once. He waited another week before he went to her office, and he stood by the desk without speaking until she had finished what she was writing down. Then she looked up at him, the pen still in her fingers, and he cleared his throat and spoke.

"There was a question I wanted to ask you, ma'am," he said, "before I finishes making up my mind. I'd like to know if there wasn't no change yet in that question you was talking about — the colored question over there?" he said.

"No," said the woman, and she looked down at the papers underneath her hand. "I haven't been notified of any change," she said.

It was the morning after that — and Janos was not in the mess hall for breakfast — that she found the envelope, with her name printed on it, lying on her desk. Inside it were the two letters, written neatly and inaccurately on copybook paper, and signed with Janos's name. They were not long — the first one merely four lines saying thank you and goodbye to her, and asking that she read the other letter, and send it on to Charlie Madden. The letter to Charlie Madden said:

Yessitday I talk to the US consil Charlie and what do ya think now? Seems my fammillys jus as good as they ever waz so Charlie I make up my mynd sudden to go back whar they waz waiting for me Im shure ya thinks its for the best Charlie so I says so long.

The woman sat there for a long time, holding the two letters in her hands.

(From New-Story)

THE OTHER FOOT

BY RAY BRADBURY

*W*HEN they heard the news they came out of the restaurants and cafés and hotels and looked at the sky. They lifted their dark hands over their upturned white eyes. Their mouths hung wide. In the hot noon for thousands of miles there were little towns where the dark people stood with their shadows under them, looking up.

In her kitchen, Hattie Johnson covered the boiling soup, wiped her thin fingers on a cloth and walked carefully to the back porch.

"Come on, Ma! Hey, Ma, come on, you'll miss it!"

"Hey, Mom!"

Three little Negro boys danced around in the dusty yard, yelling. Now and then they looked at the house frantically.

"I'm coming," said Hattie, and opened the screen door. "Where you hear this rumor?"

"Up at Jones', Ma. They say a rocket's coming, first one in twenty years, with a white man in it!"

"What's a white man? I never seen one."

"You'll find out," said Hattie. "Yes indeed, you'll find out."

"Tell us about one, Ma. Tell like you did."

Hattie frowned. "Well, it's been a long time. I was a little girl, you see. That was back in 1965."

"Tell us a white man, Mom!"

She came and stood in the yard looking up at the blue clear Martian sky with the thin white Martian clouds, and in the distance the Martian hills broiling in the heat. She said, at last, "Well, first of all, they got white hands."

"White hands!" The boys joked, slapping each other.

"And they got white arms."

"White arms!" hooted the boys.

"And white faces."

"White faces! *Really?*"

"White like *this*, mom?" The smallest threw dust on his face, sneezing. "This way?"

"Whiter than that," she said, gravely, and turned to the sky again. There was a troubled thing in her eyes, as if she was looking for a thunder shower up high, and not seeing it made her worry. "Maybe you better go inside."

"Oh, Mom!" They stared at her in disbelief. We got to watch, we just got to. Nothing's going to happen, is it?"

"I don't know. I got a feeling, is all."

"We just want to see the ship and maybe run down to the port and see that white man; what's he like, huh, Mom?"

"I don't know, I just don't know," she mused, shaking her head.

"Tell us some more!"

"Well, the white people live on Earth, which is where we all come from, twenty years ago. We just up and walked away and came to Mars and set down and built towns and here we are. Now, we're Martians instead of Earth people. And no white men've come up here in all that time. That's the story."

"Why didn't they come up, Mom?"

"Well, 'cause. Right after we got up here, Earth got in an atom war. They blew each other up terribly. They forgot us. When they finished fighting, after years, they didn't have any rockets. Took them until recently to build more. So here they come now, twenty years later, to visit." She gazed at her children numbly and then began to walk. "You wait here. I'm going down the line to Elizabeth Brown's house. You promise to stay?"

"We don't want to but we will."

"All right, then." And she ran off down the road.

At Brown's she arrived in time to see everybody packed into the family car. "Hey there, Hattie! Come on, along!"

"Where you going?" she said, breathlessly running up.

"To see the white man!"

"That's right," said Mr. Brown, seriously. He waved at his load. "These children never saw one, and I almost forgot."

"What you going to do with that white man?" asked Hattie.

"Do?" said everyone. "Why — just *look* at him is all."

"You sure?"

"What else *can* we do?

"I don't know," said Hattie. "I just thought there might be trouble."

"What kind of trouble?"

"You *know*," said Hattie, vaguely, embarrassed. "You ain't going to lynch him?"

"Lynch him?" Everyone laughed. Mr. Brown slapped his knee. "Why bless you, child, no! We're going to shake his hand. Ain't we, everyone?"

"Sure, sure!"

Another car drove up from another direction and Hattie gave a cry. "Willie!"

"What you doing way down here, where're the kids?" shouted her husband, angrily. He glared at the others. "You going down like a bunch of fools to see that man come in?"

"That appears to be just right," agreed Mr. Brown, nodding and smiling.

"Well, take your guns along," said Willie. "I'm on my way home for mine right now!"

"Willie!"

"You get in this car, Hattie." He held the door open, firmly, looking at her until she obeyed. Without another word to the others he roared the car off down the dusty road.

"Willie, not so fast!"

"Not so fast, huh? We'll see about that." He watched the road tear under the car. "What right they got coming up here, this late? Why don't they leave us in peace? Why didn't they blow themselves up on that old world and let us be?"

"Willie, that ain't no Christian way to talk."

"I'm not feeling Christian," he said, savagely gripping the wheel. "I'm just feeling mean. After all them years of doing what they did to our folks, my mom and dad, and your mom and dad, you remember? You remember how they hung my father on Knockwood Hill and shot my mother, you remember? Or you got a memory that's short like the others?"

"I remember," she said.

"You remember Doctor Phillips and Mr. Burton and their big houses, and my mother's washing shack, and dad working when he was old, and the thanks he got was being hung by Doctor Phillips and Mr. Burton. Well," said Willie, "the shoe's on the other foot now. We'll see who gets laws passed against him, who gets lynched, who rides the back of streetcars, who gets segregated in shows, we'll just wait and see."

"Oh, Willie, you're talking trouble."

"Everybody's talking. Everybody's thought on this day, thinking it'd never be. Thinking, what kind of day would it be if the white man even came up here to Mars? But here's the day, and we can't run away."

"Ain't you going to let the white people live up here?"

"Sure." He smiled, but it was a wide, mean smile, and his eyes were mad. "They can come up and live and work here, why certainly. All they got to do to deserve it is live in their own small part of town, the slums, and shine our shoes for us, and mop up our trash, and sit in the last row in the balcony. That's all we ask. And once a week we hang one or two of them. Simple."

"You don't sound human, and I don't like it."

"You'll have to get used to it," he said. He braked the car to a stop before the house and jumped out. "Find my guns and some rope. We'll do this right."

"Oh, Willie," she wailed, and just sat there in the car while he ran up the steps and slammed the front door.

She went along. She didn't want to go along, but he rattled around in the attic, cursing like a crazy man until he found four guns. She saw the brutal metal of them glittering in the black attic, and she couldn't see him at all he was so dark, she heard only his swearing, and at last his long legs came climbing down from the attic in a shower of dust and he stacked up bunches of brass shells and blew out the gun chambers and clicked shells into them, his face stern and heavy and folded in upon the gnawing bitterness there. "Leave us alone," he kept muttering, his hands flying away from him suddenly, uncontrolled. "Leave us blame alone, why don't they?"

"Willie, Willie."

"You, too, you, too." And he gave her the same look, and a pressure of his hatred touched her mind.

Outside the window the boys gabbled to each other. "White as milk, she said. White as milk."

"White as this old flower, you *see?*"

"White as a stone, like chalk you write with."

Willie plunged out of the house. "You children come inside, I'm locking you up, you ain't seeing no white man, you ain't talking about them, you ain't doing nothing, come on now."

"But, daddy ——"

He shoved them through the door and he went and fetched a bucket of paint and a stencil and from the garage a long thick hairy rope-coil into which he fashioned a hangman's knot, very carefully watching the sky while his hands felt their way at their task.

And then they were in the car, leaving bolls of dust behind them down the road. "Slow up, Willie."

"This is no slowing up time," he said. "This is a hurrying time, and I'm hurrying."

All along the road people were looking up in the sky, or climbing in their cars, or riding in cars, and guns were sticking up out of some cars like telescopes sighting all the evils of a world coming to an end.

She looked at the guns. "You been talking," she accused her husband.

"That's what I been doing," he grunted, nodding. He watched the road, fiercely. "I stopped at every house and I told them what to do, to get their guns, to get paint, to bring rope and be ready. And here we all are, the welcoming committee, to give them the key to the city, yes sir!"

She pressed her thin dark hands together, to push away the terror growing in her now, and she felt the car bucket and lurch around other cars, she heard the voices yelling, Hey, Willie, look! and hands holding up ropes and guns as they rushed by! And mouths smiling at them in the swift rushing.

"Here we are," said Willie, and braked the car into dusty halting and silence. He kicked the door open with a big foot and, laden with weapons, stepped out, lugging them across the airport meadow.

"Have you *thought*, Willie?"

"That's all I done for twenty years. I was sixteen when I left Earth and I was glad to leave," he said. "There wasn't anything there for me or you or anybody like us. I've never been sorry I left. We've had peace here, the first time we ever drew a solid breath. Now, come on."

He pushed through the dark crowd which came to meet him.

"Willie, Willie, what we gonna do?" they said.

"Here's a gun," he said. "Here's a gun. Here's another." He passed them out with savage jabs of his arms. "Here's a pistol. Here's a shotgun."

The people were so close together it looked like one dark body with a thousand arms reaching out to take the weapons. "Willie, Willie."

His wife stood tall and silent by him, her fluted lips pressed shut, and her large eyes wet and tragic. "Bring the paint," he said to her. And she lugged a gallon can of yellow paint across the field to where at that moment a trolley car was pulling up, with a fresh-painted sign on its front TO THE WHITE MAN'S LANDING, full of talking people who got off, and ran across the meadow, stumbling, looking up. Women with picnic boxes, men with straw hats, in shirt sleeves. The street car stood humming and empty. Willie climbed up, set the paint cans down, opened them, stirred the paint, tested a brush, drew forth a stencil, and climbed up on a seat.

"Hey, there!" The conductor came around behind him, his coin changer jangling. "What you think you're doing, get down off there

"You see what I'm doing, keep your shirt on."

And Willie began the stenciling in yellow paint. He dabbed on an F and an O and an R with terrible pride in his work. And when he finished it the conductor squinted up and he read the fresh glinting yellow words: FOR WHITES: REAR SECTION. He read it again. FOR WHITES: He blinked. REAR SECTION. The conductor looked at Willie and began to smile.

"Does that suit you?" asked Willie, stepping down.

Said the conductor, "That suits me just fine, sir."

Hattie was looking at the sign from outside, and holding her hands over her breasts.

Willie returned to the crowd, which was growing now, taking size from every auto that groaned to a halt, and every new trolley car which squealed around the bend from the nearby town.

Willie climbed up on a packing box. "Let's have a delegation to paint every streetcar in the next hour. Volunteers?"

Hands leapt up.

"Get going!"

They went.

"Let's have a delegation to fix theatre seats, roped off, the last two rows for whites."

More hands.

"Go on!"

They ran off.

Willie peered around, bubbled with perspiration, panting with exertion, proud of his energy, his hand on his wife's shoulder who stood under him looking at the ground with her downcast eyes. "Let's see now," he declared. "Oh, yes. We got to pass a law this afternoon no intermarriages!"

"That's right," said a lot of people.

"All shoeshine boys quit their jobs today."

"Quittin' right now!" Some men threw down the rags they had carried, in their excitement, all across town.

"Got to pass a minimum wage law, don't we?"

"Sure!"

"Pay them white folks at least ten cents an hour."

"That's right!"

The Mayor of the town came hurrying up. "Now look here, Willie Johnson, get down off that box!"

"Mayor, I can't be made to do nothing like that."

"You're making a mob, Willie Johnson."

"That's the idea."

"The same thing you always hated when you were a kid. You're no better than some of those white men you yell about!"

"This is the other shoe, Mayor, and the other foot," said Willie, not even looking at the Mayor, looking at the faces beneath him, some of them smiling, some of them doubtful, others bewildered, some of them reluctant and drawing away, fearful.

"You'll be sorry," said the Mayor.

"We'll have an election and get a new Mayor," said Willie. And he glanced off at the town where up and down the streets signs were being hung, fresh-painted: LIMITED CLIENTELE: *Right to serve customer revokable at any time.* He grinned and slapped his hands. Lord! And streetcars were being halted and sections being painted white in back, to suggest their future inhabitants. And theatres were being invaded and roped off by chuckling men, while their wives stood wondering on the curbs and children were spanked into houses to be hid away from this awful time.

"Are we all ready?" called Willie Johnson, the rope in his hands with the noose tied and neat.

"Ready!" shouted half the crowd. The other half murmured and moved like figures in a nightmare in which they wished no participation.

"Here it comes!" called a small boy.

Like marionnette heads on a single string, the heads of the crowd turned upward.

Across the sky, very high and beautiful, a rocket burned on a sweep of orange fire. It circled and came down, causing all to gasp. It landed, setting the meadow afire here and there; the fire burned out, the rocket lay a moment in quiet; and then as the silent crowd watched, a great door in the side of the vessel whispered out a breath of oxygen, the door slid back and an old man stepped out.

"A white man, a white man, a white man ——" The words traveled back in the expectant crowd, the children speaking in each other's ears, whispering, butting each other, the words moving in ripples to where the crowd stopped and the streetcars stood in the windy sunlight, the smell of paint coming out their opened windows. The whispering wore itself away and it was gone.

No one moved.

The white man was tall and straight, but a deep weariness was in his face. He had not shaved this day, and his eyes were as old as the eyes of a man can be and still be alive. His eyes were colourless; almost white and sightless with things he had seen in the passing years. He was as thin as a winter bush. His hands trembled and he had to lean against the portway of the ship as he looked out over the crowd.

He put out a hand and half-smiled, but drew his hand back.

No one moved.

He looked down into their faces, and perhaps he saw but did not see the guns and the ropes, and perhaps he smelled the paint. No one ever asked him. He began to talk. He started very quietly and slowly, expecting no interruptions, and receiving none, and his voice was very tired and old and pale.

"It doesn't matter who I am," he said. "I'd be just a name to you, anyhow. I don't know your names, either. That'll come later." He paused, closed his eyes for a moment, and then continued.

"Twenty years ago, you left Earth. That's a long long time. It's more like twenty centuries, so much has happened. After you left, the War came." He nodded slowly. "Yes, the *big* one. The Third One. It went on for a long time. Until last year. We bombed all of the cities of the world. We destroyed New York and London and Moscow and Paris and Shanghai and Bombay and Alexandria. We ruined it all. And when we finished with the big cities we went to the little cities and atom-bombed and burned them."

Now he began to name cities and places, and streets. And as he named them, a murmur rose up in his audience.

"We destroyed Natchez . . ."

A murmur.

"And Columbus, Georgia . . ."

Another murmur.

"We burned New Orleans . . ."

A sigh.

"And Atlanta . . ."

Still another.

"And there was nothing left of Greenwater, Alabama."

Willie Johnson jerked his head and his mouth opened. Hattie saw this gesture, and the recognition coming into his dark eyes.

"Nothing was left," said the old man in the port, speaking slowly. "Cotton fields, burned."

"Oh", said everyone.

"Cotton mills bombed out ———"

"Oh."

"And the factories radio-active, everything radio-active. All the roads and the farms and the foods, radio-active. Everything." He named more names of towns and villages.

"Tampa."

"That's my town," someone whispered.

"Fulton."

"That's mine," someone else said.

"Memphis."

"Memphis, did they burn *Memphis?*" A shocked query.

"Memphis, blown up."

"*Fourth* Street in Memphis?"

"All of it," said the old man.

It was stirring them now. After twenty years it was rushing back. The towns and the places, the trees and the brick buildings, the signs and the churches and the familiar stores, all of it was coming to the surface among the gathered people. Each name touched memory, and there was no one present without a thought of another day, they were all old enough for that, save the children.

"Laredo."

"I remember Laredo."

"New York City."

"I had a store in Harlem."

"Harlem, bombed out."

The ominous words. The familiar, remembered places. The struggle to imagine all of those places in ruins.

Willie Johnson murmured the words, "Greenwater, Alabama. That's where I was born. I remember."

Gone. All of it gone. The man said so.

The man continued. "So we destroyed everything and ruined everything, like the fools that we were and the fools that we are. We killed millions. I don't think there are more than five hundred thousand people left in the world, all kinds and types. And out of all the wreckage we salvaged enough metal to build this one rocket, and we came to Mars in it this month to seek your help."

He hesitated and looked down among the faces to see what could be found there, but he was uncertain.

Hattie Johnson felt her husband's arm tense, saw his fingers grip the rope.

"We've been fools," said the old man, quietly. "We've brought the Earth and civilization down about our heads. None of the cities are worth saving, they'll be radio-active for a century. Earth is over and done with. Its age is through. You have rockets here which you haven't tried to use to return to Earth in twenty years. Now I've come to ask you to use them. To come to Earth, to pick up the survivors and bring them back to Mars. To help us go on at this time. We've been stupid. Before God we admit our stupidity and our evilness. All the Chinese and the Indians and the Russians and the British and the Americans. We're asking to be taken in. Your Martian soil has lain fallow for numberless centuries; there's room for everyone; it's good soil, I've seen your fields from above. We'll come and work the soil with you." He paused. "We'll come and work it *for* you. Yes, we'll even do that. We deserve anything you want to do to us, but don't shut us out. We can't force you to act now. If you want I'll get into my ship and go back and that will be all there is to it. We won't bother you again. But we'll come here and we'll work for you, and do the things you did for us, clean your houses, cook your meals, shine your shoes, and humble ourselves in the sight of God for the things we have done over the centuries to ourselves, to others, to you."

He was finished.

There was a silence of silences. A silence you could hold in your hand and a silence that came down like a pressure of a distant storm over the crowd. Their long arms hung like dark pendulums in the sunlight, and their eyes were upon the old man and he did not move now, but waited.

Willie Johnson held the rope in his hands. Those around him watched to see what he might do. His wife Hattie waited, clutching his arm.

She wanted to get at the hate of them all, to pry at it and work at it until she found a little chink, and then pull out a pebble or a stone or a brick and then a part of the wall, and once started, the whole edifice might roar down and be done away with. It was teetering now. But which was the keystone and how to get at it? How to touch them and get a thing started in all of them to make a ruin of their hate?

She looked at Willie there in the strong silence and the only thing she knew about the situation was him and his life and what had happened to him, and suddenly he was the keystone, suddenly she knew that if he could be pried loose, then the thing in all of them might be loosened and torn away.

"Mister ——" She stepped forward. She didn't even know the first words to say. The crowd stared at her back, she felt them staring.

"Mister ——"

The man turned to her with a tired smile.

"Mister," she said. "Do you know Knockwood Hill in Greenwater. Alabama?"

The old man spoke over his shoulder to someone within the ship. A moment later a photographic map was handed out and the man held it, waiting.

"You know the big oak on top of that hill, mister?"

The big oak. The place where Willie's father was shot and hung and found swinging in the morning wind.

"Yes."

"Is that still there?" asked Hattie.

"It's gone," said the old man. "Blown up. The hill's all gone, and the oak tree, too. You see?" He touched the photograph.

"Let me see that," said Willie, jerking forward and looking at the map.

Hattie blinked at the white man, heart pounding.

"Tell me about Greenwater," she said, quickly.

"What do you want to know?"

"About Dr. Phillips, is he still alive?"

A moment, in which the information was found in a clicking machine within the rocket.

"Killed in the war."

"And his son?"

"Dead."

"What about their house?"

"Burned. Like all the other houses."

"What about that other big tree on Knockwood Hill?"

"All the trees went, burned."

"*That* tree went, you're sure?" said Willie.

"Yes."

Willie's body loosened somewhat.

"And what about that Mr. Burton's house and Mr. Burton?"

"No houses at all left, no people."

"You know Mrs. Johnson's washing shack, my mother's place?"

The place where she was shot.

"That's gone, too. Everything's gone. Here are the pictures, you can see for yourself."

The pictures were there to be held and looked at and thought about. The rocket was full of pictures and answers to questions. Any town, any building, any place.

Willie stood with the rope in his hands.

He was remembering Earth, the green Earth and the green town where he was born and raised, and he was thinking now of that town gone to pieces, to ruin, blown up and scattered, all of the landmarks with it, all of the supposed or certain evil scattered with it, all of the hard men gone, the stables, the ironsmiths, the curioshops, the soda founts, the gin mills, the river bridges, the lynching trees, the buckshot-covered hills, the roads, the cows, the mimosas, and his own house as well as those big-pillared houses down near the long river, those white mortuaries where the women as delicate as moths fluttered in the autumn light, distant, far away. Those houses where the cold men rocked with glasses of drink in their hands, guns leaned against the porch newels, sniffing the autumn airs and considering death. Gone, all gone, gone and never coming back. Now, for certain, all of that civilization ripped into confetti and strewn at their feet. Nothing, nothing of it left to hate, not an empty brass gun shell, or a twisted hemp, or a tree or even a hill of it to hate. Nothing but some alien people in a rocket, people who might shine his shoes and ride in the back of trolleys or sit far up in midnight theatres . . .

"You won't have to do that," said Willie Johnson.

His wife glanced at his big hands.

His fingers were opening.

The rope, released, fell and coiled upon itself along the ground.

They ran through the streets of their town and they tore down the new signs so quickly made, and painted out the fresh yellow signs on streetcars, and they cut down the ropes in the theatre balconies, and unloaded their guns and stacked their ropes away.

"A new start for everyone," said Hattie, on the way home in their car.

"Yes," said Willie, at last. "The Lord's let us come through, a few here and a few there. And what happens next is up to all of us. The time for being fools is over. We got to be something else except fools. I knew that when he talked. I knew then that now the white man's as lonely as we've always been. He's got no home now, just like we didn't have one for so long. Now everything's even. We can start all over again, on the same level."

He stopped the car, and sat in it, not moving, while Hattie went to let the children out. They ran down to see their father. "You see the white man, you see him?" they cried.

"Yes, sir," said Willie, sitting behind the wheel, rubbing his face with his slow fingers. "Seems like for the first time today I really seen the white man, I really seen him clear."

(From Mademoiselle)

A WREATH FOR MISS TOTTEN

BY HORTENSE CALISHER

*C*HILDREN growing up in the country take their images of integrity from the land. The land with its changes is always about them, a pervasive truth, and their midget foregrounds are crisscrossed with minute dramas which are the animalcules of a larger vision. But children who grow in a city where there is nothing greater than the people brimming up out of subways, rivuleting in the streets — these children must take their archetypes where and if they find them.

In P.S. 146, between periods, when the upper grades were shunted through the halls in that important procedure known as "departmental," most of the teachers stood about chatting relievedly in couples; Miss Totten, however, always stood at the door of her "home room," watching us straightforwardly, alone. As, straggling and muffled, we lined past the other teachers, we often caught snatches of upstairs gossip which we later perverted and enlarged; passing before Miss Totten we deflected only that austere look, bent solely on us.

Perhaps with the teachers, as with us, she was neither admired nor loathed but simply ignored. Certainly none of us ever fawned on her as we did on the harshly blonde and blue-eyed Miss Steele, who never wooed us with a smile but slanged us delightfully in the gym, giving out the exercises in a voice like scuffed gravel. Neither did she obsess us in the way of the Misses Comstock, two liverish, stunted women who could have had nothing so vivid about them as our hatred for them. And though all of us had a raffish hunger for metaphor, we never dubbed Miss Totten with a nickname.

Miss Totten's figure, as she sat tall at her desk or strode angularly in front of us rolling down the long maps over the blackboard, had that instantaneous clarity, one metallic step removed from the real, of the daguerreotype. Her clothes partook of this period too — long,

saturnine waists and skirts of a stuff identical with that in a good family
umbrella. There was one like it in the umbrella stand at home — a
high black one with a seamed ivory head. The waists enclosed a
vestee of dim but steadfast lace; the skirts grazed narrow boots of that
etiolated black leather, venerable with creases, which I knew to be
a sign of both respectability and foot trouble. But except for the
vestee, all of Miss Totten, too, folded neatly to the dark point of her
shoes, and separated from these by her truly extraordinary length,
her face presided above, a lined, other ellipse. Sometimes, on drowsy
afternoons, her face floated away altogether and came to rest on the
stand at home. Perhaps it was because of this guilty image that I was
the only one who noticed Miss Totten's strange preoccupation with
Mooley Davis.

Most of us in Miss Totten's room had been together as a group
since first grade, but we had not seen Mooley since down in second
grade, under the elder and more frightening of the two Comstocks.
I had forgotten Mooley completely but when she reappeared I remembered clearly the incident which had given her her name.

That morning, very early in the new term, back in Miss Comstock's,
we had lined up on two sides of the classroom for a spelling bee. These
were usually a relief to good and bad spellers alike, since they were
the only part of our work which resembled a game, and even when
one had to miss and sit down there was a kind of dreamy catharsis in
watching the tenseness of those still standing. Miss Comstock always
rose for these occasions and came forward between the two lines,
standing there in an oppressive close-up in which we could watch the
terrifying action of the cords in her spindling gray neck and her slight
smile as someone was spelled down. As the number of those standing
was reduced, the smile grew, exposing the oversize slabs of her teeth,
through which the words issued in a voice increasingly unctuous and
soft.

On this day the forty of us still shone with the first fall neatness of
new clothes, still basked in that delightful anonymity in which neither
our names nor our capacities were already part of the dreary foreknowledge of the teacher. The smart and quick had yet to assert
themselves with their flying, staccato hands; the uneasy dull, not yet
forced into recitations which would make their status clear, still pre-
served in the small, sinking corners of their hearts a lorn, factitious
hope. Both teams were still intact when the word "mule" fell to the
lot of a thin colored girl across the room from me, in clothes perky
only with starch, her rusty fuzz of hair drawn back in braids so tightly
sectioned that her eyes seemed permanently widened.

"Mule," said Miss Comstock, giving out the word. The ranks were still full. She had not yet begun to smile.

The girl looked back at Miss Comstock, soundlessly. All her face seemed drawn backward from the silent, working mouth, as if a strong, pulling hand had taken hold of the braids.

My turn, I calculated, was next. The procedure was to say the word, spell it out and say it again. I repeated it in my mind: Mule. M-u-l-e. Mule.

Miss Comstock waited quite a long time. Then she looked around the class, as if asking them to mark well and early her handling of this first malfeasance.

"What's your name?" she said.

"Ull — ee." The word came out in a glottal, molasses voice, hardly articulate, the l's scarcely pronounced.

"Lilly?"

The girl nodded.

"Lilly what?"

"Duh — avis."

"Oh, Lilly Davis. Mmmm. Well, spell 'mule,' Lilly." Miss Comstock trilled out the name beautifully.

The tense brown bladder of the girl's face swelled desperately, then broke at the mouth. "Mool," she said, and stopped. "Mmmm — ooo —"

The room tittered. Miss Comstock stepped closer.

"*Mule!*"

The girl struggled again. "Mool."

This time we were too near Miss Comstock to dare laughter.

Miss Comstock turned to our side. "Who's next?"

I half raised my hand.

"Go on." She wheeled around on Lilly, who was sinking into her seat. "No. Don't sit down."

I lowered my eyelids, hiding Lilly from my sight. "Mule," I said. "M-u-l-e. Mule."

The game continued, words crossing the room uneventfully. Some children survived. Others settled, abashed, into their seats, craning around to watch us. Again the turn came around to Lilly.

Miss Comstock cleared her throat. She had begun to smile.

"Spell it now, Lilly," she said. "Mule."

The long-chinned brown face swung from side to side in an odd writhing movement. Lilly's eyeballs rolled. Then the thick sound from her mouth was lost in the hooting, uncontrollable laughter of the whole class. For there was no doubt about it: the long, coffee-colored face, the whitish glint of the eyeballs, the bucking motion of the head suggested it to us all — a small brown quadruped, horse or mule, crazily stubborn or at bay. "Quiet!" said Miss Comstock. And we hushed, although she had not spoken loudly. For the word had smirked out from a wide, flat smile and on the stringy neck beneath there was a creeping, pleasurable flush which made it pink as a young girl's.

That was how Mooley Davis got her name, although we had a chance to use it for only a few weeks, in a taunting singsong when she hung up her coat in the morning or as she flicked past the little dustbin of a store where we shed our pennies for nigger babies and tasteless, mottoed hearts. For after a few weeks, when it became clear that her cringing, mucoused talk was getting worse, she was transferred to the "ungraded" class. This group, made up of the mute, the shambling and the oddly tall, some of whom were delivered by bus, was housed in a basement, with a separate entrance which was forbidden us not only by rule but by a lurking distaste of our own.

The year Mooley reappeared in Miss Totten's room, a dispute in the school system had disbanded all the ungraded classes in the city. Here and there in the back seat of a class now there would be some grown-size boy who read haltingly from a primer, fingering the stubble on his slack jaw. Down in 4-A there was a shiny, petted doll of a girl, all crackling hair bow and nimble wheel chair, over whom the teachers shook their heads feelingly, saying, "Bright as a dollar! Imagine!" as if there were something sinister in the fact that useless legs had not impaired the musculature of a mind. And in our class, in harsly clean, faded dresses which were always a little too infantile for her, her spraying ginger hair cut short now and held by a round comb which circled the back of her head like a snaggle-toothed tiara which had slipped, there was this bony, bug-eyed wraith of a girl who raised her hand instead of saying "present!" when Miss Totten said "Lilly Davis?" at roll call, and never spoke at all.

It was Juliet Hoffman who spoke Mooley's nickname first. A jeweler's daughter, Juliet had achieved an eminence even beyond that due her curly profile, embroidered dresses and prancing, leading-lady ways when, the Christmas before, she had brought as her present to teacher a real diamond ring. It had been a modest diamond, to be sure, but undoubtedly real, and set in real gold. Juliet had heralded it for weeks before and we had all seen it — it and the peculiar look on the face of the teacher, a young substitute whom we hardly knew, when she had lifted it from the pile of hankies and fancy note paper on her desk. The teacher, over the syrupy protests of Mrs. Hoffman, had returned the ring, but its sparkle lingered on, iridescent around Juliet's head.

On our way out at three o'clock that first day with Miss Totten, Juliet nudged at me to wait. Obediently, I waited behind her. Twiddling her bunny muff, she minced over to the clothes closet and confronted the new girl.

"I know you," she said. "Mooley Davis, that's who you are!" A couple of the other children hung back to watch. "Aren't you? Aren't you Mooley Davis?"

I remember just how Mooley stood there because of the coat she wore. She just stood there holding her coat against her stomach with both hands. It was a coat of some pale, vague tweed, cut the same length as mine. But it wrapped the wrong way over for a girl and the revers, wide ones, came all the way down and ended way below the pressing hands.

"Where you been?" Juliet flipped us all a knowing grin. "You been in ungraded?"

One of Mooley's shoulders inched up so that it almost touched her ear, but beyond that she did not seem able to move. Her eyes looked at us, wide and fixed. I had the feeling that all of her had retreated far, far back behind the eyes, which, large and light and purposefully empty, had been forced to stay.

My back was to the room but on the suddenly wooden faces of the others I saw Miss Totten's shadow. Then she loomed thinly over Juliet, her arms, which were crossed at her chest, hiding the one V of white in her garments so that she looked like an umbrella tightly furled.

"What's *your* name?" she asked, addressing not so much Juliet as the white muff, which, I noticed now, was slightly soiled.

"Jooly-ette."

"Hmm. Oh, yes. Juliet Hoffman."

"Jooly-ette, it is." She pouted creamily up at Miss Totten, her glance narrow with the assurance of finger rings to come.

Something flickered in the nexus of yellow wrinkles around Miss Totten's lips. Poking out a bony forefinger, she held it against the muff. "You tell your mother," she said slowly, "that the way she spells it, it's *Juliet*."

Then she dismissed the rest of us but put a delaying hand on Mooley. Turning back to look, I saw that she had knelt down painfully, her skirt hem graying in the floor dust, and, staring absently over Mooley's head, she was buttoning up the wrongly shaped coat.

After a short, avid flurry of speculation we soon lost interest in Mooley and in the routine Miss Totten devised for her. At first, during any kind of oral work, Mooley took her place at the blackboard and wrote down her answers, but later Miss Totten sat her in the front row and gave her a small slate. She grew very quick at answering, particularly in "mental arithmetic" and in the card drills when Miss Totten held up large manila cards with significant locations and dates inscribed in her Palmer script, and we went down the rows, snapping back the answers.

Also, Mooley had acquired a protector in Ruby Green, the other Negro girl in the class — a huge, black girl with an arm-flailing, hee-haw way of talking and a rich contralto singing voice which we had often heard in solo at Assembly. Ruby, boasting of her singing in night clubs on Saturday nights, of a father who had done time, cowed us all with these pungent inklings of the world on the other side of the dividing line of Amsterdam Avenue, that deep, velvet murk of Harlem which she lit for us with the flash of razors, the honky-tonk beat of the "numbahs" and the plangent wails of the mugged. Once, hearing David Hecker, a doctor's son, declare, "Mooley has a cleft palate, that's what," Ruby wheeled and put a large hand on his shoulder in menacing caress.

"She ain' got no cleff palate, see? She talk sometime, roun' home." She glared at us each in turn with such a pug scowl that we flinched thinking she was going to spit. Ruby giggled. "She got no cause to talk, roun' here. She just don' need to bother." She lifted her hand from David, spinning him backward, and joined arms with the silent Mooley. "Me neither!" she added, and walked Mooley away, flinging back at us her gaudy, syncopated laugh.

Then one day, lolloping home after three, I suddenly remembered my books and tam and above all my homework assignment, left in the pocket of my desk at school. I raced back there. The janitor, grumbling, unlocked the side door at which he had been sweeping and let me in. In the mauve, settling light the long maw of the gym held a rank, uneasy stillness. I walked up the spiral metal stairs feeling that I thieved on some part of the school's existence not intended for me. Outside the ambushed quiet of Miss Totten's room I stopped, gathering breath. I heard voices, one surely Miss Totten's dark firm tones, the other no more than an arrested gurgle and pause.

I opened the door slowly. Miss Totten and Mooley raised their heads. It was odd, but although Miss Totten sat as usual at her desk, her hands clasped to one side of her hat, lunch box and the crinkly boa she wore all spring, and although Mooley was at her own desk in front of a spread copy of our thick reader, I felt the distinct, startled guilt of someone who interrupts an embrace.

"Yes?" said Miss Totten. Her eyes had the drugged look of eyes raised suddenly from close work. I fancied that she reddened slightly, like someone accused.

"I left my books."

Miss Totten nodded and sat waiting. I walked down the row to my desk and bent over, fumbling for my things, my haunches awkward under the watchfulness behind me. At the door, with my arms full, I stopped, parroting the formula of dismissal. "Good afternoon, Miss Totten."

"Good afternoon."

I walked home slowly. Miss Totten, when I spoke, had seemed to be watching my mouth, almost with enmity. And in front of Mooley there had been no slate.

In class the next morning, as I collected the homework in my capacity as monitor, I lingered a minute at Mooley's desk, expecting some change, perhaps in her notice of me, but there was none. Her paper was the same as usual, written in a neat script quite legible in itself but in a spidery backhand that just faintly silvered the page, like a communiqué issued out of necessity but begrudged.

Once more I had a glimpse of Miss Totten and Mooley together, on a day when I had joined the slangy, athletic Miss Steele, who was striding capably along in her Ground Grippers on the route I usually took home. Almost at once I had known I was unwelcome, but I trotted desperately in her wake, not knowing how to relieve her of my company. At last a stitch in my side forced me to stop, in front of a corner fishmonger's.

"Folks who want to walk home with me have to step on it!" said Miss Steele. She allotted me one measuring, stone blue glance and moved on.

Disposed on the bald white window stall of the fish store there was a rigidly mounted eel that looked as if only its stuffing prevented it from growing onward, sinuously, from either impersonal end. Beside it were several tawny shells. A finger would have to avoid the spines on them before being able to touch their rosy, pursed throats. As the pain in my side lessened, I raised my head and saw my own face in the window, egg-shaped and sad. I turned away. Miss Totten and Mooley stood on the corner, their backs to me, waiting to cross. A trolley clanged by, then the street was clear, and Miss Totten, looking down, nodded gently into the black boa and took Mooley by the hand.

As they passed down the hill to St. Nicholas Avenue and disappeared, Mooley's face, smoothed out and grave, seemed to me, enviably, like the serene, guided faces of children seen walking securely under the restful duennaship of nuns.

Then came the first day of Visiting Week, during which, according to convention, the normal school day would be on display but for which we had actually been fortified with rapid-fire recitations which were supposed to erupt from us in sequence — like the somersaults which climax acrobatic acts. On this morning, just before we were called to order, Dr. Piatt, the principal, walked in. He was a gentle man, keeping to his office like a snail, and we had never succeeded in making a bogey of him, although we tried. Today he shepherded a group of mothers and two men, officiously dignified, all of whom he seated on some chairs up front at Miss Totten's left. Then he sat down too, looking upon us benignly, his head cocked a little to one side in a way he had, as if he hearkened to some unseen arbiter who whispered constantly to him of how bad children could be but he benevolently, insistently continued to disagree.

Miss Totten, alone among the teachers, was usually immune to visitors, but today she strode restlessly in front of us, and as she pulled down the maps one of them slipped from her hand and snapped back up with a loud, flapping roar. Fumbling for the roll book, she sat down and began to call the roll, something she usually did without looking at the book, favoring each of us with a warming nod instead.

"Arnold Ames?"

"Pres-unt!"

"Mary Bates?"

"Pres-unt!"

"Wanda Becovic?"

"Pres-unt!"

"Sidney Cohen?"

"Pres-unt!"

"L—Lilly Davis?"

It took us a minute to realize that Mooley had not raised her hand. A light, impatient groan rippled over the class. But Mooley, her face uplifted in its blank, cataleptic stare, was looking at Miss Totten. Miss Totten's own lips moved. There seemed to be a cord between her lips and Mooley's. Mooley's lips moved, opened.

"Pres-unt!" said Mooley.

The class caught its breath, then righted itself under the sweet absent smile of the visitors. With flushed, lowered lids but in a rich full voice, Miss Totten finished calling the roll. Then she rose and came forward with the manila cards. Each time, she held up the name of a State and we answered with its capital city.

Pennsylvania.

"Harrisburg!" said Arnold Ames.

Illinois.

"Springfield!" said Mary Bates.

Arkansas.

"Little Rock!" said Wanda Becovic.

North Dakota.

"Bismark!" said Sidney Cohen.

Idaho.

We were afraid to turn our heads.

"Buh . . . Boise!" said Mooley Davis. After this we could hardly wait for the turn to come around to Mooley again. When Miss Totten, using a pointer against the map, indicated that Mooley was to "bound" the State of North Carolina, we focused with such attention that the visitors, grinning at each other, shook their heads at such zest. But Dr. Piatt was looking straight at Miss Totten, his lips parted, his head no longer to one side.

"N-North Cal . . . Callina." Just as the deaf gaze at the speaking, Mooley's eyes never left Miss Totten's. Her voice issued, burred here, choked there, but unmistakably a voice. "Bounded by Virginia on the north . . . Tennessee on the west . . . South Callina on the south . . . and on the east . . . and on the east . . ." She bent her head and gripped her desk with her hands. I gripped my own desk, until I saw that she suffered only from the common failing — she had forgotten. She raised her head.

"And on the east," she said joyously, "and on the east by the Atlannic Ocean."

Later that term Miss Totten died. She had been forty years in the school system, we heard in the eulogy at Assembly. There was no immediate family, and any of us who cared to might pay our respects at the chapel. After this, Mr. Moloney, who usually chose "*Whispering*" for the dismissal march, played something slow and thrumming which forced us to drag our feet until we reached the door.

Of course none of us went to the chapel, nor did we bother to wonder whether Mooley went. Probably she did not. For now that the girl withdrawn for so long behind those rigidly empty eyes had stepped forward into them, they flicked about quite normally, as captious and as anyone's.

Once or twice in the days that followed we mentioned Miss Totten, but it was really death that we honored, clicking our tongues like our elders. Passing the umbrella stand at home I sometimes thought of Miss Totten, furled forever in her coffin. Then I forgot her too, along with the rest of the class. After all, this was only reasonable in a class which had achieved Miss Steele.

But memory, after a time, dispenses its own emphasis, making a feuilleton of what we once thought most ponderable, laying its wreath on what we never thought to recall. In the country, the children stumble upon the griffin mask of the mangled pheasant and they learn; they come upon the murderous topknot of the mantis and they surmise. But in the city, although no man looms very large against the sky, he is silhouetted all the more sharply against his fellows. And sometimes the children there, who know so little about the natural world, stumble still upon that unsolicited good which is perhaps only a dislocation in the insensitive rhythm of the natural world. And if they are lucky, memory holds it in waiting. For what they have stumbled upon is their own humanity — their aberration and their glory. That is why I find myself wanting to say aloud to someone: "I remember . . . a Miss Elizabeth Totten."

(From The New Yorker)

THE UNBORN GHOSTS

BY NANCY CARDOZO

*E*ACH TIME* the Piersons moved up to the country for the season — when their children were young, and they were still renting summer houses — the unaccustomed silence kept them awake the first few nights. Clare and Alan would joke about it at breakfast, lingering with the children and laughing behind their coffee cups, before she drove him down to his train. They had a way, in those days, of laughing at jokes without looking at each other, which, as they grew older, became more and more a dispassionate, lonely habit. Sometimes, years later, when other silences with the uneasy ghosts time had evoked shook her in the dark, Clare would remember those summer nights that had been haunted only by the voices of insects, small, yet interminable as life itself; and she would listen for the children to call, forgetting that Linda was grown up, living on the West Coast with children of her own, and that Davy, whose plane had gone down off Pusan, could never call her now. And she would reach out and touch Alan's impassive back and lie awake for a long time, trying to recall whether the road in front of a house they had stayed in, all of them, one summer in the thirties had been paved.

In 1938, the house that the Piersons rented for the season in Greens Farms seemed far out in the country. Week-end guests, driving up on the Post Road (for at that time the Parkway went only as far as Norwalk), thought they did well if they made it in two hours. But, as they never failed to tell their hosts, the quiet and the green shadows on the grass and the trace of salt in the air made the trip worth all the time and the traffic. Clare felt as if she had found a sanctuary for Alan and the children and their friends and relatives. For, after all, it was she who had discovered the Adams house, tall, white, with narrow blue shutters.

To the children, the Adams place seemed even more remote. Early mornings, when they looked out of their bedroom window across the tar-papered porch roof, spangled with dew, the silence was the silence of the wilderness. Smoke from imaginary tepees rose and lost itself in the mist, a scent of seaweed crept from the tide flats across the road. In front of the house, like a dense green wall hiding it from the road, and posted like a row of sentries down either side of the back lawn, stood pines that had been growing long before the house was built. Under their shaggy arms, the children gathered ancient scalloped cones and found the cast-off skins of locusts clinging to the bark, like brittle spectres of earlier summers. For Linda and Davy no other trees would ever seem as tall, no other lawn would have such mysterious shadows as that which spread, behind the house, out to the three stone walls, shiny with poison ivy, that bounded their "property." On the far side of the walls lay the widest meadows under the longest days.

Summer then was no hotter than it is now, but it may have been closer in temperament to the scorchers older generations recall nostalgically, along with parasols and homemade ice cream. In the Adams house was a japanned paper sunshade, left behind by some former tenant, but Alan's mother, who had been spending summers with them since old Mr. Pierson's death, refused to use it, and instead sat on the pebbly beach under a man's umbrella. It was not chic, yet Clare thought that Mrs. Pierson's erect black figure under the black silk shell gave the seascape an Old World air. (At that time, the beach was neither smart nor popular, deserted until the mothers and children arrived in the afternoon, desolate, with its unpainted wooden bathhouses, except on weekends, when the men were around and Star boats sparkled, racing out on the Sound.)

Then, as now, the season did not really begin until the Fourth of July. Days ahead, Alan and the children got in their supplies of fireworks. Whenever Clare went into the garage to find a trowel or a pair of clippers, she saw the tissue packages — red, green, and yellow, with Chinese markings — lying on the workbench among the bags of bone meal and the soiled cotton gloves. She eyed them with what she intended to be an amused scorn — the crackers, the snakes and sparklers, and the big cylinders of powder that smelled of danger and that only Alan was allowed to light. Actually, they frightened her. So long as they remained unexploded near the house, they seemed to threaten to blow them all (as Davy, who was eleven, loved to proclaim) to smithereens.

That year the Piersons had guests for the holiday, which perversely managed to fall on Alma the maid's weekend off. There were Alan's sister, Barbara, and her daughter, Gaby; "Uncle Adrian," who was not the children's real uncle but the junior partner in Alan's law firm; the Macys, who were summer neighbors, and their nine-year-old son, Ed; and, of course, Alan's mother, who was deaf and carried her hearing instrument from breakfast table to beach and all around the house. Whenever she was addressed, she would take out the small black box that held the batteries, set it on a table or the arm of a chair, unravel the wires, and hold the receiver to her ear, while her eyes followed the speaker's lips and her straight, frail body seemed to listen.

By late afternoon, the women, sitting on the screened back porch, felt as if their dresses had turned to limp, dull rags. The men had taken off their Palm Beach jackets. Their pink sunburned shoulders shone through their soft white shirts. The air smelled of burnt powder. The oily ash of snakes festooned the driveway. The children had set off all the firecrackers. Tin cans had been detonated. Gaby, the youngest, the perpetual cousin, had screamed and held her ears, and all the birds had flown, terrified, into the safety of the sky.

Then, in the renewed silence, time dribbled slowly through the pine branches. There was nothing left for the children to do but listen to the diminishing reports from neighboring lawns and wait for the daylight to die. They lolled, bored, about the porch, their bodies sticky and redolent of sarsaparilla. "Darlings," Clare pleaded, "why don't you do something? Go down to the beach and see if your castle is still there."

Linda, her hair ribbon tipsy over one ear, sighed with the impatience of an eight-year-old. "Mother, you know perfectly well the tide's been in and washed it away ages ago."

Davy and Ed refused to go swimming (too many jellyfish, they claimed), afraid that darkness might catch them unprepared. Uncle Adrian looked out at the sky that burned behind the copper screening and insisted that he smelled rain. So much gunpowder in the air was sure to bring it on before evening, he said, and they would have no fireworks after all. Gaby, who was only six, believed him and began to cry.

"Don't listen to him, silly pet," said her mother. "He's always teasing." She leaned across the unravelling wicker table and slapped

Adrian's bare arm. There was a blue serpent tattooed on his hard
brown muscle, which the children believed gave him a magic power.
It seemed bold of Barbara to touch it, and they stared. She bit her lip
and turned away quickly when Adrian grabbed at her, spilling her
highball down the front of her blue dirndl skirt. Gaby sniffled on the
back of her wrist and stopped crying.

Clare, pitying them all and feeling responsible, as usual, sent the
children off to pick some mint for iced tea. They left the porch reluctantly. Single file, they crossed the back lawn, watching for clouds
in the azure sky, their bare feet soundless on the turf. They passed the
cement birdbath and the swing, hanging motionless from the arm of a
beech tree, and disappeared among the currant bushes, where the
mint grew wild, along with sour grass and Queen Anne's lace. As
soon as the four of them were out of sight, the men stirred and stretched
their arms, the women sighed with relief.

Irene and Tom Macy, who had left their cottage baking on the
beach to spend the afternoon in the Piersons' shade, swung like love-
birds in the canvas glider. Tom fanned Irene's round, powdered neck
with his green visor. He was a research physicist — a burly, beetle-
browed man who drank copiously without a spark of inebriation; he
rode down to the city weekdays with Alan on the seven-fifty-two. It
had been Alan's idea to invite the Macys. He was impressed by scientists and admired Irene's likeness to a Renoir lady. This afternoon,
she was wearing her peasant outfit — green-blue batik skirt and a
white blouse that showed her firm, rosy shoulders. In winter, Irene
would most likely wither, thought Clare, and she considered her own
tanned arms, her pink golf dress, and her muscular legs, which still
looked sensible in slop socks and sneakers, though she seldom wore
them. She and Irene stood at opposite poles.

Clare glanced at her husband. He was stretched out in a deck chair,
one knee drawn up in his most boyish fashion, describing a case he had
handled when he first began to practice — telling the story a little
pompously, she thought, as if it had happened fifty years before, in a
dim, rich past. But no one was paying much attention. Mrs. Pierson
had switched off her hearing aid. Her eyes were closed, and, impervious
to heat as well as noise, she had drawn her black-scrolled chiffon scarf
up around her withered neck. Adrian, who had found a clean handkerchief in someone's coat pocket, was dabbing at Barbara's skirt, trying
to dry the overturned drink.

"Oh, let it be," Barbara said coldly. All afternoon, thought Clare,

Barbara had been entranced, listening, rushing to be the first to answer the phone each time it rang. ("That's not our ring," she had been told again and again. "Ours is three.") Even now, she was listening, her cool, straight features so like Alan's, but smaller and tense and wary.

"Listen!" she said. "What was that?"

"Nothing at all," snapped Alan, annoyed at the interruption.

"But I could have sworn I heard a bell," said Barbara. "I guess I'm hearing things."

"Maybe the place is haunted," said Irene Macy.

"It's not old enough." Alan had lost his story now. "Thirty years is all, I'd say. No real class."

"Poor house," said Clare. "Its ghosts are still being born." Her drink had turned warm in her hand. There were specks of sawdust in it. As usual, without Alma to remind him, Alan had forgotten to wash the ice that came from the icehouse.

"The humidity," complained Irene.

Tom stopped fanning her. "You should fuss," he said.

"It's like the jungle," Clare murmured. Mrs. Pierson switched on her earphone, which then emitted an insistent whine, as if it were demanding, inhaling sound. Her head, with its wreath of twisted yellow-white hair, was tilted toward Clare, waiting.

Clare looked at Alan, thinking, Must I? The most inane remarks had to be repeated if Mrs. Pierson demanded it. Alan leaned forward and tapped his mother's black-silk knee. "Clare said that it seems like the jungle," he said.

Mrs. Pierson's lips followed his. "The what?"

"The jungle," shouted Alan.

His mother nodded.

The children came back much too soon, grumbling about prickers and mosquitoes. They dropped their bunches of mint, crushed and darkened already, in Clare's lap. *Now* what time was it, they wanted to know.

"Twenty to six," Barbara answered, without glancing at her wrist-watch.

"You'd better wash," Clare said to Davy. He scowled. A mint leaf pasted on his brown cheek gave his face, under his indefinite, pointed brows, the look of a faun.

"And put a shirt on for supper. And shoes," Alan said, never able to resist a final admonition.

Davy scratched his smooth, round stomach. "C'mon," he said to Ed

Macy. They ran inside, and in only a moment they could be heard
scuffling on the floor upstairs. Bedsprings banged and bureau drawers
were scraped in and out.

"For God's sake!" yelled Alan. "Cut it out! We've had enough
noise for one day!"

Clare shook her head at him. How could he lose his temper over a
trifle? How would the children ever learn? He rose and scooped the
mint out of her lap, not meeting her look, and went off into the house
to get some more whiskey and ice and soda.

Linda stood by Adrian's chair. Her dress, white and sprigged with
cherries, which had belled out with starch a few hours before, had
wilted, and her knees were stained with grass. Gingerly, she put out a
finger and touched the cerulean serpent on his arm. Adrian looked at
the ruffled top of her head, confused, not quite paternal. Then he
offered her his glass. "Here, have a taste."

A blush mottled her transparent temples. She took a sip from his
glass, staring at him in solemn adoration.

"Well?"

"It feels funny going down," she said, trying not to grimace. "As if
it weren't me drinking it."

"That's only because it's the first time," said Adrian. "How do you
suppose you'll feel the first time you wear high heels?"

Linda sat down on the wicker settee beside her grandmother. Her
face was crimson.

"Gaby?" said Adrian, offering his glass to her. But Gaby, who was
as shy and unpredictable as a fritillary, turned from him and flung her
arms around her mother's waist and buried her head in her lap.

"Look out," said Barbara. "Can't you see my skirt is soaked? You'll
crease it." Gaby ran away across the porch, her brown hair fanning out
on either side of her pale, mauve-shadowed face. She squatted in the
corner where the butterfly nets were hung, licking a mosquito bite on
the back of her hand, glowering, trying, thought Clare, to look like her
father, whom Barbara had divorced in Europe that spring.

Adrian drank the rest of his highball. "I wonder how many people
are dead by now," he said.

"Don't be so gruesome," snapped Barbara.

"Well, it *is* gruesome," he persisted. "All the way up in the car this
morning, I had the radio on, and they were announcing accidents like
baseball scores."

Mrs. Pierson lifted her whining black box. "Who's driving up?"

"Death toll," Clare mouthed.

"Traffic accidents!" shouted Adrian, leaning forward, his thigh muscles strained under his tight duck trousers. "Death on the highway!"

Mrs. Pierson switched off her machine. "Terrible," she said.

Barbara's face had blanched beneath her tan. Her soft underlip trembled. Whoever was supposed to telephone, Clare decided must be coming in a car. Perhaps Adrian knew. There was something a bit sly and spurious about him, she thought — an artificial flavor, like spearmint gum. He stared at Barbara. His young, square face, under its sun-bleached cap of hair, wore a look of triumph.

"Think of something pleasant," said Clare. "Think of snow."

"It melts too quickly," said Irene Macy.

"We've never been here when it snowed," said Linda. "Could we come and see it sometime, Mummy?"

"Maybe," said Clare. But they never would.

The blood had come back into Barbara's face, but now there was a line between her eyes, which were always faintly pink and bleary, as if she had been crying or had swum too long underwater. "I suppose," she said, tapping her long red nails on the peeling arm of her chair, "if it were winter, you would sit around with your feet on the stove and talk about how cold it was."

"Of course we're dull," said Adrian. "I suppose ———"

"Oh, come," Clare sighed.

"When in the world are we going to have the fireworks?" asked Gaby, from her corner. She had scratched the back of her hand so that it bled. "Couldn't we each do just one sparkler, Aunt Clare?"

"It seems a shame to waste them on the daylight," said Clare.

"But, Mummy, it lasts forever!" cried Linda.

And, truly, it was as if time had stopped, as if this scene had all been fossilized ages before — the figures on the porch, and, beyond, the meadows of timothy and clover, and the black pine trees, like hands raised in prayer, all bathed in amber sunlight. Was it this summer or last?

"Pretty little girls," said Mrs. Pierson. Gaby sucked at the blood on her hand.

Alan came back carrying a bowl full of ice chips. " 'In Dublin's fair city, where the girls are so pretty . . .' " he sang softly in his sweet tenor voice as he gathered the empty glasses from table edges and the guests' lazy hands. His mouth is weak, like Barbara's thought Clare, with a pang of disloyalty, watching him lean over to bestow a kiss on his mother's forehead. (Mrs. Pierson never touched a drop — just a

thimbleful of wine against her papery lips on birthdays.) But he was
tall, and hard, still, with only the least beginning of a paunch — to
keep his trousers up, he would say, hiking his belt over his narrow hips.
He had been helping himself in the kitchen, she knew. Soon he would
be singing all his songs and telling all his stories.

" 'Crying cockles and mussels, alive, alive-o.' " Alan gave her a glass,
and pulled at the curls that had slipped out of her combs and down her
neck. She pushed his hand away. It was hard enough to keep her hair
up without that. Barbara's eyes, half closed, watching, seemed to say,
"How satisfying to be leaving this domestic scene, to be meeting someone tonight beside the cannon under the elms on the village square!"
Or wherever he might wait. And Clare imagined the white turnpike
leaping under the tires of the car, and the evanescent neon roadhouses
that lit the shore road.

A horsefly hit the screen and bounced off erratically into a bed of
phlox. The chains of the glider complained as the Macys pushed themselves idly with their feet. Barbara stood up. She brushed past Adrian
and went into the house. Mrs. Pierson rose also, but fragilely, gathering
the wires of her instrument and her webs of silk about her. "Come
along, lambs of the world," she said to the children. "Grandma will
read to you while we're waiting for supper." She herded them off the
porch in folds of black crêpe de Chine, and Clare felt her disapproval
of the lengthening hours of drinking float back like a wake.

"When do we eat?" asked Alan. "Just because Alma's left us
stranded, must we starve? And when it gets dark, you know, we'll
want to be done with supper."

Irene Macy leaned confidentially toward Clare. Her powder had
melted in the pink hollow between her breasts. "Just like a man, isn't it?
Can't wait to be exploding things." They smiled together. "What
can you do?" asked Irene.

Clare pulled herself up from her deck chair. "No," she said, as the
others gestured limply. "I don't want any help. It just has to be put
on the plates." From the door, she looked back at them. Alan was
holding his long head in his hands, trying to remember how a certain
tune began. The other three stared up at the cobwebbed porch beams,
with helpful expressions on their faces.

In the living room, Clare was conscious of the stifling smell of paper
window shades toasted by the sun, and the ineradicable odors that
seasons of strangers had left behind. At the far end of the room, Linda
and Gaby and Mrs. Pierson were examining the books on the shelves,

All the ashtrays were filled with the white worms of butts (she had been too sleepy last night and too busy all day to empty them), and there were rings made by glasses on the top of the upright mahogany piano. Upstairs in the bedrooms, there would be damp towels and bathing suits lying in pools of moisture on the floors, and tennis balls in clots of dust under the beds — as if, she thought, rubbing her finger along the fretwork of the music rack, as if we ran an eternal houseparty. How lovely it would be when the weekend was over and everyone had gone! She and the children would go down to the village at noon, when the stores were empty, and have tuna-fish sandwiches and sodas for lunch in the drugstore, under the soothing circling of the electric fans.

Clare looked at herself in a round mirror that hung above the cretonned sofa. The sun had drawn fine lines at the corners of her eyes, but her skin glowed in the shaded room and she smiled at herself. Deep in the mirror she could see the grandmother and the two little girls. Linda's pure, straight profile, lowered over a book, the lashes demure and secret on her cheek, gave Clare a premonition of the stranger she would become. A grievance against time that was so contrary — time that passed so slowly but would not stay — claimed her, and she glanced restlessly about the room, at the student lamps on the end tables and the Italian landscapes in brown frames that she had been meaning to put away, as she had put away the photographs of families in ladder-back chairs and of shy, cold couples in high collars. On the mantel were candle stubs and someone's pipe, fairy shells, dried starfish, a nest with a freckled turquoise egg, stones specked with mica, and a sea-gull feather. She could no longer tell which of these Davy and Linda had found and which had been gathered and forsaken by other children, other summers.

"*Heidi!*" cried Linda. "It has colored pictures." The grandmother took the book from the shelf, sat down in a leather armchair, and lifted the eyeglasses that hung on a silver chain around her neck.

Books in rented houses were only the ghosts of books, thought Clare, watching the three heads, one white, two tawny, bent beside the green glass lampshade. Shopping lists and postcards of blue-and-orange beaches secreted between their pages had much more life, and pressed, brittle rosebuds marked someone else's passionate afternoons.

"If you won't stop fidgeting, Gaby, I simply cannot read," chided Mrs. Pierson.

It was then that the telephone rang. On the third ring, Clare lifted the receiver from the hook. "Hello," she said softly. There was no

reply, only a smattering of interference on the line. She imagined a
phone booth in a bar, heat lightning flickering in the atmosphere between it and herself. Whoever was calling, not sure whether she was
Barbara or not, was waiting for another sign. Clare waited, too. She
heard Barbara's mules clopping along the upstairs hall. On the cover
of the telephone directory Clare read, "Plumber, call 237. Butcher —
South Main Street."

"Is Mrs. Colter there?" The man's voice was unfamiliar. She was
about to reply when Barbara, wrapped in a beach towel, her face lucid
with cream and almost blank without lipstick, appeared beside her.
Clare handed her the receiver of the long-necked phone, with its in-
trusive voice, and went off to the kitchen.

She took a lemon from the ice chest and sliced it on the wooden drain-
board. From the glass-doored cupboard above the one-legged sink, her
own face glimmered back at her, a ghostly reflection, indefinitely
limned but quite at home among the pink willow china that someone
with doubtful taste had chosen for this shelf years ago, and the thought
occurred to her that in some summer yet to come another tenant might
see that wavering ghost of a face still prisoned in the glass and wonder
who she was and how life had seemed to her.

Out on the porch, Alan was leading the others in bibulous laughter,
and Clare could hear Mrs. Pierson's voice, in the living room, going
steadily across the page. (Barbara's hand would be cupping her mouth
at the phone to hide her lover.)

"The best one I've heard in a long time," Alan was saying, "is the
one about the man who went to the doctor ——"

Clare put her hands over her ears. Davy and Ed ran past the
kitchen window. (How could they bear to run?) Intent on some
secret errand, they circled the lawn, a cloud of midges at their heels,
and ran under the beech tree. Clare saw the swing move as they went
by. Empty, it rocked and seemed to set the air in motion, as on some
future day the wind might stir up memories of children's games. The
boys' shadows flitted hugely over the grass and lost their heads on the
far side of the wall. The sun must be going down at last. But by the
time supper was ready it was still not dark enough to light the lamps.

"If this is like the jungle . . ." said Alan, buttering a roll. "I was led
to believe that in the jungle the sun went down quickly."

"You mean the dawn," said Clare. "Coming up like thunder."

Unlit candles stood on the long table like pale, headless sentinels.
Coral slabs of salmon in marbled skin, lettuce, black olives, gold-leafed

wands of celery, and pearls steaming, all seemed to float in the half light, the faces of the diners poised above. For a short while, the children, with napkins tucked beneath their chins, were silent, and the grown people (all but Barbara, who was upstairs, still dressing for what she had chosen to call "a sudden little dinner party") sat in a quiet that was marked only by the sounds of silver and the children's chewing, and requests for butter.

"Aunt Barbara's going to miss a good show, isn't she, Dad?" Davy spoke with his mouth full. Beside him, Ed drove his teeth into his fourth ear of corn. Linda and Gaby sat opposite, their arms around each other, whispering feverishly.

"Wherever Barbara goes, she'll make her own fireworks," said Adrian.

"She was smart to get out of Europe," said Tom Macy, brandishing his celery.

"That's one thing. Everyone's coming home."

"Like birds before a storm," said Adrian. "Or is it rats?"

"A few years ago, when Hitler was mentioned, nobody'd ever heard of him," said Irene. "Remember?"

"But we won't have another war," said Clare. "I refuse to believe it."

"Would you go, Daddy, if there was one?" Ed asked. It was his first remark at the table. His face was cherubic, like his mother's, under a feather of orange hair.

"No," Irene said, laughing. "He's too old. And you're too young."

"Adrian will have to fight our war," said Tom.

Adrian saluted across his empty plate.

"Ah, that's not fair," said Davy.

Adrian lit a cigarette. "You can have the next one," he told Davy.

"Stop talking like that," said Clare. "You've no right. As if wars would go on forever."

"No use, my dear," said Alan. "We'll always have wars. You can't ——"

"You can't change human nature," Davy interrupted, in a singsong. They all laughed uneasily, except for Mrs. Pierson, who had hidden her little black box in her lap and sat in her place of silence picking at her salad.

Gaby jumped up from her chair and ran to the window. She pressed her face against the screen and lifted her arms. "Look!" she cried. A firefly winked chartreuse and gold above her head. The other children went and stood beside her. Outside, on the darkening lawn, a host of pale-green stars came and went minutely. A hot, wet breeze bellied the curtains into the room, as if, far away, some monster had exhaled. "Come back to your seats!" said Alan. But the children did not move. Clare looked at his thin, exasperated face at the far end of the table. Darkness had deepened in the room now. It hung its veils between them, obscuring the expressions of their eyes. (What color are your husband's eyes? she asked herself. No, really now, think. What does he look like? He wears horn-rimmed glasses and a puzzled smile.) "Where is Barbara?" asked the grandmother. No one answered her. A roulade of explosions sounded from the direction of the beach.

"It's the yacht club! They're starting!" Davy and Ed hurled themselves out of the room. Linda and Gaby followed, screeching. The screen door slammed.

No one wanted dessert. (The children would have to eat watermelon all week.) The grownups drifted out of the house into the evening scents of phlox and honeysuckle, and wandered about in pairs, Alan and Irene, Tom wrapping Mrs. Pierson's shawl around her shoulders, Adrian with Clare. It seemed to her that they were like the audience at a play, strolling between acts, or perhaps the actors themselves, and she was reminded of carnival interludes at school, the kings and princesses lifting their robes as they went along the corridors, showing sneakers and Argyle socks. The light was theatrical, impartial on their faces, roseate still from the vanquished sun that bled behind the pines.

Barbara, ready at last, came out of the house and joined them. She had put on a flowered silk dress and she carried a white coat. Adrian put his arm around her. "So you desert us for a foolish grown-party," he chided.

She smiled up at him, her face transformed by something more than make-up. The diaphanous folds of her dress fluttered against her thighs and over her breast. "Gaby!" she called. "Come and kiss me good night!"

But the children had climbed up into the pines to get a better view. "I'm blowing you kisses, Mommy. Can't you see them?" The kisses flew unseen among the pine needles.

Barbara went to her mother and put her arms around her and kissed her good night on the cheek, just as she must have done when she was a child. Then she patted Alan's jaw and waved to the rest of them. "Good night! Take care!" they called as she went off toward the garage to get her car, her ankles unsteady above spike-heeled sandals. In a moment, her blue coupé slid down the driveway, Barbara's braceleted wrist dangling from the window. Clare shivered, thinking it would be cooler with the wind rushing around the car, chaperoning it like time itself, which was the enemy as well as the friend of lovers.

The men brought chairs from the porch and set them on the lawn. The children came down from the pine trees, and Tom distributed sparklers and sticks of punk. Adrian lay down on the grass at Clare's feet. "I'm too old for such nonsense," he complained. "Or too young, maybe."

Clare looked down at his hard china-blue eyes. What a self-conscious young man he was! She wondered what would become of him. Nothing at all, probably. Wherever he was, he became such a part of the local scene that it was hard to believe he could belong to any other.

The little girls were dancing with their sparklers, their feet on the turf as rapid, as resilient as the vibration of their hearts. Caby had taken off her dress, and her slip, with its buttoned shoulders an ruffles, gleamed in the dusk. A tremolo of bats dashed through the upper air. "My hair!" Irene screamed, and buried her head in her arms.

The bats were gossamer shadows, teasing each other. Off in the meadow, armies of insects were singing, and from lawns far down the road the artificial thunders rose and fell.

"Now, do be careful, Alan," said Mrs. Pierson. He was trying to read the directions for a fountain of fire. In the flare of his match, Clare saw the shape of his face, which she had almost forgotten — the hollows around the nostrils, the knotted muscles of his mouth. "Don't you remember, Alan," his mother was saying, "the time your father burned his hand so badly? We used to drive along the ocean at Asbury Park. My, they had pretty displays!"

"Do you remember the clambakes?" "Do you remember the dances at the country club?" The voices of Alan and his mother floated back and forth. The punk wafted a delicate smoke. The children's faces, their immature bones, shone through it. Clare saw Davy kneel to light the fountain, his small head lowered ceremoniously. He held his breath. Remember — remember? Would she remember this?

Now there seemed to be many more children, and unfamiliar dogs, bounding about the lawn, like released shadows. With a rush, then, the fountain put forth a tree of light.

"Oh!" cried the children.

"Lovely!" said someone. Adrian reached for Clare's hand, which lay in her lap, and held it against his cheek. He must be feeling sorry for himself because Barbara has gone off, she thought. Still, something touched her, too, as if the night deepened as the fountain died.

A pinwheel spun its arms of gold. Alan sprang from light to light, shouting orders like a brilliant child. Somewhere in the dark, Irene

was laughing. She laughed, thought Clare, as if she had a secret understanding with life, the way one might have had an understanding with
a boy long ago. Mosquitoes were plaintive. There was the sound of
slapping and Tom's voice, jubilant — "Got him full of blood!"

Alan stood with his feet wide apart, swinging the Roman candles.
Blossoms of light flew upward from his hands. All the cords in his neck
stood out. Clare leaned forward in her chair. A lost tenderness
suffused her, and she thought of the years when she had not known
him, of the little boy walking along a side street in a Jersey town, sitting
between his parents in a carriage at Asbury Park, sailor-hat ribbons
tickling his ear; she thought of the young man, earnest with ambitions
that would not be realized.

Suddenly the candles sputtered out and left him standing in the
darkness, lonely, only his white shirt and trousers showing. She would
have to remember to tell him how beautiful the Roman candles were.

The children clapped their hands. "The rockets!" they cried.
"Now let's have the rockets."

Streams of fire ripped far into the sky and dropped their globes of
color. "Where do they go?" asked a child. The luminous girandoles
leapt above them. On the lawn, the wondering faces were flooded
and frozen in light. Even after the last rocket had sailed away, a brilliance seemed to linger.

"That's all there is," said Alan ruefully. "Next summer, we'll get
more big ones. They're the best of all."

The darkness crept back into every hollow, every crevice of the
world. The strange children and their dogs disappeared as swiftly and
mysteriously as they had come, their voices echoing down the dew-
drenched roads. Linda and Gaby, drooping with sleep, were kissed
and sent off to bed with their grandmother, for it was terribly late,
Clare told them, later than they had ever been allowed to stay up
before. The Macys said good night and went off holding hands with Ed.
Alan and Adrian decided to take Davy and drive down along the shore
to see if anything might still be going on. Clare waved goodbye to
them from the lawn, blinded for a moment when the headlights hit her.

How quiet it was! The dew had washed the smell of powder away.
There was not a trace of all that light and sound. But she knew that in
the morning there would be pieces of singed cardboard in the grass and
soaking in the birdbath, and for weeks to come the children, foraging
in the fields, would find treasured husks of rockets that had not, after
all, fallen leagues and centuries away.

The lamps in the house were dimmed. Clare knew how the little girls would whisper upstairs in bed, their heads turned toward each other on the soft, brushed wings of their hair. The grandmother would be lying with her dry eyes open, listening to her memories, which were all she could really hear now, unable to sleep till everyone else was safe in bed.

We must remember to leave a light burning for Barbara, thought Clare. She sat down on the wet grass, wrapping her skirt about her knees. Nothing disturbed the night. There were the Pleiades up in the sky, and the Big Dipper, balanced above the points of the pines. Below, on the lawn, around the deserted chairs, a mist had gathered, like a trace of garments, the wraiths of all of them, spellbound still. It was impossible to believe that anything could change, that summers would not always be the same, that anyone would grow old, or go away, or die. (In those days, no one believed the world could possibly end.)

She waited, half asleep, for Alan and Adrian and Davy to come home. Not that she thought anything could happen to them, but it was pleasant to wait, with the sound of insects weaving a web of comfort over the night. Once, from the shadows of the trees, an animal cried out as if in pain. Or it might have been a bird. Then the katydids resumed their shimmering argument: she did, she didn't, she did, she didn't, she did.

(*From Mademoiselle*)

THE CLIMATE OF THE FAMILY

BY NANCY G. CHAIKIN

RUTHIE had just graduated from the University and was preparing to stay on through the summer to take at least part of her master's when she received word that her grandmother had died. The telegram reached her one hot morning in early July, and she held the yellow slip of paper in her hand steadily for a long time before she realized what it meant to tell her and what must be going on at home. It was, as all deaths realized from a distance are, a shock, and she was shaken at first with that cold, stubborn moment of disbelief which possesses the young when they are faced with the fact of man's mortality and the quicksilver elusiveness of experience in time. But once she had accepted the message, her hand began to shake visibly and her mind was flooded with the fragments of a thousand disorganized relevancies — fragments which flew out of the explosion of the shock and burrowed sharply, like so many jagged pieces, into her consciousness.

The old woman, her father's mother, was simply not the sort who died suddenly like that, when you were far away from home. She was old, it was true; although no one knew how old, because she had never been able to tell them when her birthday was (the day after the second Seder, she would say, searching for something which would relate the old Jewish calendar to the confusing new one). But she had been a woman of tremendous vitality. After her sons married and raised families, she had continued to cook her heavy, colorful European food and keep house, with painful perfectionism, for herself and her unmarried daughter Selma. She had stuffed lavish dinners into her grandchildren when they visited her, carried her rich yellow cookies to them at their homes in small paper egg boxes, run back and forth between the houses and managed, with all the scrubbing and cooking and baking, to remain a cheerful widow whose greatest joy was her children's children and greatest sorrow her unmarried daughter, who grew fat on the rich cooking. And now, when she was dead, it seemed impossible to Ruthie that the tireless heart had finally given out.

She packed carelessly — just enough to keep her for a week — and arranged to take the next train for the East. Sometimes, when you were far away from people, you forgot how they walked and looked and how their voices sounded when they talked. But she could not forget her grandmother's voice, and as she threw each article of clothing into the small weekend bag, she could hear the voice — loud and not quite old — laughing at something she had said to tease her; and she could hear it singing an old song, high and with a slight tremor but steady enough to tell you that once it had been rich and full and confident. Ruthie's father had inherited the voice and, on rare holiday occasions, he and his mother had stood together at the piano behind Ruthie as she played for them, her grandmother's voice trembling in the melody, and her father's, lower and stronger and more steady, taking the harmony. It had embarrassed her a little then to hear the sad ruin of old age in her grandmother's quivering tones, but now it only made her think with pity how anxious the voice had been, how eager and full of love and memories. It was strange: she could remember her grandmother's voice perfectly, but she could hardly hear her parents' voices at all. She closed the suitcase and went to call a cab to take her to the station, thinking of her parents and what they must be doing now.

The train ride back to the East was a long, dirty business, and Ruthie had not allowed herself the luxury of a Pullman. So she sat up straight against the fading green plush back of the seat and watched the flat Midwestern landscape streak by, feeling the soot and dust of the car in her nostrils and the grit gathering on her hands and face. At dinnertime she rejected the thought of the rocking diner, with its cups of coffee shaking, spilling, and its flat, tasteless food. Instead, she bought a cheese sandwich from a white-jacketed porter who passed through the car with a basket, and washed the gluey yellow cheese and dry white bread down with coffee, which always tasted paler, staler and colder when you drank it from a paper container. She watched the landscape darken and the light grow dim and saw in the window the reflection of her own tired, dirty face against the blackened contours of the land and sky.

It was not, she realized now, only the news of her grandmother's death which had disturbed her enough to keep her from sleeping. The affection had been strong but they had not seen each other often enough during these past four years for her to feel anything complete beyond the sense of shock. It was more, she thought with some shame, the fact that this was the first death in the family since she'd been old enough to shoulder some of the responsibility of family bereavement. And it meant — she dreaded it — at least three or four days, possibly a week, of being a mature, consoling daughter and niece, of moving carefully, respectfully around among the condolence-callers and sitting somehow through the funeral services, the ride to the cemetery. It meant — she hid her face in her hands, wondering how it would be — looking into the coffin upon her grandmother's still face.

She had been only a small child when the last death had occurred — the passing of her mother's mother. She had not gone to the cemetery, but they had let her sit in the palm-filled parlor of her grandmother's brownstone house and listen to the service. She could not remember now the words of the rabbi who had laid her mother's mother to rest, but she remembered that they had been words of praise for the woman who had been, when she was well, a prominent member of the temple. That Grandmother had been a widow too from the time that Ruthie was old enough to know her well, but she had been different from this one. Her mother's mother was a slight, doll-like woman whose pink face and white hair belied the will of iron with which she had dominated her daughter's life. Ruthie had not understood it then, but now she knew that the last few years of her maternal grandmother's life had been difficult ones for her mother; for the old woman, in her long, pain-ridden last illness, had nagged and stormed and demanded constant attention from her only daughter. But when she was well she seemed a little white-haired sprite of a creature who took her granddaughter riding through the park in a chauffeured car and bought her sweet brown popcorn with which to feed the pigeons. She had rarely come to their house, and when she did she never brought home-baked cookies (it seemed to Ruthie that her mother's mother must never have had to do anything for herself), but she would press warm, carefully folded dollar bills into Ruthie's hand and tell her to buy something with them but not to tell her mother. So Ruthie had sat in the palm-thick parlor of that old dark house and listened to the droning of the rabbi and thought of her grandmother and the tiny mother-of-pearl opera glasses she had said Ruthie must have. (Ruthie still had the glasses, in a tan kid case which was now worn and soft and creased.) And she had thought of the dollar bills, tightly folded, being stuffed into her hand. When they asked her whether she would like to see her grandmother again before she was buried, she had shouted, "No!"

"You ought to," her mother had said quietly, her face very gray under the black hat she wore in mourning. "She looks beautiful, Ruthie dear."

But Ruthie had cried, "No, no!" and hurried from the room before anyone could ask her again.

At that time she had been only six years old, and for many days after the funeral, long after the callers had stopped coming with their long sad faces and their cakes and flowers and stuffed fruits, she had lain awake at night in her room, remembering their voices as they spoke to her mother and hiding her head in the pillow as she tried to stop thinking of death and of what it would be like just *not being*. And in the darkness of her room and the suffocating, smelly warmth of her pillow, she would cry sometimes, cry aloud at the thought of what must, she knew, someday happen to her. But in the morning the sun would stream through the windows of her room and it would again seem impossible that such a thing could happen. She would think about it less and less, then, and finally she stopped thinking of it altogether. But somewhere, in the back of her mind, it had hovered and beckoned, and now she knew that she must come to grips again — less helplessly perhaps — with the inevitability of it, now that the other grandmother had died.

She was able to get a little sleep during the long, sooty night ride. But she would awaken spasmodically, hearing the faraway murmuring of one of the other passengers, feeling the cold pane of the window against which she had leaned her head, and the back of the seat, unyielding and straight. And beyond it all, round and round in her head, the voice of the other grandmother, the high, tremulous voice singing behind her at the piano:

> *Du, du, liegst mir im Herzen,*
> *Du, du, liegst mir im Sinn'. . . .*

For a long time the melody would not leave her head.

Now she could see, even before she got home and heard about this one, the difference in the deaths of the two women. The one, slight, fragile, constantly cared for until she finally almost wasted away, leaving behind the memory of the fine, aristocratic features, the tiny body that was beautiful even in age, and the impact of her strangely powerful, demanding, unbending personality. There was no doubt that

Ruthie's mother had loved her mother deeply, devotedly, but her death, after the hard years of catering to illness, had at last set both of them free. But the other one, the strong, busy, competent woman, though she was proud of her sons ("a professional man — a lawyer," she would tell them, speaking of Ruthie's father with a great smile of pride and wonder), had always been a bit humble in the presence of her daughters-in-law. And her death must, Ruthie thought, enslave them all with the guilt of the living who now cannot possibly make up to the dead for what they have done or failed to do. How, indeed, must that family feel, remembering the many times they had been ashamed of the old woman?

"If she only wouldn't push her plate away from her when she's finished eating," her mother had complained to her father over and over again, "if only she wouldn't do that." And her father had only sighed each time and offered no answer for his mother's ways.

How often the old woman had become meek and self-effacing in the luxurious homes of her sons and their wives. How often she had refused to stay for dinner, hurrying to the door so that they would not have to urge her. And how they had shamed her for running night after night from her small apartment to play poker with the other women who sat in the park in the afternoon sunlight and talked of their sons. If it had been bridge, Ruthie thought now, they could have forgiven her. But Ruthie too bore her share of guilt: she told herself now that she had never been truly malicious when she laughed at the way her grandmother tried to smoke — the awkward way in which she held the cigarette between her thumb and forefinger and put it in the middle of her mouth, puffing furiously as if it were going to go out. Nevertheless, her grandmother had taken the teasing well, had loved her and allowed Ruthie to fix her up when she came from the beauty parlor with a new permanent frizzing up the ends of her thin, iron gray hair.

"See," she would say to Ruthie, running her knotty fingers through the gray fuzz, "I ain't so ugly after all."

And Ruthie would laugh and say: "But think how beautiful you'd be, Grandma, if you'd let me set it."

Then there would be much bickering back and forth, but the old woman would finally sigh and sink back on the couch and let Ruthie rearrange the awful new permanent into a slick, smooth roll. Ruthie had never really been ashamed of her, but she had felt often how the others were and how it embarrassed them when she went to temple with them on the high holidays and after services they had to let her speak to their friends.

She remembered how it had been at temple, on those high days. After services — except on Yom Kippur when even in the reformed temples services went on all day — they would mill out into the vestibule, the women in their new holiday clothes, the men dying for a smoke, and Ruthie always a little sick to her stomach from hunger. Her grandmother would come down from the balcony — only the regular members sat downstairs on the big holidays because the temple was small and always crowded — down she would come, in an old hat with a new flower or feather bobbing above her broad, ruddy face, smiling and saying hello to everyone, kissing her sons and their wives and kissing Ruthie with a loud smack. If it was Yom Kippur they would all stay on for memorial services, not eating anything all day; but on the other days her grandmother would be persuaded to ride home with them in the car and stay for dinner. Sometimes on those days it was good: they would drink wine before the meal and after it they would all go into the living-room where her grandmother, flushed with the wine and dinner and family around her, would suddenly break into singing. Then they would all go to the piano and sing for a long time. But often her grandmother would have to be coaxed to stay at all, and then would be humble and quiet and a little ashamed for staying, and Ruthie would feel herself freezing up, like her mother, at her table manners. Now that she was dead, those curious, unpolished things she did seemed very dear.

The train rocked and racketed through the dark night, and Ruthie's back was stiff and sore when the first gray haze of daylight started to seep in through the car window and light up the sky above the clouds. After a while she made her way carefully to the tiny ladies'-room compartment and washed herself down with rough paper towels, removing the blouse which stuck to her back and her armpits. Then she took a fresh blouse out of her bag and put it on, folding the other carefully in spite of the streaks and creases already in it. Returning to her seat, she bought another cup of coffee from the porter and drank it slowly, feeling the dusty, gritty fatigue in her bones and the grime of the train rushing back to her face as quickly as she had washed it off. By mid-morning the sun was blazing in on her face, and she could already feel the hot vapors of the city upon her as the train shot into the tunnel to Grand Central Terminal. She had wired ahead, but she did not expect anyone to meet her.

Nevertheless, when she walked up the ramp from the platform with the handle of her bag sticking to the wet palm of her hand, she saw her brother standing there behind the rope, waiting.

"You didn't have to meet me," she said, kissing him and letting him take her bag from her.

"I thought I'd better," he said, smiling a little. "The funeral's this afternoon and we have to go right to the parlor."

She did not say anything then but followed him to a side street where he had parked the car.

They rode, mostly in silence, through the crowded, hot city streets, starting and stopping with a jerk as they crawled downtown and toward the bridge to Brooklyn. She felt sick to her stomach now, the way she had on those holidays riding home after temple. She thought that she would never remember the temple without feeling again that slow, rolling nausea that came over her after services.

"Have you eaten?"

"On the train. I'm not hungry, anyway."

"You should eat, you know." He offered her a cigarette which she refused. "You look thinner than ever." It was the first time he had really looked at her since they met at the station.

"Are you going to have lunch?"

He shook his head. "No."

"Then neither will I."

Anyway, they would not have had time for lunch. The bridge traffic was terrible and it was an hour and a half before the car, steaming with the heat, pulled up in front of the air-cooled chapel in Brooklyn.

There was no time to turn back. Inside, the room was dark, artificially cool and filled with palms. Her father's family sat around on chairs, not speaking. Looking over the room slowly as she entered, trying not to see the coffin right away, she caught sight of her mother and father sitting together in a corner, her father with his head down, her mother pale and grayer than she remembered, saying nothing to her father but holding one of his hands and stroking it. When they saw her and had kissed her, her mother started to cry.

"She wanted to see your diploma," she sobbed to Ruthie, "she only wanted to see your diploma."

Her mother was terribly upset, and Ruthie wished that she had never remembered the business about the table manners. Her mother had, in her own way, been close to the old lady. She searched hopelessly for something she could say to the two of them there and to the aunts and uncles whom she kissed silently, moving slowly across the room to each couple. But there was nothing, nothing at all. Her aunt Selma, her eyes large and black in her fat, sorrowful face, hugged her hard and murmured something which Ruthie could not understand. She hugged her back and kissed her and then, because she knew that they were all watching her, because she knew that she would have to do it now, she walked over to the coffin and looked in.

It had been a stroke, and the skin, always so soft and loose, was pulled tightly over the face, making the cheekbones look high and hard when before you would never have noticed them at all. It had nothing to do with the face of the bright, eager, living woman. It did not look as if it could possibly have been her grandmother; the gentleness and love had gone out of her face and what was left was only the tight white mask of an old woman who had died in pain. She saw that her arms were crossed over her bosom and that they had smoothed out the knotty look of the tired fingers. Then she looked for a long time at the gray hair, thin and wispy and poorly combed, thinking of touching it, combing it a little perhaps, but her hand would not move from her side. She knew that if she cried, it would be a terrible cry, born not of love and remembering alone but of shock and fear and pity for herself. So she stifled it and turned away from the coffin, wishing there were someone to hold on to. And there was Aunt Selma at her side, pointing to a wreath of flowers at the foot of the coffin.

"From her cousin in California," she said, looking at Ruthie. "Marty, the actor — *you* know. She would have been so proud." And Ruthie remembered how her grandmother had taken pictures of the actor out of her big black pocketbook and shown them to her over and over again.

"That's your cousin too," she would say. "How many times removed is it, Ruthie?"

And Ruthie would shake her head, not really knowing.

"Well, he's your cousin. He's an actor, a big actor out there."

The wreath was dazzling — a great swell of white gardenias which filled the room with their strong scent. And Ruthie knew that they would soon start to tinge brown around the edges and grow limp against the great purple bow behind them.

They sat in the room for a long time, hearing from the inside chapel the occasional cries of people at another funeral. It was a terrible sound, and after a while the people filed out of the chapel behind a coffin, and they could hear them mumbling and weeping as they passed the door and went down the hall.

Ruthie stayed with her mother and father and they talked a little, about school, about her degree, but mostly about her grandmother.

"She was cooking a pot roast when it happened," her mother told her, "— for a neighbor." And then her father broke down and started to cry into his long thin hands, and Ruthie still could not say anything but stood bending over him with her arms around his shoulders, feeling the body shake and sigh.

"It's the first time he's broken down," her mother told her silently, across his back, forming the words with her lips.

At last it was time for the services, and they walked into the chapel together and heard the rabbi intone the Hebrew words of prayer and the English ones of eulogy. No one cried except Selma, who shook silently, and the neighbor in the back of the chapel, an old woman who screamed out loud when the rabbi mentioned the pot roast. It was not a long service, and they filed out of the chapel slowly, feeling the impact of the still, hot air as they left the cooled building, allowing themselves to be herded systematically into the great black hired cars.

At the cemetery the air was hotter than ever, and Ruthie could feel the sun burning into her scalp through the straw of her hat. She did not hear the words of the rabbi, but when the proper time came she tossed a single flower which someone had handed to her upon the polished top of the coffin. The final words were spoken, and she turned away slowly with the others and walked with them back to the car which would take them to her grandmother's apartment, the house of mourning. During the long ride back to Brooklyn, she felt a great sense of relief and was able to smile at her father and hold his hands in hers as her mother had done.

In the apartment, when they got there, everyone was talking at once, and the cousins, whom she had hardly seen at the funeral parlor, were rushing around the apartment getting chairs to put in the living-room. The front door had been left open and several of the neighbors, passing to go to the elevator, looked in curiously. In the kitchen, one of her aunts and a woman whom she had never seen before were giving orders to her cousins Jack and Bert, who were to go out for food. She heard them ordering roast chickens and meats and cakes and fruits — enough for the whole week — and their voices sounded sure again and very business-like. What was it, exactly, that she was trying now to understand? Suddenly, somewhere along the way, it had all changed. And now it was becoming plain that all at once, as if at a given signal, the family had fought its way out of the dark and into the summer day again. The weight of the preceding hours and the heat of them seemed to have rolled off like some great boulder, and now they were strangely happy in a kind of togetherness, a bustle of efficiency and purpose, rushing around with things to be done and smiling at one another as they did them.

"Don't set all the chairs up yet," she heard an uncle call in the living-room. "Give us a little room to breathe."

And in the kitchen her aunt Harriet climbed up a ladder-chair to get some dishes down out of the yellow-painted cupboard, saying, "Did you ever see a kitchen so immaculate?"

The women all clucked over that and one of them said: "Whatever you do, when I die don't let anyone into my kitchen closets." Then they all laughed in the kitchen — not loudly but with relief and close-ness, scurrying around the small room, bumping into one another, in-specting the icebox, carrying piles of dishes back and forth, and all the time as if they were getting ready for a party. It was not out of place, this new laughter, Ruthie thought; it was good to see them that way.

In the living-room the men, more quiet than the women but somehow more relaxed too, rolled up their shirt sleeves and sat back in their chairs with the windows wide open, fanning their faces with the morn-ing newspapers.

And through both rooms, their heels clacking importantly on the bare, clean floors, the cousins hurried in and out, volunteering for errands, glad to be able to move and speak and smile again.

"There's nothing like family," she heard her mother say to someone, and then, "Has Ruthie met Cousin Sara from St. Louis? Ruthie — Sara, did you say hello to Ruthie?" And Sara told her how small she had been the last time she'd seen her — only a little baby but so smart, carrying a tune at eighteen months.

There were more out-of-town cousins than she had ever known about and she could not remember their faces and their names. But rushing back and forth, setting up chairs and tables, no one seemed to notice or care. They were all getting ready to eat together, there in that small room.

Ruthie thought of how her grandmother would have fed them all if she had been there, saying, "Eat it up, eat it all up," as she went happily from relative to relative. Soup, rich and yellow, with blobs of *kreplach* floating in it — little envelopes of soft dough filled with meat. Then chopped liver and chicken and potatoes and two green vegetables. And then the cookies and cakes — pale, flaky shells stuffed with prunes or nuts or cheese, or little round ones that melted as you chewed them — and strong coffee to wash them down. She would push the food at them until they all felt stuffed like so many bulging pillows and could not move from their seats to carry the dishes back to the kitchen. There were a few cookies now in an egg box in the kitchen cupboard. When they were discovered they were just put aside silently, and they lay in their box, light and crumbly, with nuts sprinkled over the top of them, moving around faintly in the box as it was put down, waiting to be eaten by no one knew whom.

At last the boys came back with the food order, and they laid some of it out on gleaming platters and cool white linen in the living-room. Then they all sat down and ate, talking a little but not so much as before. In the darkening room the women were grateful for the respite from the hot bright kitchen and for the cold, familiar dairy supper. But it was getting later now, and with some reluctance they crowded back after supper into the kitchen again, scraping and washing and drying until everything was clean and shining and back in the spotless cupboard. When they had finished and returned to the living-room to wait for the first callers, they sat for a long time talking quietly to one another, telling lonely little stories about her grandmother. Outside, the summer night darkened a little, its stillness broken at last by the faintest rustling of leaves as the heat lifted from the street and dissipated into the silver nightfall.

And now all that had happened, the sudden burst of relief out of the coldness of the ceremonies of bereavement into the warmth of family life again, seemed to wipe away for an instant the shock and terror and guilt which had gripped them all during the past twenty-four hours. Ruthie felt that she understood now how they were able to cope with the enormity, the terrifying inevitability of what had happened. And she was comforted here in this room at nightfall by an eager, almost desperate fragment of hope: that if she were to awake that night and once more contemplate the terrible, incomprehensible character of mortality, she would feel again the climate of this family in this room and warm to it through her old, returning fear.

(*From Harper's Bazaar*)

WOOD SMOKE

BY ANN CHIDESTER

*T*HE SEASON of fortified childishness may often be long in us When I first saw the town of San Juan del Monte in Mexico I was already thirty-eight years old; but I know now that at that time, though I thought myself mature and successful, I was only ignorant and childish.

In the first place I had no real desire to go down into Mexico. I had my own work and was impatient of interruptions of any sort, and in my heart I have never liked travel and its many discomforts. The mission to Mexico was especially distasteful to me in that it meant going to a remote town which I could not reach by rail or car. Also, it concerned my stepbrother, Philip, who had died several months before, leaving, after many years of absence, a small estate. Philip was my father's only child by his first marriage to a woman named Alice Cromwell, of Buffalo, who had died shortly after Philip was born. By the time I was born, Philip was already going away to school, beginning to be mysterious about his activities and bitter, rude and strange in our presence. From time to time my brothers and I heard from him. He worked as a coffee planter, stevedore and deck hand, a tourist guide in Italy and an archaeologist. His very presence on earth, vague and energetic, made all of us more than a little nervous. We heard from him occasionally and sent him a small check, though he did not ask for money or even bother to thank us for sending it. But it eased our consciences to do so.

My brothers and I were moderately successful in business. That summer four years ago when I went to Mexico to see about his burial and whatever estate he had left — hoping, naturally, to recuperate our investments in him — I was already well on the road to being a wealthy man. I had been taken in as a partner in a dye manufacturing firm, and

I owned a large house in the country. I was married to a well-educated, capable woman, and we had a healthy, six-year-old son. I was chosen to go to Mexico because I was the eldest brother and, since my firm had done business all over South America, I knew some Spanish. Now, I am glad in my heart that neither Norbert nor James went, for I believe they would have bungled the matter even more than I.

I was able to travel four hundred miles or so from Mexico City by rail and then by third-class bus. At the end of the bus line I found a boy who would guide me on horseback to the next town. I had written to the parish priest who had first informed me of Philip's death, and everything was arranged. The boy said nothing during the long ride, and I was weary and did not dare to drink from his canteen. The sun was hot and vicious, and my mouth tasted of bitter dust. When we reached the mission, a tall Mexican in very clean clothes came out and spoke to the boy who nodded, tipped his great sombrero politely and went his way. The tall man smiled at me and shook my hand with great respect.

I must comment here on the manner and appearance of the man who had been sent by the priest of the town where Philip had died and was buried. He was the tallest Mexican I have ever seen, and his eyes were pale blue. I learned later that possibly he was descended from Emperor Maximilian. He looked at me with keen and wondering eyes, and with a contained delight which disturbed me. I had no idea about Philip's reputation here, but I doubted very much that he had done well. Still, the guide's friendliness was wonderful. That night I slept on a rope bed in the mission. I was bruised, and the night winds off the desert kept me awake, and through the night I saw strange, quick visions of my childhood as though (unconsciously) I was trying to recall everything I had ever known about Philip.

In the early morning when the dust blew through the decayed walls, the padre came out before the sun and blessed the burros, the horses, the guide and myself in that order and rode with us to the place where he turned to go down into the valley. We set off over the mountains. My guide, Juan Chavez, questioned me slyly about myself and considered my replies in long silences. At last he told me, as though revealing something sacred, that he had known my brother very well.

"He was a friend of everyone, *señor*," he said. "He is well known everywhere — *El Borracho*."

"*El Borracho?*" I said, startled, and yet in myself I felt a certain shameful satisfaction. Now, I can see how horrible this feeling was, but at the time I think that I wanted to be certain of something about Philip.

Most of all, I wanted my own impression of him confirmed. "You called him *El Borracho* — the drunkard?" I asked.

"Everyone knows him by that name. He had always, even to the very end, a miraculous talent for tequila. A wonderful thing to see in a *Norteamericano*."

He then told me of Philip stumbling over the surrounding mountains in a kind of blind, burning delight night and day. Apparently, he had managed to uncover a few Aztec remains and had drunk himself into gaiety on pulque. Perhaps he felt his exile terribly. Juan described him as being tall as a tree but thin as a man's arm, with golden, curly hair like that of a child and eyes like those of a young woman waiting for love. He said that his memory was venerated because he had been wonderfully clever with animals, children, the old and the sick and also because he had taught the village dancers to do the Highland fling to the weird, nasal music of the local *mariachi* bands. Later I learned with surprise — a businessman has little contact with the world of archaeology and such — that Philip had a flawless reputation for sobriety, brilliance and attention to his work. In his own town, however, he was called *El Borracho* with respect and affection, and it was because of him that Juan Chavez had left his town and offered me his immediate, unreserved friendship. He believed that all foreigners were like Philip.

One may travel to many places; but when one goes down into an ancient, remote place, that which is most ancient in oneself is awakened. As we came over the last hill, having traveled for five days, sleeping in wayside towns and missions, the old colonial town appeared to me like Rome, though it was very small with nothing of the international city about it. Still, there in the distance were the three foothills and all around were many churches — the pink marble spires of the *Parochia*, the rounded dome of the ancient *Oratoria*. The air was vibrant with the sounds of many bells and had the substance of eternal spring with an odor of flowers and wood smoke. The whole town lay in a dreamy mist of this smoke, illumined here and there by a patch of many-colored flowers; and there was a magnitude of animal sounds — dogs, chickens, burros and children, and somewhere a woman wept softly as though in complete desolation. The air trembled with life.

I knew, then, how that Englishman felt when he first came upon the strangeness of Shangri-La in Tibet. There was snow on the peaks here, too, and I felt that all my life I had lived with a memory, a desire, for this place; and envy stirred in me of Philip, the idler and wanderer, who had spent years here. Turning, then, I saw in the dusk the great statue of Saint John which dominated the scene. It was set so high on the mountain I wondered how it could possibly have been carried there, an enormous pink block of stone with green lines from the weather running through it. The face was easily visible, the strong features like those of an Indian and the body and head turning as we moved so that the eyes appeared to follow everywhere.

Juan smiled with pride. "He is our patron," he explained. Children at play looked up into that face, and mothers with newborn babies took them out into the street for the saint to see. Men in acts of crime and passion often stopped dead under the severe gaze of their saint. At death, one naturally turned to look last upon the face of the saint. It had been carved by a young peasant who had been left in the street bleeding to death during the great Revolution of 1810. Saint John appeared to him wearing only a loincloth and carried him to this far mountain town. The town had been renamed in the saint's honor, and he was their patron whom they venerated daily.

Wearily, then, we made our way down the steep streets paved with ancient smooth cobblestones along the edges of which ran open sewers and trailing vines of bougainvillea. We passed the ducal residence, a vast and decaying wall through which we saw charcoal fires and smelled the odor of cooking and heard the sleepy murmur of children. Next to this, broad and imposing, stood the residence of the former bullfighter who now raised bulls for the arenas of Mexico and old Spain. By this time the sky was dark blue and the stars large and near, and we went down into the plaza where a *mariachi* singer leaned against a banana tree in the plaza garden and sang of a lost love with red lips and a black, black heart.

We turned into the ancient inn, a *posada*, which had once been the house of a Spanish count and still retained the old patio, fountains and trees. I went with a gnarled brown *mozo* to care for the horses and to check my bags while Juan sought out the owner of the inn, a man with an enormous belly and the black cross of Ash Wednesday still on his forehead though it was ten days gone. Several burros and saddle horses slept in the corral, and just beyond it, over a low wall, I saw, with a sense of having gone swiftly backward in time, the old priest walking in the monastery garden. He was pacing off his daily office. He wore a rusty cassock and a black biretta shaped like an outsized mushroom. He seemed a thousand years old in that smoky air.

It was then as I watched the priest, wondering if he could be the one with whom I had corresponded, that I saw the blind boy for the first time. I thought that he, like the priest, was praying. In my exhaustion I did not look carefully, though I was impressed with the aspect of the boy, graven and still, as he sat in the lantern light not moving his lips or striking any formal attitude in the way of other unfortunates and beggars in this country. Here, as everywhere, along the walls that were older than anyone knew ran the rich, heavy drape of bougainvillea. That night I slept in a room off the patio which had once been the study of the old Count of Cruz who, over two hundred years ago, had brought his Indian bride to this house. I slept as in Paradise to the gentle sounds of the animals in the corral and the faintly audible, rhythmic murmur of the priest's matins. There was always a lot of politics in the company for which I worked. That is to be expected. I had succeeded only by wits and maneuvers, and there were many men who knew the work better than I. Still, as I slept, all the confusions and competitions fell from me, and I existed as myself alone without any of the accustomed props of my position at home. It is a rare, dangerous feeling. A few natives came by candlelight and lamplight to peer at me through the iron bars of my window and door as I lay sleeping. Their soft, respectful voices came in soft waves of sound, and I felt an awakening companionship with them, and then I slept deeply again.

In the morning Juan Chavez was waiting for me with an air of proud excitement. He had slept outside my door all night on a straw *petate*, though he owned a small house down from the inn near the Church of the Three Bells. "You will need me, *señor*," he said. "I will help you to know all you must know. I will also tell you stories of the old haciendas and relate local scandals and warn you against thieves, murderers, beggars and witches." He was telling me more than this. He was saying that he would be my faithful friend and guide, serve me well in his own town and pray for me daily at Mass. The old innkeeper came to me, bowing, and escorted me to my table where a breakfast of hot baked fish, eggs cooked with rice and tomatoes and peppers, *tortillas*, strong, hot black coffee with a pitcher of hot milk, and a rare, sweet meat with stuffed peppers and boiled onion all stood steaming and fragrant under the pecan tree. This was served grandly with both Juan Chavez and the innkeeper standing well back into the patio corridor watching and murmuring in admiration.

The owner poured me yet one more cup of coffee which was as strong as raw whiskey to my mild tongue, and then both he and Juan began to ask about Philip. What was he like as a boy? Was he brave? What about our family? As we talked, the two boys came into the patio, Eduardo and the younger one whom I had seen the first night, the blind boy who had been born during an eclipse of the moon. They wore poor, clean rags and were shy and barefooted, and their feet were superbly calloused against all sharp stones and dangers. They were

Juan's sons, and he introduced them with shy pride. Their aunt, an ugly woman whom many men had loved, preferred to care and cook for her nephews and pray in the church for hours with her arms rigidly outstretched. "A saint of a woman," Juan said with a worldly shrug, "but a terrible woman just the same."

I showed no impatience to see Philip's grave, for I thought they had their own ideas about showing it. Also, I did not ask about his house and land, for I knew that to show impatience is to profess to greed. Besides, it was pleasant there. A heavy lassitude dragged at me as though I were drowning in the light of the patio, in the air and colors and odors there. Until now, I had assumed that my business about Philip would be a matter of two or three days, no more, but I began to sense that the matter was too delicate to be rushed. The eyes of the two men and the two boys lingered fondly on me. In an hour or so the old priest I had seen the previous night with the blind boy came in and was introduced. Still smelling of communion wine, he sat at the table with me and sipped coffee.

"The women have gone to put flowers on his grave," the priest said. "We shall go later. You have not seen the house or the land?"

"Not yet," I said. "You see, Padre, Philip was my stepbrother. We had the same father, but we were never close."

"He spoke of his brothers," the priest said.

I was surprised. "We — there were times when we, my brothers and I, wondered about him."

The old priest had a broad brown face and delicate hands which were held quietly. He raised them now as though in protest. "You wondered?" he asked.

"Well, you see, we thought of him as a tramp, in a way. We never knew what he was doing and we heard so seldom; and when we did hear, we thought he needed money. Because we did not know him or to what purposes he meant to put the money, we never sent very much."

"Ah, but you will come to know him here. It is not too late," the priest said. He looked off into the morning brilliance at the far end of the patio as though he saw Philip standing there. Indeed, I had much the same feeling. "He brought water in pipes to this town. He taught the ranchers how to restore the land and to plant to prevent erosion. He imported mulberry bushes, excellent for our climate. He taught many to read and write, lifting the dark veil of ignorance from their eyes, for grown men and women here had never learned. He loved everyone and was well loved. You will know him."

"Yes, I see," I said uneasily.

I did not at this time go into the matter of Philip's finances. I reasoned that he would have many debts and I would be lucky to recuperate anything at all and luckier still if I did not have to pay all his debts. It has been my experience that men who want to change the world, though they may succeed and be revered for it, are almost always poor and change the world by using other men's money. The reformers die in debt. It is a bitter truth. Something, however, in the old priest's gaze went into me like a sword, and I felt that he knew my thoughts and despised them. But at that moment I was greeted respectfully by the chief of police, the mayor, the old lawyer who was the priest's twin brother, the two wealthiest ranchers and a handsome young man who spoke English and was going away to a Texas university in the fall. Then the priest, Juan Chavez and I rode through the village and called upon the sister of Jesús María Montalban, who had been a famous opera singer and was now a monk in a Peruvian monastery.

These formalities attended to, Juan spoke to the padre, who nodded and we rode to Philip's house. I must confess to an extraordinary sense of discomfort at this point. All of these people were very poor, poorer than people of our country can even imagine. They lived, many of them crowded together, in huts with dirt floors. They cooked over poor little fires and slept on the ground curled together like animals. After all, Philip was my stepbrother, and I did not want to live forever in the discomfort of thinking that he had also lived in such a miserable fashion.

It was, however, a small pink house where a beautiful, graceful woman, perhaps no more than thirty and dressed in mourning, came daily to clean and put flowers about. Philip had saved her small son when he fell into the river. He had breathed his breath into the boy. A few years later the boy had died of the mysterious, mortal fever common to this region, and now this lovely widow mourned both of them, her son and the ghostly breath of Philip which had died in the boy. The house was like a shrine. It dazzled me. Flowers of the town — dark red, brilliant yellow and many-colored blue — were everywhere, and over everything was a soft, pale light from the pink walls. Philip had brought the best of himself and his inheritance and culture to this remote town. For the first time in my life I felt confused and desperately inadequate. I was a stranger on earth. I was made as welcome as an ambassador — all because of Philip, whom I had always thought of with scorn and shame. It was a new and profound experience for me.

"You must live here, too," the widow insisted. Her eyes were black with pale golden lights. Respectfully, but conscious of her womanliness, she led me from room to room and pointed out Philip's favorite chair made of mahogany and smooth, tight leather. There was a neat pile of dry wood cut to his specifications, for he had loved fires all through the night and well into the cool mornings. Here stood his favorite carved wood *santos*, and here was his bed in the high *torreón* that looked out over the old town and seemed to stand at right angles to the statue on the mountain as though these two, Philip and the saint, had often conversed. I stared at the blue serape worked with a design in gray of the birds of the region. I could imagine the blond, curly head lying there. The very air breathed of him who had so successfully recreated himself and left his legend behind. I was disturbed in many ways, for I had been prepared to find a wasted, disgraceful life for which I would have to be apologetic to those who had known him here.

His image in that house seemed to go before me, golden and ghostly. It lured and teased me. The two boys, Eduardo and the blind boy, waited anxiously. They wanted me to live here, for this house was like a magic place for them, awful and at the same time fascinating. It is strange now that the blind boy, to whom I do not recall ever speaking directly, is the spectre of my mind, the one who haunts me to this day as the personification of all my guilt. He was always just within reach of his brother — a brown, wiry little man with a handsome, dreamy face and eyes the color of mountain opals, neither smiling nor tearful, but always there even as he is now always in my mind.

Eduardo brought my canvas army bag down from the inn, and the widow took out my clothes and hung them in the sun. Then the three of us, followed by the town dignitaries, rode to the summit where they had buried Philip directly under the eyes of their statue, as though they wanted him to continue his daily communion with their saint. They had marked his grave with a complicated design of stones and carved his name *El Borracho* in ornate letters on a polished piece of marble. The priest said prayers there just before sunset, and we all went down in silence when the red sun turned the great mountains to fire. When, as we neared the house, I asked the priest about the cost of such a funeral, the coffin and the funeral services and the burying fee, he looked at me in silence for a moment.

I explained, "In my country it is proper for the relatives to pay the expenses when a man has left no money for them. We take care of our own, Padre."

"But he was ours, *señor*," he said gently. "We knew him better than you did."

"But there was his illness, too. I would pay for that. Juan Chavez and the widow took care of him for almost six months when he had the fever. They sat with him at night — you said so yourself — and they fed him and paid for the herb medicines he needed. I am here expressly to settle his debts."

"You must ask them, then," the priest said. "The widow loved him — and so did Juan."

It is this which I do not understand and which is so hard to combat. I went through Philip's papers carefully, and there was no authority given to me or to anyone to sell his house in order to pay off his debts. He wanted the house left as it was, with his books and wooden saints and furniture and clothing for anyone whom the padre, Juan Chavez or the widow might desire to live there. He wanted the rancher who worked his land to remain there. I was his guest here though he was dead and had never been my guest for so much as a meal or a night's rest. Though I spoke to both Juan Chavez and the widow, they would take no money from me, and there was hurt pride in their eyes when I asked them. These people were very poor. I knew that Juan and his boys ate cooked cactus and *tortillas* and a little meat now and then. They were poorer than anyone in the city where I live, and one always hears that Mexicans are lazy, cheats and thieves; but still they would not take a cent from me though I tried to press money upon them. My gifts to them were taken reluctantly — a few clothes for the boys, a new serape, some fresh fruits from the market and dress material for the widow. They all looked back at me in silence as though they failed to understand my reasoning, my efforts to pay Philip's debts.

My business there took no more than a week, but I lingered. I read Philip's notes on how to enlarge the water system for the town, a suggested care and treatment for the fever from which he had died, plans for crop rotations and how to expand the mulberry crop. In all cases I was surprised at his knowledge of agriculture, history, engineering and medicine. I reasoned, too, that if I lingered a while and came to know the people better, I might finally be able to pay his debts. He owed the lawyer for a horse, a rancher for two pigs and a sheep. He owed the tailor, the baker, the blacksmith, the storekeeper and the mule driver who brought wood from the hills, but they all said the same — they had no memory of such matters, though they were all so poor and threadbare, their charity was a living miracle of daily deprivation.

We were a curious little group in Philip's house, almost like a family living there with the splashing fountain in the patio and the leafy avocado trees shading us. This was the life of a village don. I was deferred to and my advice sought, and everyone was polite before my ignorance. I did not know if a girl should marry in the full of the moon or when the rains would come or how to increase the produce of eggs. Philip had known about such matters. In the evenings Juan Chavez and his boys sat about the fire and entertained me with local legends. The older boy, Eduardo, was very bright and fresh, and his father kept a heavy hand on him. The blind boy had nothing to say but seemed happy merely to sit there in the firelight like the ghost of my own boyhood or like the conscience of my secret self. Others came, too. The chief of police told sadly and beautifully, between sobs, of the death of a young bandit only last month. The priest told of a maiden lady who lived in the far valley and could speak with birds. His twin brother, the lawyer, spoke wittily of the scandals of the old royal families, and each in his turn wanted to know about my country — Philip's country — and his boyhood and exploits.

You know how it is when you are far away from home. You speak as though your own country is without fault, a perfection, even though you know it is impossible. Still, everyone with a heart loves and marvels at his own country. In the firelight of Philip's house there was a simple companionship the like of which I have never known, not even in the war. We all told things about ourselves which we would not have otherwise revealed. Their credulity and native wisdom provoked a marvelous sense of life in me and an inner peace. I remained almost a month with them and gained a fuller knowledge of my stepbrother, finding a pride in him and loyalty to him which later I could never quite explain to my younger brothers. And I came to know something of myself as well.

I tried again, before parting, to repay Juan Chavez and the widow and to pay for Philip's burial and his many debts, but they eluded me. They looked away when I spoke. They were embarrassed that I would think so much about money, and in the end the debt was not repaid. None of us had realized a cent from his estate, but we had the peace of knowing he had not wasted himself and lay in a respectable grave in a land he had loved among people devoted to him.

For a time I heard from the old priest. He told me that Juan Chavez had died of the same fever that had killed Philip, and then he wrote to say that the boys' aunt had married a rich rancher and now sat in the patio of her hacienda barking orders, dressed night and day in violently colored silks from Mexico City and passionate woolens from Oaxaca. She had become the opposite of her habitually devout self and no longer cared for the boys. I sent money for their care to the priest. Soon after that the old priest died in his sleep, and the mayor of the town wrote me; but it seemed ill-advised to send money to a politician, and in time I no longer heard from that town.

All of this happened over four years ago, but I often think of the town and how Philip lived there for many years on the charity of those impoverished people who cared for him and buried him. They had received me like a prince and would never let me pay for the food, the service or even the horse I rode. I have asked myself a thousand times how I, an American businessman traveling and living for a short time in a foreign country, am to blame in any way for the poverty and ills of that town. It was not I who caused Juan Chavez' child to be born blind; and if he were not blind, would I still feel this great concern for him? Why am I plagued by the memory of the starving children, the crippled and blind, the poorhouses and the sight of funerals almost daily?

Still, I continue to think of these matters. My sleep is often disturbed by the vision of that high, ancient world of the mountain town. Something like a sturdy amber wave rolls into my sleep and over me and leaves me awake and confused. Do all Americans traveling abroad have this same feeling of guilt? After all, I say to myself, one cannot give to *all* the beggars. Sometimes isn't it wiser to let matters lie as they have lain for centuries? Why stir up a furious dust of activity which may go all wrong in the end?

But I will never be the same again. I do not know if there is a word in any language for my feelings or if this is something very ancient and inherited in me or something altogether new or something that has happened to me alone and is unknown to others. But it remains with me — the vague odor of wood smoke, the momentary sharp memory of my brother's house, the sense of a debt unpaid and something undone that ought to have been done and a sentiment that makes me strongly aware of being an American. I do not know, though, the exact name for it.

(*From Epoch*)

THE MOTION OF FORGETFULNESS IS SLOW

BY CHARLES EDWARD EATON

*T*HEY MET at the Atlantico, one of Rio's most popular night clubs. They knew from the beginning why they were sitting next to each other, and this enabled them to dispense with the stiff and tedious preliminaries of conversation and be almost immediately easy and informal. Their hostess, Jacqueline Laurent, was a garrulous, masculine Frenchwoman of forty-five, a refugee, somewhat bitter about life, but still a great arranger of romance, an authority on the principles of life, although she had no lover at the moment, and it was doubtful whether she would ever have one again. Some said she was a Lesbian, but that was probably untrue since it would have been too easy and almost natural for her, and she was a woman who enjoyed what was most difficult for her to do. Her preoccupation with love had made her widely and ardently social, and she was a familiar figure of café society. Though people feared her, knowing that she could be vicious or benevolent according to whim, they were always glad to be entertained by her because she was never dull. With her love of intrigue, she never gave a party that did not have its implications of the destruction or arousal of a *liaison* between at least one of the couples present.

She had chosen the proper time for this particular conspiracy. A few weeks later, and it might never have happened. But tonight, success was probable. She knew it, they knew it, and as a consequence, the surface of the evening moved rapidly. Since she liked them both so well, she had gone to some trouble to inform and prepare them carefully beforehand so that nothing would go amiss. Ingrid Lombard was an old friend from the pre-war days in Paris, and Robert Atherton, a young journalist with the Office of the Coordinator of Inter-American Affairs, had won her sympathy not only through his personal charm but because he was a type which she liked, very blondly and brightly American, evoking sentimental memories of her life in the United States when she toured the country on the old Keith vaudeville circuit singing French songs.

Jacqueline knew, and she was satisfied now that they knew what she called the "circumstances." A week before, Ingrid's husband, Monsieur Charles Lombard, had left for Paris, recently occupied by the American army, and it was understood that he would not return. Monsieur Lombard was a handsome man of fifty, a painter of minor talent but much ego, possessed of the aloofness and confidence that are often so attractive to women. Ingrid had met him ten years before when she had come from Sweden to study art in France. Out of her respect and need for love she had made of him, in her mind, something he was not, but something she could love, and they lived rather happily together until his selfish possession of her was sated. Now at thirty-nine it was hard for her to lose him, and for the moment she had almost ceased to exist since she realized that the world of her invention, of which he was the center, had really never had any validity at all. There is nothing lonelier than living among the ruins of belief and because she could not bear this loneliness she had come to Jacqueline's party.

Robert Atherton had not known much about love when he came to Brazil. Like many young Americans of thirty, he had slept with a girl or two, but the relationship had always been of short duration, rather frantically and hectically physical — the kind of experience that later enabled him to understand what a Brazilian friend meant when he said that love in America was usually a matter of athletics. The girls he had known at the University had been wholesome, usual in opinion and attitude, pretty but sexually rather dull, and he had lost interest in them quickly. Not long after his arrival in Brazil, he met Yvonne Vautier, who had come to Rio to visit friends and been stranded there by the outbreak of war. She was urban in manner and outlook, small, unathletic but firm and trim of figure, and had a very intense color of red-gold hair and brilliant blue eyes. She was two years older than himself, had been married once and in love several times. She liked Robert, understood him quickly, and became his mistress after six weeks. They had a *garconnière* together, and Robert went through a complete experience of love, beyond the merely sensual, beyond the spirit of youthful adventure, and knew for the first time what Europeans meant by falling in love mentally as well as physically. Jacqueline, who was a close friend of Yvonne, had enjoyed every stage of the affair, thinking it a perfect union of Old World–New World. She foresaw what would happen to Robert when Yvonne found it necessary to return to her aging parents in Paris, was ready with comfort after the departure and, finally, the party and meeting with Ingrid.

They knew, and yet they had come, were studying, and were going through with it. They knew it was one of Jacqueline's little amusements, and that it might be desperate for them, but there was a chance it might not be, and nothing was worse than shutting the door completely and admitting that it was over, that one had been loved and now was not loved and might not love again since love was miraculous and even haphazard and accidental and not to be expected more than once in a lifetime. No, it was better to pretend that the door was still open in a place where self-deception was possible, where there were people, music, and motion — pretend, at least for tonight, that circumstances were still fluid, that it should and would happen again, that it might happen more beautifully than before.

The party of six couples, all foreigners, was masterfully engineered by Jacqueline, although she was not really interested in any of them except Ingrid and Robert who were the nerves in the body of the group. It was their presence alone that excited and stimulated her and enabled her to play with skill the part of the gracious hostess, knowing that the whole elaborate social texture of eating and drinking, gesture and small talk had a purpose and center of intensity, a covert drama which was of her own instigation. As they talked, they were conscious of the fact that through the sound and action of others present, in intrusions and withdrawals, the unpredictable pattern and direction of reciprocal speech, the sudden close-knit vocal unanimity, Jacqueline was listening to them with a focus of attention, central and direct beneath its superficial digressiveness.

They knew that they were being used, and they did not care. They knew that Jacqueline was increasing the sense of her own power by finding them, for the moment, at least, pliant in her hands. If things worked out as she intended, she would never let them forget it. No, she would never let go of them. But sometimes it is better to be used than to remain inert since movement is life, and in both of them there had been a great and sudden slowing down, so that memory receded into the past hardly at all and the present was stagnant, as if the means of extending feeling had been shut off within the blood, leaving in the heart neither the possibility of death nor birth. Jacqueline promised to unlock this rigidity. So being used was moving and better than being still at the point where one could not move voluntarily, the point where someone outside had to play Fate and free the congealing of circumstance.

Inside where there were music and light, and whisky had loosened the tightness of thought, it was possible to feel the surface of life moving, not quickly yet, but mobile again and moving toward the old rapidity. It was possible to believe this even more securely, knowing that Jacqueline was helping it happen. Jacqueline, too, from the outside believed, and it is the viewpoint beyond the personal which supports confidence. Yes, she was very sure. When they left at midnight their sense of identity which had been hard and stopped was fluid again, lightened and diluted in the hazy but swirling suspension which alcohol makes in the mind. The past did not weigh as much as it did, so that they felt that they could move through it or around it and that it was not anymore oneself lying in a closed small place. And Jacqueline was standing there, telling them goodbye, sure of it, smiling and solicitous like an accomplice. The last thing they saw was her mouth with the heavy black down on the upper lip, smiling and obscene in the foreground, and if it had not been for the whisky they would have been embarrassed.

Then in the cab they were not so sure of motion, although the physical movement was there in the rolling of the wheels along the Avenida Atlantica, down the damp curve of the beach in the phantom-dim light. Through the open windows the rawness of the sea came in. The apartment houses were all dark and like a huge cliff on one side, and there was heaviness again everywhere. By contrast, the sea was loose and flatulent, having no thrust and incisiveness where it struck the ponderous earth, pouring on the sand a white spray without power. They said nothing and sat apart, strange and stiff, on either side of the seat. It was not a long drive, but it felt long and stretched out as though the pace of the moments had shifted again and was going slower and slower and might stop altogether. The driver sat at the wheel, rigid, tense, non-communicative, strangely so far for a member of his trade, and seemed to lean with intensity on the gas feed like a man who kept his feelings distended in order that they might remain fluent at all in a night of thickening dross.

Ingrid had an apartment in the hills above the city. Most of the foreigners lived there because of the long open view of the sea, the lighter air, and the feeling of being above the tropic languor of the beaches. But tonight the fog and sea-mist were reaching up into the higher air and were curdling around the tops of the hills, and it was hard to imagine that morning would ever open the sky again and that the harbor would lie there below in a rippling scarf of blue, fluid with outward going ships and racing light.

When the cab stopped at the top of the hill before the entrance of the apartment, laboriously and massively as though the functions of the engine had finally been choked with night, Ingrid said to Robert quietly, "Come in. Come in and have a drink."

"All right," he said, and they went into the dark entrance without looking to see whether the cab moved on.

Inside it was better with the rawness of the damp air leaving their skin and the warm interior light, and they could forget a little the strange solidification of the drive up the hills away from the music and movement of the nightclub and Jacqueline, glowing triumphant, transmitting impulse and impulse as though her body were the channel for the current. But now it was better again, although the house was not cheerful. It was furnished as a foreigner might furnish a house, thinking of home. There were things that recalled Sweden and Paris, and they looked dead and rootless here, as they would have in any of the fashionable apartments of the city where one always sensed beneath the structure of modernity the jungle earth, unreceptive to anything that was superimposed and of its own. But more than this, the living room where they were sitting was cheerless because of the things that were missing, little things that had indicated two were living here, closely and intimately, and whose absence now said one, and one alone, one, now and perhaps forever, alone.

She had nothing in the house but gin, and it was bad to mix it with the whisky, but there had to be somewhere to start from and this was not like the nightclub at all but a sliding backward to a point where the emotions were once more constricted, and they would not have been able to start again without something to drink. But as the gin awakened the ebbing, warm radiance in their bodies, they wanted to talk and to knit the nightclub feeling and the feeling of now together. And he began to see her for the first time through his own eyes, not remembering very much of what Jacqueline had told him to think, and he wondered whether she was seeing him similarly.

The reddish hair and the blue eyes, he was thinking. *Like Yvonne, and yet not like her, not like her at all. The red hair and blue eyes of Sweden. Not Paris. No, not from Paris. Not delicate and very slender-compact. Not small of shoulder and breast. Not the small mouth and the blue eyes with a film of the sea across them. But very kind and generous like her body, filling the sofa with abundance and the wish to give it and the feeling that her abundance lies fallow and unclaimed.*

And now, perhaps she was thinking — still remembering partly what Jacqueline had said, not being able to forget the other one, the one before, as women are never able to forget the other one wholly — *he is thinking of her. And is needing not to think of her, not to remember because it hurts, but to touch and be touched, finding the under-depth and the inner, healing, pain-forgetting heart of touch. Wanting to forget, being young, and not yet all-despairing. Remembering and not wanting to remember how love suffers. But remembering and still remembering. Being young, uncynical, and what I would have wanted of love.*

Then they were speaking aloud, but it was difficult for Jacqueline was not there, transmitting impulse and impulse, joining their diffidence through the force and confidence of her personality. It was difficult because there was a feeling of guilt beneath their being together. A feeling of betrayal and shame at trying to forget too soon, and yet, undyingly the wanting and willingness to love, the furtive hope of filling the image in the heart with another image, of blending form, gesture, and word upon the memory of another form, other gestures, words that were now a consummation and a death, inert and final, forcing upon the mind the recognition of not-love, the fear, hardest to bear, that love lies in a compartment of the soul severed from current-consciousness, suspended and immobile in the enslavement of memory.

The music of the *samba* came in through the open window, primitive, simply melodic, without rhythmic sophistication, unabashedly and unashamedly sensual. In the night that had seemed to be going solid and weighted it was a cry that said the darkness had not died, that the body of the night had heart-life still.

"There's a *batuque*," she said, singing the refrain. "*Quero chorar, nao tenho lagrimas.* I want to cry, but I have no tears."

"That's Brazil," he said. "More deeply Brazil than anything else I know."

"Yes," she said. "I'll miss it when I leave. I won't miss much else — not any longer. There was a time when I would have, but not now. How I hate the *gran finos* and their silly floating-flower lives, the false-front of the Copacabana, like a stage setting imported from Europe. And how I hate myself for ever thinking I wanted it all." She paused and listened to the music once more, "But I want to remember that crying. I don't ever want to forget that."

"They laugh so much here," he said. "No wonder in their music they want to cry and don't have any tears."

The women's voices carried the words, soaring and quivering, seeming to fall back into the deep and resonant under-boom of the talking, wanting to listen to the music.

"When Charles and I first arrived, I liked it better here than any place I had ever known," she said finally. "Somewhere in the back of the mind, all of us dream of a country that is love's. Perhaps it is because in the fairy stories we read when we are children love makes everything beautiful. The witch is really only a princess in disguise, the Beast a Prince Charming. And, of course, where they live happily ever after is the most beautiful country on earth. We will always remember this country. It is the one place we can never forget. I suppose I thought I had found it once and for all when we came to Brazil. The mountains, the sea, the clear blue of the sky, were fabulous, the perfect background for what I was feeling. Finally, the landscape was not background but part of the feeling itself as though there was nothing antipathetic in the world and I could reach out and touch a rock, a flower, a tree, and know it to be love's. Now I don't feel that way any more, and I can't really see Brazil at all. I suppose that is why I want to leave it. I don't like hospitality, and I want to see again."

She spoke now without pausing, without even waiting for the conventional linking sentences that he might have inserted. It was not a monologue of self-absorption or indifference but of intense awareness of his presence, of an urgent sense of the need for fluency between them which she, being on the surface at least less constricted and diffident than he, must supply. Consequently, she talked steadily, intimately, and inclusively lest a silence occur, as in the car on the way to the apartment, and an intangible thickness coagulate and make communication slow to a laborious stop.

"When Charles told me four months ago that he wanted to go back to Paris, I knew he would not take me with him," she said. "He did not say so then, but I knew that he would expect me to understand in time, and that I would not go. He was French all the way through, very passionate, very complete in love, and very sure when it was over. My use was a thing of time, neatly measured so as not to last one day beyond boredom.

"To be the lover who does not lose it takes precision in judging others and the incapacity for regret, and Charles always saw things with a terrible precise clearness. He was very afraid of growing old, and I had begun to remind him of the fact that he would. No man wants to live in a museum of what he was. He can go back there in memory but not live there. Charles saw the future clearly. It was my fault that I kept it vague and undefined."

He was glad that she was talking, since he himself was not ready to talk, being closer to memory, and he knew that she would come, as she had, to that point in the past where the rupture was, the point from which they must, if ever, proceed. He was thankful for the flow of her words. The ample talkativeness of women, he thought, is often a thing to be thankful for. In a moment of tension, it will do its best to push remembering forward into not-remembering or spread it horizontal and thin like water on a dry field to be slacked up and lost from sight. Silence is the cause of much of our suffering, the keeping of grief within us, acute, perpendicular, unreleased, and women, he felt, know this better than men.

But, though he had not spoken, he knew that she was aware of the intensity of his response. It was she, ostensibly, who was moving them toward a starting point but the tempo and extension of her conversation would not have been possible without his sympathy. Her words were the surface motion, but a hidden current, intuitive and deep, like a belt under a revolving tableau of figures and scenes, was moving them into conjunction.

When she paused at last for breath, they were once again, for a moment, silent, but the silence was not empty or formal but quivering with the reverberations of her words. She sat loosely against the sofa, her figure nowhere strict and taut, not fat but well-rounded, the body of a woman, who, without fear of falling into excess, could stretch the sweetness of her sense a little beyond denial.

There are no rough edges in her, he thought. *She is gentle and hurt. Hurt and not able to hurt in return. The muscle of her heart is rich and strong but tired from loving, enduring, and not wanting to hurt. Now she is missing, needing, the serenity of affection. Can I open in her the sealed up power of touch again? Can I kiss her, touch her, taking the darkness of sensation into another darkness until there is warmth and the denial of darkness? To do this, to need to, to want to love again, to try in a passionate wanting.*

He moved very close to her, and put his arms around her. He did not look into her eyes because of his embarrassment and because he was ashamed of his desperation, of his desire to commit so soon a betrayal, of his wish to flood his loneliness with sensuous oblivion. Suddenly he was hearing, "Slowly, Robert. Not so fast. Wait a little." Said gently, tenderly resistive, at the same time that she rose and went into the other room.

Before they lay down, she lit a candle and placed it on the table beside the bed. At first, he was shy about the light, but then he was not, for it left them visible to each other and yet indistinct, hardly familiar at all, more like dream-figures, even strange to themselves, and perhaps this was better and easier for not remembering. The candle had been used before and was encrusted with its own wax flesh and relic-weeping, and he thought that everywhere you looked in the world, at any hour, there was something broken, torn, crying, or frozen in an attitude where the crying had stopped. It was right that she had lit the candle, alive again now and liquid with fresh tear-form droppings, gleaming through all its cylindrical shape, dully so at the base, tipped with a tiny, molten self-destroying crater where the flame, like an element antipathetic to the entombing wax, was almost disembodied from the wick. Without this light and its training it would have been impossible, at first, to have stayed in the room. The night would have been too dense and they would not have been able to endure the muffling darkness without the wavering, shadow-shimmering flare of the candle whose almost incorporeal lucence moved, probing and pliantly caressive over the walls, bed, table, over them where they lay, as though to enter once more the thingness, the body, that it would but finally, death-fearing, could not leave.

She did not undress entirely but lay there partially hidden from the candle-glow like one who knew light and the absence of light, not calculating the risks, being incapable of doing so, but not rushing toward them either, knowing the pitiless price one pays for wanting to possess the beautiful whose possession always quivers with not-possession, bringing the final soulless wish not to have possessed at all.

As he looked at her, very quiet and waiting, with the light on her reddish hair, everywhere on the broad surface of her face except the recesses of her eyes which were dark and closed, he knew that he would always remember her saying, "Slowly, Robert. Not so fast. Wait a little." Not harshly spoken, but gently admonitive, as those who have suffered will admonish others who have also suffered but not so greatly as they.

Then she put out the light, and there was a moment of strange waiting and perilous equipoise in the darkness. And when he touched her, the touch of another was there. And when he kissed her, it was illusive and unreal since he could not kiss through memory, since he could not touch her really at all, suddenly in the darkness remembering, not being able to forget, feeling that forgetting, in a lifetime, would hardly move fast enough or far enough to leave behind in silence one word of all that remembering.

And where his hand, his physical hand, reached — but without feeling — to accomplish the touch, he could imagine that she, too, would put her hand into another hand, and that their past lives were locked in a trance out of which they looked, as from imprisoned sleep, into the outrageous, shame-haunted, pent-eruptive world of dream to see the fictive motions of their present lives.

It was then that he remembered — as memory will always make you remember a clear indestructible moment of the past just when the present struggles toward freedom — the departure and final passage of the boat seen from the window of his hotel, the boat, white, compact, poised like a bird on the water. The realization and shock-vision that within the boat was the other form, the other face, the absolute evidence of love. Within the boat moving, at first, slowly, almost laboriously and reluctantly, then quicker, more quickly, quicker, more quickly, quickly, quickly, quickly, until the sky at the far end of the harbor cracked open and, in a moment and forever, the boat drained out of consciousness.

Afterwards, it was very quiet in the room. They lay there silently, unstirringly, as though in the darkness they were being watched hostilely from above. It was a long time before he dressed, and he began to wonder why she said nothing. But then he knew that her quietness was not anger, not silent reproach, not exclusiveness, not indifference, but deep patient waiting, the acceptance of not-possessing the recognition of the vastness between one life and another.

At the door she kissed him softly, without passion, and he wanted to cry out and shake his body for its obtuseness and his heart for its backward looking, but he did not. He could not. The sidewalk toward the city was steep and damp, and he had to walk down through the thick fog slowly, very slowly, to keep from falling.

(*From The Hudson Review*)

CHILDREN OF RUTH

BY GEORGE P. ELLIOTT

*R*UTH ADAMS, a vigorous woman of fifty-five, had lived all her life in the same house and intended to be living in it when she died. The house suited her tastes and needs to perfection; it was spacious and well proportioned, it had no needless decorations yet it served the requirements of comfort, it was entirely respectable yet admired by persons of every taste. It was, in fact, a part of herself. When she tried to imagine herself without her house, she did not know who she would be; it was her scholar's books and her painter's brush and her farmer's soil. Her attachment to it was so strong that she refused to go as delegate to out of town conventions, no matter how worthy the cause at hand; in defense of her refusal, strange in one who took so many good causes to her heart, she argued that in order to effect one's ends at a convention one must use every device of unscrupulous politics, compromising, if only in that corrupt practice, one's most cherished beliefs. This is true; however, it is doubtful if she would have objected so strenuously if she had not been reluctant to leave her house. It is notable that, whenever a convention of the sort that interested her was held in San Francisco or Oakland, she made her influence felt in ways that can only be called political. Chief among these ways of hers, though she was not conscious of duplicity or of putting on pressure when she did it, was her inviting key delegates to visit her, or even to stay at her house, during the convention. The commodious grace of the house and her assurance in it exercised an influence which only most insensitive or hostile delegates could resist.

Twice in her life Ruth had been tempted to leave her house, each time because of the love of a man. The first occasion had been when she had barely emerged from girlishness and had not yet emerged from her girlish love of a college companion, Luke Adams. It was during

the First World War; they felt hurried, they married; Ruth had produced a daughter and was pregnant with a son when Luke enlisted
and was shipped overseas. Luke contracted tuberculosis in the trenches;
at the war's end he was dying in a hospital in France, and it was then
that Ruth was tempted to leave her home for a long voyage overseas.
But the doctors assured her the trip could not save him; and since both
the babies were sick with flu at the time, she stayed home where she
belonged and let Luke die by himself. She grieved over his loss and
reproached herself for not having gone to him; but the reproaches had
so little substance that she eventually forgot them, and the loss while
great enough at the time gradually came to seem less and less devastat-
ing to her. Luke by inclination and temperament had been destined
to a prominent position in the YMCA; while the YMCA was a virtuous
organization in Ruth's view, still as the years went by her taste inclined
more and more towards a headier sort of man than it was likely to
produce.

The other temptation had been in 1930 when she had fallen in
love for the second time. It was with a major in the Army, a large,
indocile, irresponsible, domineering man named Frederick Kotowski.
She disapproved of his profession, his philosophy and his effect upon
herself; yet when he demanded that she marry him and go off to China
where he was being stationed, she almost went. In fact she put her
house up for sale and began packing her dishes. She was with child
at the time and her friends kept telling her how right she was to marry
Kowtowski; but when at the last she decided not to go with him but
to stay in her home and bear a child out of wedlock, her friends, such
as did not fall off, began applying the ephithet courageous to her.

The epithet stuck: when a few years later she had alone and unaided
dug up the evidence to convict three city officials of embezzlement, the
local newspaper too applied it to her; and her defense of Japanese-
Americans at the beginning of the second World War won for her the
final laurel of fugitive fame: favorable epithets in *Time* Magazine ("grey-
haired, brave Ruth Adams . . ."). So she had preferred her snug house
to the danger and mystery which loving Kotowski meant; she wrote
him after the child was born and never heard from him again. In 1942
the child, Erasmus Oliver Adams, received notice that his father had
been killed in the Philippines and that he was the beneficiary of a
$10,000 life insurance policy. She put the money aside for the time
when he would need it, spent half a day wondering why she had ever
loved a man like Kotowski, and turned back then to helping the Japanese-Americans. For their sake she thought of flying to Washington,

where she might put the pressure on some senators and bureaucrats; but she did not trust herself so far afield, and she sighed with relief when she was told she could not get priority to travel on the planes. And now she was as active as ever, except that she had to rest for a couple of hours every afternoon; as active but not quite as self-assured, for the Japanese-American battle, which she had of course lost, had made her realize for the first time that the collective fate of the people of Oakland was scarcely at all in their own hands: during the nineteen-forties a great many gears were stripped in that fine Machine of Progress, though not all of them.

The house she lived in had been built by her father shortly before she was born. Her father, Orestes Stull, had been an advanced architect of the time and had made a great deal of money from the designing of private houses for the well-to-do of Berkeley and Oakland. He refused to design public buildings in a style acceptable to city officials of those gingerbread decades; and despite his vogue among the expanding class to which he catered, he was never left completely free in his designing of houses. Always the husband insisted upon a bay window, or the wife declared she would die without a rear staircase, or they both agreed that the fireplace should be in a wasted corner. Throughout the 80's his fame and fortune grew, and by the early nineties he had the money to build for himself the house at 17 Denver Place, the home which he had been perfecting piecemeal in the houses of others.

It was built of redwood — an ancient, rather dark, straight-grained wood — and there was no part of it which was not useful, functional. Still, though every beam had its use, some of them might have been larger than necessary because to him they looked better large; some of them might have been placed at a graceful angle and not at the angle of greatest efficiency; they had an architect's rather than an engineer's usefulness. The living room was spacious and low of ceiling for those times; to keep it from being gloomy, Stull had put casement windows along two walls; one side yielded a view of lawn and trees and the other a small prospect of the Bay. It was neither a formal nor an intimate room but either as one willed, and it was always beautiful. One ate in the kitchen, which was huge and airy. The kitchen was redwood too, unpainted; as coolers and gas ranges and refrigerators and mixmasters kept being invented, Stull and Ruth after him had them incorporated into the paneled walls. One had the impression of cupboard doors clean yet darkened by the years of cooking in that comfortable room and bright pottery on open shelves and large workboards; and none of that surgery feeling, glistening and well arranged, which is a kind of ideal nowadays: shining implements and white purring machines and housewife in white smock and clocks and a deadline for dinner, all for lamb chops and peas. In the Stull kitchen guests frequently sat till midnight talking over coffee; the chairs were kitchen chairs and a great deal better for thinking in than right-angle dining-room chairs or an overstuffed davenport. In every bedroom there was a copy of a painting on the wall, a Turner countryside, a Cézanne still life, some Audubon birds. The study was lined with books, the cellar was stocked with canned fruit and a barrel of apples and a few cases of wine, the attic was full of odds and ends of furniture and boxes full of old curtains or, later, of Stull's manuscripts and drawings. Ruth had a great many photographs on the walls of her room of each member of her family, of her friends, of the Parthenon and ruins of Rome and Mont St. Michel; she kept them all and added to them as the years went by; she seldom really looked at them but she would have been diminished by their absence. From the outside the house was dignified but unostentatious; indeed to the owners of the mongrel imitations which surrounded it, it appeared plain. To them its comfort without their antiseptic luxuries was a sort of perversity, its flagrant honesty a temptation and a threat. Neither Stull nor Ruth nor Ruth's three children ever made friends with their neighbors.

Ruth's friends were scattered throughout the Bay Area; and, while she had no secret requirement that they should live in houses like her own, decent and dignified, yet most of them, as it turned out, did. Some lived in apartment houses and some in stucco coops, one in a tenement and a few in shacks; but most lived in houses solid and separate; and her oldest friend lived in a house only slightly less beautiful than her own. Though she was no snob and though she had never in her life said so to anyone, she could not imagine a better way to live than this; and she had decided long ago that she had a right to it. Whenever someone who had not yet made a treaty with his sense of injustice asked her how she could bear to live thus when so many must exist in the hovels and caves of poverty, then she would answer that all should be able to live as she did, that the sacrifice of her happiness would not ease their misery, that progress was a leveling upwards. She was her father's only child — her mother had died in childbirth — and when he had died he had left her this house and a fine income from the rent of several apartment buildings. Some of these apartments had declined into tenements and most were hideous, but they were better managed and cheaper than any others in town; when she was challenged for living off these rentals, she answered, justly, that it was a deplorable injustice, which, having inherited, she did with as best one could do; under another landlord her tenants would be worse off. When her older son, Eugene Gracchus, suggested once that she donate the apartments to their tenants, she was not even ruffled; it was logical in a way, as most of his ideas were, but like much logic it went counter to all her experience.

Her public life was a matter of committees and civic agencies and the expression of upright opinion. Hers was a philosophy full of sympathy and eschewing scandal, of hope and good works. She was in excellent health, she was an example of virtue and good fortune yet such an example as to baffle envy; she was respected more than most of us are and was hated less. Yet she was not a happy woman because of her children.

It is a Sunday afternoon in September, somewhat misty, as hot as it is likely to get in Oakland; there is a little breeze in from the sea; climate is not one of the enemies here. Even so, Gene is wearing the blue wool turtleneck shirt he usually wears around the house. He has never been a seaman; he likes this shirt because he is seldom too warm, and because his neck is long and thin and easily chilled, and because he is used to it. Gene is well over six feet, but he is so thin and pale that he gives the impression not of being tall but of being too long. Ruth is still lying down, on a cot in the back garden, waiting for the family to gather for dinner, as is their custom on the Sabbath. This dinner is about all that remains for them of that fourth commandment which their puritan ancestors made so much of once long ago.

"Mother."

His voice, which is not low, rises to its treble when he is excited in any uneasy way. It is high now.

"Hello, dear."

With a quick gesture Ruth lifts her arm from across her eyes, and quickly turns her head to look at him. She is ready to relax again if he has nothing important to say.

"Does anything need to be fixed for dinner?"

His huge, smooth bluff of a forehead is wrinkled. She can tell that he has something to say which it will take him many indirections to get at. She lays her arm by her side and stares up through the branches of the cherry tree spreading above her.

"No, dear. Miriam will help me get things ready."

"Well, Dorie will be here before long."

Dorie is his fiancée.

"I suppose."

It is Dorie's habit, three Sundays running, to arrive too late to help in the kitchen; the fourth Sunday she will come so early as to do more than her share. Gene has not noticed this habit of Dorie's. Ruth has; her "I suppose" is rather dry.

"Is E. O. going to be here for dinner?"

E. O. is Erasmus Oliver, who has exacted from everyone but his mother the obligation of calling him by his initials. He has told his friends that his father was a Texan who named him, in the Texas fashion, by initials only.

"He said at breakfast that he would be."

The puckered lines about her mouth, the combined result of determination and false teeth, become more puckered yet as she speaks of Oliver — with the determination of hiding the pain which thinking of him gives her.

"Is he going to get a new motorcycle?" asked Gene, though he knew the answer. His intention with these questions — at least what he accomplished with them — was to make his mother as little at peace as he himself was.

Ruth, however, did not understand about such tactics and would not have believed them of Gene if she had been told; she answered therefore truthfully and painfully.

"I will not give him the money. That is not quite correct, I will do everything I can to prevent his owning a motorcycle. It is not the money. He says he will work for the money." She turned more directly toward Gene. "What can he do now? He has no training."

"He knows all about cars. Maybe he'll get a job in a garage."

"If that's what he wants," she answered. But the sadness was all in her eyes; her voice and mouth were controlled and allowed Oliver freely the right to work as he wished.

"There's nothing wrong with being a mechanic," Gene said.

"Nothing at all. It's the motorcycle that's so wrong. Everything it means."

She closed her eyes. Gene took a last puff on the cigarette he was holding and flipped it into the shrubbery. He walked restlessly to the other side of the cot and looked down at her.

"Mother," he began, his voice pitched a little higher than before.

"Yes, Eugene?"

"You know that I've been having good results in my chess lately."

"Yes, dear."

"The next international tournament is to be held in Tokyo."

She could not see how that information affected her. She did not answer.

"I have been invited to attend with the American team."

"Really?" She half sat up with excitement. "You would be with the masters then?"

"Yes. I think it may have some importance for my future."

Ruth saw little point in chess, except as a way of relaxing; but if Gene was going to take chess seriously, it was obviously best for him to be very good at it. Her congratulations were sincere, but as always when she spoke of chess there was a note of bewilderment in her voice.

"I am so glad for you. I hope with all my heart you do well. Do you know anything about the others?"

"Oh yes. There will be some excellent Russian players there. The great Polish master is dead."

"Well," she said, reclining again, "it makes me happy to think of you being there."

Gene's brow wrinkled again, in irritation; he thought she was deliberately not helping him, whereas in truth she did not know he wanted her help.

"The point is, Mother, I haven't the money to go."

Now for something as important to him as this Ruth would never have denied him the money, and Gene knew it. But Ruth herself did not know it, though he thought she did. He thought not only that she knew it but that the long process of reasoning herself into it, which she always went through, was a method of reproaching him. She had nothing like reproach in her mind; she was, though she did not know it, providing her conscience with good reasons for giving this money to him.

"How much more do you need, dear?" She put her arm back across her eyes; all he could see of her face was the rather stern-looking mouth, which irritated him too.

"Five hundred dollars. I've looked into the cost by boat. I'd rather not fly."

"When is it to be held?"

"Next May."

"You would have to leave in March."

"I'd rather go in February. As long as I'm there I'd like to see something of Japan."

She was silent. It was in her silences that he felt the reproach most keenly, the reproach of being thirty-three and good for nothing. A chess player. Lives in his mother's house. Doesn't even earn his own

living but lives off the rents of houses which his grandfather paid for.
A professional amateur. Couldn't get a good job if he wanted one.
"Then you would get married next summer."
"Yes."
In Ruth's mind, conscience was still tipping the scales. She had
promised her sons to double their incomes when they were married.
She thought what she allowed them was sufficient, and for simple
tastes it would have been; neither of them had simple tastes. Also,
she had promised a very heavy contribution to the American Civil
Liberties Union for the prosecution of some white farmers who were
combining to ruin the Japanese farmers in their county. She felt she
ought not spare the money from that lawsuit for Gene's happiness.
"Of course," he said, "I could borrow it. But I'd rather not be in
debt when I marry."
His features seemed to crumple when he said this. Overtopped by
his huge forehead they looked squeezed down by it, pushed together by
too much intellect and anxiety and reproach. She could hear all this
in the quaver in his voice, as of one who holds back tears or rage, and
she could not bear it.
"No, son, no. You may have the money. I hope it gives you great
satisfaction."
Her voice was steady and ungrudging; not very warm, but then it was
never a very warm voice.

Gene walked off, not very happy. He stood looking at flowers for a
time. Now on a lovely afternoon when there is nothing to do, one is
supposed to enjoy natural life whether in a garden, a park or the countryside; and Gene had often done so, or thought he had. He was especially fond of going with Dorie to the Golden Gate Park and walking
about or sitting on the lawns all an afternoon, and when he had been a
child his mother could give him no greater treat than to take him to
the country for a day. Now he stood looking at a bank of wistaria and
felt nothing; he was too honest to pretend he was liking the flowers, but
he was mystified, as he had been before, at his own emptiness, its cause.
What he lacked was eyes of another to see through, warmth of another to
feel the beauty through, another's openness to open him. He stood
staring dejectedly, and at the sound of his sister's maternal yoo-hoo and
her children's yelps, he ran upstairs to his room. He liked Miriam but
she showed him nothing; he was fond of George and Penny but children's candor alarmed him a little; and he thought her husband Bill,
who was an actuary and a ski enthusiast, to be a thumping bore.
He found Dorie writing at his desk.

"Dorothea!" he exlaimed. "When did you come?"

"Hello, Gene." She looked at him a little abstractedly. "I had to finish a letter to Pris and all the dogs in town were barking under my window. Do you mind?"

"Of course not. Go ahead."

He walked over and patted her shoulder; she squeezed his hand with a rather mechanical affectionateness and turned back to her letter. Gene lay on his bed looking at his room, which, though he had lived in it for twenty-nine years, pleased him as the wistaria was supposed to have done.

He liked the roof-beams above him and the redwood paneling; he found the irregularities in its shape, caused by two closets, to be a convenience as well as a guard against the boxlike effect a room can give. He liked the Klee painting he had on the wall over the desk and the Braque over the bookcase; the books, which were not numerous but very well used; the piano, which he had learned to play on as a child and still did not neglect; the confusion of equipment in the corner where he was himself assembling the best possible record player; the low chair and ottoman; the plywood chess board stuck behind the bookcase and the cheap chess men, chipped and dirty, scattered on the desk; the rugless floor; the hard mattress; Dorie at his desk. Liked everything in the room — which almost contained his life — except himself. As he lay on the bed, pleased with what he had done and what he was going to do but not with himself doing it, he realized that it would take more than an absent-minded pat on the hand from Dorie to make him feel good again.

She had stopped writing for a moment and sat gazing out the window.

"What are you saying to Pris? Give her my best."

"What?" said Dorie turning toward him and focusing her eyes on him.

"I said, what are you writing to Pris about?"

"Oh nothing much."

"Well, come over and give me a kiss. I'm a little low."

"I'm busy, darling."

"What are you writing about? Your bridal plans?"

He though he was being ironic, but as often happened to him his irony was neither strong enough nor delivered in such a way as to make its intent clear. People would take his ironies straight, or think he was being facetious, or ignore them altogether. Dorie took this one straight.

"In a way."

"What do you mean?"

"Well, I was telling her the possibilities in this house, when we ever get a chance to fix it over."

He reared up in dismay.

"What do you mean? What's wrong with it as it is?"

This house had sheltered him all his life, he liked it, it had been kept in good repair. He could just conceive of living in another house, but this one he could not imagine improved by anyone and certainly not by Dorie, whose taste, though he loved her, he deplored.

"I was telling her what a distinguished-looking room the living room would be if the walls were white plaster and maybe, though I'm not sure, if the ceiling were white too, in between the beams."

She stole a look at him; she knew she was trespassing and wanted to see how he accepted it. His forehead was wrinkled, his eyebrows were raised, he was stroking his jaw with one finger; it was an expression and gesture characteristic of him when he was observing or trying to understand something. She went on.

"The kitchen of course would have to be redone from one end to the other. It's hopelessly out of date." He did not even blink. "I think those brown shingles on the outside walls are very drab. Wouldn't it be more striking to put grey composition shingles over them?"

"No," he said, whinnying with annoyance.

"They're fireproof too."

"My mother would never consent to modernizing this house, and besides she has three children. Why should we have it to ourselves? You're wasting your time."

"It's terribly dark and gloomy. The only thing it has is a good floor plan and lots of windows, but it's terribly inefficient. It's *slow*, if you know what I mean."

"I don't and I don't want to." His voice was at the top of its register but not loud. "And even if we inherit it I wouldn't agree to a single one of your ideas. I like it and I feel an obligation not to change it."

She saw it would be a long campaign. She chose to be feminine at the moment and went over to kiss him.

"You're too late for that," he said pushing her off. "Besides, you ought to go down and help mother and Miriam."

"All right, darling. Just one kiss to show you love me."

They kissed. She coquetted with him a minute, shaking her hair in his face and biting his nose with her lips; he smiled. She went back to finish her letter and he watched her.

Gene was a great watcher; his favorite way of dealing with his fellows was to watch them. People at concerts, at ball games, at church, skid-row bums, a class of deaf and dumb children being herded through the zoo, pregnant women standing in street cars, children playing paper dolls or chasing each other, himself in a mirror, his mother, Dorie now. He prowled the city like a photographer, looking; and he saw as well as a good camera. Not as a good photographer, but a good camera, for there were too many things which he was afraid of for him to be able, as a good photographer must, to love or pity or censure — or, most god-like of all, to forgive — all that he saw so very clearly. Mostly he saw curiosities and matter for jest. He would follow a woman with a cleft palate and a Louisiana drawl as she bought food from counter to counter in the Tenth Street Market, watching her anger and timidity with clerks and listening to her cloud-like words form and amalgamate and seem to mean something and dissolve: she became a joke to tell. He liked to get a glimpse of people who had not pulled their blinds clear down undressing for bed, not for pruriency's sake but because they looked so ludicrous scratching, yawning, half-naked, so much like each other. It is true of course that he was not always just the camera; a mother with her baby, a Negro in a streetcar full of whites, or always a blind man, such as these he saw with more than his physical eyes. But now as he lay watching his fiancée, it was a joke for himself that he was after.

"Dorie," he said, "can you move around this way a little. I like to look at your leg like that."

Flattered, she obliged him, but it was not her legs he wanted to see. They were plump and not well tapered at the knee and ankle; crossed as they were now, the fleshy calf was pushed out of shape, and besides the crossed leg stuck out at an angle of pure vulgarity. It was not her legs he wanted but for her to think it was; also he could get a better profile of her whole person thus. It was a pleasant, rotund little profile; after a child or two it would be dumpy. The babyishness of her face was accentuated by her soft and fluffy hair and her ready smile; as Gene knew, the babyishness was flatly contradicted by the coolness and judging in her pale blue eyes. She was concentrating on her letter, or seeming to; he could see her glance, however, rest on her leg from time to time. She adjusted her skirt so that it came down a little further over her untrim knee. As though tired of her shoes she slipped them off; her arched feet were her prettiest point, her feet and the coloring of her skin like a fresh strawberry peach. When she, so nonchalantly, dropped the shoe off, Gene felt that his joke had worked; content, he went to the window to watch the family in the garden.

His tall and slightly stooped sister and his dumpy little mother were just turning from a flower bed to go into the house. They were talking; he could tell by the way his mother was patting the back of one hand in the palm of the other that something had put her out of patience. Bill was on the cot reading the Sunday paper, and the children were climbing the apple tree. A sprinkler was revolving sedately in one corner of the lawn. It wasn't much of a scene, no cleft palates or goiters in it, but Gene was feeling a sentimental glow over it as he watched — sentimental because, if he had been down in it, it would have seemed quite different to him, full of little dangers to be guarded against. Dorie, ignored, left her letter and came to stand beside him.

"How can Miriam look so sleek, a mother of two kids?" she said in her unbabyish voice, with a lingering on certain vowels that some women learn at sorority houses and neglect to unlearn afterwards.

Miriam was sleek after a lean fashion. If you were in the mood to see her that way. Gene was not. He was thinking Miriam looked well groomed or chic.

"No," he said contemplatively, "she isn't a bit frowsy, is she?"

He went over to the confusion of wires about the record player and began doing something. Dorie looked to see if her slip was showing and returned to the letter, but she could not concentrate on it any longer. She put on her shoes and before going downstairs she went over to kiss Gene. He was still annoyed at her; he responded to her kiss with some amorous horseplay of a kind she disliked. But their parting sounded amiable enough. Dorie because she was still making amends for her earlier trespass, Gene because he thought he was being ironic in his amiability, and because it is so risky not to be amiable.

"And the American Medical Association?" Ruth was saying, tapping one hand nervously in the other.

"I'm afraid they'll be against it, but one can never be sure."

"On the contrary, one can be quite sure. I'm grateful for organizations like the AMA and the American Legion. You always know precisely where they'll be and what they'll want and how they'll go about getting it, and you always know that in a pitched battle they'll win."

"Mother, I never heard you sound so cynical."

"It's called realistic," said Ruth very dryly.

"Mother!"

"Go ahead, my dear, take your own path. If I were thirty-five I would do it as you are doing it. By the time you've learned all the tricks for yourself, you'll be taking naps every afternoon too."

"You think," said Miriam a little timidly, "that I've just been wasting my time? I hoped ——"

"Nothing of the kind. You will have awakened a few more people to their responsibilities."

Miriam groaned.

"You might even succeed," said Ruth.

"My God! I want to get something done! Awaken people to their responsibilities."

"Think of it this way, if it makes you feel better. I do sometimes. In every good deed you do, by just so much do you retard the progress of corruption."

Ruth was very fond of this sentence, and Miriam had heard her say it a score of times before; yet never had it penetrated so far as it did now. She groaned again; there was not a trace of humor in this groan as there had been in the first one.

"Pay no attention to what I've said, dear," said Ruth. In a rare demonstration of affection, she kissed Miriam on the cheek. "I'm out of sorts today." And then, with an association of ideas she herself did not recognize, her voice changing with the change of subject, she added: "Did you know that Gene is going to Tokyo next spring to attend the chess tournament?"

"No!" Miriam exclaimed, relieved to have something cheerful to exclaim at. "The world championship tournament?"

"I believe so. He'll marry Dorie when he comes back."

"Mother!" yelled George. "Look!"

He was straddling two limbs high up in the apple tree. He achieved the effect he desired: the women came squawking in alarm to get him down, and he in an affectation of being disgruntled lowered himself to a safer limb. Bill had fallen asleep with the paper over his face, and Penny was sitting in the lowest crotch of the tree eating an apple. Surveying their work with approval and possessive pride, the mother and daughter turned to the kitchen.

Dorie entered one door as they the other.

There was an involuntary change in Miriam the moment she saw Dorie. Miriam too had attended a sorority in college, though only for a year; and although she had hated the sorority and although she was not proud of the accomplishment, she could be as shellacked, as hard, as stamped by the great machine, as the next woman, and in Dorie's presence she assumed that smiling and vacant-hearted type she deplored. All during the preparation of dinner the two kept up a chatter about food and clothes, meaning nothing but that they did not like each other.

It distressed neither of them, but only Ruth; Ruth did not chatter, and she would never have permitted herself to dislike her daughter or her future daughter-in-law — except perhaps when she first woke up in the morning, when all things seemed worse to her and at the same time less hopeless. Yet, even so, there was something in Ruth which was not unlike their machined perfection. Her undemonstrativeness might have become their empty assertions of affection: there were too many darlings in their acquaintance; they so loved to do this or that; things were too frequently charming. Her reserve, which was a respect for the privacy of others, might have become their dreadful intimacy, which permitted them at a bridge table to describe their husbands' potency, and their yet more dreadful aloneness when trouble marked them and left them only the hard and hollow sympathy of their friends. Her house might not have meant to her grace and a decent life but have been a cause of pride, as it would have been for them, a thing of which others should be made envious.

Sometimes as she was lying in bed the first thing in the morning it seemed to Ruth that those who like Dorie and Miriam would arrogate to themselves this air of cold superiority must surely be mean spirits, but later in the day she would reprove herself for her unkind thoughts and remember their excellences. What she found very hard to forgive in them was the pride they took in their meanness: snobbery is a small but nasty version of that most cardinal sin.

"Mother," said Miriam as she was prearing the salad, "I do hope E. O. gets here for dinner." Her tone of voice was warm and genuine for she was fond of her younger brother, and furthermore it was a tactful thing for her to say. She had noticed his absence, she had observed her mother prick up her ears when a car seemed to be stopping in front of the house, she knew how much her mother counted on these family dinners; more, she knew with what pain her mother would account to them for his absence at table. But lest it seem tact and only tact she added, what was perfectly true but did not have to be added, "He's so nice with the children." In it all there was nothing but affection and honest feeling. Yet she could be so catty and unkind as to make Ruth sick at heart.

And Dorie, though the cattiness seemed more natural to her, had far too much strength of character actually to become the role she played. Her baby face, her smooth manner, her naïve opinions on public matters, these were devices she used to get what she wanted. In her first husband she had married the type which fitted the type she seemed to be; he was a handsome, country-club, fun-loving dealer of a man, a successful broker, a baffled husband, and venal to his marrow. She had divorced him, and now what she wanted was Gene, no one knew why, not even Gene, no one but herself and she could not have explained it with her impure, machined vocabulary which had no words for motive as complex as this. Without the words for an idea it is very difficult to have the idea at all; she called it love, though she knew that love was the least of it, and everybody was satisfied but Ruth.

The family sat down to dinner half an hour late, but without Oliver.

Oliver was in quite another part of town, one where he felt more at home than in his mother's house. He was at Iggy's Igloo down on East Fourteenth Street. The hot rod gang usually hung out at Sleepy's, on Ninety-Second Avenue below East Twelfth Street; but Oliver and his best friend Jack felt they had got beyond the hot rod stage, so they went to Iggy's, a motorcyclists' hangout. They were not contemptuous of hot rods by any means; a hot rod can kill you as dead as a motorcycle, but, it was their opinion, it would not kill you quite as soon. The way they put it to themselves was: A rod's okay, but there's more kick in a bike. After Oliver had wrecked his third rod he had not built up another but was saving himself for a motorcycle; Jack had traded his rod in before he had wrecked it, and now had an old but still lethal English bike.

A little after noon they had roared up, Oliver sitting behind Jack, to Iggy's, revved her up and turned off the ignition so she would back-fire, and gone in for some beer. Iggy did not care whether they were under age as long as they sat in the back room to drink the beer.

Iggy was alone at a table in the main room, half asleep over the Sunday paper.

"Hey Iggy!" shouted Jack.

"What's the matter, man?" said Oliver. "Stay up too late last night?"

"Well, boys," said Iggy pushing himself to a standing position, "is it beer already you want today?"

"You got it, man," said Oliver snapping his hat at Iggy, "you got it Two of the brew."

Oliver had been wearing for the past couple of days a very small black bowler cocked over one eye. It was held in place by an elastic

that went around his head; upon the slightest provocation he would
pull it away from his forehead and let it snap back. His intention was
to set a new fad, but the fad wasn't taking on much. The hat was
decidedly silly, and most people, even most motorcyclists, do not like
to look silly, in their own eyes at least. Oliver, however, rather liked to
make himself look silly: he had a pervasive sense of his own unimpor-
tance, which he could make good use of only by seeming to ridicule
himself. Yet he was not a buffoon; he would not obtrude himself upon
other people as much as a buffoon must. His attitude was: I'll go along
with everything and have a good time and be one of the boys, but if
I happen to become the center of attention somehow or other, I'll be all
prepared to be laughed at. Consequently he wore a small, tight smile
on his lips nearly all the time, embarrassed, deprecatory, supercilious,
ironic, friendly, depending on how you looked at it. Consequently too
he was a leader of his friends only in the matter of fads; there he was
ahead of them all.

They went into the back room and sat at a small round table with a
red check cloth on it. On one wall there was a shelf with two large
and handsome steins on it, and on the other walls were rather soft
photographs of Bavaria.

"Hey, Iggy," said Oliver when the beer arrived, "anybody been
around yet?"

"No, today you are the first."

"What's the matter, Iggy?" said Jack jovially. "You're droopy.
Best friend die?"

Iggy smiled and shrugged his shoulders; but his watery blue eyes
behind their glasses said, though not to them exactly: To an old exile
all friends are dead. He went back to his paper.

"Hey," said Jack to Oliver, "you get the money for a bike?"

"Naw, I can't get my hands on it till I'm twenty-one."

"Your old lady won't give it to you?"

"Naw. I'm going to get me a job."

And Jack laughed, with a sort of bellowing formality recognized by
them as expressing incredulity.

"Oh, E. O., what you going to be this time, a garbage collector?"

Oliver's tight little smile, which had nothing to do with mirth, tried
to be supercilious, tried to suggest he knew something that Jack couldn't
guess. But Jack wasn't fooled; since he had known him, Oliver had
kept none of his jobs for more than a few weeks. Oliver had picked
fruit, driven a delivery truck, been a surveyor's helper, washed dishes,
worked in a cannery, worked in a warehouse, and held a dozen more

jobs like these; either he had simply not showed up for work one day or he'd been fired for loafing, or else he'd earned as much money as he'd wanted at the time and then had formally quit.

"I got me an in at the Plumbers' Union," he said. "They make good dough."

"Yeh?" said Jack full of doubt. "How you going to get in?"

"I know somebody who knows somebody."

Jack shrugged with apparent indifference.

"How good of a bike you going to get?"

"I figure I'll borrow me seven hundred dollars and pay it back in a year. That'll get me a pretty fair motor."

"Nobody'll lend you seven hundred."

Oliver just smiled. Jack shrugged again; it was his favorite gesture.

"You got one lined up?"

"No," said Oliver leaning forward, "but I know what I'm going to get when I lay my hands on that ten thousand. I'm going to get me a chrome job, with a straight pipe and a butterfly cut-out. . . ."

He'd been through the catalogue of his motorcycle's charms so often that both he and Jack knew it by heart, but the more elaborate and set his imaginings of it the keener was his anticipation. He had hardly got started on his recital when some one came in the front door. A melodious, feminine voice spoke to Iggy; Oliver continued, unconsciously raising his voice a little. When he had quite finished, Jack suggested his favorite variation, harder but puncture-proof tires; Oliver responded, "Aaah, I'll get me a new set of tires every month." And the curtain to the back room parted to a young woman in motorcycle clothes. She was brown-skinned and had short black hair; she was strong and carried herself like a man, though her figure was amply female; her eyes were dark and bold, her face was impassive, and her thin lubricious lips scarcely moved when she spoke.

"Hi, Jack," she said; she seemed to be trying to make her beautiful voice harsh but succeeded only in making it sound flat and strained.

"Hello, Jo Ann."

"Who's your friend?" she said pointing at Oliver with the glass of beer in her hand.

"E. O. Adams. Come on and sit down."

"E. O. Adams? I've heard about you."

"This is Jo Ann Rakoczi," said Jack.

Oliver's little smile tried to express indifference but he only looked pleased.

"Pleased to meet you," he said. "You have a nice motor."

She nodded and looked at him without expression. Oliver was excited, for he had seen her at the head of her gang a dozen times, fearless and confident it seemed to him; he had seen her perform a perfect figure eight in the middle of East Twelfth Street, stopping the traffic with complete nonchalance. He thought she was beautiful, and she would have been beautiful if it had not been for the hardness with which she shellacked herself and which Oliver admired in her.

Under her gaze he did not know what to say; he knew that boasting would not succeed with her, and he felt that the exaggerated cowardice with which he sometimes talked about his hot rod exploits would not amuse her. So he said nothing but only stared at the ring on her hand. Saying nothing became Oliver; he was well-built and handsome, and though he sat in a sort of slouch and though his face was marred by a scar on the cheek, he looked like a strong man affecting indifference to his strength. His embarrassment, which was really a kind of modesty, seemed to Jo Ann, disguised as it was by his smile and his slouch, a kind of indifference to herself; to overcome this indifference without seeming to became her immediate object.

"You're all alone?" asked Jack.

"Yes," she answered. "We had a party last night. Everybody else is still laid up from it."

"Sit down," said Oliver dragging a chair into place with his foot.

"Thanks. Say," she said to him, "it sounds like you're after a pretty sharp motor."

"Yeh. I'm coming into some dough in a few months."

"What you got now?"

"Nothing. I wrecked my last rod, but I'm tired of rods. Kid stuff."

"Oh I don't know," she said looking at the scar on his cheek. "I got up to a hundred and thirty-five out in Richmond one time in a rod. Brakes wasn't worth a damn either."

"Oh, yeh," said Oliver hastily, "*high-grade* kid stuff, but a bike's got more kick to it."

"Oh, yeh," said Jo Ann, "a lot more kick."

"A lot more," said Jack.

"I know a guy," said Jo Ann, "that's got a damn good motor he'd probably sell. Want to go see it?"

"How much he want for it?"

"Four hundred. It's a good machine. Not as good as mine except on turns. It's a little heavier. But it's got as much soup as I've got."

"I got no money."

"Borrow some. Get a job."

"Of course, this one would just fill in. I'm coming into some real money in a few months."

And suddenly, with a boldness that astonished himself, Oliver looked down straight into her eyes and then at her lips.

"Sure," he said as though he was meaning something else. "I'll come with you. Give me a ride?"

"Sure."

Oliver turned to Jack.

"You got anything to do?"

"No," said Jack getting up expectantly, "I got nothing to do."

"Well, find something, man," said Oliver winking at him in such a way that Jo Ann would not see it. They left Jack crestfallen.

Oliver had never intentionally been so rude to anyone before in his life. He judged that any man whom Jo Ann admired would do things like this and he winked to soften the unkindness to his friend. But as they roared away toward Alameda, his conscience was uneasy.

He yelled in Jo Ann's ear, intending to say, How long have you known Jack?, but saying instead, "What's Jack to you?"

"When we used to be kids, we were neighbors. What's it to you?"

"I don't know. He's my buddy."

"Yeh, but he hasn't got much nerve."

They didn't speak again because of the noise, but Oliver felt impelled to tell her one of his what-a-coward-I-was stories, impelled by an obscure sort of loyalty to Jack whom he had betrayed and who was cowardly too, and by a sense of flying under false colors now with Jo Ann. So when they stopped in front of Jo Ann's house in Alameda, he told her, with grotesque exaggeration, how he had been so frightened in a time-run on the Richmond streets once, because the hot rod before him had blown a tire and rolled over, that he had cut his rod out at eight-five with the excuse that his supercharger had gone on the fritz. The story was true; but he told it so quietly and with such great exaggeration that Jo Ann thought he was making it up to defend his friend; she thought he was saying, "Even a brave man can lose his nerve sometimes," and she admired him for his loyalty, his honesty and his courage.

The motorcycle for sale belonged to Jo Ann's brother, who was at sea. Oliver climbed on it and followed Jo Ann up the steepest streets to Skyline Boulevard, and there he performed feats which froze his guts with fear and at the same time flushed his face with pride. But the only tribute that he won from her was when he performed a power spin that nearly pulled his left leg off.

"Say," she said, "that's good. You ought to get a steel shoe."

"I will," he replied, "when I get me a real bike."

And he roared down the winding road so fast he had to clench his teeth to keep them from chattering but always with the tight little smile and always ready to wave nonchalantly at his friend who was not afraid. She was not afraid in truth; she had discovered exactly how good she was on a motorcycle, and she would do anything up to her limit and nothing beyond it. She was as afraid as Oliver of seeming afraid; but she was wiser than he, less reckless, for he was afraid not only of fear itself but of the danger as well; that was an emotion she had not felt, purely and simply, for years. A rock in the road was something to avoid for her; for him it meant five painfully broken ribs or a broken neck.

At about three-thirty, feeling hungry, they roared down the hills to 17 Denver Place and roared up the driveway to the garage just as the rest of the family were starting to eat dessert.

"That's where my room is," he said to Jo Ann, pointing to the room over the garage; then he led her into the dining room.

"Hi, Mom," he said snapping the black bowler at her; she had begged him the day before not to wear it in the house. "This is Jo Ann; Jo Ann, my mother. Those are the rest of my family."

Ruth concealed the hurt she felt and said how do you do in an even voice. Gene looked at Jo Ann in her jeans and kidney belt and tight man's shirt, at Oliver, at his mother; he said nothing but watched them all three closely, holding his eyebrows very high. Miriam was furious, said nothing, glared at Oliver. Oliver missed none of their reactions.

"You got to the pie already," he said. "We'll go out in the kitchen and get some of the stuff that's left over."

"I'll fix it for you here," said Ruth. "I can easily lay another place."

"Don't bother," said Oliver. "Jo Ann can dish it up. Anyway, we aren't dressed for the occasion." He leered at Miriam, who was as always well turned out. "I'm thinking of buying her brother's bike."

"What?" said Ruth in a sharp constrained voice.

"Sure," said Oliver; it was easier for him to say these painful words to his mother in front of everyone and casually, for he knew that she could not reproach him openly here and now. "He's at sea and it's a good job."

"Please, Oliver," she said, "for my sake ——"

And no one knew what was threatening Ruth at that moment — Oliver because he dared not see it, Dorie because she did not wish to, Gene because it was so risky — no one but Miriam. Only she saw on Ruth's face the dark shadow pass, heard in Ruth's voice the cracked will, felt in her own sympathetic heart the stark and nameless fear. Stark: she put her hand on her mother's arm and held it tightly; nameless:

when she saw Ruth's self-composure return, she did not seek to name that fear but to forget it.

All this took but a few moments. Oliver snapped the bowler again and pushed Jo Ann before him into the kitchen.

Oliver accomplished a great deal in this minute of boorishness; and it was boorishness: he knew the amenities and had violated them for his own purposes. For one thing he infuriated his sister, and that was always worth the trouble. For another, he put his mother in her place for not giving him the money for a motorcycle; of course she did not know that the pain he was giving her was for that reason, but he knew it and felt that it justified him in what he did. But only barely justified him, for he had another reason for his behavior, of which he was not aware: his family was certain to disapprove of Jo Ann; by hitting first he protected himself against their disapproval, especially against his mother's, which he could hardly bear. He need not, of course, have brought Jo Ann here at all, but he wanted to impress her with his mother's house and the style in which they lived. Though he himself lived in an uncharming room littered with bolts and dime magazines, he was proud of his mother, her house and her life; it all seemed useless to him, but pretty: to Oliver, part of the prettiness of a thing was always its inutility.

And then too he wanted to seem strong and dominating and indifferent in the eyes of Gene and Jo Ann. With Jo Ann he succeeded; with Gene he failed completely. Oliver held Gene in a peculiar respect; for, though he was contemptuous of Gene's physical frailty and what seemed to him his unmanliness, yet he was rather in awe of Gene's intellect. "He's a brain," Oliver would tell his friends, who all felt about a brain as he did: after all scientists are brains and everybody knows about scientists. But even about his unmanliness Oliver was not sure; after all Gene always managed to get women to go around with, and here he was engaged to quite a good-looking one. More, Gene had been in the war and Oliver hadn't; it is true that Gene, who had been conscripted against his will, had spent his time in an office decoding messages and not out shooting or bombing the enemy, but still decoding messages is sort of like the FBI and everybody knows about the FBI. Perhaps worst of all was that Oliver knew of no way by which he could hurt Gene, short of knocking him down, but Gene could make Oliver very uneasy simply by raising his eyebrows high and staring right at him as though he were decoding him. Therefore Oliver was trying to appear tough in Gene's eyes now; he would have winced almost physically if he had realized that Gene was pitying his shaky bravado.

With Jo Ann he succeeded, however. Jo Ann would never have been allowed to speak so rudely to her mother, who was old-fashioned about teaching children their manners. Jo Ann thought that Oliver kept his family in their place; she took Ruth's silence for submission to his domination, though it was far from that, and admired him for it. Therefore when a little later Oliver slapped her on her ample bottom as she was leaning over to pick up a spoon, Jo Ann did not hit him fiercely as she would normally have done but said menacingly and close to him, "What'd you do that for?" And when he grabbed her and kissed her, she kissed him back. It was hard to make her submit, but once down she was fierce in demanding that she be held down hard.

Jo Ann was not alone in thinking that Ruth had submitted to Oliver.

"Mother," said Miriam indignantly when Oliver and Jo Ann had disappeared into the kitchen, "why do you let him get away with stuff like that? It's terrible."

"He's a man now," said Ruth gravely. Her lips were pursed up with pain but her eyes and voice were steady. "He's free to do as he wishes, as you are, my dear."

But Miriam fumed on, outraged and inconsistent. As a mother she gave Penny and George even more freedom and indulgence than she herself had been allowed when a child; she put up with their rages and insults with great equanimity, acceded to many of their wishes, and let them have very bad manners. But she could not bear to think that at the age of twenty they would still be capable of such behavior as this of Oliver's; according to her scheme, will should automatically assert itself at some point in a child's career, bringing with it good manners, respect for convention and a sense of adult responsibility. It all seemed so simple to Miriam because she had been contented with herself most of her life. Contented, she could afford, when she wished, to seem considerate of others, which makes up for any amount of technical flaw in manners. She might have bethought herself, had she not been so satisfied with her lot, that one who is truly guided by a code of behavior, as she thought herself to be, need not and can not employ that code of bitchery she used so readily with Dorie; that Oliver, who was far from content with himself and had like herself been allowed much freedom as a child, was behaving perhaps more crudely than she behaved with Dorie, but no worse. Instead of so reflecting, she indulged herself in that sort of indignation which comes not from seeing injustice done but from seeing someone else betray one of your placid beliefs as you might have done it yourself.

"Mother, I think this knuckling under to Oliver is a shocking dereliction of duty on your part."

"Do you? To my mind, love for my children is more important than any duty, and love forgives." But she spoke with a voice in which there was more censure of Miriam than forgiveness of her, and furthermore her practice as a mother had been the reverse of this statement.

"One of your duties was, as you saw it, to love us," said Gene blandly. "Always. And don't forget — Miriam is your child too."

Ruth felt that if she stayed at this table any longer she would break down. Without excusing herself she went to her room and lay on the bed. When Miriam had accused her of neglecting her duty, Ruth had felt unfairly blamed; she had done something wrong, so she deserved blame; but it had been an error in judgment and not in intent, so she deserved commiseration as well. And when Gene had said that she should have forgiven her child Miriam too, she knew that he had said it not because it was true, though it seemed to be true, but because it would hurt. So, as she lay on her bed, it seemed to her that Oliver's cruelty, so much more childlike, so much less willed than theirs, was the action of one to whom she had done some secret injury that neither of them understood and neither had wanted; and as she lay there love for him filled her heart and dread of the damage she was yet to do.

Miriam, full of wrath — wrath the greater for the moment of dread she had felt on her mother's account and had then put out of her mind — went into the kitchen and asked Oliver in an affable voice if he had heard that Ruth had given Gene the money to go to Japan for the chess tournament; she did it not to wound Oliver but to cause her mother trouble. She succeeded.

At first, in his generosity of heart, Oliver rushed in and congratulated Gene on his good fortune; and there was a general concord for a time, with Jo Ann silent on the sidelines ingoring the children who wanted to talk to her. But this amity did not suit Miriam at all. As she stood at the front door with Bill — they were leaving the children till evening while they went to a cocktail party — she said to Oliver with a burst of machined enthusiasm: "Now you can get the money for a new motorcycle, E. O. Maybe Jo Ann's brother's."

Oliver was happy, but Gene saw what she had done.

"Good-bye now," said Miriam sweetly. "Take good care of my children."

She took Bill in tow and left.

Gene and Jo Ann were silent, for their separate reasons. Dorie was in a friendly mood and tried to start a conversation: that Ruth and Miriam had done rather badly elevated Dorie's spirits, though she herself had done nothing, whether good or bad. But no one took her gambits.

Oliver would have had he not been moved by desire; on pretext of showing Jo Ann around the place he took her up to his room.

The children, under the supervision of Gene and Dorie, who were doing dishes, seemed quite content to play by themselves in the back; it was a mild evening, and there were very few ways they could hurt themselves except on the motorcycles beside the garage, and those were forbidden them; Dorie went to the back door once in a while to glance at them. One time they ran up the stairs to Oliver's room, but he had locked the door as he always did whether at home or abroad; Dorie saw them coming down the stairs again and ordered them to stay away from his room.

Her feeling of elevation had not left her, and with it was coming a feeling of amorousness. The soft and pleasant air, the absence of anything urgent to do and of anyone to impress herself upon, Gene's rather attentive glances at Jo Ann before she had disappeared with Oliver, the not having made love for a long while, all these combined to turn her mind to lovemaking. So when Gene, as they were finishing the dishes, began some of his amorous horseplay, which meant this time not that he was annoyed with her but that he was ready if she was and if she wasn't she could tell him to quit, no harm done, Dorie responded in the way that meant she was ready too — that is, she began to talk in a serious manner about all the arrangements, the ways and means, the possible obstacles, who might interrupt, ought anything else to be done first. Dorie was not afraid to talk about love; on the contrary, with fearless frankness, in a special tone of voice, she would scrutinize all the mechanics of lovemaking with that dispassionateness which, like a shamed but flagrant nakedness, can be so sure a safeguard for one afraid of love itself. It was a chilling beginning all in all, and Gene was, as usual, chilled.

Their arrangements were made. She was to go to his room and wait for him there till Ruth awoke. She would be safe there, for Gene allowed no one but Dorie, not even his mother, to go into his room ever. When Ruth came down, he told her that he didn't know where Oliver was and that Dorie had gone home and then went up to his room and Dorie.

While the small children were still in the house, to be watched and read to and fed, Ruth was in a happy frame of mind. But after Miriam and Bill had returned after dark and picked the children up, Ruth suddenly felt empty and nervous. She wandered through the house disconsolately, nor did its familiar beauty please her at all; for in it, hiding in it, holed up in it as it seemed to her, was her son Gene who, though a full-grown man, did nothing but play chess. For all she knew, indeed she was sure of it, Dorie was in his room with him. Not even as an excuse to herself did she disapprove of their lovemaking; yet she could not remain in the same house with them. More deeply than she knew, she, who had not had a man for twenty years, resented this woman of Gene's. Outdoors, she saw the gleaming handlebars of the motorcycles and knew that up in his room Frederick Kotowski's son had taken a woman, and knew furthermore that if she asked him he would deny it. She did not know why her sons thought they had to deceive her.

She lay down on the cot, for it was still a warm night. She was conscious only of the bright stars and of the darkness in which they were lost, and she felt not just in words but with her whole heart that it had been better for her if she had never been born.

As she lay there she heard the door to Oliver's room open; she could see him descend the stairs and go to the dark house. The light went on in the kitchen, and she could hear him opening cupboards and clashing silverware. She arose and went in the back door.

He started when she came in.

"Hi, Mom. Where've you been?"

"Lying on my cot in the back yard. It's a beautiful night."

"It sure is."

"Do you want me to fix you a little snack?"

He could not refuse her without an explanation of why he wanted to take a double portion to his room to eat; rather ungraciously he thanked her and sat down.

"Where's Gene, Mom?"

"Up in his room, I think. Miriam and Bill came for the children a little while ago."

"They're mighty sweet kids. Penny's the cutest little girl I ever saw."

"She's awfully fond of you, Oliver."

"Yeh," he said with pleasure, "she is."

A little silence began, which both of them tried to think of a way to fill. Pleasantly Ruth began another subject for small talk, a movie she wanted him to see; it was a short-lived topic too.

Oliver thought that his mother was going to reprove him for coming to dinner late, entering rudely and with the black bowler on, and bringing in Jo Ann so brusquely; as their mutual uneasiness increased, as he gulped without pleasure the good food she prepared for him, he began to think that she wanted not to reprove him openly but to punish him by making him thus uncomfortable, and this deviousness he resented.

She, on the other hand, had no such intention at all — quite the reverse. In the sadness that had overcome her as she was lying on the cot, it seemed to her that everything that had gone wrong with her children must surely have been her own fault, though she did not understand what she had done and knew she had not done whatever it was intentionally. She too was thinking of his cruelty this afternoon, but she felt that somehow she had made him do it to her; her pain she could stand, every mother must, but the thought that she had driven him to it, against his own nature, she could not bear. She wanted him to forgive her for having made him do it, and she thought he understood her impulse and rejected it; mistakenly she thought the sullenness of his mistaken resentment was unforgiveness, and her feelings of guilty failure deepened.

But while these complex misunderstandings made a barrier between the mother and son, they were not the chief danger; that was too great for either of them to face before they had to. That was the event which Oliver's resentment and Ruth's sense of failure were preparing them for; it was painful and wasteful, and neither of them wanted it and both felt it was coming, and nothing anyone could have done could have prevented it.

"Hey, Mom," Oliver said forcing himself up from his sullenness; there had been a long, grave silence which he felt he should interrupt by a triviality, but the pressure that made him speak was so great that it was no trivial thing he said. "Hey, Mom, Sis says Gene's going to go to Japan."

"Yes," she said brightening. Both of them respected Gene's intellect; that was something in this strait.

"Will he ever be the world's champion, do you think?"

"I certainly hope so. But he seems to think he never could be."

"Well, it'd be swell if he could." He had finished eating. He should have left his mother before speaking again, before the danger had been exposed and run toward; but that would have happened only if he had known what he was about to do, and he did not.

"How much money will it take him to get there?"

"I don't know, dear. He had to have five hundred dollars from me." She ought not have said that last, but it was true and she told the truth, and it took the last step in the dark, the step that both of them had been dreading in that way only with which one dreads a sure pain.

"Well, gee, Mom, that bike of Jo Ann's brother's only costs four hundred. Let me have it, will you? It's only fair. I'll pay you back when I get that ten thousand."

With all her heart she wanted to say yes, here it is; he would have loved her then and forgiven her. But she had decided long ago that it would have been wrong for her to encourage him in his destructive passion for fast cars and motorcyles; she felt it to be her duty to try to restrain him from his desperate courses until he had matured a little and straightened out. She had told him all this before, more than once; but he was nearly a man now, he would have his $10,000 soon. She could have given in without any great sense of shame. She probably would have given in, had it not been for one thing: it would have been a method of bribing his love, more, of bribing her own conscience, of cheating her sense of failure, and that her pride would not let her do. So once again she allowed her duty to thwart her impulse; while her understanding of her duty was very likely sound and good, her impulse was sounder and better yet, for her impulse was usually to do something for someone and her duty was usually, it seemed, to abstain.

"No," she said. "You know how I feel about your motorcycle, Oliver. Won't you please me just a little ——"

"What the hell!" he shouted suddenly and stood up. "Gene gets this, Gene gets that, now he gets five hundred dollars and I don't get a dime. What kind of a deal is that?"

"Oliver! Do not speak to me in that tone of voice."

"Why not?" he shouted louder yet, there was a meanacing expression on his face; he could be heard throughout the house. "Why not? Tell me that. I've always got the short end of the stick and I'm sick and tired of it. Okay, you can take your money and shove it. I'm getting out of here."

"Oliver, I'll put five hundred dollars in the bank against your name. It's not the money. I just don't want you to kill yourself with those machines."

"What I do is none of your business." There were tears, not only of rage, in his eyes. "I never asked to be made a bastard but you made me one and the least you could have done about it was to be a mother to me. Okay, play your damn favorite. I won't bother you any more."

He went to the back door. Crying, Ruth held to his arm.

"Forgive me," she said, "forgive me."

"I wouldn't forgive you," he said, "if you was dying. I couldn't. You made me. I won't be back either."

Gene and Dorie heard the shouting. Dorie was frightened and urged Gene to go down and make peace. He told her to be still. They lay in bed in the dark, listening. Not until the motorcycles had roared away did Gene arise.

"Get dressed." He whispered though he was positive that his r̲
was still in the kitchen. "I'll keep her talking in the kitchen til̲
creep out the front door."

"Why can't I just stay here as I always do, till she goes to bed?"

"When she's upset she even comes into my room."

This was not true. He only wanted Dorie to leave him alone.

In his turtleneck sweater and tennis shoes, holding a cigarette in fingers that were not entirely steady, his eyebrows very high on his high forehead, he entered the kitchen. Ruth did not take her face from her hands; she was still crying.

At first he did not know what to do. He walked over to the sink to knock the ash from his cigarette. It occurred to him to pat his mother on the shoulder, but he decided against it; had he been in her place he would not have wanted to be patted. He could think of nothing to say. He felt chilly, though it was warm. He put out his cigarette and stood with his hands in his pockets, watching her. It occurred to him he ought to leave her alone. So he went out from the kitchen and walked through the house aimlessly. He found himself oppressed by the house, the dark inward spacious house; but he could not go outside because there was nothing at all out there but dark. He turned on the lights in the living room, but the dark redwood panels seemed to absorb the light. He wished, for the moment, that this room, that all the rooms in the house, were white and geometrical as Dorie wanted them to be. It was not ordered enough for him now; it allowed him to be whatever he chose to be within its own broad limits, and he did not know who he was. He had to go back into the kitchen where his mother was, but he needed an excuse to return. He discovered that he was hungry. He returned and ate a ham sandwich.

At last she raised her face to look at him; he was washing his long fingers under the tap. Her eyes were puffy and red, and the puckerings about her mouth was replaced by ugly swellings and teeth marks in her lower lip. She looked at him beseeching mercy. In his high-pitched, exact, merciless voice he answered the look.

"Well, you and Oliver seem to have had an argument."

He thought, and no one else in the world would have thought then, that he was being ironical and light; but these bad ironies of his were sharp knives with notched blades.

"He has left home, Gene."

The pathetic are ugly if you close your heart to them.

"Well, he's nearly of age."

"He hates me. Why does he hate me?"

"Oh, well, he's hot-tempered."

o, he is not. What shall I do?"

ike a man in a well, she clutched at a rope to find it a snake falling
ck in with her. Gene shrugged.

"Why?" she said. "I taught him what was right and wrong. Why
does he choose this?"

"Why didn't you offer him the motorcycle he wants? He'll get one
anyway. Do you think it is right to make him feel bad about what he
loves so much, just because you don't approve of it? Why indeed?"

"If I had given him what he wanted, I would have been ordering
him in a way. Surely it is better to let him be free." It was her last
appeal.

"It is worse to subvert," he said.

She looked at him almost blankly.

"Did I not leave you all free to choose?"

"You cut our anchors. That is different."

"Is it not the noblest thing for a man to be free?" she cried out over
him.

"Yes," he said and drew in his neck like a turtle, "yes, Oh God, yes."

"Gene," she said bitterly, "my son is full of hatred for me. He has
left me. Why has he done this?"

She called Oliver "my son" as though Gene were her enemy, and
indeed for that moment he was not her son but her conscious enemy.

"Do you understand what I'm saying? Does it mean anything more
than words to you?"

In his highest pitch he answered, "Try to take some nembutal,
mother. Sleep is the best restorative."

"Sleep," she said with such bitter scorn as he had never heard from
her, "sleep."

She put her face back into her hands, and her shoulders shook.

He went to his room and the sixty-four squares and thirty-two men of
chess. He set himself to work on trying to find, for the hundredth time,
the weakness in his own variation of the Ruy Lopez opening; but the
chess could not keep him from hearing his mother's movements. He
heard her when she came up the stairs, slowly, heavily; he heard her dial
a number and talk in a low voice to someone; he could not tell who it
was, but from her voice he guessed it was some friend, some old trusted
friend; he wanted to open his door and listen to her conversation but
he had not the nerve. She went up to the attic then and moved something heavy; he was racked with curiosity to know what she was doing,
what was happening in the long silences between the rustling and shifting
noises. Perhaps she was looking at old pictures or reading old letters;

he could not imagine what else she could be up to. But at last she ca[me]
back down to her room and was silent. After an hour he opened [his]
door and looked down the hall; there was still a crack of light under he[r]
door. He applied himself to the Ruy Lopez, knowing that he could not
sleep until her light was off. But nothing could keep him from listening
with all his might for her movements.

For he knew that this was for Ruth a night like two others he could
remember. One had been when the first Japanese-Americans had been
taken off to the Relocation Camps; the other he remembered from his
childhood, the night after Sacco and Vanzetti had been executed. All
that night he had slept badly and full of dread, for whenever he had
awakened he had heard his mother walking up and down in the house,
and sometimes she had cried out in a terrible voice, "What is wrong?
What is wrong? What should I have done?"

THE FIRST FACE

BY ELIZABETH ENRIGHT

*W*HEN she opened her eyes the next time she saw that day was coming, for the air beyond the hospital window had lightened into a deep, shadowless blue-violet, so newly begun that the lights along the bridge had not yet been turned out. At this moment, balanced between night and day, the bridge itself was a surprise. She had been too preoccupied to notice it when she came here, hours ago. How many hours? She did not know.

"What time is it?" she asked.

"Nearly seven," her husband said. "I'll have to leave in a few minutes."

The bridge was wonderfully beautiful. In the cold winter air, its many lights trembled and quivered like stars; it was as if all the constellations of the sky, with their different-sized stars, had come down and arranged themselves in this great, horned, scintillating arc. Its brilliant, glittering beauty was one more thing — a crown for all her happiness. Never had she been so happy. She tried to tell her husband.

"I feel so — I can't describe to you how marvellous I feel."

"I know," her husband said — yawning, for he had been up all night, "You've told me."

"Have I? How many times?"

"Oh, fifteen or twenty." He smiled at her. "Off and on, ever since they brought you down."

"But isn't he wonderful?" she asked. "Didn't you think he was wonderful?"

"Of course. He's a beauty," her husband said. "His ears are nice and close to his head, too. Some of them have ears like Chihuahuas."

"Perfect little ears." She sighed with joy, and looked back at the scintillating span beyond the window.

After her husband had gone, she still lay staring at it. This was one of the few moments in life when the present could not be outshone by any dazzle from the future. Here she was, lying like a huge sea shell washed up by the highest wave, empty but still ringing from the tides. Before her eyes, the lights winked out along the bridge. It was daytime in earnest, and where there had been a sparkling crown, there was now a peaked gray carcass. Already from within it came the steady mumbling of early traffic. The window curtains suddenly blew forward on a draft as the door opened and the nurse came in.

At ten o'clock, a small basket on long stalks was wheeled in. Within it lay her son, neatly covered with a white cloth, like a new loaf of bread in a pan. There was no sound from him, no stir beneath the cloth.

"He sure is sleeping it off," said the nurse. Her voice was like coal going down a chute.

"Yes. Hurry. Let me see."

The nurse twitched back the cloth and tipped the little basket up on its frame.

Her son lay on a slant, his head turned toward her.

"Ten minutes, I'll be back to get him," the nurse said. "O.K.? Can't have him very long this first time."

She held her breath until the nurse departed; then she raised herself and leaned forward to look.

His eyes were closed. He was deeply asleep and absolutely still. None of the tiny tremors, the fleeting grimaces of earliest infancy, disturbed his flawless calm. The veins on his eyelids were lavender, and fine as silken threads; the nostrils were round in his blunt nose. His lips were firmly closed, and, folded on his breast, his hands were scaled and wrinkled, like the paws of an old turtle. She could not hear an inkling of his breathing, and only the soft pulsing of the fontanel on his domed head attested that life was at work in him.

It was the expression of his sleeping face that impressed her. It was — "majestic" did not seem too serious a word. For this was a face of total calm, a face where doubt had never yet been seen. One might have called it stern, but sternness presupposes an attitude towards acts or beings, whereas he had just accomplished the first and most important act of his life, willy-nilly, and as for beings, he was not so much ignorant as innocent of their existence. All at once, she realized that this must be the visage of the unborn, that he was still so new he had not quite outgrown it. In the latter weeks, as his features had become perfected, this must have been the look he had worn, lying in the oceanic fastness of the womb, sustained beyond doubt or question, assured as no caress or mortal word could ever reassure him. In his lifetime, he would hear and say the hackneyed word "security" a hundred thousand times, perhaps, never quite forgetting that once it was no word but his own kingdom.

That was the meaning of the look, the look of austere, undamaged peace that he would not wear again until, when life was over, he lay dead. And then it would mean nothing.

She put out her hand and laid it over the crumpled paws on his chest. Beneath them she could just detect the hasty, tiny tripping of his heart — the only hasty thing about him. He did not stir.

The draft announced the nurse. She slapped in loudly on her rubber soles. She entered and moved and spoke as though she knew all about reality and had discovered it to be made out of white tiles, ice water, and hundred-watt bulbs.

"Well, time's up," she called vigorously, at the bedside. "Time to take your boy friend back to the bull pen. Here you go, brother."

Two large hands seized the edges of the basket and adjusted it so briskly on its frame that the baby's head wobbled like an egg in a tossing nest, but still he did not wake.

At six o'clock, when her son returned, she heard him before she saw him. An angry chirping sounded from the basket, and when the nurse lifted him out, his whole head, right to the nape of his neck, was rosy purple with anger. His hands were the same color, and even the toes of his bare feet were dark as red kernels of Indian corn. The nurse (another woman, this time, older and gentler) folded him up carefully in a white blanket, then held him in her hands, watching him remotely, though with pleasure.

"Oh, give him to me, please!"

The next second, he was laid beside her, warm with outrage. His fingers closed fiercely around her thumb, and on his features, as his open mouth searched for her breast, there was an expression of determination and impatience that nobody had had to teach him.

After his short span of sucking, he seemed exhausted and content, and fell asleep at once within her sheltering arm. But this was sleep upon another level. His face was continually crossed with little squalls — premonitory frowns, grimaces, and flickering, mirthless smiles. His eyelids trembled, and his lips worked reminiscently. The look of masterly peace was gone, and she would never see it on his face again.

(From Northern Review

THE CONVERSION OF WILLIE HEAPS

BY HUGH GARNER

I COULD SEE Willie coming along the road from his place, walking fast like he always did. His long legs were jerking back and forth above his broken shoes and his tangled hair hung in a bang just above his wide-staring eyes where it had been cut by his mother, Mrs. Heaps. His mouth was hanging loose like it usually was, and even from a distance you could see his long brown teeth that were always wet like a panting dog's.

Although he was thirty years old he didn't seem much older than me. My father said that it was silly for a full-grown man to play with a twelve-year old boy, even if Willie *was* a little simple, but he was the only real friend I had, and we had lots of good times together. In the winter I went with him on trips to town, and during the summer we would go fishing down to Allison's dam, or woodchuck hunting in the fields around our place.

He was an expert at gelding colts, and once or twice a month during the summer he would take me with him to other farms around the district. I used to watch him with my tongue between my teeth as he operated on the young horses, his hands as gentle as a mother's, hating to cause any more pain than was necessary.

The first time I saw him working on a colt it made me sick and I vomited in a corner of the yard. Willie told me I couldn't go with him again if I acted like that, so I was careful from then on and it never bothered me again.

When Willie got up to our place he stood in the road and shouted to me to come with him.

"Where to?"

"Down to Angus Gordon's place."

"I'll have to ask my mother," I said.

"Hurry up then. I want to get going before it's dark," he shouted impatiently.

My mother heard our voices and came to the screen door, wiping a plate with a dish towel.

"Can I go with Willie?" I asked.

"Oh — I guess so," she answered, not wanting me to go, but not wanting to stop me either. She shouted, "Hello, Willie!" as she spied my friend standing in the road.

He didn't answer. It seemed that he could never get used to talking to grownups.

"Don't you be late home, young man," my mother warned me as we set off up the road.

I waved to her and hurried along, trying to match my stride with Willie's.

He was excited about something, and he kept turning his head in my direction, trying to make up his mind to tell me what it was. Sometimes he acted like that, worrying about a secret thing until he almost burst with the burden of it.

"We've got a new preacher at the Pentacostal," he said finally, grinning with relief now that it was out.

We climbed the torn wire fence that separated our land from the old disused railway spur.

"The preacher's name is Reverend Blounsbury," he said as we slid down the grassy bank to the tracks.

"What happened to the other one?" I asked.

"Who, Mr. Oldsworth? He's gone to the city. Reverend Blounsbury is a better preacher anyways."

"Is he a real minister, with minister's clothes?"

"He don't need 'em," answered Willie.

"Why don't he? My minister wears them."

"He's God's servant. He don't need 'em."

On Sundays Willie went with his mother and father to the Lost Souls Pentacostal Mission in Brantford. They never missed a service there, and Willie had told me several times about people being saved by the blood of Jesus Christ, which would cleanse you of all impurities and make you ready to meet your Maker on the judgement day.

Willie was thinking hard about something, and now and then he'd swallow and his neck would twitch with excitement. After a long silence he said, "I got saved last Sunday."

"How do you get saved?"

"You go and kneel down at the front of the Mission," he asnwered.

"Is that all?"

"Everybody sings, and sometimes the women cry."

I cut off the tops of some wild mustard with a long willow whip I'd picked up. "How many times you been saved, Willie?" I asked.

"Oncet. Oncet is all you can be saved," he said, looking at me as if I should have known.

"Was you scared much?"

"Nope. Ain't nothing to be scared for."

"Do you believe in that, Willie?"

"Sure I believe in it — hell!" he asnwered, with mild disgust at my ignorance.

"That makes you sure you're going to heaven, don't it?" I asked.

"Yep," he answered. He walked very fast and I had a hard time keeping up with him on the old cinder roadbed.

"Does the new minister save anybody at all?"

"Yep. He's a better preacher than the other one."

"Is that all they do at the Pentacostal, Willie?" I asked. We went to the Presbyterian Church in Simcoe, and I had always wondered why his church was so different from ours.

"No, they sing and the minister says a sermon. On Sunday he talked about sinning. He says it's a sin to go out with a woman 'cause Jesus didn't do it, and it's sinful when men do it."

I couldn't imagine our minister talking about that stuff in church. I thought about this as we hurried along the track, the cinder dust billowing up from our feet and the old musty-paper smell of the burdocks filling the narrow right-of-way.

"I wish we didn't have to go down to Angus' place," I said. "Some of the fellows are down catching bullfrogs at the dam. Perry got one last night as big as a saucer."

"They don't know nuthing about catching frogs," said Willie. "You wait an' see what we catch tomorrow night."

He told me how he would do it. He would sneak up behind them and throw rocks into the swamp ahead of the frogs. Then when they jumped in his direction he would catch them in a long strip of weighted lace curtain. Willie sure knew lots of tricks like that. I was glad he was my friend and let me go places with him. There'd be no fun at all without Willie.

When we reached the bridge across the tracks he pulled me up to the road. He was thin but he had a lot of strength. He lifted me clean off the ground with one hand.

"How old is the colt at the Gordon's, Willie?" I asked as we turned up the road to the farm.

"I dunno. There's two of 'em, Angus said."

"It must hurt them, eh, Willie?"

"For a while, I guess. They get over it."

"What does it do, Willie?"

"Makes 'em big and quiet. They can't work good unless they're cut."

The dirt road was warm through the rubber soles of my sneakers. It was the kind of summer evening that usually comes before an electrical storm. The sun was lying low behind a grove of hardwood and high in the sky the clouds we called "washboards" were pink in the evening light. Over the low spots in the fields high-climbing swarms of gnats boiled and tumbled in the warm air. The crickets whistled at us from every fencepost as we hurried along the road.

"I feel sorry for the colts," I said. "It don't make me sick no more, though."

"Don't you get sick again or else I won't bring you."

"I ain't gonna be sick no more," I answered. I didn't want to get Willie mad at me.

There didn't seem to be anyone home at the Gordon's when we got there. We could hear the cattle and horses stamping in the stable beneath the barn.

Willie knocked on the kitchen door, but there was no answer.

"I hope they're at home," he said. "I don't want to hafta come over here again next week."

"Maybe they'll be back soon."

"We ain't got much time to wait 'cause it'll soon be dark."

"They'll come in a minute," I said hopefully.

Willie was getting mad, and I could see the big blue veins in his neck beating like the devil. When he was mad there was nothing to do but keep out of his way. One time it took three men to hold him when he was mad.

"I won't come over again next week," he muttered, kicking at the bottom step beneath the door.

"Maybe they'll come home soon, Willie."

"Why didn't they wait! Why'd they go away when they knew I was coming over!"

He was getting madder every minute. It would be dark soon and I didn't want to be alone with him if he got real mad.

"Can't you do it anyways, Willie?" I asked, trying to quiet him down.

"Oh, why didn't they wait!" he cried. He kicked at the step again, harder this time.

"Let's do it, Willie," I pleaded. "My mother told me not to be late getting home."

He was no longer listening to me. "They could have stayed in!" he cried. "Angus Gordon is a sinner anyways!"

I could see his shoulders working under his blue denim jacket and I was afraid to have to go home with him unless he calmed down. He wouldn't hurt me when he was all right, but his mother told me once to stay away from him when he took a spell.

"I'm going to fix them colts anyways," he said, striding towards the barn.

"That's right, Willie. We might as well," I answered as I tried to keep up with his grown-up strides across the yard.

Willie opened the stable door, and the colts whinnied from the darkness. I groped around on the shelf near the doorpost, trying to find a stable lamp.

"I can't find a lamp, Willie!" I shouted at him, my voice showing me how scared I was. I tried to follow him with my eyes so I'd be ready to run if he turned on me.

"I've got one," he said, and I could see him in the light of a struck match as he struggled with the chimney of a lantern.

When the lamp was lit I looked around the stable. The colts were tied at the end of a short row of stalls. There was also a team of horses and a big Holstein bull.

"Help me out with them," he shouted, and in the light from the lamp he looked crazier than he ever had before. I hesitated near the door.

"Come on, come on, we can't stand here!" he cried. "There is too much sin around here! Angus is a poor sinner an' we gotta help him before he's punished by God!"

"Let's wait until another time, Willie," I pleaded.

"We may be too late. Now is the time!"

"I don't want to," I said, afraid to leave the open doorway.

"You gotta. There's too much sin. Oh, Lord, help the poor sinners!" he cried.

The horses were scared, lifting their feet from the floor, their heads high and their eyes bright in the lantern light.

He brought one of the colts into the yard and we got him down and hitched his feet. Willie was singing a hymn and he walked around in quick little jerks, doing all the work himself. He worked fast. The colt snorted and stretched his neck when it was done.

"You'll never sin!" Willie cried. "You'll never sin, little horse!"

The sight of Willie moving around the yard with the short knife in his hand, singing his crazy hymns all out of tune, scared me half to death. This was a different Willie than I had known before.

He turned the colt loose and I opened the gate, letting him through. The next colt was harder to manage, but with my help Willie got the rope around his legs.

"Glory!" Willie cried when his singing stopped. "No more sin! There'll be no more sin!" He fitted the words into another crazy tune.

He did the other colt, but it took him much longer this time. While I held the lantern I shivered at the sight of his crazy hands and at the sound of his tuneless mumblings. It was quite dark now outside the pale circle made by the lantern and heavy clouds were blotting out the sky.

When he finished his job I led the colt out through the gate and came back to Willie. "Now we can go, Willie," I said eagerly.

"Hallelujah! I'll not let them sin!" he shouted. "I can stop all the sin in the world!"

"Sure you can, Willie," I agreed. "But let's go home now."

"Not yet. I've got work to do. Glory!"

"Come on, Willie, please!"

"No, not yet."

I stared around me at the darkened buildings, praying that the Gordons would come home soon. Across the fields I could see a light in the kitchen of the Turner house a quarter of a mile away. Though it was far it made me feel a little better to know that I wasn't completely alone.

Willie ran into the stable again, shouting about sin. I followed him as far as the door, and when I looked inside I nearly fainted at the sight. The lantern was standing on a ledge and Willie held the knife in front of him. His body was stooped and he was walking slowly toward the big black and white bull.

"No, Willie!" I cried in terror. "No!"

"The world is full of sin! Oh, Lord, help me to stop the sin of the world! Glory!"

"Please, Willie! I think I hear Mr. Gordon coming!" I lied.

"Angus Gordon is a goddam sinner! We're all sinners! I have the power to stop all sin! Oh hallelujah!"

He caught the bull by the tail, and it bellowed and swung its haunches against the wall. A cloud of dust rose from the floor and the stable was filled with the noise of the big beast banging against the timbers. The horses were stamping in their stalls. I saw Willie trying to get into position to use his knife and I began to scream.

Then I turned my head so I couldn't see him any longer, but I could hear the bull bellowing and banging around and the snorts of the frightened horses.

Suddenly he came running towards the door, the lantern swinging in his hand. "The Lord be praised!" he cried. "No more sin!"

I ran across the yard as fast as I could and climbed over a fence into a pasture. Hiding behind a post I watched Willie standing there with the lantern lighting his legs.

He began circling the yard. His hymns and the bellows of the bull were so loud that I thought every living thing in the neighborhood must be listening. I watched him heading towards the pigsty and I shouted to him, but he made no sign that he heard me. There was the click of the latch on the pigsty door, even above the other noises, and the lantern disappeared inside, lighting up the cracks between the boards.

There were some grunts at first, then startled squeals. The bellows of the bull grew weaker, but the night was filled with the squeals of the hogs and the noise of them butting against the walls of their pens. Now and again there was the sound of Willie's singing, but his songs no longer had any understandable words.

I looked around me in the darkness, hoping I'd see somebody coming across the fields. Willie stayed in the shed a long time, the pigs squealing and grunting, and his crazy tunes rising and falling across the yard.

I wondered what Mr. Gordon would do to us. We'd be arrested! I'd tell them that I didn't have anything to do with it. Anyways I was only a boy. I wouldn't do a thing like this.

The place was a bedlam. Every animal seemed to sense what was happening and they were all trying to break out of their pens and stalls together.

Willie came out of the pigsty, swinging the lantern around his legs. I wondered what he was going to do next. Then I heard another door opening and there was the sound of hens clucking and the swish of wings against wood.

The henhouse door swung open and he came out again, the lantern held high so that I saw his face. He was completely crazy now, his eyes bugged out from his head and his mouth slobbering as he sang his tuneless songs. He peered around him in the darkness, and the light from the lantern shone on a frantic white hen that was running back and forth against the wall of a building. He ran towards it and his lamp blinded the hen so that it stopped running long enough for him to grab it. He dropped the lantern to the ground and picked the bird up by the neck. Then he stared into the sky and screamed at the top of his voice, at the same time pulling the head from the hen. He threw the wriggling body from him, where it flopped along the ground, and stooping, picked up his lantern once more.

He held the light high and began calling my name. At times he got mixed up and called the names of other people who lived in the neighborhood, crying out that they were all sinners. He began to search for me in the darkness, and I pressed myself down in the grass to hide. When he came closer to me I stood up and backed away from the fence. He saw me then and his face broke out in a horrible grin. "Come on, poor little sinner," he coaxed as he stumbled in my direction.

"No! Go away!" I screamed, hating him now so that I forgot I had ever liked him. He was a complete stranger to me, a crazy loathsome stranger, I'd never seen before.

His look changed from crafty friendliness to horrible rage and he roared a string of filthy curses. His mumbling lips were covered with spit, and he threw himself against the fence, crying and cursing together.

I turned and ran as fast as I could across the uneven ground, trying not to scream and give away my position in the darkness. I don't remember all of my flight but I was so scared that I took a large patch of skin off my back going through a rail fence, and didn't realize it until later. In my imagination Willie was right behind me with his knife.

I don't know how long it took me to get to the Turner place. I was sobbing and panting with fear as I made for the house, slapping at the Turner's dog which was barking at me and trying to grab my legs. Bert Turner let me in the door, and I collapsed on a chair in the kitchen.

"What's the matter, boy?" he asked, staring at me.

"It's Willie — Willie Heaps! He's gone crazy! He — he's cutting all the animals at the Gordon's. He's killed the pigs and chickens too!"

"What did he say?" asked Mrs. Turner, entering the kitchen.

"It's Willie Heaps," Bert answered. "I'd better telephone his father."

After they bolted the door I sat on the chair crying and shivering with fright. Mrs. Turner gave me a cup of coffee but I was too weak and shaky to lift it to my mouth. Bert called my family on the phone, and my father and Edgar the hired man came for me in the car.

A search party was out all night looking for Willie and warning the neighborhood to be on guard against him. Early next morning Mr. Summerville the police chief in Cumberford got a message that Willie had been found in a ditch by a farmer, self-mutilated and nearly dead from loss of blood. An ambulance was sent from Brantford and they took Willie to the hospital there. He died the following night.

My mother made me go to the funeral, but I refused to look at Willie in his coffin. Mr. and Mrs. Heaps were crying and carrying on, and shouting to God to call Willie to his side.

A tall skinny man in a black shiny suit introduced himself to my mother and father as the Reverend Blounsbury, Willie's minister. He had a turned-on smile and a long thin nose that seemed to be running but wasn't.

"And this is Willie's little friend, is it?" he said, putting his hand on my shoulder.

My mother nodded.

"Poor child, to be bereft of a friend so soon in life," he said. "But don't grieve, lad, Willie now sits at the right hand of his Maker. He had been saved, you know."

My mother nodded again.

"And how about you? Have you been converted yet, young man?"

"No!" I cried, shaking his hand from me and edging to the door.

"Why, what's come over that boy!" exclaimed my mother.

I ran out of the house and down the road towards home. I hated them all: Willie, Mr. and Mrs. Heaps, my mother and father, and especially the Reverend Blounsbury. Why couldn't they have left Willie alone, I asked myself. Why couldn't everybody in the whole wide world leave everybody else alone?

(*From The Atlantic Monthly*)

WEEKEND AT GRIMSBY

BY MARTHA GELLHORN

THIS WAS the shapeless weather all travellers dread. A smeared grey sky closed down over the smeared brown land. Cold leaked around the window frames and the door of the railway carriage. England looked larger, flatter and more desolate than was either possible or fair. No one should move in November, Lily Cameron thought. She was full of hate for this weather, this opposite of scenery, the still pain of the cold, and wondered why she moved at all, any month; even June was a nice time to stay in one place.

There was no law which forced her into English railway carriages in November. Nothing prevented her from buying or renting another house and living in it. But the question was: where? There had been a villa, an ancient stone barracks really, in Fiesole; a glassy flat in Paris; a grim little dump constructed of marshmallow sauce at Praia da Rocha, the bottom edge of Europe where Portugal caved into the sea; a house, dainty and dead, in London; and luckily no house on that jaunt to the glamorous Orient; and only a hotel suite during the brief visit home, if New York had ever been home. It was some sort of record in case you went out for records: four dwellings and a romp around the world in four and a half years, or since May 7, 1945, to be exact. I might as well keep moving, she thought with disgust, it's less trouble.

Then she revolted against this vision of herself as a female Flying Dutchman or Wandering Jew. Stop being pathetic, she thought, sell your violets somewhere else. There was a reason for being on this train. If your friends were too broke to come to you, you went to them, even if they lived in Grimsby, Lincs. You looked forward to a jolly meeting of ectoplasms. Stop it, she told herself again. I am going to Grimsby because I want to. I know what I am doing. It is the one thing I am still useful for: to remember.

How did the English survive their ghastly climate? She stamped her feet furiously, and in so doing kicked an inoffensive stranger good and hard on the ankle. "I beg your pardon," Lily said.

A pink-cheeked lady, sitting on the opposite mottled plush bench, smiled politely and returned to her book. This is not the first time I have visited Grimsby, Lily Cameron informed the lady who read with determined attention. Do not imagine Grimsby awaits me as a delectable surprise. However, I was not a ghost going to a reunion with fellow ghosts, when I came here before. That was during the war, madam, and a type of English bomber, called as I remember the Lancaster, a graceless square job, took off from fields up this way, nightly, for the city of Berlin. I had friends then, as I have now, except at that time my friends were alive or dead, but not in the present intermediate state. I had friends who flew those Lancasters, and I travelled to Grimsby one year to spend Christmas with them. You would hardly believe how gay we became on Spam, and blotting-paper bread and marge, and the one rationed egg, and very little liquor, since liquor was scarce for the working soldiery. We had a lovely time, and that night, or rather the next black morning, all the planes came home, so it was a perfectly delightful Christmas and I returned to London in fine spirits.

Then, three days later, a letter arrived from Andrew, who was Group Captain, written in that neat English handwriting which they all have, rather like pursed lips, and most unsuitable to their personalities. It said: "You will be sorry to hear that John Wakeford was lost over Berlin the night of twenty-seven, twenty-eight." Sorry to hear. You could call it that. Though to tell the truth, Lily said to herself, one did not mourn the dead then. There was no time. I do not need to apologize: I have been mourning them for almost five years. Or probably mourning is not the right word: they live with me.

Sim would be waiting at the Grimsby station which resembled a mine shaft except that it was horizontal. When last seen, six years ago, Sim was brown and astonishingly elegant in khaki trousers and bush jacket and black beret, carrying for practical reasons an Egyptian fly whisk, a horse-hair plume tied to a bamboo stick. Lieutenant Prince Simon Mitrowski and his Regiment, the Polish 12th Lancers, had by then fought and bounced all the way from Africa in Staghounds, vehicles which were laughingly described by their users as armored cars. That was in Italy, where the war was most intimate and perhaps most senseless.

And I was a pretty sight myself, Lily thought, in my neat little khaki suiting and my honorary black beret. Me and my canteen, and no one can say that I did not handle the war well; I was the very acme of shrewdness, they should have had me on a Planning Board. For witness the efficient way I advanced myself from Naples and Rome until I landed where I wished to be, in a line regiment of lovely goofy Poles, with sea-bathing thrown in, at least in the summer. I knew what I wanted; in those days there was something to want.

Could this train actually be stopping again? Here we are at another of those glorious stations which dot the English countryside, and there is that broadcast female voice, so civil and so ladylike, telling the traveller what to do. Change here for; on track two; all passengers. A couple puffed their way into the glacial compartment. Grains of rice dropped from their clothing and both wore wilted gardenias, in buttonhole and bosom.

Would you believe it? Lily asked herself. Would you think that a man and a woman, in their fifties, both so ugly that a solitary life in a cellar would seem their destiny, could go forth and marry each other, and display on their faces this look of embarrassed delight? The woman could hardly breathe for her chins and the heavy box of her breasts. She wore an electric-blue satin dress under her black coat, and her ankles rolled over the sides of her sensible black oxfords. The man was thin, with a neck that would not stay in place and supported his head loosely. His teeth were all out in front and long and yellow, and his hair either grew or was cut so that it started well up his head and sat on top like a parrot's crest.

They did not talk but, whenever they looked at each other, a secret and silent giggle shook them both; and the woman's face was purple with pleasure. Presently, seeing that the lady in one corner was reading, and the lady in the other corner turned toward the window, they reached for each other's hands, and two large swollen-jointed shapeless paws met and held. And both, with fierce discretion, looked at the floor as if they did not know they were holding hands at all.

What do you have to do, what do you have to be? Lily wondered. Must you be poor and ugly and fifty and a native of Lincolnshire, in order to trust life? The present was all right by those two, it was fine, it was the best; they had just made the final statement of confidence, they had married. I must tell Sim. What would she tell Sim? Two people got married. Yet Sim would understand how mad it seemed; like putting all your money in a bottle and throwing it into the ocean, or spreading your arms to fly off a building.

The bridegroom stretched his rubber neck and placed his narrow tufted head on his wife's bosom, and slept. For a time she guarded this precious burden, then slept too. In her corner the American woman took off her shoes, flighty slippers of black suede, and rubbed her feet which could be seen, red-painted toenails and all, through the fine stockings. Then she pulled from the rack a large dark mink coat and wrapped it around her as if it were a rented steamer rug. She became a small mound of brown fur.

The train advanced slowly, coldly, through Lincolnshire. Lily Cameron pushed aside her coat, sat up, and said to no one, "Two hours late. I ask you."

The bridegroom, very brave but not facing her, said, "Grimsby's next, miss."

End of the line, and the night leaking rain, and the cold would hang like a roof of stone over the town. Poor Sim; there were gayer places to be ghosts in.

The bridegroom helped the two ladies with their luggage, while his wife beamed approval of his good manners. Lily Cameron followed last, and felt the rain on her face, and saw the murk of the station and the jumbled people in raincoats, everyone looking pinched and dim, and going home to nothing tolerable. She did not move; Sim would find her.

Then she saw him, and though he was changed, he was as she remembered. He came down the platform, under the feeble bare light bulbs, and was very tall and moved with the grace he had. Sim waved and walked faster and then he was kissing her on both cheeks and saying "Lily, dearest Lily."

Lily returned, instantly and with joy, to where they had been before. There were the narrow roads deep in flour-white dust, and the regiment moving like a gypsy caravan, but screaming sirens and flying their red and blue striped pennants, from one encampment to one farther ahead. They were always busy with the ways and means of life; setting out, after suitable lies to superiors, in a scout car to bargain with peasants for a goose and for wine, since every night, simply by being night and they still together, was cause for a celebration dinner; and afterwards they lay in a haystack and could not see the dust and the sweat dried, and they listened to the men singing Polish love songs and the sad but loving songs about home; and cursed the English artillery which chose to settle behind them and make deafening noises that were an outrage in the soft Italian sky. When Sim's squadron was in reserve she would go to their field in the early morning, with plans for a swim on the forbidden Adriatic beaches, not yet de-mined; and find Sim asleep in a shallow pit beneath his Staghound, lying between the driver and the gunner, as cosy as the three little bears. And he would get up, wearing the frayed white silk pyjamas which he had kept all the way from home, via Tobruk, and be immensely charming and invite her to breakfast as if his Staghound was a castle with rose gardens.

And there were Stash and George and Mike and the Chaplain and the Bloody Colonel and Skinny, the gentle gloomy batman, who was the kindest man in the regiment, and Paul and the baby jeep-driver, Lubo, who wanted to become a medical student when the war was over. They were all young and greedily in love with every day they had. In memory, the hard and the ugly and the stale were forgotten. Death had no place, no one could have died. And there had never been any winter.

"Oh Sim," Lily said, and put her arms around his neck and felt she had come home, to that distant place where she lived.

"We should get out of this rain, darling, don't you think? I have a taxi. Everything is beautifully laid-on, you will see the efficiency. We are going to my house. The Bloody Colonel is waiting for us."

"A party! How sweet of you, Sim! I didn't even know he was here."

But in the taxi, she was shy and could not think of anything to say. They had shared no taxis in their past. Sim chatted easily, asking about her life, and she told him of the different countries, the various houses, all the faces. She must have lived it in her sleep, since she could hardly remember where the years had gone. But she knew every farmhouse, every village, every road and lane and field and beach, between Pescara and Rimini.

"My dear," Sim said, "I cannot imagine anything more wonderful. I so long to travel that I would be excited to go to Birmingham. But we are stuck here, with our fish."

"What fish?"

"They are plaice. I am sure you have never eaten them, no one would except the English, who are the bravest people on earth but have strange eating habits. The Bloody Colonel and I are the business managers. We have two boats. Stash and Mike and four men from the Third Squadron run them. I tell you, it is a disaster."

"But why, Sim?"

"The plaice don't stay where they used to; it is very hard to find them. Then there is always a storm and something falls out of the engines. We will remain in Grimsby our entire lives, trying to catch enough plaice to pay for the boats. Although it is better in Grimsby than on the boats; thank God I was too clumsy to fish, so they made me second business manager."

"And the Bloody Colonel?"

"He is very happy because he has become a painter. He goes to Lincoln to night school, and paints beautiful pictures of apples and cups and sometimes portraits of Pilsudski. He does not mind, now that he has Art."

"I can't believe it."

"You will see. Tomorrow there is a special exhibition for you, at his house. Tomorrow also we will have a sightseeing of Grimsby."

"Are you sure Grimsby's still here?" There was certainly no sign of life around them; even the road was invisible.

"On the other side of the street, please," Sim said to the driver.

Sim paid the taxi and opened a low wicket gate; she could see the dull shine of a cement walk. Suddenly, from somewhere farther ahead in the darkness, a firecracker exploded, followed by a Roman candle which climbed two feet and fell in a sputtering faint curve. A Polish word, obviously blasphemous, greeted this performance. There was now a string of firecrackers, sounding rather fretful and then, quite handsomely, two globs of colored fire and a little plant of flames flowering from the ground.

"Fireworks!" she said, seized with giggles.

"It is the Bloody Colonel. He has planned this for days, but forgot the rain."

They ran down the walk and a man emerged from a shadowy hut, a tool shed or chicken coop, and shouted with laughter and said, "It is like Fourteenth July, no? Hello, General, Hello General," and threw his arms around Lily and hugged her.

"Now we go inside," the Bloody Colonel said, "and drink and drink."

She felt Sim's pride, as he walked before her, leading the way into his home. There was a narrow hall, with a carved varnished side table, and room for nothing more except hooks to hang the essential raincoats. A stairway mounted one side of the hall; you had to wedge yourself past it to the second door, which Sim opened.

"The library," he said.

Since the whole house was built for midgets, the size of the room was proper. As furniture there was a day bed, serving as couch, a bulging brown leather-covered armchair, a desk, a bookcase, two straight chairs and too small tables. A Polish flag was tacked to the wall, and photographs of men and women and children and laughing groups of skiers and huntsmen and Lancers stood or hung in every free space. Orange curtains, of a thin unlined material, covered the window and a striped woven arty blanket and odd colored pillows covered the couch. The rug was a purplish thing, intended to be Oriental. A miniature coal fire burned on the hearth, and there was the smallest bottle of gin Lily had ever seen, like a gift sample given away to new customers, and three unmatching glasses, on a tray beside the couch.

"It's absolutely charming, Sim."

"It is rather cosy, isn't it? We fixed it up with bits and pieces we found in the secondhand shops."

"This is a beautiful house," the Colonel said solemnly. "Not like mine."

"How is yours, Marek?"

"Mine is full of dirt, ugly, everything broken, cold, disgusting. Sim makes this beautiful house. We come here always to be in a beautiful place."

"Do you want to go to your room, Lily?"

"Later, darling." Give me time, give me time until I can see it as beautiful too. "It's so lovely and warm. What a heavenly room, Sim." There could not be too much of this; he would not doubt her.

They now heard weak radio music, coming through the paper-thin wall that joined this house to the next.

"My neighbors," Sim explained. "They have a nice little girl called Dorothy."

"The people in Grimsby are good to us," the Colonel said. "We are here much time, General, in camp, before we get these fine suits of civilians."

"A cocktail, Lily?"

"Yes please, Sim. Oh my, this is the first time I've been comfortable in England."

Then Marek Starecki, who had named himself the Bloody Colonel long ago, gave the signal: do you remember. And they were showing her photograph albums of the others and the places they had all been, and there were pictures of her too, looking, she thought, forty years younger, how was it possible that she had been so young at twenty-nine and so immeasurably old at thirty-five. Each blurred snapshot of a shell-pocked Italian village, with the same square white-in-the-sun cement buildings, the same dilapidated streets, clogged with their same equipment of war, was a clear and separate and wonderful memory. They laughed with pleasure again at jokes which could never have been very funny; jokes about the chaplain and about Stridek the boxer who married a Polish WAC and was lightly but inconveniently wounded the day after, and jokes about how the Bloody Colonel believed his jeep to be invisible; and no word at all about Michael who had been blown up on a mine and flung, headless, into a tree because that day they were bored and went exploring down leafy deserted lanes, full of military ardor and nonsense; and nothing about the two brothers, the young ones whom Skinny so loved, who were booby-trapped into soggy red messes trying to open the door into a house where a woman was screaming. Only the laughter and the friendship remained, and the unreasonable mocked-at but triumphant feeling that anything was possible after the war.

"Here is my house in Poland," Sim said. "The one in the country where I grew up. It was a nice house."

It was a house built perhaps three centuries ago, for the enormous familes of the Mitrowskis. The photograph was poor; you saw a vast faded building, with many square windows and arched doors, and a terrace, on which stood two figures wearing high boots and wee Norfolk jackets, like ancient schoolboys.

Sim looked at this picture with tenderness, as if he could pass through it into the house and his father's voice would boom orders any minute, and his mother would preside placidly at an immense round table, where the ten children gathered for tea.

"First the Germans had it, then the Russians had it. If it is still left, I do not know who has it. I missed it, for a long time, but now I have this house of my own," Sim said, and put the picture away.

"Who is this one?" the Bloody Colonel asked, showing her a photograph of a very thin, uniformed young man, with wild light eyes, astride a monumental horse. Sim quietly left the room; he did not want Lily to notice his going.

"I don't know him," Lily said.

"It is the Bloody Colonel!" He shouted with laughter. "It is the Bloody Colonel when Lieutenant of Cavalry."

"Marek! You look as if you were going to eat the horse."

The Colonel studied the picture, laughing happily, seeming not reminded that he had always been an officer of cavalry, until armored cars replaced horses, and now was an officer of nothing.

"More vodka," the Colonel said, filling her glass with gin. "Like those bad Russians."

And Sim, she thought, has one brother in Scotland on a farm, and one brother in China doing who knows what, and one sister with a Buchenwald tattoo on her arm, and that's the lot; but perhaps four out of ten was a good score for a family. And the Bloody Colonel had the fish and his painting, but nothing else; still it was the same proportion really, he had only two children and a wife to lose.

"I think," the Bloody Colonel said into the silence, "in two three four years maybe, when the fish are good and we pay for the boats, we go to fight the Russians."

"Not me."

"Not you, General? Who gives coffee and cigarettes and nice things to the Lancers?"

"I don't know. I'm going to an island, made entirely of salt, in the Dead Sea. I'm against war. Nothing good comes of it. Afterwards."

"After? What do you think, such an intelligent girl, they make wars for something? They make wars because that is what men like, they make a war so they get some excitement first before they die; or they only live and die, that is nothing much. General, General, what friends you have now? You are always a happy girl. Why are you talking of after?"

My friends, she thought, are you and those like you, the people who used to be. Am I supposed to welcome more wars, so more ghosts can be manufactured? I don't even like ruined towns, I find nothing attractive in ruins. I see no point, she thought angrily, no point, no point.

"Madame est servie," Sim said, from the hall.

There were two red candles in cheap brass holders on the small table in the dining room. More of the costly coal burned in the grate. There was a tablecloth, and paper napkins, and something, perhaps a packing box, also covered with a white cloth, pulled up near the table so that Sim could serve without moving. The feeling was that the servants had been sent away, since this dinner was to be an intimate feast. On Lily's plate, an iridescent apricot-colored glass saucer from the local Woolworth's, lay a small booklet. It was made of dark blue cardboard with a raised gilt figure of a girl in pantaloons, shawl, and a poke bonnet.

Lily opened it and saw, in Sim's agreeably illiterate hand: Menu. Lobster à la Tobruk, cutlet Alamein, legumes Cassino, salade sauce Ancona, tarte Mitrowski, Claret, Champagne, Napoleon Brandy, Cigars. They watched her as she read, with their own indestructible gaiety, waiting for her applause.

"But what a chef you have!" Lily said. "Darling, you spoil me."

"Nothing is too good for our General," the Colonel said. "Only I wish Stash and Mike did not go out on the bloody boats, so they are here for the party."

"You'll stay until they come back, won't you, Lily?" Sim asked.

"It depends," she said, not daring to say "no," not with this feast and these candles before her. They had done this all for her, who was nothing, nobody, insignificant even as a ghost. They had schemed and saved to make this welcome; how lonely they must be if her coming was such an occasion.

"I want my Tobruk lobster," Lily said, and Sim flourished before her a small glass plate with two pieces of bright canned lobster adorned with a pompon of mayonnaise. Not on the ration, she thought quickly, but so expensive; and the meat had used both their rations probably for a month, and Sim had shelled the peas which did not turn out very well and looked grey, and Sim had washed the lettuce and sliced the stunted tomatoes and arranged them in petals, and Sim had fancied up the bakery shop tart with maraschino cherries and powdered it with a snow of valuable sugar. She was not hungry, she was the opposite of hungry with her throat shut to food, but she ate everything; such cooks, she said, such regal fare; such quantities; but they should leave Grimsby at once and open the finest restaurant in London, Paris, Rome. The claret was raw, yet watery, and when it was time to open the champagne she prayed that the cork would pop. I will do anything, she prayed, if only the cork will pop.

They were very gay; Sim loving to be host in his own home, at his first real ambitious party; the Colonel delighted to show off the English he had acquired in the last four years, and delighted to remember and remember. Her smile felt carved on a glass face; her laughter had a sharp false ring. Yet it had been so natural to laugh before; she remembered the three of them on leave in Rome in the dazzling summer of 1944 and she laughed harder, higher, so as not to cry.

Then Sim was saying, "Shall we have coffee in the library?" and they moved to the room with the bookcase, for coffee and chemical-tasting brandy. Now they were quieter and she was only there as a listener, while they talked of Poland and Russia and the Regiment and the future of plaice in Grimsby and how maybe Australia was a fine country for emigrants. Lily felt she was failing them; she should have been able to dredge up, from these separated years, stories that would keep them laughing.

They had finished the remnants of every bottle in the house and the Bloody Colonel was happy and fairly drunk. At three in the morning, he said he must go home, and they made many loving farewells, wedged together in the hall. They would come to the Colonel's home, at noon, for the Art Exhibit.

"My poor Lily, you are exhausted. We have been dreaming of you for weeks; and then Marek and I do all the talking when we know everything we have to say by heart. It is too stupid, I could shoot myself. And you must be so bored."

"Darling, how could I be bored with you and the Bloody Colonel? Only I am tired. I have been awake such a long time."

"It is Stash's room when he is here," Sim said, opening a door in the second-floor hall. "And there is the bathroom, across there. Should I light the hot water?"

"I'm too sleepy even to brush my teeth," and she looked at this room and knew the mattress would be stuffed with railroad tracks, and looked at the varnished chipped dresser and the bare table and the single rush-bottomed chair, and, on a tin trunk beside the bed, a water glass with a rose in it.

She turned and put her arms around Sim and kissed his cheek and hid her face against his coat because now she was too tired to keep back the tears. But Sim took this differently, and held her very close and said, in the softest voice, a new one, "Darling?"

She became crafty at once; it was necessary to escape from this, and escape with gentleness. She imagined that Sim needed a woman, since Grimsby would scarcely be a gathering place for available beauties, and she guessed he was sick with loneliness.

"My dear Sim, my dearest Sim, I'm sorry." There were no suitable words.

"I've never forgotten you, Lily."

And I have never forgotten anything, she thought. But she knew what Sim meant, and she was shocked. How could he, as persuasion use the perfect and admirable past now in this grey time? For he was reminding her that once, returning with Stash and George and Lily smuggled along, from a night patrol, a moonlit night when every shadow had been ominous and they came back, having accomplished nothing, relieved not to be tense and watching and frightened, gay as people can only be when there has been danger and they are out of it, that night he had walked across the field to her distant tent; and once, after they had tiptoed hand in hand, making jokes but very nervous, on a beach empty except for the Germans' abandoned barbed wire, and had blown up on no mines, and swum in a lukewarm sea under streaming sunset clouds, once there, on the still warm sand. They had been lovers; but they had never been in love. They were great friends, and both were handsome and gay and wild; and this had been part of their immense joy in being alive and in owning their bodies and those intact. Whereas, in a frigid box of a room, in Grimsby, making love with Sim would be an act of pity on both their parts, or an act of desperation. They had been, in that other time, too good for pity or desperation.

She moved away from Sim, and lit a cigarette and smiled uneasily and said, "Lieutenant dear, don't let's get things mixed-up."

Prince Mitrowski had known a great many Anglo-Saxon women and they no longer surprised him. Lily would, of course, be in love with someone as he might have foreseen. And Anglo-Saxon women apparently had a deep-seated objection to going to bed with a man, during the time they were in love with another man. This was an unwritten rule they followed and there was little or nothing you could do about it. But so tiresome; here they were in a remote uninteresting town, they were old friends, and the normal thing, as anyone except an Anglo-Saxon woman could see, was for a pretty female and a healthy male to make love, especially if they had a whole house to themselves. He had rather counted on it; he retained a most pleasurable memory of Lily's body, aside from all the memories of her which were like his love and loyalty for the men in his Regiment; and he was disappointed.

Still, he was too fond of Lily to be angry, and too sure of himself to be offended. She was not an ignorant silly girl who could be talked around. But he was puzzled; he found Lily unlike herself. A black Paris dress and good sparse jewels were preferable to a khaki uniform; she looked wonderfully cared for, not older only more arranged. The peace agreed with her; she had a fine life, travelling wherever she wanted to go, yet she was sad. Perhaps the man she loved did not love her. Was that enough, nowadays, to make people unhappy?

"Where's your husband, Lily?" Sim said, also lighting a cigarette. She sat on the steely bed and he sat on the rush-bottomed chair, and she felt the draught through the closed window and thought, oh my God how late it is, but if talk will make this easier, let us talk.

"I really don't know, Sim. I haven't seen him for years. We were divorced right after the war, you know."

"Are you still in love with him?"

"Dear Sim, I can't remember if I ever was. It's so long ago." In another life and another world, and then there was the war, and she had met many men who were what Charles wanted to be or said he was, but were it without effort. The war had served as an anesthetic to the operation of cutting off a marriage.

"What became of that American, that P-47 chap, the fair one?"

"His name was Robert Allen." But that was in Germany, had she written Sim about Robert?

"Where is he now?"

"He's dead," Lily answered in surprise. Anyone ought to know that much. It was normal to be dead.

Ah, Sim thought, that is it. She loved the American pilot, I remember her letters. I might have understood without asking her. The way she cannot live anywhere and is always alone; the way nothing interests her except the war. All the time I wondered how a woman who has everything, good looks and friends and money and a passport, dared to carry sadness around with her. Poor Lily, poor good Lily, it's too heavy a price for the war. Lily was explained; if you loved a dead man, naturally you were not alive. I must tell Marek. Lily was always so kind to us and when she needs help we have not comforted her.

He saw Lily's face differently now and was startled to find it hollowed and blanched with fatigue or grief. How could I not have noticed, he thought, I am too selfish.

"Go to bed," Sim said, and pushed the rush-bottomed chair neatly back under the rickety table. "Sleep well, darling," and he kissed her forehead.

Lily took his hand and held it against her cheek and said, "I love you very much, Sim. I always will."

"My General," he said gently, "I know."

Standing in the hall, with her door closed behind him, Sim thought, with anger and sorrow, war is too hard on women, no one realizes how hard it is on women.

Lily took off her clothes, shivering in the cold stale smoky air of the room, and hurried into bed. She turned out the lights and the cotton blankets were weightless and she might as well have been lying naked on the floor. She rose in the dark, found her coat, put it on and climbed back between the coarse sheets. She was trying to will warmth into her body, when she heard Sim go softly down the stairs. Later she heard a distant clanking from the kitchen; he would be washing the dishes at four in the morning, so she would not know that he always washed the dishes, and be sorry for him. It was contemptibly unjust that life should be easier for a rich ghost than for a poor one. That was the final limit; there ought to be economic equality for ghosts and all should have enough money since they had nothing else. Mink makes a nice nightgown, she thought in bitterness, and slept.

It seemed no more than half an hour later when Sim, looking polished and awake, touched her shoulder and offered her a great white china cup of tea. Something like daylight came through the window.

"It's a lovely day," Sim announced. "It's not raining."

Evidently, in Grimsby, all a day had to do, to be admired, was not rain. Lily felt her face sticky with the make-up she had not cleaned off, and her mouth foul with drink and cigarettes, and she hated having Sim see her like this, until she decided it was good for him, let him realize she was no dew-laden blossom and he would not regret the night.

"There is hot water and when you are ready, there is breakfast downstairs."

"Thank you, darling, I'll hurry."

You are old, Mother Cameron, she told herself. The back aches since it is unused to railroad-track mattresses; and it is terrible not to have enough sleep; and I am frightened of the day ahead, Grimsby and Marek's pictures and the long effort to be bright and merry at the spectacle of two men buried alive.

But she worked carefully on her face and put on a simple grey jersey dress for which she had paid Molyneux more than, no doubt, the value of all Sim's plaice, and went downstairs hoping that even her heels on the uncarpeted treads sounded joyful. Sim again had the meal ready in the dining room.

"There's an egg," Sim said quickly. "I never eat them, bad for my liver."

"What a luxury, Sim; I didn't expect two feasts," and she thought: I could get eggs from Janet's farm in Buckinghamshire and have them shipped here. It must be possible, and of course packages from New York. And blankets and plates, and other womanly little house-warming presents, which could hurt no one's pride.

"We should go to Marek's soon, Lily. He is so excited to show you his pictures. I hope you will like them. It is not far; we could walk."

"I'm longing for a walk. I'll get my coat."

Sim stopped, on the pavement before his house, so that she could see his domain well, in its entirety. Of course he would know which was his, Lily thought, because it's on the corner. There were fourteen houses, joined together in a row, on each side of the street. They were identical: red brick with a pointed roof, a small bay window on the first floor and a door, two windows on the second floor, green woodwork, and a low picket fence surrounding a patch of what would be grass later on. And not a tree in sight.

"I didn't know how wonderful it was to have a house," Sim said, looking fondly at his brick box. "I had a few things to sell, so I could make the first payment, and now I'm buying it by the month. It is a remarkable system they have here. Of course Grimsby is not a very amusing place but it makes all the difference if you have your own house. A house is so interesting; I can't think why I never noticed that before, in Poland."

"Yes, I know," Lily said, and knew that she knew nothing. Slowly, she began to feel herself alone, far away, hiding in a country never invaded, while others fought.

She liked walking with Sim, it reminded her of how they had walked in that brilliant Italian summer. Their steps matched and she ignored the straight streets, with never a curve, never a surprise. The difference between the streets was only that some of the houses were yellow brick instead of red. This scandal of ugliness was so complete that it ceased to have meaning, as scenery in a dream is unimportant. It was all a dream; they were two disembodied memories, walking anywhere, telling each other wisps of fairy stories, the gossip of a previous life.

"We are almost there," Sim said suddenly. "A friend of ours will be at Marek's house. Be nice to her, Lily."

"Darling, what an amazing thing to say! Have you always found that I was beastly to people?"

"No, of course not. No, really, Lily. But you see, this friend is only a girl, she's twenty-two. She is a stenographer in the bank, and her father has a small shop here. Marek and I are fond of her. She's sweet, Lily, but she will be frightened of you. I mean, she has never been anywhere except Grimsby. Her legs are very ugly."

"I can't see what possible difference that would make to me. I don't give a hoot about women's legs."

So he thinks I'm a snob now, and he would never have thought that before. Really, men are a caution. How guilty and mean I felt last night, and all the while Sim is well fixed-up with a local.

"You're cross."

"I am not," Lily said crossly.

Then they were standing before the Colonel's house, which was like Sim's, except older, and yellow brick trimmed with black woodwork.

"We go in," Sim said. "Marek rents the first floor to a nice young couple; the husband was on Anders' staff as something or other. Be careful not to fall over the pram."

The stairs were dark and steep. There was a curious smell and Lily remembered Marek had said it was a dirty house.

Sim began calling, in Polish, as they neared the top of the stairs. He led her down a hall to a room which ran across the front of the second floor. The furniture appeared to have been thrown in rather than placed and the disorder was astounding. Sim left her here, to find the Colonel. Lily could hear Sim down the hall saying, "Get up. Get up. There is nothing to drink except beer. Beer for breakfast is unhealthy.

"If we had gin It would be different. Oh Grace, good morning," a false careful voice, Lily thought. "Yes, what a good idea."

Lily had time to look at the Colonel's paintings which were standing on chairs and against the wall at one end of the room behind his easel. There was a green and purple and black face, on the easel, an unfinished canvas. The other pictures ranged from correct sail boats and glorious apples to muddy Impressionist landscapes and angular street scences.

Sim came back, followed by a girl carrying a tray. The girl was almost as tall as Sim, perhaps six feet tall, and enormous. Lily could not help looking at her legs, and they were more like tree trunks than any legs Lily had ever seen. Her body was built on the heroic scale of the Winged Victory and though, Lily thought instantly, she would be colossal in Greek draperies at the top of the stairs at the Louvre, you did not expect to meet a Greek statue in Grimsby, wearing ugly patent-leather slippers and a slate-blue crepe dress, foolishly looped up on one side, foolishly pulled to a vulgar neckline, beneath the powerful perfect throat.

But what was even more incredible than this noble size was the girl's face. It was oval and her skin was without make-up or even powder, and the cheeks very pink, perhaps because it was hot work to make coffee in Marek's little kitchen, perhaps because of meeting Lily. Her brown hair was parted in the middle and hung in natural waves almost to her shoulders. A mistake, Lily thought, I ought to tell her; she should wear her hair up so you could see the line of her head and throat. And her eyes were dark blue, absolutely honest, absolutely trusting. Her mouth was as good and as gay as a child's. Seeing her face, you forgot at once that this girl was a giantess, and felt she was small and much too young and vulnerable.

Sim made introductions: Miss Needham, Mrs. Cameron. The girl
said "How do you do," and then, in shy explanation of the tray, "Marek
will want coffee, I think. He said he was drunk last night." Her voice
was unadorned and direct, as honest as her eyes.

"Could I have some too?" Lily asked. That Sim should have found
this girl, this particular girl, was what she could not believe. Sim.
Imagine. Sim who had only known women like Anne Marie and
Lorna Charters and Bianca and all those, the sleek the chic the elegant
the quick the clever the witty the greedy the lazy the artificial. Or
herself, herself also, and perhaps she belonged with the others. But
never anyone like Grace Needham; what had happened to Sim that
he could find Grace Needham?

The Bloody Colonel hurried in, his thin grey hair brushed flat as
always, his worn blue suit pressed as if he still had a batman to keep him
smart, and he kissed Lily and made apologies.

"I was too excited, I can not sleep, so I think: now I will again paint
Pilsudski. I did not go to bed before it was daytime."

He turned to look at the unfinished green, purple and black canvas
and Sim moved to stand beside him.

"It is better," Sim said gravely. "The moustache and the hair are
very good. It is better than the last one."

"Oh?" said the Colonel.

"It isn't like any of your others," Grace said. "It's altogether different, isn't it, Marek?"

"Mm," said the Colonel. It was a pleased sound.

The three of them looked at the painting, as if they expected it to
move or speak. They had forgotten Lily.

Marek does not surprise this girl, Lily thought, she expected him to
happen, she expected to be on hand and serve him. And she is proud of
Sim, that's how she loves him, not because he is hers, but because he is
Sim and will always stand and fight. It does not matter how Marek
paints; painting is another country to fight for. And I am like some
miserable desk General who arrives for twenty-four hours, well-fed
and rested, and goes no farther forward than Division. I am not helping anyone to fight for anything at all. It is no wonder they have forgotten I am in the room.

You think always in terms of war, Lily told herself, the war is over.
The war was so easy compared to this that they ought to reverse the
words; this is much harder and longer than war ever was. I couldn't
get a job in this kind of war; no outfit would have me. They have
Grace, naturally they found her.

The Colonel turned the canvas upside down and said, "It looks as good this way." He has had a fit of rage, Lily thought, he knows how far it is from his mind to his hand. He is furious with rage as he used to be when the banks of a river held up the Staghounds and the engineers didn't arrive; or when they couldn't get the Germans off that hill with the tower on it. Only rage; nothing in him gives up. And she thought: how clever Sim is, how wise. Bravery is what he honors, and he recognizes it anywhere except in himself, so he is spared the poses and lies of the people who only want to love bravery and only want to be brave. How could I have gone along thinking Sim was sweet and charming and generous, but never guessing what he really is. You are not his kind, she answered herself, that's why.

"Now we have had breakfast," the Colonel said suddenly, "we will have beer." Grace went to the kitchen because she always looked after them, and what they wanted she gave them; she was at home in this war. Sim worried that Lily would think Grace a joke, and be charming to her, and Grace would feel it (she was very conscious of her size and her legs) and he could not bear to have Grace hurt. But if Lily had come and gone, and they had hidden Grace, that would have hurt her more.

He meant to warn Lily, but he was not sure where the danger lay, so, to his surprise, he announced: "I am *Mister* Mitrowski and Marek is *Mister* Starecki, now."

We are what we are, he thought, with nothing to make us look better. It is enough for this girl. No one must condescend to her. She is the same as we are.

"Mr. Mitrowski," Lily said, her eyes hot with embarrassing tears, "Mr. Starecki, I never loved you more."

The Colonel began to talk, very fast, his English confused and heavily accented, and he was showing Lily his pictures, explaining when he had painted them, why they were bad, and what he must learn.

"Next year, when the fish are better," the Colonel said, "we will have money and we will go to the galleries in Paris and Italy. We can travel cheap, Lily?"

"Oh yes, certainly," Lily said, ashamed that she did not know.

"We will go in the summer when Grace has her vacation; she will want to see the pictures too. She is so interested in painting as we are."

"Yes," Sim said, although he thought the business was more likely to fail than to give them money for a trip. And if it failed, he would probably lose his house. I cannot lose my house, he thought, I will not lose it.

But no one said, for talk's sake, for fun, to be cosy: and you come too,

Lily. Of course not, Lily thought. I am an intruder. I do not deserve to be here, you have to earn it. Nothing was changed; it was only harder and secret. They were the same men, as solid as they had been at Tobruk or Alamein or Cassino. Since they had never turned and run, why should they now? Grace had joined them, for the endless duration. You had to stay and live it, you had to share it with your friends and love them more than yourself, then you belonged as Grace did. I must get out, Lily thought, I am scared, I don't know who I am.

They lunched at the Crown Hotel which was the most expensive place in town, and Lily guessed at once that they never came here, but naturally they would offer her what they could not afford for themselves. The dining room at the Crown was full of silent eaters, all looking as if the food disagreed with them and Sunday was a punishment. The waitresses were insolent and slow and disliked the foreign merry manners of these Poles. Lily hated the waitresses and wanted to tell them to honor their betters and bring beer at once when it was asked for; and the meal was disgusting, all white, everything white, and lukewarm and thick.

She saw how cheerfully Sim and the Colonel matched coins and added and got enough for the bill. And how Grace behaved, quietly and easily, knowing what money they had and did not have and how hard the week would be, but able to arrange it for them somehow. They will eat scraps at Sim's house, and wash the dishes together, and talk of Marek's painting and how they are going to Italy and tomorrow morning Grace will go to the bank and Sim and Marek will go wherever they manage their fish, and none of them will despair.

Let them win, Lily thought, Oh God, let them win. Before, she had been part of the winning, but now, somehow, somewhere, she had lost her place; she had demobilized herself.

Sim walked ahead with Grace; there was just time to walk to Sim's, pack Lily's suitcase, and take a taxi to the station. They had urged her to stay but she said she could not, so many errands, she said, you know how it is. What am I trying to think, Lily wondered. Oh yes, Grace's legs look perfectly all right. They are hers and how she is, is all right.

The Colonel was not talking. Lily saw him staring at the street, the houses, the sky, and knew he was thinking of colors and what you could do with grey. With an effort, the Colonel abandoned the street, and took Lily's arm.

"General, you are sweet to come to us. It made us happy."

"Thank you, Marek."

"They walk well together."

"Yes."

"One day they will marry."

"What?" It could not be her voice, squeaking like that.

"Why not? She is not Princess or Countess; she did not go anywhere; she has no dresses except three, all ugly. And she is a good woman, everything is good. She loves Sim: she is not afraid of what life he will have."

"I didn't mean that."

"It is different, Lily. You must be a Pole perhaps to understand. We come very far away, but that is not strange to us. We always go back but maybe not the same ones who go away. Sim knows. Grace knows this too; she is not a Pole, but she knows, for Sim. For you it is the same life as before. That is good. That is what we all like, but it does not happen so."

Ah no, Lily thought, you are wrong. She might have cried out in pain, it was so clear in her face. The Colonel remembered then what Sim had told him, hurriedly, in Polish, when the girls went to fix their hair before lunch. Sim had been useless for Lily, too, or so he said. They were only concerned with their own lives, their own little problems. Their problems were nothing and would be solved. But how did a woman learn to stop loving a dead man?

"I am sorry, Lily. We hope it comes better for you. Everybody must forget something, Lily. It is not possible to live if you always remember."

What is he saying, Lily thought. Her legs felt cold and weak; the streets went on and on, where was Sim's house. Why is he telling me this?

Grace must have packed for her. There was more gin; she could taste it burning in her mouth. She did not listen to the men, nor hear her answers. She believed she could hear the minutes ticking in her tiny silent watch. It was raining again, she noticed, as they drove through the cold identical streets, and the station held its own cloud of train smoke and looked as it had when she arrived, dark, and full of jumbled pale people, in raincoats. The ladylike broadcast voice told them where to find the train for London. Sim walked up and down the long train while she waited with the Colonel and Grace, out of the rain. Sim reported he had found an empty compartment and led them, carrying her suitcase.

Then she was inside the familiar varnished box, leaning out the door, while they stood with the rain making pearls in their hair. The three of them, all so tall, united, with laughing faces, called good-bye.

"It's been lovely," Lily called back. "Such a wonderful weekend! We'll meet soon, won't we? Darlings, take care, darlings, thank you, good-bye, good-bye."

The noise of the train cut off their words, the lowering smoke blurred them, and they were three distant figures under the feeble bare light bulbs.

Lily closed the window and sat down, with her feet on the opposite bench. Her feet were wet, London was hours and hours away. A hot bath, she thought, trying to imagine comfort, and a hot toddy and a hot-water bag.

I have made a cruel mistake, she told herself. She was whispering in the silence of her mind. There is no one to remember for, or no one to remember with; everyone must forget. The dead are dead, there is nothing to be done. And the ghosts, the others she believed were like herself; had she pursued them, saying: Ghosts, Ghosts, when they only wanted to live?

She was not rejected by the ghosts, who would be too kind for that, but she knew she must leave them. How did you pick up the habit of living, once you had lost it? How did you live with yourself after you had guessed for the first time, with disbelief and certainty, with horror, that you were a coward?

She shut the door into the corridor, pulled the shades to hide herself from passing people, and turned off the light. Shrivelled with cold, she lay under her coat, sick with cold, sick with weariness, sick of all the journeys. And watched the rain, like melting grease against the dark window, and the night too dark to see.

(From Prairie Schooner)

ALWAYS GOOD FOR A BELLY LAUGH

BY EMILIE GLEN

*T*HE MAN was a circus on blades, his solemn tussles with the ice good for a belly laugh at every flop. Night after night, skaters going round and round Rockefeller rink left off to watch; people jammed the red rail, threw a cordon of laughter around the Plaza above; diners in the French and English grilles on either side of the rink were convulsed behind plate glass.

"Must be a funny man from some ice show," the onlookers speculated. ... "Hired by the rink perhaps." ... "Looks like an undertaker in that dark homburg." The skaters pieced together what they could learn of him.... "Harvard graduate" ... "Statistician with some brokerage house in Wall Street" ... "Commutes from Montclair."

The formality of this bone of a man in Brooks Brothers clothing, his air of having just emerged from a board meeting to pay his respects to the ice, that was the architecture for his comic fall. He was anyone in authority you'd want to pull the rug out from under, but before you got there he pulled out his own rug in a fight for balance that laid him low.

In a bit of business with tight-wrapped umbrella and bulging briefcase, he would come out on the ice with a carriage so erect that he all but leaned over backwards, a fall from his eminence unthinkable. Or he would clap a Tyrolean hat on his head, and consult endlessly unfolding time tables and road maps before mounting an imaginary bike and plunging toward the plate glass of the English grille.

Whenever he rested by the rail, his precise features in repose verging on good looks, most skaters by-passed him as if their laughter had thrown up a barbed-wire entanglement between them. In the skatehouse they acted embarrassed to see him sitting there packed tight in his reserve.

Travers knew his effect on the other skaters; he had felt that way himself when he went back to the theater for something he'd forgotten, and an unshaded light was a cold eye on the empty stage.

The laugh was on him two seasons ago when all this started, not controlled by him, but on him. He had come down to the rink with his wife and two boys. Harriette had refused to change from her lacy pumps into rented skates with their green-painted heels. "You'll never catch me making a fool of myself out on that ice," she'd said, "for the whole world to see."

When he was thirteen he could have skated dizzying circles around both his boys, but out there on the ice for the first time in twenty-five years, he could scarcely keep his feet. His long habit of carrying himself straight as a flagpole threw him ludicrously off balance, as he could see by the mirrored columns in the grille, and hear by the laughter all around. The old balance came back to him fast enough, the knee bend instead of the swing from the hips, but he still played the beginner just for laughs, that red rail like a little red schoolhouse where he studied the comedian's art.

As blade and ice fused in a power that sent him in a glissando across the rink to roars of laughter at his pretzel-like knotting by the rail, he felt the power of that great gold Prometheus up there above the fountain, his gift to mortals not mere fire for their cook stoves but the fire of laughter.

Back by the skate-house Harriette had covered her disgusted little nose with her veil. His boys weren't laughing either, not even nine-year-old Brock. In his own childhood he might not have been as clever as some others, but he knew the give-and-take of laughter. He'd do anything to get laughs — mimic, grimace, let himself in for bad marks by muffing translation, making such ridiculous mistakes that even his teachers had to laugh.

What he'd do for a laugh all but prostrated an Averill family, accustomed to laughs as discreet as their coughs whenever they couldn't avoid seeing the joke. Averills never clowned; they sat on the bench, ran for office, founded colleges, but they never clowned.

"We're not amused," his mother would say at his groping humor, and when his father died, he and his younger brother were locked in such a struggle to be first with their mother, her idea of head of the family, that he turned into quite a somber young man.

As for girls, if you wanted them you couldn't be both clown and lover, catching them up in your arms while you sprawled at their feet. Besides, the Averill in him was not amused. He had no use for funny men either, regarded them as low life. Broad humor was something to discard along with growing pains even if it left him without anything in which he excelled. He had started out a whiz at track until the doctor said his heart couldn't take extraordinary strain. "Nature has compensated for a slight valvular lesion, but if you don't favor your heart a bit, compensation will no longer work for you."

Tonight he felt the soaring power of his skill as the laughter from above fell in leis about him. Almost three seasons now, he'd worn them — his alone ever since he'd slipped back without Harriette and the boys to try out his clowning.

In high silk hat and his grandfather's silver-headed cane, he was dancing around in gingerly rhythm, stiff as a ruler about to take the measure of the ice, when his mother and sister came down to the rail. He wouldn't stop off yet, not while the laughter of the crowd was feting him. No one from his other life had any business thrusting in here, making him feel it was a vice to get laughs, like hitting the bottle or taking up with some woman when you had a perfectly good home.

Snow crystals cut by the blades of many skaters tingled like the laughter. He felt power, felt smoothness, felt rhythm beneath his blades. His mother and sister standing there as if they were no part of him, he'd make them laugh, rip it out of them. In every fall from his height it was his family who fell, generations of pride going down with him; his younger brother's plaster pomp went crashing while he, Travers, rose — rose to his skill, his comedian's art.

Hanging onto his silk topper and holding fast to his grandfather's cane, he began to fold, give way, melt into the ice, laughter wrapping him round like warm quilting. As he went through the droll business of righting himself without loss of hat or cane, he glanced across to his mother and sister. They were frozen at the rail. The crowd was with him, their laughter the streamers drawing him around in carnival mood before he could catch his breath. Here he was king — those two would have to wait for their audience.

Harriette might as well be frozen at the rail along with them. Since their marriage she had become more one with his family than with him. Her sense of fitness was tight as her bra; you couldn't shake up laughs. When Harriette — never to be addressed as Hat or Hatty — had been one of the battery of stenographers in his uncle's brokerage house, her eyes looking up at him had been blue fields of adoration. She was his short stuff, a nestling kitten like the one he had sneaked home in a big paper bag — all his, if his mother would let him keep a stray.

Like the kitten, she turned out to be more the family's than his, often looking past him to his brother as head of the family, copied his mother and sister with alarming results, a little thing trying to dress tall and

talk overbearing, catching up their mannerisms faster than their manners, and affixing her own funny idea of fitness. She made delicious
errors in her reach for big words, her rule-book parties. It was fun to
guide her tastes as that anxious-to-please little frown drew her tendril-
like brows together. She had a morning face, so fresh and pink it needed
very little done to it, her hair, fine-skeined. He had never let her alter
her child's bob to one of his sister's striking coifs. Oh, he loved her all
right — it would never be another woman — just this, this ice fever.

The last time Harriette or the boys had ever come down to the rail,
he had perfected his routine enough to want them to see his act, to let
go a little, then a little more until they were laughing with the others.
As pre-schoolers their laughter romped all around his antics, but exposed to Harriette and his own family, they winced at loss of dignity,
especially in their father. That night, only his youngest had let out a
belly laugh — hastily sucked in — at his solemn contemplation of a
small globe of the world in his hand while his skates were about to slide
out from under him.

Whether his family laughed or not, when the flags of all nations
took the gusts of the Plaza as if whipped by the laughter going around,
it was life itself to be out there on the ice. All thought of Harriette and
the boys glanced off his blades, went swirling away with the snow
crystals that stung his face like a flying theater curtain. On blades, the
oldest laugh routines were new as if you were the first comic who ever
flopped for a belly laugh.

Back by the rail his wife and mother were inclining their heads, yet
lowering them in a way that told him they were overhearing chatter
about him. "Bones," he'd overhead himself called. "Bones" . . .
"Bonsey" . . . a nickname he hadn't heard since his clowning school-
days.

A long line of Averills skated around with him, and whenever he
fell, they all sprawled. If he'd kept his dignity, his name on the door
might be up with the members of the firm, one day, instead of at the
lower left, but his legs were too long and restless to be wedged in at a
statistician's desk; he could only wander from it when the ice waited
for him, neat as a poker chip, smooth as a watch crystal.

The instant he lost his job, his brother spread a landing net, ready
to take him into his firm. "In those brother teams," he'd heard said
often enough, "one is usually the brains, has to carry the weight." He
wasn't going to be the lesser brother.

With the first cut of his blade, this new season, Harriette, who always looked to him for decisions, made one of her own. "I'm not going on like this. Your brother will arrange a divorce — see that the boys are looked after." Not a lone decision then, his brother had helped her along with it.

When he saw that she meant what she said about the divorce, he stayed away from the ice, looked for a job so fast that he fancied himself on skates along the smooth marble corridors, gliding from frosted door to frosted door; even practised a spin while waiting for the elevator.

Harriette — he couldn't imagine any kind of life without his short stuff, her hair in its child's bob, soft as a kitten to the touch. And the boys, he wanted to be with them constantly throughout their growing years; he wanted them to be *his* sons. Just the same it was no good making him choose — not yet. He could only try to hang onto both, like the hat and cane that sent him headlong to the ice.

Forced evenings at home wrapped all the disconsolate times when skating sessions were called off because the sun had melted away the ice or the rain was beating down on it. Everything about the house was static, waiting — the smoothed bed-spread, the crystal centerpiece, Harriette's fingers on the glassine cover of a rented book. In a cell where he could neither stand nor sit nor breathe, all of him was out there soaring across the ice.

Night after night he would close his eyes to such a reeling head that he was no longer lying motionless; he was some sort of toreador who had slain boredom, and was being borne up on the laughing shoulders of the crowd. On his job interview, next morning, he would act fuzzy, played out, a bad forty risk.

The ice he wore lightly as a charm on his watch chain — his jewel, his diamond, the perfect circle. Fast ice, slow ice, it was all his, the fast ice of April, a mirror lake for a swan-like glide ending in a fall that left him wringing out his trouser cuffs; slow ice, hard, resitant, his blades scrabbling for a foothold as he skated under the giant Christmas tree when he should have been home decorating his own. Whatever the season he always skated away with the laughs. After all the reticent years, it was good to be out there making an unholy show of himself.

Each time the men cleared the ice between sessions, obliterating the skaters' marks, a bit of himself was obliterated. Summer could only be a fretful waiting. He would stand looking down on what used to be his watch-crystal ice, now mushrooming with umbrellaed tables, Muzak still playing its skating rhythms, attendants turning the hose on boxed trees and plants instead of ice for the session.

One indoor rink stayed open in the summer, but only a few un-smiling skaters went around in the damp mausoleum air, condensation from the ceiling dropping on them like cold sweat.   Seeing himself in the fearsome expanse of mirror, he was so lean and sorry-looking that he wondered why anyone ever laughed.

"Travers — Travers — here." His sister cast off her usual come-to-me attitude through a slightly unbalancing lean over the red rail, but in an elegant reach of her leopard sleeve, she tried to rake him in with a croupier's gesture. He could have felt close to Roz if she'd let him. She was something of a comic jack-in-the-box, too, the lid secured ex-cept for an occasional rusty-springed quip.

In a running slide across the ice he lurched to the rail where his mother and sister stood, doffed his silk topper and fell flat to laughter they gathered their furs against.   That might be a creeper of a smile across Roz's face except that she always had the look of smiling her disdain.   One smile from Roz would mean more than the roars of all the rest.   As children, when he had the school-yard in laughter, Roz would just walk away.

No, he'd spare them nothing; he'd go through desperate attempts to right himself, and flop again, and again, bringing their pride down with him.

"Get up — will you get up?" said Roz.

He just squatted there at her feet, partly to catch his breath.   That shortness of breath was getting more bothersome, and the swelling in his ankles made them feel ready to burst his laces.

"This is the only place we can find you, these days," said his mother. "We have something urgent to discuss."

"Won't you step into my office?" he panted, doffing his topper again.

His mother had a way of looking past him, her profile the only part of her face he ever called up.   The fullness of her gaze had always be-longed to his brother.   "Don't you think so, Brock?" she'd say.   "What's your opinion, Brock?"   Brock couldn't help her now, as she stood there in the conservative sealskins worn by generations of Averill women.

Roz looked past everyone, past him now to remark, "Mighty short of breath, aren't you?   And your color — it's blue.   Your heart's not up to your clowning."

In the mirror column beyond, he could see that his skin had a faintly bluish cast like the remains of clown's paint.   "Reasonable exercise, yes, your heart has compensated to that extent," she was going on, "but not this — this unholy show."

Harriette had gone through the same thing with him, adding sobs to her sound effects. "It's not just the fool you're making of yourself, the career you're tossing away — my having lost you — it's what all this may do to your heart." Poor short stuff, she'd only miss what little there was of his brother in him.

The crowd above was clapping for him . . . "Hey, Topper, do your stuff." . . . "Get going, High-hat." . . . "Shake a blade." . . .

"Why, that rabble is actually calling for you," said his mother, "as if you were some sort of paid entertainer."

"Let's go into the English grille," said Roz, "where we can be semi-private."

Pell-mell on the points of his skates he headed for the plate glass of the grille, glumly inspected the diners, making a pretzel of himself to scan a menu in someone's hand, pulled out empty pockets, tipped an apologetic hat, and slunk back to his mother and sister, turning the spotlight of laughter on them.

"Travers, listen to me," said his mother. "It's not too late even now. Harriette says she'll call off divorce proceedings if she has any assurance you'll stop playing the clown."

"A good way to convince her is to land a job," said Roz. "I've just heard of an opening. No, your brother has nothing to do with this. Just get in touch with a Mr. Donaldson of Donaldson and Struthers, 51 Pine Street."

Travers did a back flip away from them — out to a nice round belly of a rink — a belly full of laughter.

In a leap that powered his blades, he took a sudden turn off the ice to the skate-house. As he opened his locker, Roz came to the doorway. "Leaving?" she asked.

He was too short of breath to do anything but shake his head, No. By the time he'd exchanged his topper for a homburg, his cane for a *Wall Street Journal*, Roz was gone from the doorway.

Coming out on the ice, he saw that his mother and sister had moved to a more inconspicuous curve of the rail. He unfurled his *Wall Street Journal* and dallied about on the ice so absorbed in stock quotations that he tripped, righted himself, tripped again. That should blast laughter out of those two. He looked across the ice. They weren't at the rail, or by the skate-house, or in the English grille; they weren't anywhere.

The rink was all his again. Later, he might regret this — the finality of their leaving, what they'd say to Harriette — later — now his blades were too swift for awareness of anything but the ice — all thought of the boys lost in the laughter that ringed him round. He had the crowd on the point of his blade. The season was only just beginning — he'd have a long run. This was his glittering stage, and the stars above were bits of smooth, fast ice, a million rinks awaiting his blades; and he'd skate from star to star along a milky way of laughter.

People in the Plaza above pushed and jostled for a better look at the funny man's new routine, laughed their insides out at his solemn business with the newspaper, his pencil worrying at the margin. Then the rarest yet — a regular dying swan, a droll collapse, his homberg rolling off. Usually so careful of his props, he let the newspaper get away from him, sheets flying high as a kite, tangling around the legs of skaters as guards went on frantic chase. His impeccable timing was off, too; he stayed down too long in a tedious gasp for breath. They began to clap for him, the steady clap, clap, clap of a movie audience for a broken film to be spliced.

A waltzing couple skated over with his crushed homberg, bent over him as if in real concern, motioned for the guards. They helped him up, his legs weak as macaroni. This was no act — this was on the level. Of course he could be faking a collapse at the stock-market news, but the guards didn't think so. They brought him into the skate-house, and laid him on a bench out of sight of the other skaters.

The crowd waited a long time for his reappearance, but he didn't come back on the ice that night. Those who waited above the skate-house saw the two men help him carefully up the stairs, his face a deathly blue.

"Heart attack," the manager said. "We brought him around."

"You won't see that bird on the ice again," said one of the skaters.

"I don't know," said his partner, tightening her laces. "I don't know. I think he's a chronic like us, and when you're a chronic, there's no place else."

The rink settled to its round of skaters throughout a winter so cold that few but the regulars came out on the ice, and almost no spectators stood in the down-drafts from the great buildings above. It was no place to go for laughs anymore. Without their funny man, the skaters looked like a bunch of bedraggled stooges.

Along in April when the tulips by the Prometheus fountain were bobbing stiffly as beginners on their blades, he came out on the ice one Sunday evening in the striped trousers and cutaway he must have had on that morning as church usher, convulsed them with a best-man-at-the-wedding routine. He marched cautiously up the aisle, shaking imaginary rice from his handkerchief, fumbling through his pockets for the ring.

His blades gliding faster and faster, he caught up with a skater in white, and just as he was about to kiss the bride, pretzeled down at her feet, untwisted himself, knotted, flopped — the laughs all his.

(From Town and Country)

BRAHMIN BEACHHEAD

BY NANCY HALE

*F*ROM INSIDE* the privacy of his dark glasses Christopher Lake, crouching in the hot sand with his bony knees under his chin, watched Betty Fellowes make her morning entrance on the beach — the little beach, *the* beach of Harm's Shoals.

It was high noon. The happy few who had always summered at the Shoals lay blissfully stretched out under the red sun in a state of shared grace — old friends, old companions-at-arms against the intruder, a special breed of Harm's Shoals Bostonian.

Chris watched absently but critically as Betty slapped down the stone steps to the sands in her beach sandals, shuffled across to her particular rock, spread the contents of her beach bag around her, opened her bottle of oil, and began to anoint her bountiful person.

"Well! What do you all think about the people in the Wigglesworth house?" she inquired. "*Les Irlandais?* I mean, really!"

The little beach was the social club, the forum, the daily newspaper of Harm's Shoals. All summer long its habitués lived the life of the sun — lazy, relaxed, calm — beside the beautiful sea; and, as they stared out toward the wreck of the Liberty ship that had driven onto the breakwater last winter (some said for salvage), they discussed each day some new, urgent topic and passed, as a body, upon it — the Bikini bathing suit worn by the Sturgises' weekend guest, the false eyelashes on the blonde at the Inn. On such matters as these a judge presided, a jury found guilty or not guilty, and each of them there was judge and jury too.

Chris picked his bottle of baby oil out of the sand and rubbed some more of it on his thin and aging shanks, turning slightly to hear what would be the response to Betty's opening.

"I don't see why it couldn't have been somebody *possible*. The bank had no right to sell like that without consulting any of *us*," Julie Jones began. "The only thing we can do, I suppose, is simply to forget these people live here at all."

The Wigglesworth house was one of those directly abutting the little beach and its owners could walk straight out from their front lawn down to the sand.

Betty shuddered. "Ugh! I can't help it, I think that race is the *worst*. Dirty, dishonest, lying. I simply have an instinctive aversion to them, that's all."

"Not instinctive, darling," somebody objected. "It was borne in on us as children with the procession of biddies passing through our kitchens. Do you remember how they always smelled?"

"And Catholics!" someone else contributed.

"Not that, darling. Catholics can be all right."

"French Catholics, yes," Betty declared. "Italian Catholics. Any kind of Catholics, but not *Irish* Catholics!"

"You're as bad in your way as an anti-Semite," Christopher put in. He said it idly, without caring, simply to contradict Betty, whom he liked to put in her place. He knew all about the Dolans having bought the Wigglesworth house, but he had not come to any definite position about how he stood on the matter.

He was far too worried about himself to care.

He crouched, isolated inwardly from the life of the beach, feeling like a magician who has lost his magic. As the debate waged fast and furious, he leaned his cheek on his palm, in a lifetime's characteristic pose.

For thirty summers, ever since he had come back from his student days in Paris, Christopher Lake had been the moving force, the life, of Harm's Shoals. He lived, a bachelor, in the little house overhanging the cliff — La Gaviota he called it, for it perched there like a gray-and-white sea gull. And for all those years he had been, in the little, close-knit colony at Harm's Shoals, its celebrity, its artist, its contact with the slightly alarming world of art.

Not that being a painter would have admitted Christopher to the inner circle. Its members were conventional, conservative, voted Republican, kept servants, deplored change and Mayor Curley. It was no artist's colony.

But Chris had been born one of them. He was the son of old Mrs. Cabot Lake, whom all of them remembered as the *grande dame* she had been. Chris was entirely eligible socially. The Lakes were as good a Boston family as any and Chris had never been involved in any kind of scandal — the sort of thing one associated with artists. As a matter of fact, his name had never even been mentioned in connection with that of any woman, except, of course, his mother's.

He was, in fact, a gentleman, a gentleman-painter, and one whom the great, mysterious world of art took seriously. All of them had read the reviews of his one-man shows in New York, where he wintered. It was most impressive.

But beyond all this, Chris was the moving spirit of the Shoals. He lifted them out of their slight boredom, out of the tiresome way things had of becoming monotonous. He *invented* things, that was it: it was he who always had the ideas for all the best parties, Betty's sailing picnic and Julie's moonlight clambake. He had rearranged Mona Potter's whole way of dressing and doing her hair — with delightful results. He shook them up, he introduced change when change was needed and the Shoals-Bostonians had not the faintest notion of how to bring it about. He was a pearl in their midst.

His worries, just now, were entirely private ones. Only he knew that he had not sold a picture in four years; that he had not been able, really, to paint one in five. *He* knew; it gnawed at him.

It was not just the pictures; it was everything. He had lost his feeling, he had no bright ideas, he had lost his magic. Things simply did not *come* to him any more. He felt tired, and empty, and frightened.

It was only a question of time before these people too realized what had happened to him — that he was painted out, played out, burned out somehow. And then what would become of the blessed satisfaction of his summers? He would have lost his function in Harm's Shoals, as innovator, mover, and shaker; as celebrity and pearl of parties.

It never occurred to him that they would have any use for him — these dear old friends of his — under such circumstances. He would simply lose all: his gift and his friends too.

Was he too old? Why had his daemon deserted him now? Was he going to pieces? He was only sixty-one and many artists were prolific at that age. Why had the color gone out of the world around him?

It was like a cancer of deep anxiety. Life was unthinkable to him if he was not to be an artist, of pictures and of parties. For what would he be then?

He shrank and ducked at the very possibility of facing the answer to that question. It was something that he had always rejected.

To avoid that answer he threw his attention back to the debate on the beach, on the subject of the Irish. Nobody, he hoped desperately, would be able to see how wretched he was or how frightened. His eyes sought the irregular bulk of the wrecked ship out at sea. He felt as lost

and abandoned as that. What good was a ship that could not sail?
What use an artist who could not create?

". . . Boston politics," somebody was saying. "They're at the bottom
of it. Corrupt, dishonest . . ."

"They simply won't do," Betty Fellowes said firmly. "That's all. I
shan't call."

Chris looked at her with dislike. Betty was the wife of Heber Fellowes
and perhaps next in social cachet at the Shoals to the sacred Percival
Heath, who seldom even graced the little beach with his presence.

Who did she think she was? Chris thought, his dark mood focusing
into vindictiveness. Originally she came from Brockton. She had
only *married* Heber Fellowes.

Simply in order to contradict her again, Chris said, "You can't
condemn a whole nation like that. I'm afraid you're given to generali-
ties, Betty. You don't use your mind."

"Of course that's sense, Chris," Julie Jones said. "But none of us is
very sensible about the Irish. For instance, you hear people talk about
Irish charm. Charm!" she rolled her eyes up. "They simply haven't
been brought up, as we were, in Boston."

"Charm," Chris repeated, absently.

And, all at once, with that one idle word, something happened inside
him, mysterious as flint and steel's collision. He moved sharply in the
sand and sat up straighter.

What lights the spark in an artist's mind? What is that magic? What
opposites unite?

The object seems to be bathed in radiant light, discerning, adorning.

Suddenly Chris saw the Dolans in his mind's eye — he had only seen
them once, on the road, — with a kind of love, a feeling familiar to him.
He saw them obscured, as though enclosed within a block of marble;
their true potentialities hidden; their wonderful, radiant, special individual *selves* unseen behind a muck of prejudice, of phrases about the
Boston Irish. Something inside him yearned for their release; something longed for them to be seen for what they truly were but he did
not even know what that was.

Only, to that frivolous man, it seemed unbearable that this gift of
God should be unrecognized. And in that same split instant he felt
himself a sculptor, one who could chisel the marble and bring forth
what was hidden within, disclose the beauties latent in the stone.

It seemed to Christopher Lake that this was, for him, the most important thing in the whole of life. When the spark lights, the artist recognizes it.

The debate on the beach was wearing out. In a moment somebody would say something which would finish it for all of them. They would have made up their minds about the Dolans.

"*I* shall call," Chris said slowly and felt all of them turning toward him in surprise. "I met them on the road and they are charming. Not at all what you think. You mustn't allow prejudice to blind you to something delightful. He's a very cultivated man — owns that big music store on Boylston Street. And she is a beauty. A real beauty. An *Irish* beauty," he added and saw them all stare.

Everyone began to gabble, then, while Chris sat still. He had dropped a bombshell. He felt the seed of his new idea begin to swell within him, silently, wonderfully. From despair, he had by a miracle found heaven, a new kind of heaven to this old painter. Once more he had lifted the Harm's Shoals people out of their old ways, out of their rut and their Bostonianism.

That afternoon he did not even pretend to go to the moors on one of his abortive sketching trips whereby he had tried to keep the secret of his artistic impotence from the others. He dressed in the white ducks and white sneakers which were *de rigueur* in the consciously simple life of Harm's Shoals. Promptly at four he presented himself at the front door of the old Wigglesworth house — that door so familiar to all of them, where they had yelled, as children, up at Sneaky Wigglesworth to come on out, where they had gathered for old Mr. Wigglesworth's French evenings, so very long ago.

He did not expect the house to be the same; he did not even want it to be the same. He was excited. He was ready to accept anything; it would be grist for his mill. Inside him the spark was blowing into a flame.

Elizabeth Dolan came to the door, with an expression of some surprise. She did not know, he thought, what was in store for her. She undoubtedly had no idea of being accepted here. They probably intended to bring down their own Irish friends from Boston for company. Such as these never had been accepted in Boston; why should they be here, by more of the same?

Chris wore his most cordial smile. "How *do* you do?" he said, "I'm so glad to see you. I hope you're getting settled in this dear old house. It's nice it has been bought by people who will appreciate it."

He walked in past her and past the little girl who had followed her mother to the door. "How do you do?" Chris said to the child, who replied, "Hi!"

That, Chris thought swiftly, would have to be translated out of bad manners into a refreshing freedom.

"What a marvelous piano!" he cried, entering the old living room, now so changed.

Mrs. Dolan smiled and sat down opposite him. It was true, she was beautiful. She was smart, as no real Bostonian could be smart, in a dark-blue linen frock; her gold hair, parted in the middle and drawn down, shone like fine brass wire. Her smile was faint and almost dreamy; her expression, cherishing and arch. The fey look, he thought.

"I hope you won't think we've ruined it at all," she said.

How sweet of her!

"But on the contrary . . ."

The piano, concert size, had the most prominent position in the room. Gone were the Victorian sofas, the red corduroy upholstery; instead the room was furnished with modern furniture, the sort of thing one saw in copies of *House & Garden* but not in one's friends' houses. It was all extremely attractive.

A man stuck his head into the door, then entered. "This is Mr. Dolan," Elizabeth Dolan said, and Chris, not wincing, stood to shake hands with the short, dark man with a clever blue-eyed face.

"You're the painter, of course," Luke Dolan said. "I saw the show of yours at the Whitney — was it three years ago?"

"Four," said Chris.

He sat down beaming and warm inside. He lit the cigarette Dolan offered him. The man really was cultivated.

The child, whom they called Mickey, burst into the room again and went to her mother with some fishhooks, interrupting the conversation with a plea of her own. The parents made no protest against her behavior.

That will have to be both translated and changed, Chris thought. But the work will be a joy!

Luke Dolan suggested drinks and Elizabeth brought whisky and soda. I must tell them about sherry at teatime, Chris thought, looking round the room as he sipped his highball.

"We must have a musical evening soon," Chris said, nodding at the piano and smiling. "I could even, perhaps, attempt one of your re-corders. You play the fiddle?"

"I do," said Dolan. "My wife is the pianist and Mickey is studying the flute."

"How delightful!"

"I wonder," Dolan said. "You don't by any chance play the cello?"

"I'm afraid not."

"We need a cello."

"Percival Heath —" Chris said before he could think. He stopped short, his pleasure faintly fogged over. That snob. Who cared about him? What if he played the cello? Chris would not finish telling the Dolans that. It was always best, he had found, simply to forget about Percival Heath. God knew the Dolans were not likely ever to so much as meet him.

The old wound in Chris stopped throbbing as Luke Dolan, quite simply, yawned.

Goodness! he thought. Dear me! I suppose we can put that down to unaffected Irish charm. Child of nature and all that. Already he felt proprietor of all that was here.

And so, when there came a knock at the door, and Elizabeth Dolan went to admit none other than Betty Fellowes, come to call in the white wash dress and white sneakers of Harm's Shoals afternoons, Chris felt a modest gratification. People had made up their minds to call.

That was in late June. By the middle of July it was obvious that the Dolans were not only accepted, they were a triumph. "The Irish" was now a term of loving familiarity used by Julie Jones and the others on the beach. "Oh, but we *must* have the Irish," they would say. It was the thing, to speak of Lizzie's chic and Luke's wit and of that impish little girl. It was new and gave them such a sense of broadened horizons. Once more Chris had served them well. The Dolans were included, were wined and dined (fancy asking the Irish to dinner!), and in everyone's mind it was understood that they belonged to Chris. They were his. "Your darling Dolans," people called them.

Chris was no longer unhappy. He was happier than he had been for years. This was almost better than painting! For was not this art in terms of living flesh and blood, the release of delightful beings from the petrified block of obscurity which had concealed them? He felt the joy that accompanies the act of creation. He felt a sense of sustaining virtue: he had overcome the sin of prejudice in others and, for himself, he had the feeling that he was saved.

He was busy all the time in giving little touches to his work: Mickey's lack of discipline . . . Luke's yawns and his table manners . . . the Dolans' little social gaffes — these things had to be made to seem unconventionally amusing in themselves but also gradually eliminated at the source.

He realized he had an ally in this in Lizzie Dolan. She was a clever woman, besides being beautiful. Like all clever women she was suggestible and much could be conveyed to her with a look, a quirked eyebrow. She was no fool; of course she wanted to make her family's way in the society which had so miraculously been opened to them. Chris simply let drop little hints about things, little oblique references, and was gratified to see that things did change. The round soupspoons at the Dolans disappeared; the child did not interrupt so often; Lizzie herself now referred to Luke as "Luke" or "my husband."

Never had a summer been so happy! He felt not only happy but powerful; not only powerful but good. Was he not giving happiness to others, lots of others? No life could compare with that of an artist's, especially of one who had found he could work in the medium of human beings.

Even that little private sore spot seemed to have stopped hurting.

With August the summer grew even hotter. The days were long and lazy under the sun; on the little beach they oiled their bodies and turned to brown another side; they planned a clambake for next week. The nights turned cooler in that northern latitude, the Milky Way creamed in the summer sky, the moon came out, and people gave evening parties.

Lizzie Dolan accepted just enough and then gave just the right sort of party, a musical evening — Mozart and a little Bach. How rewarding these intelligent people were! How pleasant that they were musical! The party made a new sort of entertainment at the Shoals, for no one else played an instrument.

Except, of course, Percival Heath — up there in his white house on the hill, occasionally appearing, silent and supercilious, on the beach.

As if anyone cared.

The snob!

Thank God, Chris thought devoutly, that I am not so limited. Thank God I am an artist — free — and no snob, certainly.

Forget him.

In August people in bathing suits brought picnic luncheons down to the beach and ate lobster salad and drank cold beer. By now everyone was one shade or another of mahogany. O blessed sun! They all belonged to its cult, and offered their bodies up to its blessing, to its subtle alteration of them.

Out on the breakwater the wreck seemed to diminish day by day as the big seas beyond the breakwater washed incessantly against it. They all stared habitually out toward the horizon from the sands; the sea was as blue as an alcohol flame.

"Chris, how would it be if I was to have a bit of a binge for a few people

over at Revere Beach one evening?" Lizzie Dolan asked him over
picnic sandwiches. "Wouldn't it be a change, shake us up perhaps?"
"Oh, *no*, darling!" He put his sandwich down from his mouth.
"What an *awful* idea! That would never do. That loathsome, noisy
place. And roller coasters . . ."
She laughed at him, her blue eyes shining in the sparkling sun. She
wore a stark black bathing suit and her white skin was only lightly
tanned. These fair Irishwomen!
For a moment he felt quite angry at her for her idea. It did not fit at
all, her plan. His scheme was quite otherwise. His beautiful distinguished picture . . . How *dare* she!
But then he saw that she was, quite sweetly, smiling, with no thought
of going on with her disapproved idea. Very teachable.
He put his lettuce sandwich back to his lips and was about to bite
when a voice, familiar and disturbing, made him stop again.
It was Heath, descended from his Olympus for one of his few swims
in company. Very tall, spare, impassive, he was coming down the
beach in shorts with a towel over his arm.
Why does the very sight of him upset me so? "You know why quite
well," said a voice. And memory treacherously brought up the awful
scene, the awful words . . .
"Lake, will you please take your hand . . ." Heath's voice. Oh, at
least ten years ago, fifteen?
O ghastly memory, O shame. Blot it out, shut it out, kill it. It
never happened. Be gone shame, horror, at what I did. I reject the
memory. I never did it.
Turn shame to hate.
The snob!
And because in moments of stress it was impossible for Chris to be
silent, he began calling to Heath and making introductions. "I say,
Heath, I don't believe you've met our new neighbors at the Shoals.
Mrs. Dolan, Mr. Dolan, and this is Mickey."
"How d'you do?" said Heath in his cold voice. "How are you,
Lake?" And he turned away.
Damn him to hell for darkening the sun!
He could not help watching Heath go down to the water and begin
his long, slow swim.
I don't want to look at him.
He reached out and took Lizzie Dolan's hand and squeezed it.
"Darling, you look perfectly charming in that black bathing suit."
She smiled delightfully.
God bless God for sending me the Dolans. They appreciate me.

They *recognize* me. What an idea! He moved sharply out of his musing. It is I who have recognized them.

On a late afternoon near the end of August, Chris was wandering down the road enjoying the prelude to sunset across the moors and thinking vaguely of dropping in on the Dolans to go on with an argument he and Luke had been having over Whistler's value as a painter. He had not yet made up his mind whether to do this or to continue walking down to the cliff to look at the sea in this light (for he might even begin to paint, soon) when a sight met his eyes that for an instant paralyzed him.

There it stood like doom. Percival Heath's ancient, immaculate blue Packard, before the entrance to the Dolans' house.

He was in a sort of frenzy, a sort of panic, alone on the road.

Heath? There? What was he doing? What were *they* doing? Had he called? He *never* called. He had never called on Chris . . . What were they talking about? Him? What had he told them? Were they laughing at him? Or worse? Heath *never* made friends with strangers.

He tried to tell himself that some contingency of which he knew nothing had occasioned a moment's stop at the Dolans'. He walked on down the road, actually trembling, and went out to the cliff and stared unseeing at the surf below. But, after a while, a terrible magnetism drew him back.

The immaculate, old-fashioned, and snobbish car was still there.

Chris looked at his watch. At the least, Heath had been there nearly an hour. It was impossible, so awful as to be untrue, for Heath to be closeted now with his darlings.

He started to go in, to join them, to indulge his agonized curiosity. But somehow, he could not do it. He felt like a shy and left-out child.

Instead, shamelessly, he skirted the back of the Joneses' place and went across the connecting lawn, looking to see if he could catch a glimpse of anyone through the windows. He could not.

But he heard, instead, the sound of music within: a piano, a violin, a cello. And bitter, bitter jealousy overwhelmed him. They've discovered a bond. And I'm left out. I won't have it!

That night he slept wretchedly, turning and waking and lying, eyes open, in the darkness. All his summer's happiness was gone. He felt bereft, deserted, and stripped of all power. He felt old.

In the morning he assured himself that he had been absurd. The only thing to do was somehow to take possession of this new development in the Dolans' lives and go on exactly as before.

Telling himself that all was the same, he ran over to the Dolans' after breakfast, which had become a custom with him. He was fond of helping Lizzie with the flowers, following her around the house while she attended to things, chattering with her of plans and of personalities.

Elizabeth, in a white beach robe over the bathing suit she had put on for the morning, arranged a bouquet for the dining room table while Chris sat in one of the side chairs, his legs crossed, smoking a cigarette. The morning sun struck on her brass-wire hair and made it an aureole. Her piquantly beautiful face was bent over the flowers as she listened gravely to what Chris was saying. Mickey ran in and out from the kitchen, *not* interrupting. Bit by bit, Chris relaxed. Lizzie turned, leaning on one hand on the table, explaining to him what she intended doing about the calendulas. Chris was about to rise and go out into the garden with her, to go over the ground.

Then the telephone rang, and he knew, instantly, who it would be.

He had not been able to bring himself to mention, even casually, that visit of Heath's yesterday. The old, disciplined habit of forgetting about Heath was so strong that the never mentioning him persisted. Besides . . .

"Yes," Lizzie said now. "Yes, Oh, yes indeed! That sounds perfectly delightful. . . . Of course we won't forget. Goodbye, Percy."

Percy! Chris was holding himself together bodily.

"That was Percy Heath." Lizzie said. "We're to dine there Tuesday."

Dine! Percy! And I have *never* been invited to dine at Percival Heath's, God knows.

Lizzie was still speaking. "Shall we look at the border, then?" she asked. "Or will we go down to the beach?"

. To his horror he could not answer for a moment.

"Chris dear . . . are you ill?"

"By no means," he said gaily, suddenly able to speak. "I'm on the crest of the wave. But I *have* got masses to attend to at La Gaviota. So, if you'll excuse me, I'll see you on the beach later."

Death would be better than to let her know, let her see.

He went home and drank a glass of gin and lay down on his bed for a time. His heart pounded from the unaccustomed drink.

Around noon he made his appearance on the beach, where he remained for the rest of the day; on deck; in view. His lips uttered witticisms. Nobody could have guessed what was happening within him.

In the late afternoon, in the cool twilight, Chris sat all alone on the little beach. Everyone else had gone; even the children had taken their pails and gone up to supper. The summer dusk, now almost of autumn,

hovered sweetly and sadly. The small waves splashed against the hard
sand left by low tide.

It was the first time in the day that Chris had allowed himself to be
alone. All afternoon behind his casual front the ebb and flow, the re-
lentless terrible progression of his emotions had gone on without check.
All day his jealousy and humiliation had flowed rhythmically; his pride
and his impatience ebbed — all within the sealed casket of his personality. And slowly, like the eternal march of the tide, the progress of his
mood had marched from shock into despair into outrage.

Until now he was left alone on the little beach of Harm's Shoals, alone
with his gathered and ripened anger. And all of it had been agony,
and this, too, was agony, to him. What had they done to him? To
leave him thus, ruined? It was unendurable, his position. They . . .
he was not sure, now, whether he meant the Dolans, who he felt had
betrayed him, or Heath, his archenemy.

A tiny voice, a whisper of the ebb, said: "But it's really such a little
thing, what's happened; it's nothing. . . ."

And the swelling power of the flow pressed on: It isn't little, it's my
whole life. Mysteriously he knew it to be true: it *was* his whole life,
somehow, what had occurred.

It was something like a stuggle between enormous forces, creation
and destruction, and he the one to be destroyed or saved. It was by
no means little. He, the creator, the artist; or he, the nobody, the old
finished wreck.

I *must* be an artist, he thought desperately, just as he had thought it
before the providential advent of the Dolans.

But now things were changed. He had built them out of nothing into
acceptance, and it was as though the figures had picked themselves up
from the paint on a canvas and walked away into their own lives. His
creatures had deserted their creator and left him dry — left him for
his enemy . . .

The last whisper of the ebb protested: "But I would be glad for one
of my pictures to go out into the world, leave me, make its own way . . ."

But this was different. This was flesh and blood.

And it was as if, in leaving him, they were taking his own flesh and
blood with them. It was as though in helping them he had somehow
helped himself, raised *himself* out of a shameful obscurity, endowed himself with value and with life. And as though that were why he suffered.

His anger mounted higher.

It was quite clear to him that, if it had not been for him, the Dolans
would never have caught on at Harm's Shoals, never in the world. That
morning when their fate had been lightly tossed about in the conversa-

tion on the beach, it was he who had stepped forward and tipped the balance for them. And if they had not been accepted they would never have so much as met Percival Heath — for that matter, he had actually introduced them. Their very existence here was his doing. How dare they move away, on their own, when they owed him everything!

Chris stared blindly at the little waves, through the gathering twilight. And slowly something seemed to rise to strengthen him.

It is not too late. I created them; I can destroy them.

And a faint echo of the ebb cried, wept: "But I am an *artist.* . . ."

The day for that is over, his mind continued inexorably; there is nothing left but this; there is, however, this.

And he felt a new sort of power swelling in him, slow and dark, bringing strength to his body, exhausted from the long day.

He stared at the waves.

It shouldn't be hard. Only a few anecdotes about their unfortunate manners — Paddy manners, he would call them. A self-deprecating little reference to the mistakes one could make about people. "I was so wrong. After all, they simply won't do." Luke's yawns in people's faces; his failure to deal with dessert fork and knife properly; Mickey's brattish behavior. "But, after all, one shouldn't have expected anything better from a Paddy." It would be easy.

They would, all of them, the old guard on the little beach, simply relax into what they really were, what they were before Chris had lifted them out of it: Bostonians, brought up from childhood with sullen, dirty, dishonest, Black Irish biddies in the kitchen. This was their prejudice, this was their background. Now they could sink back into it, at a well-chosen word from Chris.

Heath, he thought, Heath might remain friends with the Dolans. But the world of Harm's Shoals, that little, sacrosanct world, would drop them. And who cared about Heath?

Chris knew, now, what he had to do. His long day of turmoil and unease was settled.

In the twilight he leaned, relaxing, on his elbow, his cheek propped in his palm by lifelong habit, and reflected upon the comforts of snobbery. Snobbery was a kind of refuge, a harbor. It was safe. Thank God, there was one realm in which one could rest upon the knowledge that *this* was done, and *that* was not done — a harbor in which one might rest in one's old age in the confidence that the rules had been made long ago and one need not worry about them. All one needed to do was the sort of thing one did do. Now he was not helpless. He had his power.

He looked out over the ocean and for a moment had a pang of fear. He thought, in the half-light of dusk, that the wrecked Liberty ship out on the breakwater had finally washed away entirely. He seemed to follow it in imagination, down through the strata of the deep, washing farther and farther down through green oblivion. But then he looked harder and saw, in the failing light, that the wreck was still there.

(From New Mexico Quarterly)

WHAT'S IN A CORNER

BY PHILIP HORTON

MR. WRIGHTMAN climbed into his bed next to the window and with a long sigh composed himself in his usual posture: hands clasped across his chest, legs close together and ankles crossed. He had once read somewhere that such an arrangement of the body in a cruciform pattern regularized the flow of one's psychic energies, and if his wife sometimes observed from the adjoining bed that he looked "just plain dead" lying there with his eyes closed and his mouth slightly opened, this only served to confirm his sense of profound relaxation.

The truth was Mr. Wrightman believed in ritual. It represented — as he had long since tired of explaining to his wife — the principle of pattern and therefore of order, and provided a stable framework within which one could collate, arrange and subsume the disorderly experience of everyday life. The posture of his body right now, for instance, he liked to think of as subsuming the psychic energies flowing through it. (For a moment he actually saw, pulsing from the toes of his crossed feet to the tips of his spread elbows and thence to the crown of his head, small scalloped waves of pale fluorescent light.) Meanwhile the posture of his body was contained and subsumed by the quiet rectangle of the bed and the similar shapes of cool sheets and warm blankets carefully aligned and tucked in; and the bed in turn, parallel to the wall, was subsumed by the shape of the room, and this by the shape of the house, which itself faced squarely on a street parallel to many other streets. . . . Mr. Wrightman gave a small sigh of pleasure, and in the act of groping on the night table for another tangerine his wife looked up from her book.

"Sleepy, dear?"

He lay very still, taking care not to interrupt his regular deep breathing. The sharp fragrance of tangerine and the sound of succulent munching reassured him for a moment; but his failure to reply hung uneasily in the air.

"De-ear?" Her voice was tentative, considerate. "Now dear, don't go and go to sleep. I'm almost finished my chapter and then we can have a nice cuddly chat." She paused, then added coyly, "Or maybe, if you like we could play the game."

Feeling the prying force of his wife's eyes on him, he bent all his will towards appearing even more profoundly asleep until the turning of a page told him he was safe for a few more minutes. But her last words had thoroughly chilled him and the fluorescent sense of well-being was gone. There were, he reflected bitterly, certain "cuddly" attitudes and impulses so firmly rooted in the deep animal recalcitrance to order and system that they could never be successfully subsumed in any reasoned way of life; and the "game" was pre-eminently among them. In a way, he supposed, it was a kind of perverted ritual, a ritual of unreason, like a black mass, full of obscene and malevolent parodies of the real thing. He sighed again, but this time inaudibly, with his internal organs. The posture of his body, now willfully fixed for fear of betraying wakefulness, weighed on him like a *rigor mortis*, and from time to time he could hear a faint whispering noise which presently he identified as his wife's toenails scratching absently at the sheets of her bed.

In his mind's eye he saw her as clearly, as immemorially as Whistler's portrait of his mother, but how different. She was sitting cross-legged near the head of her bed in a great swirl of blankets and sheets and pillows, crouching over her book like an animal and rocking back and forth with a gentle rocking-chair rhythm. Tossed in the wild convolutions of the bedclothes appeared the flotsam and jetsam of her evening's amusements: the rinds of several tangerines, a crumpled pack of cigarettes, the wrapper and gummy remains of a chocolate bar, discarded books and magazines and the mutilated ad section of the evening paper. And on the night table between the two beds, like a senseless salvage, a wet tea bag, an empty cup, an apple core already turning brown, and tumbling out of an overflowing ash tray a jumble of nasty balls of used Kleenex.

Mr. Wrightman itemized the familiar disorder with mingled affection and despair. Among the books he noted, as usual, Henry George's *Progress and Poverty* which his wife, when she read it at all, read backwards in order, as she explained, "to understand his premises in the light of his conclusions"; the *Garden Encyclopedia;* a whodunit by Dorothy Sayers; *Barchester Towers,* as a standard soporific; and the *Kinsey Report,* which she was now reading admittedly as a counterirritant to *Woman: The Lost Sex,* and which judging from her little grunts of triumph and contempt was admirably filling its role. He had often remarked that the more absorbed she became in her reading the more frequent and varied were the noises she uttered. In fact, in all her more responsive and unreflective states she was addicted to making obscure animal noises, her vocal cords responding as mindlessly as the strings of an Aeolian harp to the unpredictable gusts of her emotional life.

Suddenly the light went out. He lay quietly, trying anxiously to fathom by the complicated series of sounds from the next bed the drift of his wife's intentions. The brisk, blubbery noises of the nightly facial suggested she was widely and vigorously awake. On the other hand, what followed — the heavy thud of the *Encyclopedia* slipping to the floor as she humped herself down in the bed, succeeded by the lesser retorts of Henry George and Kinsey and the swishing avalanche of papers and magazines — seemed to bespeak a blind and drunken determination to sleep at all costs. The alternatives hung suspended in the darkness along with the sticky fragrance of apricot face cream which was now beginning to settle over his bed like a creeping fog.

"De-ear? . . . Are you really sleepsy, dear?"

He made no answer, miserably taking the full measure of her determination from the extravagant gentleness of her voice. She was going to be sweetly reasonable.

"Now dear, you can't really be asleep. You've been lying there like dead for the last half hour, flat on your back without so much as budging, and people just don't sleep that way."

She herself slept like a disorderly fetus, Mr. Wrightman thought, some sort of animal fetus, a panda or a honey bear.

"It's unnatural," she went on, "and besides I've seen you often enough when you're really asleep. In the morning you're spread out all over the bed like a great octopus going every which way. I just know you're not really asleep, now are you?"

And supposing he was, thought Mr. Wrightman. He couldn't very well answer the question without coming awake, in which case he wouldn't any longer be asleep. The profound illogic and duplicity of his wife's insistence suddenly smote him with a great indignation. It was more than he could bear.

"I am," he declared in a flat bitter voice, "profoundly and irrevocably asleep. Please do not disturb."

She sniggered into her pillows. "Now don't be angry, dear. You see, you weren't really asleep after all."

The complacency of this left him speechless, and his wife, sensing her advantage, pressed on quickly.

"Now let's play the game, dear. Just once. Just a little short one . . . and I'll begin."

This was what he had dreaded. It was not The Game, which at least had the virtue that it couldn't be played in bed, but *her* game, learned in the provincial hinterland of her childhood, which one night in the fourth year of their marriage she had abruptly rediscovered in the cluttered attic of her mind and had brought down, so to speak, to install prominently in the foreground of their daily lives, like the whatnot in the corner of the dining room which she had inherited with all its silly gimcracks from the Roxbury farm. And like the whatnot, he loathed it for its shameless quaintness, its blatant and abysmal frivolity. But now there was nothing for it; he was caught again and his wife knew it. He could hear her settling voluptuously into her nest of blankets and making those queer laryngeal noises which frequently, and particularly in bed, signalled her preliminary dealings with a complicated idea. Presently she was ready.

"I've got something that begins with 'C.' "

"Animal, vegetable, or mineral," he replied, feeling all sorts of a fool, but determined to make short shrift of this nonsense.

"Vegetable," she said promptly.

"Is it in this room?"

"Yes."

"Is it an article of furniture?"

"No."

"Is it on or in any furniture, or is it a part of any of the furniture?"

"No, dear." She was obviously quite pleased with herself and her voice came to him half muffled by the blankets.

"Is it on me?" He thought of the cord of his cotton pyjamas.

"No, dear."

Suddenly he was sure he had it. She was always wearing one or more of her little side combs to bed, forgetting to take them out, the way she often forgot to take off her dressing gown. Once on coming home from a late party she had even worn to bed a small black toque so that awakening the next morning, he had had the shocking impression of seeing a lumpy little man in a black cap sleeping in her bed.

"It's one of your combs," he declared, and at once saw his mistake. His wife giggled.

"Don't be silly. They're made of tortoise shell; they're animal."

He grunted. "How would I know? They might be made of wood pulp or rutabagas or God knows what these days."

He remembered bitterly the night he had staked his all on a silk ribbon, pure animal product of the worm, he had thought, and how his wife in the midst of the subsequent row had thumped downstairs to lug back Volume XX, SARS to SORC of the *Encyclopedia Britannica* in order to read him, as if reciting the Doxology, the article on "Silk, Artificial." "Vegetable," she had wound up triumphantly, "it's as vegetable as a cabbage."

Thoroughly aroused now to his danger, he hoisted himself on one elbow and peered carefully about the shadowy room. He would go about this business systematically, relentlessly. He divided the room lengthwise, then crosswise, and taking each of the four quarters in turn tried to eliminate in a series of rapid-fire questions each vegetable item beginning with "C" which, visible or invisible, he knew to be in the room or which — as he grew more desperate — he thought might figure to the highly imaginative and cloudy mind of his wife as being in the room.

At first his method worked quickly, with a bright air of ease and efficiency, like a new toy or an outboard motor, but after several minutes it began to show embarrassing pauses and finally sputtered out in random guesses and expostulations. He felt himself floundering, and the room of a sudden appeared very small and bare. Meanwhile, he had learned only that "it" was plural (there were apparently several of "them" distributed with maddening impartiality in every quarter of the room); that they were "not useful, but terribly important in an aesthetic and mechanical way — I mean I don't use them myself, ever"; and that they were very large, "maybe twelve feet long." It was this last simple item of description that finally reduced him to silence, and gave him his first premonition of something terribly wrong. The full enormity of it did not strike him at once; he sensed rather than saw it, his befuddled faculties groping about its large and simple proportions like the hands of a blind man until, abruptly, he sat bolt upright in bed, remembering clearly that the dimensions of the room were only fifteen by eighteen and the beds a modest six and a half by three. Yet there were several, she had said, there were several of these gigantic objects in the room. This way, he felt, lay madness. He made a last despairing gesture in the direction of reason.

"Did you," he said, and was surprised to hear his voice, half suffocated by emotion, come out as a hoarse whisper, "did you say twelve *feet*?"

The heap of blankets in the next bed stirred slightly and gave out a small murmur. Having by now achieved a thoroughly "cuddly" state of being, she had clearly lost interest in the outcome of the game and was about to fall irretrievably asleep. He had suffered this peculiar form of humiliation more than once before and at the prospect of again finding himself arguing heatedly, idiotically, with the darkness was seized with violent panic.

"Damn it all," he shouted, "wake up!" He swung his feet to the floor and leaning over her bed began to shake her back and forth. "You wake up and stay awake till we're finished with this business."

Her head appeared, all unexpectedly, halfway down the opposite side of the bed.

"Stop it! Now you stop it, Fred, you're hurting me. Can't you see I was just about asleep?"

"Asleep. . . ." The audacity of it fairly choked him. Reaching over, he took a firm grip on the nape of her neck. "Now look here, Susan, did you or didn't you say these things were twelve feet long?"

"What things? . . .Oh those; why of course I said so. You can see for yourself."

"Oh I can, can I?" He exerted a strong uplifting pressure on her neck and brought her struggling into an upright position. "Well then, let's just look at this thing together. Where, in this cubicle, are there several objects twelve feet long that I fail to see?"

She continued to struggle about sturdily. "Let me go, Fred, let me go and I'll tell you. Really I will."

He held her fast. "I don't want you to tell me," he said pleasantly with a fine free sense of contradicting himself. "I simply want to play the game."

"Well I don't, I want to go to sleep. And besides you don't know *how* to play, all you want to do is argue, argue, argue . . . and bully me. Now let me go," she panted, "it's the corners I meant, so there."

"The what? What corners?"

"The corners of the room, you — you big dope. There, there, there and there." She waved her free arm wildly around the four points of the compass, then feeling his grip loosen, dove quickly under her blankets.

For a moment he was stunned. There was indeed something terribly wrong here. He sensed enormous discrepancies of viewpoint and focus; deranged perspective swinging wildly like searchlights in the night sky;

and something even more cosmic, the metaphysical shadows of Mr. Eliot, falling with perpetual frustration between the substance and the reality. He grappled with it stubbornly.

"Nonsense," he declared. "Who ever heard of a corner twelve feet long?"

His wife's head darted savagely out of her burrow. "It goes from the floor to the ceiling, doesn't it?"

Again he sensed a mysterious angle of vision, and shifted quickly to more solid ground.

"Anyhow, a corner's hardly vegetable, it's *mineral*. It's made up of plaster and sand and stuff like that. It's *obviously* mineral." He was angrily aware of an almost pleading note in his voice. But it did him no good, for his wife, it appeared, had thought it all out.

"Oh, but that's different, that's the *outside* corner. I'm talking about the *inside* one, the one made of wall-paper and mouldings and that's just as vegetable as your old plaster is mineral, and besides. . . ."

"Oh, no you don't, Susan, you don't get away with that." Mr. Wrightman felt a last flicker of rage. "That's just about the silliest damn thing you've said all night. Outside corner, inside corner! Where do you think we are anyway, behind the looking-glass? Where I come from a corner's a corner, and it's made of plaster and lathes and incidentally decorated with paper and moulding, and it's mineral . . . or if you want to be really pedantic about it, it's mineral and vegetable and you know it as well as I do. And furthermore. . . ."

"And furthermore," hissed his wife, starting upright from her blankets, "I don't know anything of the kind and I won't be bullied any longer. I know what I meant and I still mean it. And just because you come along and choose to describe a corner as if it were a *wall* and put your own constrictions on it. . . ."

"Constrictions," he shouted, "Oh God, that's wonderful, that's priceless. . . ."

"That's right," her voice soared still higher, "laugh at me, bully me, push me around. That's a nice way to play a game. Just because I won and had to tell you the answer, you have to have your nasty little revenge and sit there and . . . and make fun of me."

She collapsed into her blankets with a wail, and Mr. Wrightman recognizing in the tremulo of her last words a really serious danger signal, rose hastily from the edge of her bed. The finality and the injustice of his defeat were now equally obvious.

"Go 'way," she whimpered, "just go 'way and leave me alone."

He turned and climbing into his own bed, stretched out flat on his back. After a moment he crossed his ankles and having pulled the covers up carefully under his chin, folded his hands on his chest. The posture was really very comforting and seemed at once to ease the pounding of his heart; but behind his closed eyes his mind flickered restlessly with a dim phosphorescent light, illuminating by fits and starts a broken chain of reasoning, a shadowy objection, a magnificent but decapitated rebuttal.

After some time and without his making the slightest effort there emerged with a sweet serene clarity the explanation of it all. It was really very simple. And with understanding came forgiveness: he felt a friendly need to communicate his finding to his wife.

"After all, Susan, if you had been really fair, you would never have chosen a corner in the first place."

"Well . . . why not?" She was still petulant, but ready for reconciliation.

"Because a corner, my dear, is not a proper object."

"What is it then?"

Mr. Wrightman paused, embarrassed. He suddenly realized he hadn't thought it all the way through.

"Well, it's a . . . how shall I put it? It's an arrangement of space. That is, it's not actually an object in and of itself, like a chair or a table, but is made up of two objects, — the two walls — coming together at an angle. So you see. . . ."

He was ready to elaborate, no matter how shakily, on this interesting idea, but she began to giggle into her pillows.

"Oh Fred, you're really too funny. Not that it makes any difference and you know I don't care one way or another, but after all, a house, I suppose, is a proper object, and what's a house but a bunch of corners stuck together with walls? And now, for heaven's sake, let's go to sleep. I'm simply exhausted." She stopped giggling and blowing her nose vigorously into a fresh Kleenex, dropped it in the direction of the night table and withdrew with unmistakable finality under her blankets.

For a brief moment he had it in him to rise once more to the attack, to denounce and reduce her prideful irresponsibility, but the impulse was followed at once and quite unexpectedly by a profound purging sense of the frailty of human nature. What reason and order could not subdue charity could at least transcend.

"Yes," he said, "yes, I suppose you're right."

But as he said it, his eyes, wide open now in the darkness and moving almost furtively as if to escape his detection, sought out the far shadowy corner of the room and he had already begun to wonder.

(From Harper's Magazine)

THE SEARCHERS

BY SUSAN KUEHN

THERE WAS no trace of Danny. He had been lost six hours by then. Lights swung in the darkness as our search party found the way back along the trail we had cut in entering the woods. Mud, caked by water, made my feet so heavy that it was hard to lift them each time. I touched my face, expecting to find a growth of beard, but there was only dirt. All around, there was the green smell of water, of sweat and damp wool clothes and always the scent of the wet, decaying earth. We came on the clearing of my father's farm suddenly to see it filled with people and alive with moving lights.

When my sister June hurried toward us, her hair was mussed up, and the wet night air made it spring up around her face. "What did you find, Graden?" she shouted.

I had to tell her there was no sign of her son. June was eight years old when I was born, but now I felt like the oldest. "We'll find him," I said. "Don't worry." But it was like talking to a stone.

She nodded, and some life came back into her face when she clutched at my arm. "You're not going to give up? You can't leave him alone in the woods at night."

"There must be fifty people out there now. They told us to turn back and get some rest."

"Graden, I'm sorry. I guess I'm half out of my mind," she said. She looked around the crowded yard. "Where's Kendall?" she asked, hunting for her husband. "I don't see him anywhere."

"He wouldn't turn back. He's still out there."

I looked at the dirt-smeared faces of the other men in the half-brightness of flashlights and lanterns and saw that most of them had long red scratches on their foreheads and cheeks. I felt my own face and took my hand away when I touched a gummy line at the jaw. A dot of

caked blood lay in my palm. Everywhere in the woods, the branches
had reached out to hold us back. Sometimes they held like rope around
the waist, and we had to push hard to free ourselves, but there always
would be the little, soft-looking ones that were the worst after all, because they clawed at our faces and clothes. Danny's little light sweater
would be chewed to pieces by those thorny green branches alone. He
was only six years old.

Women who lived near enough to make it had come, bringing food
and coffee that we swallowed standing up that night, because the
ground was cold, and there wasn't anywhere else to sit. A truck moved
into the yard, carrying army cots, and we learned we were supposed
to sleep there.

But I couldn't sleep for blaming myself. Danny might have been
here now if I hadn't broken my promise to him. When June and her
family drove up from Chicago, I had helped Danny build a little house
in our back yard. It was going to be a copy of our place, front porch
and all, and when he started working on it, Danny forgot all about his
toy model car collection. "You promised me you'd help with the
house," he had said that morning. But I had to be a big shot because
it was Saturday noon, and drive into Byron City in Kendall Jackson's
blue Buick Riviera for everyone to see. I had bought Danny a can of
brown paint at the hardware store that morning, to make up for leaving
him behind. I felt it still in my pocket when I rolled over on the cot.

I opened my eyes to see June moving around the yard with the other
women, pouring coffee and saying nothing. Inside the house, her little
girl began to cry, and June hurried inside, coming back to stand in the
doorway with Marcia in her arms.

"What are they here for?" the little girl asked. She stared at us.
"When's Danny going to come to bed?"

"Never mind." June's voice was flat. She looked like Dad then,
with the bones sticking up through her skin, and her lipstick gone.

"It's not fair for him to stay up later than me." But Marcia didn't
complain when June took her back inside.

June had been shouting for Danny when Kendall Jackson and I
drove back from Byron City. Dad had been watching him when he
disappeared, but Danny had gone so quickly that there was no way of
telling which direction to follow. Help had come fast. All afternoon
a string of cars drove up the bumpy dirt road that led off the highway.
Nap Stoner came with Sherman Blatnik, his deputy. Sherman had
brought his two bloodhounds with him — queer, ugly dogs with big

muscles and sagging faces. I suppose it was the first time Sherman Blatnik had seen June in all the time she had been gone, but all he did was ask for something of Danny's so he could give the scent to the bloodhounds. She brought out his pajamas. They were blue, with little figures of Mickey Mouse on them. The druggist, Everett Handler, and the Cranstons had come over right away, and in the middle of the afternoon, forest rangers and game wardens began to turn up. Just before it got dark, National Guardsmen came. As each group started out, Nap Stoner or Sherman Blatnik had given a pistol to the leader. When Danny was found, there would be four shots.

I could hear Dad's voice again as I lay on the cot. "This picture was taken in April, when Danny was in his school play," he said. "He's got real light curly hair. You'll be able to see it against the trees." His one good hand couldn't hold the picture still. "I told him to find me a little piece of wood for his house. I thought he was just going around the yard," he said, and you could tell by the way he said it that he had gone through the story so many times that the words didn't have any certain meaning for him any longer. "I just turned my head not more than fifty, sixty seconds."

I could hear Marcia sobbing inside the house. "Was she outside with them when it happened?" Nap Stoner asked.

"She's too young to understand. She never says the same thing twice," June answered. I watched her high heels sink into the earth beneath the sparse grass. "She thinks it's some kind of game."

"I just turned my head not more than fifty, sixty seconds," Dad said. He sat in one spot, not moving except when he turned to peer into the black edge of woods. And he was listening. I could tell that. Then he stood up and wandered off to the left.

"Where are you going?" Nap Stoner asked.

"Over to those spruce trees. I think he must have gone into the woods there."

"We've looked there," Nap told him. "The hounds didn't even get a scent."

"I was sure it was over there," Dad said, walking back to his seat. I noticed then that it was a stuffed parlor chair he had brought out from the house and set on the ground. I could remember when Mother picked out the red slip-cover material, and it looked crazy to see that chair sitting there on the grass.

I watched Everett Handler lie down on the cot next to mine. He was an ugly, good-natured man with scant, light eyebrows and lashes around his pale blue eyes, which gave the appearance of being all white.

Before June had left for Chicago, she used to take me in town with her and buy me a coke at Everett's drug store while she would leaf through the movie magazines. That was one thing you could say about Everett, that he never complained when you looked through magazines you didn't buy. After June finished paging over the pictures of the stars, she would hold her chin up and throw her hair back over her shoulders. She combed her hair a lot those days.

What was it like for her, I wondered. When June married her boss in the Chicago insurance company, Dad and I hadn't gone. Instead, we used the train tickets and clothes money to buy a silver tray. Dad asked her to visit us, and once it looked as if they were coming, but at the last minute they couldn't make it after all. We didn't really believe they would come this time either until we actually saw them drive into the yard. Kendall Jackson had a little, trim mustache that reminded me of a movie star, but I couldn't remember just who. And although June didn't go into town and say hello to people she knew, she seemed glad to be back.

But there was one thing she didn't mention, and finally Dad spoke about it. "You didn't ask about Sherman Blatnik," he had said that morning in the kitchen.

She held a wet glass out in front of her. "How is he?" she said.

"He used to drop in and ask about you before you got married," Dad told her. "He's got a good farm and some hunting dogs."

I had watched her move back and forth from the cupboards. I liked the striped skirt and the high heeled pumps she wore. "I'm glad he's doing well," she had said.

I lay on the cot, watching the sky and wishing I could fall asleep instead of thinking. When I saw the lights coming out of the trees, I thought maybe I had slept and turned the stars upside down in my mind so that they were on the earth instead of where they were supposed to be. But they were only more flashlights.

It was funny, I thought, how everything had happened at once. Dad got crippled in the tractor accident, and June went to Chicago. That morning, Danny had asked Dad why he couldn't move his arm. June had told him not to ask such things, and it surprised me to see her face get so red.

When someone touched me and said it was time to start out again, it was early morning. During the night, tents had been pitched across our property, and big food tables had been set up close to the house, where men now stood in a line waiting their turns. Nap Stoner was talking to some groups of men, new arrivals who had driven in that morning, and getting them ready to start into the swamp. Some of them I knew, and most of them I didn't.

"I've never seen so many men together like this except once," Mr. Cranston said when we were waiting in the coffee line. "It was a posse for a killer."

We started out again. The balsam and cedars were far enough apart at the edge so you wouldn't think they were dangerous, but the woods were a tangle further in. The ground was springy and wet all the time, no matter how little rain we had, and a storm two years before had knocked brush and trees down over holes so you could fall down twenty feet if you slipped into one of them. Sometimes, if a dog got lost and didn't return, people belived that this place was where it went. I had gone in there once, daring myself, but the thick tangle of trees made me turn back. I had cut in only far enough to say I had been inside. Even though it was bright outside, the trees were dark and wild-looking. Shaggy and massed together, they had a coldness about them. You could smell them, the oldness and the stale, molding pull in the nostrils.

Nowhere, even at our place, had there been a footstep of Danny's to follow, and we didn't see any now except for our own, looking like blurred scars in the muddy earth as we moved along. Although it was warm for October, it was moist inside the woods, and I put on the jacket I had tied around my waist. The land sloped downward toward a cedar bog. Danny had been wearing green overalls with a jersey of the same color, but everything here was green — dark, pale, medium green. I hunted for a glimpse of his blond hair, and once I thought I saw it and shouted, but it turned out to be a clump of yellow leaves. A hole in my boot sole began to leak water until my right sock was wet through. I couldn't remember what kind of shoes Danny had worn.

All morning the woods were full of sound. Our group had Everett Handler, Joe Cranston, and his father in it. I didn't know the others by name. The men kept on shouting, but they stopped when they were too out of breath to keep on moving and call for Danny at the same time. I saw that Everett was getting winded already from so much walking. Finally, Mr. Cranston called back to us to rest for a minute. Although he was pretty far ahead, I could hear him talking to Everett.

"It's funny it would come down to her depending on us," he said.

"That must be almost ten years ago," Everett told him.

"That doesn't change it any," said Mr. Cranston.

We started out again. As I watched birds skim out of the trees and flutter against the leaves, I envied them because it would be so easy to fly and not fight through the wet, uneven ground as we had to do. A bee would buzz around my head, or a mosquito would sing in my ear so that it was a relief when it finally stung me and died with my slap. But the sound that I heard all the time was the noise of my own breathing. I kept wishing that I could put one foot down after the other and be sure I was stepping on something safe and level and certain. It was funny how, in a clearing, a spot a hundred yards away could look so comfortable, but it was just as full of briers as the rest of the land when we reached it. It was all a web of twigs that cut against our faces.

I left my jacket hanging on a tree, because it was too heavy and caught too many thorns. Since it was red, I knew I could find it again. The ground broke away when I moved down a steep hill toward the creek in front of me. The grade was so sudden that my shoulder nearly touched the earth, and the wet, black dirt crumbled under my boots to roll into the ravine below. Then my feet, that had been so sure before, couldn't keep up with the speed I was traveling, and I found myself rolling too, but never as fast as the crumbling earth that slid and ran down the hill before me. I fell all the way, and my mouth was full of dirt when I stopped. More stones broke loose under my feet. With a wrench inside me, I heard them drop and roll against the rocky edge of a hole I might have stepped into myself. When I looked down into the hole, I didn't find what I was looking for and yet afraid to see. He wasn't there.

It was easier to move down a hill than to go back up again. I couldn't find anything to cling to. Small plants growing on the hillside pulled loose in my fingers as I grasped them. I walked in the creek, because there were fewer branches there to slap against my face and catch on my clothes. Finally, I found myself standing in water that reached only an inch below the top of my boots. I tried to climb the steep slope of brown earth, but it broke apart underneath my feet and sent me back again to the water with a splash. I stood in the creek again, watching water drip into the pool at my feet. There was no way of knowing how long I stood there, too tired to move right away and wondering how soon the water would rise above my boots. The sky was nearly hidden by the trees, and I had no watch. I didn't feel as if I had a bit of strength left. Sometime later, I saw a root embedded in the ground, the only thing I hadn't noticed before, and I held it in my right hand and put my left behind me for leverage. The root held, then moved out of the ground. I held it with both hands for the last try, but it pulled loose and dangled from my fingers.

When I got my breath back, I dug my hands into the ground, clawing it while I crawled up the hill. It worked. But when I went to get my jacket, it was gone. I wondered who could have taken it, because I had the right tree for sure. Didn't I? I couldn't remember, and I knew I, too, was lost.

Terror came sudden and swift when I saw I had closed myself in with branches. Where was the opening? How had I come into this place at all? When I tried to part the thorny branches, they caught at my sweater and pants like barbed wire so I couldn't move. They made holes in the cloth and worked their way past the material into my skin. As I clawed, searching for an opening, a branch snapped against my eyeball. For a long time, I was afraid to open my eye for fear it would fall out.

The smell of molding ground was heavy around me. I looked down to see a fresh footprint in the wetness, but I realized almost right away that it was my own. I had made it only a few minutes before.

"Danny!" I yelled. I knew now how scared he must be, how tired and wet and scratched. "Danny!" Far off, I could hear the shouts of the men. What if Danny, too, tried to shout at us and was caught somewhere in a hole so he couldn't move? I moved, to hear the marshy ground suck against my foot. It wasn't safe to stay there. I yelled out for Danny once more and heard something come through the twigs and dry branches. They crackled like fire as they broke. It was Everett Handler, panting as he cut away the branches to free me. He had found my jacket. It had been only a couple of yards away all that time, and the men, too, were closer than I had thought. It took us only about fifteen minutes to get back to them. Because there was no place to sit down, they half-leaned against the birch trees surrounding us. The birches weren't strong enough to hold our weight, but the other trees had too many needles to be comfortable. A few of the men were smoking.

"Do you remember the time the little girl got lost over near Pear River, and they found her just as good as new?" asked Everett. He wiped his steaming face against his sweater sleeve.

A few of the men remembered.

We came out of the woods for the second time on Sunday afternoon, to meet the faces of Dad and June. Their eyes were dark, made small by lack of sleep. Marcia knew what it was all about by then.

"Danny!" she called as she ran over to the edge of the woods. "Come back and finish your house." June had to run after Marcia and catch her in her arms to keep the little girl away from the trees.

"Danny, why don't you answer?" she shouted, trying to get away from June. "Mother, can't you make him *talk* to me?"

But most of the time, Marcia stayed close to the house and didn't complain when one of the other women watched over her to give June a rest. Jackson spent nearly all his time in the woods. When his group came in, he would join another, eating whatever food he could find to carry.

The damp night air was no good for Dad, but he wouldn't go inside. That night I found him standing in the yard, looking at a mound of stones and wood.

"Danny's house," he said. "He never got to finish it. Do you suppose he tried to build something out there?"

"It's going to be all right," I told him, and thought of the water holes inside that were deeper than a man is tall. "We're going to find him."

"I shouldn't have asked her to come back at all," Dad said.

Word came on Monday night that one of Sherman Blatnik's hounds had struck a fresh trail on the ground above the cedar bog. When Nap Stoner's party came back with the news, June stepped forward as if she couldn't quite believe it. Nothing would stop her from going out herself as we all started back toward the woods.

"Why don't you stay here?" Kendall asked her. "If we get a track, I'll let you know."

"I've been here too long. I've imagined myself out there so many times that I might as well be," she answered, and there was no way for him to keep her back.

She moved ahead as fast as anyone, although her feet kept slipping, and her breath came in jerks.

"You're tired already," he said.

"No," she said sharply. "Leave me alone."

"I've done all I could," he said. "I've looked until it doesn't seem possible he's in there at all. He had his toys. Why did he go looking for a piece of wood?"

"He was building that house. Maybe he liked it because I used to live there. Isn't that a reason?"

"But he had his toys. I don't understand it."

"You shouldn't keep asking that," she said. "Maybe he'll tell us himself. Maybe they'll have found him when we get there."

"Don't," he told her, and the word was like a shout. "Don't even hope until we *know*."

"You don't think we'll find him, do you?" she asked.

"We can't be sure until," and he stopped for a second. "Until we get there and find out."

I walked behind them, swinging my flashlight off toward the trees. Everything seemed much stiller than it was by day. Kendall lit a cigarette, and the smoke curled up as if it were climbing the beam of light. I turned the flashlight on the ground. It was funny to see my own feet come out of the dark, as if they weren't part of me any longer. There were bonfires in the swamp, and you could see them shining through the trees. They were beacons for Danny and places where the men could warm themselves and dry their clothing. Guides and trappers were crisscrossing the ground when we got there. I heard Sherman Blatnik's voice before I saw him.

"The dog's lame, but we've got to hold to the scent while it's warm," he was saying. Then, in the swinging gleam of a flashlight, I had a glimpse of his cap and his dark face, made darker by a growth of whiskers. I watched June rush toward him, while Kendall walked over to Nap Stoner. Looking at her and Sherman Blatnik, I wondered if things might have been different if he could have done as much for her ten years ago as he did now.

"What have you found out?" she asked.

"Nothing yet," and his voice was soft. I watched him take June over to the nearest bonfire to wait while the search went on. Then he came back to the dogs, and I could see her, huddling her hands into her sleeves as she stood with her back to the fire.

Each minute could bring Danny or another sign, but the minutes went by empty until Sherman Blatnik's dog went completely lame. Someone was sent back for fresh hounds, because Sherman refused to give up until another dog came to pick up the scent. But it was no use. The first hound simply couldn't go on, and when they came back with another, the trail had been lost.

I think that was the time when June gave up hope. She left the fire and didn't look at anyone. She didn't seem to feel even Kendall's arm holding her to keep her from stumbling. Once I saw her pull her arm away from his. It was a long, terribly quiet walk back. All through the woods, it smelled like decay.

When they told Dad that the scent had faded, he was quiet, and I was afraid he was going to collapse. He gripped the stuffed arms of his parlor chair, just staring into those trees. I noticed he was trying to say something to June, but he couldn't seem to get started.

"I tell you it's my fault," he said finally.

"Don't blame yourself," June said in a strained voice.

"I've got to tell you," he said. "I dozed off for a minute in the yard. That must be when he wandered off."

Something flickered up on her face to fade out there. "Asleep?"

"I was happy, I guess," he said, as if he were apologizing. "It was nice out, and I was thinking that you were home again. And Danny was out there playing next to me. I just dropped off."

June's face was all closed up so you couldn't see anything in it. "I understand," she said.

More men kept on coming every hour. An airplane flew over the next day to help guide search parties through the densest part of the woods, although we probably didn't cover more than six square miles altogether. The mosquitoes got worse every time we went in. I thought of Danny's thin jersey almost all the time, but the idea of what must be going through his mind was something I didn't want to think about.

A photographer who had driven up from Minneapolis edged around, taking pictures. He got Dad to stand at the place in the yard where he had first missed Danny. Then he had June pose for him, and somebody brought Marcia out to be in the picture. At the entrance to the woods, the men's feet had worn a heavy band of bootprints into the grass Dad and I had planted. The prints were ground into the earth, and they looked more like huge toothmarks than anything else.

All day long in the woods, the sky had the same color. It appeared in scraps between patches of interlaced branches above our heads, always gray, although the gray had a glow behind it at noon. The brightness behind the sky went away as it got later. It was flat gray just before it turned dark. Old leaves of red and yellow had fallen into the mud where they seemed to be melting into the ground as if they had been chewed. That night was bad, worse than usual, because a mist crept into the trees. And we were so tired by then that it didn't seem worth it to stand in line for food any more, and time passed steadily without any sharp moment. They were all alike.

I was asleep when I heard the pistol shots. When I was on my feet, I heard them again, and the people rushing toward the wood made me certain that it had been no dream. But instead of four, they came two at a time. It was Jackson who suddenly got excited this time.

"Did you hear it?" he shouted at June, although she was beside him.

"Yes," she said. "I heard the shots." But her voice didn't lift to his.

Somewhere near the house, I heard the women start a hymn that was sung at the Lutheran church in Byron City. Men left their cots to dash off into the swamp. I felt a long shudder of relief run through me like a chill.

Jackson was gone when I looked again for him. As I ran toward the balsam trees at the swamp opening, the shouts had died down, and there was only the women's singing and another sound, the heavy breath of Everett Handler beside me.

"I wonder why it was only two shots," he said.

"They add up to four," I told him. "That's the signal."

"But they weren't together."

We moved faster than we ever had, along a trail that had been cleared out by four days of men passing through. Before we had gone half a mile, lights came toward us, and I saw Mr. Cranston and Sherman Blatnik carrying Nap Stoner.

"Nap fired those shots," Mr. Cranston said. "Fell in a bog and maybe broke his leg."

"Go and tell her," Sherman told me. "It was no signal."

Danny would not be found. The hounds followed scents, then lost them again as they trailed off into nothing. It was like looking for something lost inside the house that was there a minute ago, and finally searching places where you knew it couldn't be. They brought in the dogs to rest. Their flews hung down so far it was a wonder their collars didn't choke them. By Wednesday, all the hounds were lame and couldn't keep on. The National Guards started to leave, and when their leader said that Danny couldn't still be alive, he said just what most had been thinking.

Nap Stoner had sprained his ankle when he fell, so Sherman Blatnik took his place and said he would keep on going. The guard members went away because they had done their best while there was the most hope, and people from the resorts began to drift off, too. Once the feeling started to grow, there was no holding it back. As each group slipped away, Dad tried to make them see that Danny was big and strong for his age and dressed in warm enough clothes to keep him alive. Finally, the Byron City group started leaving on Friday, not long after we heard Nap Stoner had pneumonia. They remembered searches for other children who were never found.

Sherman Blatnik told June the men would give up the search by nightfall if they weren't any luckier than they had been up to then. There hadn't been a sign — no discarded jersey or lost shoe fallen in the trailless woods. Although I expected June to speak she didn't but looked at Sherman and nodded. It was Dad, instead, who tried to argue with the men.

"Give it one more day, why don't you?"

"There's no use," Joe Cranston's father said.

"He just wandered off in a minute. He couldn't have gone so far that you could miss him," Dad said. "I just looked away for a couple of seconds."

Dad didn't say any more after that. He just looked from one face to another, searching for something he never seemed to find, because he finally turned away and walked into the house. I'll never forget how strange that red parlor chair looked then, standing alone on the bumpy ground. As he went in, I thought the sky grew darker, dim somehow. When he was gone, Jackson tried to keep the men going.

"We can't stop now," he said. "We'll never know what happened to him if we do. I've got money." It was the first time he mentioned what we all took for granted.

"It wouldn't do any good," Everett Handler said when it seemed that no one at all would answer. "How can you spread any amount of money among so many men?"

"It can be done," Jackson said, but June stopped him.

"No," she said, "they don't ask for pay." Then she looked straight at us, and in spite of the men's talking about her going away from Byron City as she did, they couldn't say she wasn't strong. "It has to be stopped sometime. You can leave now. It won't help to stay for nightfall." I looked at her and expected her to scream out, and I finally wished she would let go, but her face was tight.

Most of them turned for home them. "I've got to get back," Everett said in his gentle voice. "My wife can't handle the drug store alone." His big face was splotchy, and I suppose the week had been harder on him than he ever let on. Four men stayed. Besides myself, there were Jackson, the newspaper photographer, and Sherman Blatnik. I never thought of stopping. I was afraid to, because then I'd imagine how different things would have been if I hadn't gone into town in that fancy Buick. And I had thought I could make it up to him with a little can of brown paint. The others had their reasons clear enough. One had to finish up his job, and the other wanted to show that he wasn't holding what had happened almost ten years ago against anyone. And there was Jackson, who would keep on going as long as he could. But I wondered if the men who weren't with us any longer hadn't been the best of the group. They had stayed all that time, although few of them had ever seen Danny, and though some blamed June for leaving their town.

The sky, drab all day, seemed to draw into itself as we walked toward the woods for the last time. Suddenly something damp was cold against my face, and it was snowing. Hopelessly, we stood and watched the loose, filmy mass come down, sparse at first and then quickening until it spun at us with frantic force. It hung to the shoulders of our coats and began to cover the ground.

"That means it's freezing," Jackson said in a dead voice. "We might as well give up."

Although it was mid-afternoon, the sky turned dark. As I watched Sherman Blatnik and the photographer drive off, the snow slanted down against the road. Nobody was in the yard any more, not even the chair was left.

Jackson went in, and I watched the lights turn on inside our house. He and Dad sat across the room from each other. I saw June touch Dad's shoulder, and she tried to smile. I went in then, and at the doorway I took off my cap and shook it to get off the snow. Some of the flakes had melted already, and I watched one cling to the damp wool, stretch out and hang there before it fell to the floor. That was what losing hope looked like.

(From Today's Woman)

THE CALL

BY BETHEL LAURENCE

*T*HE BELL was ringing. Again. The room was dark, and there seemed to be nothing in it but the swelling of the bell and its reverberations in her body. And then again. And over and over and over again.

She had been asleep when the telephone had begun to ring. She had seemed to recognize it at first in the pit of her stomach and then later with her ears.

Now she began to whimper. She was on her stomach, her elbows bent, her arms pressing against her ears, her body taut and still except for the spasms which shook her middle.

She turned over and sat up in bed. She lifted the strands of short blond hair and removed the little pieces of cotton that had been pushed into her ears. Reaching down, she picked up the quilted satin house coat which lay at the foot of the bed. She pulled it around her tightly, not because she was cold, but because it seemed to offer her protection.

She got up and walked to the telephone. It was just a plain squat red hand phone, yet it seemed to have taken on character. She looked at it and waited, and then she lifted the receiver and said, "Hello."

It was his voice, low and slow and monotonous.

She listened. The first time it happened she had put down the receiver and cut the connection. Now she often thought of cutting him off again, but somehow she always stayed on listening. She never said anything but her initial, "Hello." Even that was unnecessary. He knew who would be there. She knew who would be calling. His last remark she never answered. When he said, "May I come up now, Ann?" she felt the heat flooding her face and the perspiration coming through to the rayon satin house coat. And that was when she would put the receiver down, gently into its cradle.

Tonight was the same. Unhurriedly, quietly, "You are going to die, Ann," he said. "You know that, don't you? It will be very horrible. I would like to tell you more about it." She waited until he had asked his question, "May I come up now, Ann?" and then she clicked the phone, cutting off the sound of him, yet still hearing him because the words were there, familiarly clinging to her like the perspiration on the house coat.

She started to walk toward the door and then she thought, No, I won't do it. I won't try the lock again. I've tried it four times and I know that it is locked and I won't indulge myself again.

She went to the wall and started to press the light switch, and then she thought, No, I won't do that either. He might be standing out there on the street, waiting to identify the apartment, attempting to spy on me. She wanted to creep to the window and peer out into the narrow, gray, only half-illumined street of Greenwich Village to see if he really might be waiting there, but she was afraid that a flashlight might flare up from the street below onto her face. So she went to the sofa, the one that did not open into a bed, and she sat there in the dark, shivering in her heat.

She tried not to think of the things he had said, but the words were swarming all over her. For the hundredth time she tried to imagine — who was this man? And why was he calling her? What did it mean? And why was it happening? And then again and again she tried to tell herself that no, it was not true; she was not growing mad.

"*You are going to die,*" the words had said.

And there was no one but her to hear them. No one to swear that they were being said, to share their terrible secrecy or to help her if they were true.

She got up and walked back to bed. She lay there, still thinking of his words until the imagined sound of the telephone drowned them out and then the words surged back, drowning out the telephone. Then she turned over on her stomach and pressed her palms deep, deeper, into the flesh of her ears.

When the light came in through the window next morning, she got up and went to the end of the room and closed the window without looking out. She fixed her breakfast and began to dress; then she went to the telephone and called her office and told them that she would be an hour late for work that morning. She was nervous and she knew it, and she had a sore spot in her stomach where her excitement had concentrated and her girdle now pressed against it and antagonized it.

She was dressed in her light blue suit; it was sleek and fitted, a Sunday suit, but she thought that wearing it might help to assuage her nervousness. She pulled the comb tightly through her short blond hair, trying to force into place the curls that she had ruffled through the night. Her blue eyes looked deeper for lack of sleep, and the usually perfect bow of her mouth had a jagged rise where her hand had slipped with the lipstick. She erased and redrew it as best she could, and then she walked outside, down to the street.

She walked two blocks, turning off into a little side street where she entered a door and stood by a high counter until a man in police uniform came up and asked her what she wanted.

Her chest was constricted as though she were about to tell a lie.

"Lafferty," she said. "Detective Lafferty."

A short man with a round face and a rounded stomach came out. All of his features were round and even his hands gave that effect.

"Yes?" he said.

"Lieutenant Lafferty," she began, "I'm Miss Mason. I've spoken to you on the telephone."

He looked at her blankly. "Yes? Won't you come in?"

She followed him through a hallway into a smaller room and sat down on a chair next to a desk.

"Now, what was it about?" he asked.

She sat straight, her feet in a line, her knees strained together. "I live down here in the Village," she said. "Just two blocks away. I telephoned you a couple of weeks ago about some phone calls I've been receiving. Don't you remember?"

His face looked undecided.

"Threats," she said. "No, not threats exactly. Information. I am going to die." Small circles of moisture appeared on her face. "A man keeps calling up and saying I am going to die. At all hours of the night."

"Ah, yes," he said, "I remember which one you are now."

She held her eyes down as though afraid he might ask her to repeat what she had just found so difficult to say.

"So he's still calling?"

"Yes. He is."

"Well —" He moved toward the chair facing the desk. He sat down on it. "I'll tell you frankly, Miss Mason, there is very little we can do about it."

She rubbed her hands against the soft leather of her purse.

"We have several similar cases right now, but our hands are rather tied on them." He swung his chair around, confronting her. "You see, unfortunately with these dial phones, the connection is broken the minute he hangs up, so there is no way of tracing the call."

She nodded her head and looked at her nail marks on the leather bag.

"However, there are several things that I might suggest." He twisted a pencil slowly between his fingers. "One is that you simply ignore the phone at these hours. That would be the simplest method. Nerve racking, maybe — but simple."

"I know," she said. "I've thought of that. But you see, Lieutenant, I have a sister who lives in Wilmington. She's very ill. They might call me at any time. I keep thinking, this may be the time. And then I have to get up and answer that telephone."

"Oh, I see." There was a long pause. He switched the pencil to the other hand. "Miss Mason," he said, eyeing her speculatively from behind the point of the pencil, "before we go any further with this case, there is one thing which we must ascertain. Are you absolutely positive that you don't know who this man could be?"

"Oh, yes. Yes, I am."

"Are you absolutely positive that no one, to your knowledge, would want you to die?"

"Oh, yes. Yes, I swear it!"

His eyes rested on her again for a second. "You're an extremely attractive young woman. It's not unlikely that you would have — admirers — jealousy, no doubt —"

"I'm afraid you don't understand, Lieutenant." She leaned forward, clutching the purse. "I'm fairly new in town. It's not easy meeting young men in a city so large." She tried to keep the regret from creeping into her voice. "No. I'm afraid there is no love life. No complications."

His right eyebrow lifted higher than his left.

"I know what you're thinking." The small circles of moisture spread into one large pool on her face. "But I wouldn't be fool enough to lie to you, Lieutenant, when I'm so very frightened."

"Very well." He seemed satisfied now. "Then I still think as I did before that you're the victim of some prankster. I can only tell you this — it is not uncommon. Single women, Miss Mason, who are listed in the phone book like that, are quite often the target of calls from jokesters, cranks and lunatics. In practically none of these cases would the offenders actually resort to any form of action. They're simply telephone-happy, you might say. It's unfortunate — but true, and we're in a bad spot with them. We get hundreds of these cases. . . ."

"Well, that isn't very satisfactory," she said, "when you're the target."

"On the other hand, it isn't entirely hopeless. There are several things I might suggest. One is that you get a friend to stay with you. Arrange with a neighbor to get into their apartment. When he calls you, hold him on the phone, get the friend to call here on the other phone and we can check into the conversation and trace it back."

She held her purse in front of her hands to conceal the fact that they were quivering. "That would be awfully complicated," she said. "I don't know if I could arrange it."

"Well, we could give you another number and keep you out of the book, a silent number, known only to your friends."

"But Lieutenant," she said, "practically the only friends I have are from out of town. They come to town and try to call me. No one could ever reach me then."

He shrugged his shoulders.

". . . And besides, Lieutenant —" She leaned toward him. "All of these things. He should be punished. He —" She stopped and caught her breath; then she spoke a little more slowly. "What I'm trying to say is, after all, if this man has my telephone number he also has my address. He might be lurking outside my door. He might actually be planning on killing me. The very least he's trying to do is to drive me out of my mind! The very least —"

The detective stared at her for a minute. "Well, there's only one way I know of catching him, Miss Mason." He stopped twirling the pencil. "And that might be very difficult. It would require a lot of co-operation on your part and a lot of —" He stopped himself. "Shall we say — courage, Miss Mason?" He smiled. "That's it, courage."

She looked at him.

"That would require your asking the man to come up to your apartment the next time he asks you. Then telephone me immediately. I promise to get there right away."

Her lips parted, showing her teeth.

"If I'm not here, the other man will come. I'll leave instructions. In all probability the man has no intentions whatsoever of actually coming. And certainly not of killing you. This will simply scare him away for good. In any event, we're only two blocks away. Even if he's right across the street from you, not much could happen in that length of time."

Her lips parted farther.

"At any rate," he told her, "this is all I can suggest. We have no other method of coping with the thing. Of course, it requires a lot of — did we say, courage, Miss Mason? — to handle the situation. Do you think that you could handle it, Miss Mason?"

Her nails dug deeper into the leather bag. "I — I don't know. I don't know if I could go through with it or not. I'm afraid." She stood up. "I could try though. I could always try. I'll have to think about it though. I could let you know."

She held out her hand. "Thank you very much. You'll hear from me. You'll surely hear from me." She started out the door. Then she turned back. "Leiutenant," she said. "You'll be there? Or the other gentleman? You'll surely be there? You won't leave me stranded?"

He smiled. "I promise you, Miss Mason. I can promise you that."

"All right," she said. "Good-by, Lieutenant." She went out the door.

The room was still that night. He didn't call. But she slept almost as poorly as if he had. She lay in the bed and waited for him. But the next night she fell asleep after midnight, and that was when he called.

She heard the ringing of the telephone and she put on her house coat and went to answer it. She held the instrument to her ear and listened. She waited until he said, "May I come up now, Ann?" Her lips parted loosely and so did her teeth. But she couldn't speak, she couldn't form the words. She hung up without asking him.

She went back to the bed and she lay there thinking how fortunate it was for her that she hadn't been able to ask him. For you never could tell what might have happened. She shuddered and covered her eyes and tried not to imagine what might have happened. She felt sick with fear and revulsion and the horrible loneliness of having even your aloneness threatened.

Three nights passed before he called again. Each night she sat up and waited for him, not even making the studio couch into a bed, just sitting up with her clothes on, sometimes making herself a spiked cup of tea, sometimes knitting on a sweater, but most of the time just sitting there, waiting for the telephone to ring.

By the time she lifted the receiver on the third night, she was almost anxious to speak with him. She had cleared her throat before going to the telephone. When he said, "May I come up now, Ann?" she hesitated, and then said, "Yes." There was not a normal amount of voice there, but there was enough to be audible. He didn't say anything.

He just hung up. The conversation on his part was no different from usual. The entire conversation had been no different from usual, except that she had said, "Yes," in a voice fairly audible.

The detective's number was written on a slip of paper beside the telephone and she dialed the number and told him what had happened. Then she went into the dressing room to put away the pearl brooch that her mother had left to her. Her hands were restless and seeking for action, so she went into the bathroom to wash out some clothes. And all the while she was thinking, He won't come. He certainly will never come. He certainly doesn't intend to come here.

There was a knock at the door, a soft, considerate knock. She wasn't sure that she had really heard it. She turned off the water. There was a knock again. She put the undergarments, still dry, back into the hamper, closed the lid and put the soap flakes and scouring powder back into place. She went toward the door, starting to turn around, wanting to run back to the bathroom and lock herself in.

She walked into the foyer and opened the door.

He was standing there.

She thought, It isn't too late. I could still slam the door. And then she looked up at the boy. He was tall, very tall, and young. He was under thirty, just a few years older than she. His nose turned up; it was childish, undeveloped. His hair waved nicely. He had no particular coloring in either his eyes or his hair or his skin. His mouth was wide and fleshy. It didn't seem possible to her that he could have spoken the way he did until she looked at the deep fleshiness of his lips, and then she could picture the voice coming out of them and the words running over them.

"Won't you come in?" she said.

He walked through the doorway.

"Won't you sit down?" she said.

He looked around the living room, and then he sat down on the studio couch that opened into a bed.

She sat on the chair opposite him, nearer the door.

"The buzzer," she said. "It didn't buzz from downstairs. How did you get in?"

"Oh, a lady let me in. She had her key, so she let me in with her. She said I had an honest face."

She smiled and then stopped quickly, staring at his face. "What's your name?" she asked him.

"George."

Her head felt light, light as paper. "George," she repeated.

"That's right." He smiled at her. The smile was young, even younger than his face; his voice was more alive than it had been on the telephone. She began to wonder if perhaps this were the wrong boy; if perhaps he had been sent by someone else.

"You didn't think I would come?" he asked.

"No. No, I —"

"I almost didn't. It was Arthur," he said.

"Arthur? Arthur?" She relaxed a little against the back of the chair. Then there actually had been some other person; George was not altogether responsible. Perhaps he was not responsible at all. This made it easier, somehow, to be in the same room with him. For it was Arthur, the unseen, who was at the root of all this. Her mind was fuzzy and confused, and yet it seemed right that it should not be this boy. It was the unknown Arthur with whom she had to contend. She sat there watching him, surprised at herself for thinking at a time like this that perhaps if he were just a boy, a nice boy whom she had met at a party or somewhere. . . .

"That's right." He gazed at her; he seemed to be admiring her.

"You're a very attractive girl," he said, "to be living here all alone —"

The room was warm and she didn't want to walk past him to open the window. She rubbed her hands together. "I — I don't understand," she said. "This — Arthur? And you . . . you don't look . . . that is, you don't act — I don't understand," she said.

"Perhaps I could explain."

"Yes!" Her whole face was eager. She leaned forward, waiting. For now there would follow, of course, some logical explanation. She had the same feeling of relief which she sometimes experienced while trying to awaken herself from a dream. Knowing that there was, after all, some goal of reality, some reasonable escape, if only she could pull hard enough.

"Yes," she was saying. "Yes! Perhaps you could. Please. Please explain."

He grinned at her again.

Her body was stretching toward him. "You didn't really say those things? It wasn't really you?"

"Well —"

"You'll have to talk faster. We haven't got all night."

He crossed his legs, still grinning. "Why not? I figure we have."

"No." She sat back. "No. You'll have to take my word for it. You'll just have —

His eyes distended. He jumped up. "I get it. I'll be going." He headed for the door.

"No!"

He stopped and turned toward her, holding out his hand. "Then give me the keys."

"No. It isn't that. The door's not locked." She could see the door keys with the string upon them, lying, as they always lay when she was home, on the table nearest the door. "It's just that —" She stood up. "If you go now, there's sure to be trouble. But if you stay —" She walked toward him. "If you *really* weren't the one who said those things, if you could explain, then maybe I — I —"

There was movement in his eyes, in his body, back and forth, from her to the door.

His face relaxed. "To tell the truth," he said, "it would be darn silly for me to run away. I haven't anything to hide. And if I run away, they might think I have. But this way, I can explain."

"Yes." Her breathing was lighter. "I'm sure you can."

He walked back to his chair.

The buzzer was buzzing. For the downstairs door. She remembered then that she had not told the detective about that downstairs door; she had forgotten to give him the key.

There was no color in the boy's face except for a red spot on each cheek where the blood had gathered. He sat down slowly on the edge of one of the chairs.

"Honestly, Miss Mason," he said. "Arthur, he's my roommate, he and I just pulled this thing as sort of a lark." His eyes moved to hers. "You'll have to believe that. We didn't stop to think that maybe you'd take it seriously and call the cops and all. We —"

"Oh." Her breathing was still light. "Then it wasn't you. It was Arthur I spoke to. I'm so glad."

"You see, when we got back from the Army things were —"

"Oh, you were in the Army."

"Yes." He moved forward, covering less of the seat. "Well, things were pretty dull around here, and then one night we were sitting around and talking about psychology and people going mad and things like that. And Arthur said, why anybody could drive anybody mad. It was very simple. Fear, he said. Fear could drive anybody mad. Fear of death. I said that it was a lot of tommyrot and Arthur said that he could prove it. 'Take anybody,' he said. 'Take —' "

The buzzer buzzed again.

George turned to look at the button on the wall. "And then we picked you out of the phone book and —"

She was staring at his face. Very carefully. Then she got up and went over to the wall and pressed the buzzer.

"But honestly, Miss Mason — Ann," he said. He followed her. "We didn't mean any harm by it. Honestly." He touched her on the shoulder. "I didn't think that it would really hurt anybody. And Arthur seemed to get such a big bang out of it. We were buddies in the Army and —"

"It's nice you were in the Army," she said.

He looked down at her, his head cocked to one side, his eyebrows lifted, his eyes searching. "It will never happen again. Please believe me," he said. He held up his right hand. "Before God," he said.

She stood there watching him, surprised at herself for thinking at a time like this that perhaps if he were just a boy, a nice boy whom she had met at a party or somewhere. . . .

There was a knock at the door.

She met his eyes and they looked straight down, studying her.

"Before God," he whispered.

She took his hand and led him into the bathroom and then went through the foyer and opened the door.

Lieutenant Lafferty was standing there; she had hoped it might be the other detective. He was breathing hard. "What happened?" he said.

"Oh, I — I was — was —" she waved her fingers. "Indisposed," she said.

He glanced around the room, "Where is he?"

"He?" She looked at the detective's round fat stomach and she thought how silly to be afraid of a man with a comedian's stomach. "Oh, he didn't come. You were right about it."

The detective turned and stared at her. The blood flowed in waves through her body. "He'll never come now. I'm sure he won't," she said.

He tapped his hat against his knee. "Well, maybe he'll come later. Maybe he hasn't got here yet. I'd better stick around."

"Oh, no. No!" She could hear her heart pounding. "I'm sure he's not coming. He said five minutes. He said, 'I'll be up in five minutes.' So I'm sure he's not coming."

"Well, as long as I'm here —"

"No. Please." She was walking him back to the door. "I'm tired and I'm nervous and I do want to go to bed. I'm beginning to feel ill.

Nothing can happen now, I'm sure. Good night, Lieutenant, and thank you very, very much." She held out her hand.

"All right, Miss Mason. Good night. I'll stick around outside for a few minutes to see that everything is all right, and then I'll phone you when I get back to the station. I'm glad that fellow turned out to be a false alarm for your sake. Get some rest now."

He went out, putting on his hat.

She waited until she heard him getting into the elevator, and then she went to the door of the bathroom. "You can come out now, George," she said.

The door to the bathroom opened and George walked toward her.

"You'd better leave," she told him.

"All right," he said, "if that's the way you want it."

He stood there.

"You'd better leave," she said again. "The detective is going to call in five minutes; I want to be telling the truth when I say you're not here. I've lied enough for you tonight." She was suddenly drained and exhausted by the encounter; even conversation was an effort.

"Sure thing," he said. He walked toward the door and she put her head in her hands in relief. "I don't want to bother you any more," he said. "Especially after you've been so swell."

She followed slowly behind him.

When he got to the door, he turned around. "I don't know what to say, Ann. Except that it really was swell of you. And we certainly didn't mean any harm. You see, you'll have to try and understand. It's just Arthur's ego or something. He seems to have this feeling that he has an unusual influence on people, and then he just has to try it out every once in awhile." His hand was on the knob. "And you know, in a way, he has. I didn't really want to come here tonight and then, all of a sudden, he had me really wanting to come. Arthur is like that."

"Well," she said uneasily. "Well."

"Anyway, I'd like you to know that we do appreciate what you've just done. I — I'd like to apologize for both of us, for the trouble we've caused you, and to assure you that it certainly won't happen again. I —" He stood there for a minute. "I guess I really don't know what else to say." He held out his hand. She took it and felt it and then let it go again.

She leaned against the door. "Good night, George."

"Good night, Ann."

He went out.

She waited to hear the latch click before she turned and walked away.

She sat down on the couch and supported her head against the pillows; then she got up and took the pillows off and started making the couch into a bed.

The phone rang and it was the Lieutenant. "He's not here," she told him. "Thanks for your concern. I think that this will be the end of him now. Thanks again, Lieutenant. Good night."

She finished making the bed and climbed into it without even cleansing her face. Her body was limp; she was too tired to think of the boy and talking to him had somehow taken the meaning from the calls and the words.

It was all over now, the fright and the feeling of helplessness and the nagging, insidious awareness that she was slowly losing her reason. She could forget the whole thing now. The telephone calls soon would become no more than an incident, relegated to the back of her mind, remembered only occasionally. They would be nothing much then, just items from storage, something to be looked at and wondered at and then put back into place.

She felt relaxed and comforted and she fell asleep like that.

When she awakened it was still dark and the air lay lethargically over the room. There was the sharp, clear sound of a mouse or of a key scraping against a lock. She listened, not quite believing. Then she raised her spine to the pillow and her hand shot forward and turned on the lamp beside the bed. Her eyes sought out the table where the key — the door keys with the string — had lain.

There was an ash tray there and the smooth surface of the wood and the shine of yesterday's polish. And nothing more. . . .

Her arms fell limply back to the bed and her back crouched against her arms, and she lay like that in frozen silence, her eyes bulging with terror, watching the door as it began slowly to move toward her.

(*From Harper's Magazine*)

CYCLISTS' RAID

BY FRANK ROONEY

*J*OEL BLEEKER, owner and operator of the Pendleton Hotel, was adjusting the old redwood clock in the lobby when he heard the sound of the motors. At first he thought it might be one of those four-engine planes on the flights from Los Angeles to San Francisco which occasionally got far enough off course to be heard in the valley. And for a moment, braced against the steadily approaching vibrations of the sound, he had the fantastic notion that the plane was going to strike the hotel. He even glanced at his daughter, Cathy, standing a few feet to his right and staring curiously at the street.

Then with his fingers still on the hour hand of the clock he realized that the sound was not something coming down from the air but the high, sputtering racket of many vehicles moving along the ground. Cathy and Bret Timmons, who owned one of the two drugstores in the town, went out onto the veranda but Bleeker stayed by the clock, consulting the railroad watch he pulled from his vest pocket and moving the hour hand on the clock forward a minute and a half. He stepped back deliberately, shut the glass case and looked at the huge brass numbers and the two ornate brass pointers. It was eight minutes after seven, approximately twenty-two minutes until sundown. He put the railroad watch back in his pocket and walked slowly and incuriously through the open doors of the lobby. He was methodical and orderly and the small things he did every day — like setting the clock — were important to him. He was not to be hurried — especially by something as elusively irritating as a sound, however unusual.

There were only three people on the veranda when Bleeker came out of the lobby — his daughter Cathy, Timmons, and Francis LaSalle, co-owner of LaSalle and Fleet, Hardware. They stood together quietly, looking, without appearing to stare, at a long stern column of red motorcycles coming from the south, filling the single main street of the town with the noise of a multitude of pistons and the crackling of exhaust pipes. They could see now that the column was led by a single white motorcycle which when it came abreast of the hotel turned abruptly right and stopped. They saw too that the column without seeming to slow down or to execute any elaborate movement had divided itself into two single files. At the approximate second, having received a signal from their leader, they also turned right and stopped.

The whole flanking action, singularly neat and quite like the various vehicular formations he remembered in the Army, was distasteful to Bleeker. It recalled a little too readily his tenure as a lieutenant colonel overseas in England, France, and finally Germany.

"Mr. Bleeker?"

Bleeker realized the whole troop — no one in the town either then or after that night was ever agreed on the exact number of men in the troop — had dismounted and that the leader was addressing him.

"I'm Bleeker." Although he hadn't intended to, he stepped forward when he spoke, much as he had stepped forward in the years when he commanded a battalion.

"I'm Gar Simpson and this is Troop B of the Angeleno Motorcycle Club," the leader said. He was a tall spare man and his voice was coldly courteous to the point of mockery. "We expect to bivouac outside your town tonight and we wondered if we might use the facilities of your hotel. Of course, sir, we'll pay."

"There's a washroom downstairs. If you can put up with that —"

"That will be fine, sir. Is the dining room still open?"

"It is."

"Could you take care of twenty men?"

"What about the others?"

"They can be accommodated elsewhere, sir."

Simpson saluted casually and, turning to the men assembled stiffly in front of the hotel, issued a few quiet orders. Quickly and efficiently, the men in the troop parked their motorcycles at the curb. About a third of the group detached itself and came deferentially but steadily up the hotel steps. They passed Bleeker who found himself maneuvered aside and went into the lobby. As they passed him, Bleeker could see the slight converted movement of their faces — though not their eyes, which were covered by large green goggles — toward his daughter Cathy. Bleeker frowned after them but before he could think of anything to say, Simpson, standing now at his left, touched his arm.

"I've divided the others into two groups," he said quietly. "One group will eat at the diner and the other at the Desert Hotel."

"Very good," Bleeker said. "You evidently know the town like a book. The people too. Have you ever been here before?"

"We have a map of all the towns in this part of California, sir. And of course we know the names of all the principal hotels and their proprietors. Personally, I could use a drink. Would you join me?"

"After you," Bleeker said.

He stood watching Simpson stride into the lobby and without any hesitation go directly to the bar. Then he turned to Cathy, seeing Timmons and LaSalle lounging on the railing behind her, their faces already indistinct in the plummeting California twilight.

"You go help in the kitchen, Cathy," Bleeker said. "I think it'd be better if you didn't wait on tables."

"I wonder what they look like behind those goggles," Cathy siad.

"Like anybody else," Timmons said. He was about thirty, somewhat coarse and intolerant and a little embarrassed at being in love with a girl as young as Cathy. "Where did you think they came from? Mars?"

"What did they say the name of their club was?" Cathy said.

"Angclcno," LaSalle said.

"'They must be from Los Angeles. Heigh-ho. Shall I wear my very best gingham, citizen colonel?"

"Remember now — you stay in the kitchen," Bleeker said.

He watched her walk into the lobby, a tall slender girl of seventeen, pretty and enigmatic, with something of the brittle independence of her mother. Bleeker remembered suddenly, although he tried not to, the way her mother had walked away from him that frosty January morning two years ago saying, "I'm going for a ride." And then the two-day search in the mountains after the horse had come back alone and the finding of her body — the neck broken — in the stream at the foot of the cliff. During the war he had never really believed that he would live to get back to Cathy's mother and after the war he hadn't really believed he would be separated from her — not again — not twice in so short a time.

Shaking his head — as if by that motion he could shed his memories as easily as a dog sheds water — Bleeker went in to join Gar Simpson who was sitting at a table in the barroom. Simpson stood politely when Bleeker took the opposite chair.

"How long do you fellows plan to stay?" Bleeker asked. He took the first sip of his drink, looked up, and stared at Simpson.

"Tonight and tomorrow morning," Simpson said.

Like all the others he was dressed in a brown windbreaker, khaki shirt, khaki pants, and as Bleeker had previously observed wore dark calf-length boots. A cloth and leather helmet lay on the table beside Simpson's drink, but he hadn't removed his flat green goggles, an accouterment giving him and the men in his troop the appearance of some tropical tribe with enormous semi-precious eyes, lidless and immovable. That was Bleeker's first impression and, absurd as it was, it didn't seem an exaggeration of fancy but of truth.

"Where do you go after this?"

"North." Simpson took a rolled map from a binocular case slung over his shoulder and spread it on the table. "Roughly we're following the arc of an ellipse with its southern tip based on Los Angeles and its northern end touching Fresno.

"Pretty ambitious for a motorcycle club."

"We have a month," Simpson said. "This is our first week but we're in no hurry and we're out to see plenty of country."

"What are you interested in mainly?"

"Roads. Naturally, being a motorcycle club — you'd be surprised at the rate we're expanding — we'd like to have as much of California as possible opened up to us."

"I see."

"Keeps the boys fit too. The youth of America. Our hope for the future." Simpson pulled sternly at his drink and Bleeker had the impression that Simpson was repressing, openly, and with pride, a vast sparkling ecstasy

Bleeker sat and watched the young men in the troop file upstairs from the public washroom and stroll casually but nevertheless with discipline into the dining room. They had removed their helmets and strapped them to their belts, each helmet in a prescribed position to the left of the belt-buckle but — like Simpson — they had retained their goggles. Bleeker wondered if they ever removed the goggles long enough to wash under them and, if they did, what the flesh under them looked like. "I think I'd better help out at the tables," Bleeker said. He stood up and Simpson stood with him. "You say you're from Troop B? Is that right?"

"Correct. We're forming Troop G now. Someday —"

"You'll be up to Z," Bleeker said.

"And not only in California."

"Where else for instance?"

"Nevada — Arizona — Colorado — Wyoming."

Simpson smiled and Bleeker, turning away from him abruptly, went into the dining room where he began to help the two waitresses at the tables. He filled water glasses, set out extra forks, and brought steins of beer from the bar. As he served the troop, their polite thank yous, ornate and insincere, irritated him. It reminded him of tricks taught to animals, the animals only being allowed to perform under certain obvious conditions of security. And he didn't like the cool way they stared at the two waitresses, both older women and fixtures in the town, and then leaned their heads together as if every individual thought had to be pooled and divided equally among them. He admitted, after some covert study, that the twenty men were really only variations of one, the variations, with few exceptions, being too subtle for him to recognize and differentiate. It was the goggles, he decided, covering that part of the face which is most noteworthy and most needful for identification — the eyes and the mask around the eyes.

Bleeker went into the kitchen, pretending to help but really to be near Cathy. The protective father, he thought ironically, watching his daughter cut pie and lay the various colored wedges on the white blue-bordered plates.

"Well, Daddy, what's the verdict?" Cathy looked extremely grave but he could see that she was amused.

"They're a fine body of men."

"Uh-huh. Have you called the police yet?"

He laughed. "It's a good thing you don't play poker."

"Child's play." She slid the last piece of blueberry pie on a plate. "I saw you through the door. You looked like you were ready to crack the Siegfried line — single-handed."

"That man Simpson."

"What about him?"

"Why don't you go upstairs and read a book or something?"

"Now, Daddy — you're the only professional here. They're just acting like little tin soldiers out on a spree."

"I wish to God they were made of tin."

"All right. I'll keep away from them. I promise." She made a gesture of crossing her throat with the thin edge of a knife. He leaned over and kissed her forehead, his hand feeling awkward and stern on her back.

After dinner the troop went into the bar, moving with a strange co-ordinated fluency that was both casual and military and sat jealously together in one corner of the room. Bleeker served them pitchers of beer and for the most part they talked quietly together, Simpson at their center, their voices guarded and urgent as if they possessed information which couldn't be disseminated safely among the public.

Bleeker left them after a while and went upstairs to his daughter's room. He wasn't used to being severe with Cathy and he was a little embarrassed by what he had said to her in the kitchen. She was turning the collars of some of his old shirts, using a portable sewing machine he had bought her as a present on her last birthday. As he came in she held one of the shirts comically to the floor lamp and he could see how thin and transparent the material was. Her mother's economy in small things, almost absurd when compared to her limitless generosity in matters of importance, had been one of the family jokes. It gave him an extraordinary sense of pleasure, so pure it was like a sudden inhalation of oxygen, to see that his daughter had not only inherited this tradition but had considered it meaningful enough to carry on. He went down the hall to his own room without saying anything further to her. Cathy was what he himself was in terms which could mean absolutely nothing to anyone else.

He had been in his room for perhaps an hour, working on the hotel accounts and thinking obliquely of the man Simpson, when he heard, faintly and apparently coming from no one direction, the sound of singing. He got up and walked to the windows overlooking the street. Standing there, he thought he could fix the sound farther up the block toward Cunningham's bar. Except for something harsh and mature in the voices it was the kind of singing that might be heard around a Boy Scout campfire, more rhythmic than melodic and more stirring than tuneful. And then he could hear it almost under his feet, coming out of the hotel lobby and making three or four people on the street turn and smile foolishly toward the doors of the veranda.

Oppressed by something sternly joyous in the voices, Bleeker went downstairs to the bar, hearing as he approached the singing become louder and fuller. Outside of Simpson and the twenty men in the troop there were only three townsmen — including LaSalle — in the bar. Simpson, seeing Bleeker in the door, got up and walked over to him, moving him out into the lobby where they could talk.

"I hope the boys aren't disturbing you," he said.

"It's early," Bleeker said.

"In an organization as large and selective as ours it's absolutely necessary to insist on a measure of discipline. And it's equally necessary to allow a certain amount of relaxation."

"The key word is selective, I suppose."

"We have our standards," Simpson said primly.

"May I ask just what the hell your standards are?"

Simpson smiled. "I don't quite understand your irritation, Mr. Bleeker."

"This is an all-year-round thing, isn't it? This club of yours?"

"Yes."

"And you have an all-year-round job with the club?"

"Of course."

"That's my objection, Simpson. Briefly and simply stated, what you're running is a private army." Bleeker tapped the case slung over Simpson's shoulder. "Complete with maps, all sorts of local information, and of course a lobby in Sacramento."

"For a man who has traveled as widely as you have, Mr. Bleeker, you display an uncommon talent for exaggeration."

"As long as you behave yourselves I don't care what you do. This is a small town and we don't have many means of entertainment. We go to bed at a decent hour and I suggest you take that into consideration. However, have your fun. Nobody here has any objections to that."

"And of course we spend our money."

"Yes," Bleeker said. "You spend your money."

He walked away from Simpson and went out onto the veranda. The singing was now both in front and in back of him. Bleeker stood for a moment on the top steps of the veranda looking at the moon, hung like a slightly soiled but luminous pennant in the sky. He was embarrassed by his outburst to Simpson and he couldn't think why he had said such things. Private army. Perhaps, as Simpson had said, he was exaggerating. He was a small-town man and he had always hated the way men surrender their individuality to attain perfection as a unit. It had been necessary during the war but it wasn't necessary now. Kid stuff — with an element of growing pains.

He walked down the steps and went up the sidewalk toward Cunningham's bar. They were singing there too and he stood outside the big plate-glass window peering in at them and listening to the harsh, pounding voices colored here and there with the sentimentalism of strong beer. Without thinking further he went into the bar. It was

dim and cool and alien to his eyes and at first he didn't notice the boy
sitting by himself in a booth near the front. When he did, he was surprised — more than surprised, shocked — to see that the boy wasn't
wearing his goggles but had placed them on the table by a bottle of
Coco-Cola. Impulsively, he walked over to the booth and sat across
from the boy.

"This seat taken?"

He had to shout over the noise of the singing. The boy leaned forward over the table and smiled.

"Hope we're not disturbing you."

Bleeker caught the word "disturbing" and shook his head negatively.
He pointed to his mouth, then to the boy and to the rest of the group.
The boy too shook his head. Bleeker could see that he was young, possibly twenty-five, and that he had dark straight hair cut short and
parted neatly at the side. The face was square but delicate, the nose
short, the mouth wide. The best thing about the boy, Bleeker decided,
were his eyes, brown perhaps or dark gray, set in two distorted ovals of
white flesh which contrasted sharply with the heavily tanned skin on
the cheeks, forehead and jaws. With his goggles on he would have
looked like the rest. Without them he was a pleasant young man, altogether human and approachable.

Bleeker pointed to the Coca-Cola bottle. "You're not drinking."

"Beer makes me sick."

Bleeker got the word "beer" and the humorous gulping motion the
boy made. They sat exchanging words and sometimes phrases, illustrated always with a series of clumsy, groping gestures until the singing
became less coherent and spirited and ended finally in a few isolated
coughs. The men in the troop were moving about individually now,
some leaning over the bar and talking in hoarse whispers to the bartender, others walking unsteadily from group to group and detaching
themselves immediately to go over to another group, the groups usually
two or three men constantly edging away from themselves and colliding
with and being held briefly by others. Some simply stood in the center
of the room and brayed dolorously at the ceiling.

Several of the troop walked out of the bar and Bleeker could see them
standing on the wide sidewalk looking up and down the street — as
contemptuous of one another's company as they had been glad of it
earlier. Or not so much contemptuous as unwilling to be coerced too
easily by any authority outside themselves. Bleeker smiled as he
thought of Simpson and the man's talk of discipline.

"They're looking for women," the boy said. Bleeker had forgotten the boy temporarily and the sudden words spoken in a normal voice startled and confused him. He thought quickly of Cathy — but then Cathy was safe in her room — probably in bed. He took the watch from his vest pocket and looked at it carefully.

"Five minutes after ten," he said.

"Why do they do that?" the boy demanded. "Why do they have to be so damned indecent about things like that? They haven't got the nerve to do anything but stare at waitresses. And then they get a few beers in them and go around pinching and slapping — they —"

Bleeker shivered with embarrassment. He was looking directly into the boy's eyes and seeing the color run under the tears and the jerky pinching movement of the lids as against something injurious and baleful. It was an emotion too rawly infantile to be seen without being hurt by it and he felt both pity and contempt for a man who would allow himself to display such a feeling — without any provocation — so nakedly to a stranger.

"Sorry," the boy said.

He picked up the green goggles and fitted them awkwardly over his eyes. Bleeker stood up and looked toward the center of the room. Several of the men turned their eyes and then moved their heads away without seeming to notice the boy in the booth. Bleeker understood them. This was the one who could be approached. The reason for that was clear too. He didn't belong. Why and wherefore he would never know.

He walked out of the bar and started down the street toward the hotel. The night was clear and cool and smelled faintly of the desert, of sand, of heated rock, of the sweetly-sour plants growing without water and even of the sun which burned itself into the earth and never completely withdrew. There were only a few townsmen on the sidewalk wandering up and down, lured by the presence of something unusual in the town and masking, Bleeker thought, a ruthless and menacing curiosity behind a tolerant grin. He shrugged his shoulders distastefully. He was like a cat staring into a shadow the shape of its fears.

He was no more than a hundred feet from the hotel when he heard — or thought he heard — the sound of automatic firing. It was a well-remembered sound but always new and frightening.

Then he saw the motorcycle moving down the middle of the street, the exhaust sputtering loudly against the human resonance of laughter, catcalls, and epithets. He exhaled gently, the pain in his lungs subsiding with his breath. Another motorcycle speeded after the first and he could see four or five machines being wheeled out and the figures of their riders leaping into the air and bringing their weight down on the starting pedals. He was aware too that the lead motorcycles, having traversed the length of the street had turned and were speeding back to the hotel. He had the sensation of moving — even when he stood still — in relation to the objects heading toward each other. He heard the high unendurable sound of metal squeezing metal and saw the front wheel of a motorcycle twist and wobble and its rider roll along the asphalt toward the gutter where he sat up finally and moved his goggled head feebly from side to side.

As Bleeker looked around him he saw the third group of men which had divided earlier from the other two coming out of a bar across the street from Cunningham's, waving their arms in recognizable motions of cheering. The boy who had been thrown from the motorcycle vomited quietly into the gutter. Bleeker walked very fast toward the hotel. When he reached the top step of the veranda, he was caught and jostled by some five or six cyclists running out of the lobby, one of whom fell and was kicked rudely down the steps. Bleeker staggered against one of the pillars and broke a fingernail catching it. He stood there for a moment, fighting his temper, and then went into the lobby.

A table had been overthrown and lay on its top, the wooden legs stiffly and foolishly exposed, its magazines scattered around it, some with their pages spread face down so that the bindings rose along the back. He stepped on glass and realized one of the panes in the lobby door had been smashed. One of the troop walked stupidly out of the bar, his body sagging against the impetus propelling him forward until without actually falling he lay stretched on the floor, beer gushing from his mouth and nose and making a green and yellow pool before it sank into the carpet.

As Bleeker walked toward the bar, thinking of Simpson and of what he could say to him, he saw two men going up the stairs toward the second floor. He ran over to intercept them. Recognizing the authority in his voice, they came obediently down the stairs and walked across the lobby to the veranda, one of them saying over his shoulder, "Okay, pop, okay — keep your lid on." The smile they exchanged enraged him. After they were out of sight he ran swiftly up the stairs, panting a little, and along the hall to his daughter's room.

It was quiet and there was no strip of light beneath the door. He stood listening for a moment with his ear to the panels and then turned back toward the stairs.

A man or boy, any of twenty or forty or sixty identical figures, goggled and in khaki, came around the corner of the second-floor corridor and put his hand on the knob of the door nearest the stairs. He squeezed the knob gently and then moved on to the next door, apparently unaware of Bleeker. Bleeker, remembering not to run or shout or knock the man down, walked over to him, took his arm and led him down the stairs, the arm unresisting, even flaccid, in his grip.

Bleeker stood indecisively at the foot of the stairs, watching the man walk automatically away from him. He thought he should go back upstairs and search the hall. And he thought too he had to reach Simpson. Over the noise of the motorcycles moving rapidly up and down the street he heard a crash in the bar, a series of drunken elongated curses, ending abruptly in a small sound like a man's hand laid flatly and sharply on a table.

His head was beginning to ache badly and his stomach to sour under the impact of a slow and steady anger. He walked into the bar and stood staring at Francis LaSalle — LaSalle and Fleet, Hardware — who lay sprawled on the floor, his shoulders touching the brass rail under the bar and his head turned so that his cheek rubbed the black polished wood above the rail. The bartender had his hands below the top of the bar and he was watching Simpson and a half a dozen men arranged in a loose semi-circle above and beyond LaSalle.

Bleeker lifted LaSalle, who was a little dazed but not really hurt, and set him on a chair. After he was sure LaSalle was all right he walked up to Simpson.

"Get your men together," he said. "And get them out of here."

Simpson took out a long yellow wallet folded like a book and laid some money on the bar.

"That should take care of the damages," he said. His tongue was a little thick and his mouth didn't quite shut after the words were spoken but Bleeker didn't think he was drunk. Bleeker saw too — or thought he saw — the little cold eyes behind the glasses as bright and as sterile as a painted floor. Bleeker raised his arm slightly and lifted his heels off the floor but Simpson turned abruptly and walked away from him, the men in the troop swaying at his heels like a pack of lolling hounds. Bleeker stood looking foolishly after them. He had expected a fight and his body was still poised for one. He grunted heavily.

"Who hit him?" Bleeker motioned toward LaSalle.

"Damned if I know," the bartender said. "They all look alike to me."

That was true of course. He went back into the lobby, hearing

LaSalle say, weakly and tearfully, "Goddam them — the bastards."
He met Campbell, the deputy sheriff, a tall man with the arms and
shoulders of a child beneath a foggy, bloated face.

"Can you do anything?" Bleeker asked. The motorcycles were
racing up and down the street, alternately whining and backfiring and
one had jumped the curb and was cruising on the sidewalk.

"What do you want me to do?" Campbell demanded. "Put 'em all
in jail?"

The motorcycle on the sidewalk speeded up and skidded obliquely
into a plate-glass window, the front wheel bucking and climbing the
brick base beneath the window. A single large section of glass slipped
edge-down to the sidewalk and fell slowly toward the cyclist who, with
his feet spread and kicking at the cement, backed clumsily away from
it. Bleeker could feel the crash in his teeth.

Now there were other motorcycles on the sidewalk. One of them
hit a parked car at the edge of the walk. The rider standing astride
his machine beat the window out of the car with his gloved fists. Campbell started down the steps toward him but was driven back by a motorcycle coming from his left. Bleeker could hear the squeal of the tires
against the wooden riser at the base of the steps. Campbell's hand was
on his gun when Bleeker reached him.

"That's no good," he yelled. "Get the state police. Ask for a half
dozen squad cars."

Campbell, angry but somewhat relieved, went up the steps and into
the lobby. Bleeker couldn't know how long he stood on the veranda
watching the mounting devastation on the street — the cyclist racing
past store windows and hurling, presumably, beer bottles at the glass
fronts; the two, working as a team, knocking down weighing machines
and the signs in front of the motion picture theater; the innumerable
mounted men running the angry townspeople, alerted and aroused by
the awful sounds of damage to their property, back into their suddenly
lighted homes again or up the steps of his hotel or into niches along the
main street, into doorways, and occasionally into the ledges and bays
of glassless windows.

He saw Simpson — or rather a figure on the white motorcycle, hel-
meted and goggled — stationed calmly in the middle of the street
under a hanging lamp. Presumably, he had been there for some time
but Bleeker hadn't seen him, the many rapid movements on the street
making any static object unimportant and even, in a sense, invisible.
Bleeker saw him now and he felt again that spasm of anger which was

like another life inside his body. He could have strangled Simpson then, slowly and with infinite pride. He knew without any effort of reason that Simpson was making no attempt to control his men but waiting rather for that moment when their minds, subdued but never actually helpless, would again take possession of their bodies.

Bleeker turned suddenly and went back into the lobby as if by that gesture of moving away he could pin his thoughts to Simpson, who, hereafter, would be responsible for them. He walked over to the desk where Timmons and Campbell, the deputy, were talking.

"You've got the authority," Timmons was saying angrily. "Fire over their heads. And if that doesn't stop them —"

Campbell looked uneasily at Bleeker. "Maybe if we could get their leader —"

"Did you get the police?" Bleeker asked.

"They're on their way," Campbell said. He avoided looking at Timmons and continued to stare hopefully and miserably at Bleeker.

"You've had your say," Timmons said abruptly. "Now I'll have mine."

He started for the lobby doors but Campbell, suddenly incensed, grabbed his arm.

"You leave this to me," he said. "You start firing a gun —"

Campbell's mouth dropped and Bleeker, turning his head, saw the two motorcycles coming through the lobby doors. They circled leisurely around for a moment and then one of them shot suddenly toward them, the goggled rider looming enormously above the wide handlebars. They scattered, Bleeker diving behind a pillar and Campbell and Timmons jumping behind the desk. The noise of the two machines assaulted them with as much effect as the sight of the speeding metal itself.

Bleeker didn't know why in course of watching the two riders he looked into the hall toward the foot of the stairway. Nor did it seem at all unreasonable that when he looked he should see Cathy standing there. Deeply, underneath the outward preoccupation of his mind, he must have been thinking of her. Now there she was. She wore the familiar green robe, belted and pulled in at the waist and beneath its hem he could see the white slippers and the pink edge of her nightgown. Her hair was down and he had the impression her eyes were not quite open although, obviously, they were. She looked, he thought, as if she had waked, frowned at the clock, and come downstairs to scold him for staying up too late. He had no idea what time it was.

He saw — and of course Cathy saw — the motorcycle speeding toward her. He was aware that he screamed at her too. She did take a slight backward step and raise her arms in a pathetic warding gesture toward the inhuman figure on the motorcycle but neither could have changed — in that dwarfed period of time and in that short, unmaneuverable space — the course of their actions.

She lay finally across the lower steps, her body clinging to and equally arching away from the base of the newel post. And there was the sudden, shocking exposure of her flesh, the robe and gown torn away from the leg as if pushed aside by the blood welling from her thigh. When he reached her there was blood in her hair too and someone — not Cathy — was screaming into his ears.

After a while the doctor came and Cathy, her head bandaged and her leg in splints, could be carried into his office and laid on the couch. Bleeker sat on the edge of the couch, his hand over Cathy's, watching the still white face whose eyes were closed and would not, he knew, open again. The doctor, after his first examination, had looked up quickly and since Bleeker too had been bent over Cathy, their heads had been very close together for a moment. The doctor had assumed, almost immediately, his expression of professional austerity but Bleeker had seen him in that moment when he had been thinking as a man, fortified of course by a doctor's knowledge, and Bleeker had known then that Cathy would die but that there would be also this interval of time.

Bleeker turned from watching Cathy and saw Timmons standing across the room. The man was — or had been — crying but his face wasn't set for it and the tears, points of colorless, sparkling water on his jaws, were unexpectedly delicate against the coarse texture of his skin. Timmons waved a bandaged hand awkwardly and Bleeker remembered, abruptly and jarringly, seeing Timmons diving for the motorcycle which had reversed itself, along with the other, and raced out of the lobby.

There was no sound now either from the street or the lobby. It was incredible, thinking of the racket a moment ago, that there should be this utter quietude, not only the lack of noise but the lack of the vibration of movement. The doctor came and went, coming to bend over Cathy and then going away again. Timmons stayed. Beyond shifting his feet occasionally he didn't move at all but stood patiently across the room, his face toward Cathy and Bleeker but not, Bleeker thought once when he looked up, actually seeing them.

"The police," Bleeker said sometime later.

"They're gone," Timmons said in a hoarse whisper. And then after a while, "They'll get 'em — don't worry."

Bleeker saw that the man blushed helplessly and looked away from him. The police were no good. They would catch Simpson. Simpson would pay damages. And that would be the end of it. Who could identify Cathy's assailant? Not himself, certainly — nor Timmons nor Campbell. They were all alike. They were standardized figurines, seeking in each other a willful loss of identity, dividing themselves equally among one another until there was only a single mythical figure, unspeakably sterile and furnishing the norm for hundreds of others. He could not accuse something which didn't actually exist.

He wasn't sure of the exact moment when Cathy died. It might have been when he heard the motorcycle, unbelievably solitary in the quiet night, approaching the town. He knew only that the doctor came for the last time and that there was now a coarse, heavy blanket laid mercifully over Cathy. He stood looking down at the blanket for a moment, whatever he was feeling repressed and delayed inside him, and then went back to the lobby and out onto the veranda. There were a dozen men standing there looking up the street toward the sound of the motorcycle, steadily but slowly coming nearer. He saw that when they glanced at each other their faces were hard and angry but when they looked at him they were respectful and a little abashed.

Bleeker could see from the veranda a number of people moving among the smashed store-fronts, moving, stopping, bending over and then straightening up to move somewhere else, all dressed somewhat extemporaneously and therefore seeming without purpose. What they picked up they put down. What they put down they stared at grimly and then picked up again. They were like a dispossessed minority brutally but lawfully discriminated against. When the motorcycle appeared at the north end of the street they looked at it and then looked away again, dully and seemingly without resentment.

It was only after some moments that they looked up again, this time purposefully, and began to move slowly toward the hotel where the motorcycle had now stopped, the rider standing on the sidewalk, his face raised to the veranda.

No one on the veranda moved until Bleeker, after a visible effort, walked down the steps and stood facing the rider. It was the boy Bleeker had talked to in the bar. The goggles and helmet were hanging at his belt.

"I couldn't stand it any longer," the boy said. "I had to come back."

He looked at Bleeker as if he didn't dare look anywhere else. His face was adolescently shiny and damp, the marks, Bleeker thought, of a proud and articulate fear. He should have been heroic in his willingness to come back to the town after what had been done to it but to Bleeker he was only a dirty little boy returning to a back fence his friends had defaced with pornographic writing and calling attention to the fact that he was afraid to erase the writing but was determined nevertheless to do it. Bleeker was revolted. He hated the boy far more than he could have hated Simpson for bringing this to his attention when he did not want to think of anything or anyone but Cathy.

"I wasn't one of them," the boy said. "You remember, Mr. Bleeker. I wasn't drinking."

This declaration of innocence — this willingness to take blame for acts which he hadn't committed — enraged Bleeker.

"You were one of them," he said.

"Yes. But after tonight —"

"Why didn't you stop them?" Bleeker demanded loudly. He felt the murmur of the townspeople at his back and someone breathed harshly on his neck. "You were one of them. You could have done something. Why in God's name didn't you do it?"

"What could I do?" the boy said. He spread his hands and stepped back as if to appeal to the men beyond Bleeker.

Bleeker couldn't remember, either shortly after or much later, exactly what he did then. If the boy hadn't stepped back like that — if he hadn't raised his hand. . . . Bleeker was in the middle of a group of bodies and he was striking with his fists and being struck. And then he was kneeling on the sidewalk, holding the boy's head in his lap and trying to protect him from the heavy shoes of the men around him. He was crying out, protesting, exhorting, and after a time the men moved away from him and someone helped him carry the boy up the steps and lay him on the veranda. When he looked up finally only Timmons and the doctor were there. Up and down the street there were now only shadows and the diminishing sounds of invisible bodies. The night was still again as abruptly as it had been confounded with noise.

Some time later Timmons and the doctor carried the boy, alive but terribly hurt, into the hotel. Bleeker sat on the top step of the veranda, staring at the moon which had shifted in the sky and was now nearer the mountains in the west. It was not in any sense romantic or inflamed but coldly clear and sane. And the light it sent was cold and sane, and lit in himself what he would have liked to hide.

He could have said that having lost Cathy he was not afraid any longer of losing himself. No one would blame him. Cathy's death was his excuse for striking the boy, hammering him to the sidewalk, and stamping on him as he had never believed he could have stamped on any living thing. No one would say he should have lost Cathy lightly — without anger and without that appalling desire to avenge her. It was utterly natural — as natural as a man drinking a few beers and riding a motorcycle insanely through a town like this. Bleeker shuddered. It might have been all right for a man like Timmons who was and would always be incapable of thinking what he — Joel Bleeker — was thinking. It was not — and would never be — all right for him.

Bleeker got up and stood for a moment on the top step of the veranda. He wanted, abruptly and madly, to scream his agony into the night with no more restraint than that of an animal seeing his guts beneath him on the ground. He wanted to smash something — anything — glass, wood, stone — his own body. He could feel his fists going into the boy's flesh. And there was that bloody but living thing on the sidewalk and himself stooping over to shield it.

After a while, aware that he was leaning against one of the wooden pillars supporting the porch and aware too that his flesh was numb from being pressed against it, he straightened up slowly and turned to go back into the hotel.

There would always be time to make his peace with the dead. There was little if any time to make his peace with the living.

PALO

BY WILLIAM SAROYAN

*T*HE OLD BOY HIMSELF, bored worse than ever, and annoyed because something was the matter with the brakes, something more was the matter with them that was going to cost more money, more of the stuff he'd been having too much trouble trying to get all his life, and because the windshield wiper wasn't wiping, the cars coming in the other direction weren't dimming their headlights — they ought to know enough to dim their headlights — so that slipping through the hills, slipping around the curves of the two-lane highway in the hills, he could not see, he could not see the white line on the edge of the road.

The radio, which ordinarily helped dispel the boredom, was no help at all now, although it was tuned to the proper station, the one that played records of good music from six-thirty in the morning to midnight. Now, though, it was the half-hour for children, which was something else again.

He was late, too. He was supposed to see Doc at Doc's office at six-thirty, but it was almost that already. His neck, where it was attached to his head, was hot, and he knew that meant he was tired. He was especially tired of looking at the frosty windshield and not being able to see past it.

He drew up on the side of the road, got the S. P. Railroad face towel he used for a cleaning cloth, rubbed the windshield inside, then got out in the rain and rubbed the outside until the glass should have been perfectly clear, but after he got back into the car and began to go again the grit was there again. He had to laugh and curse General Motors or whoever it was that couldn't make a windshield that a driver could see through in the rain. He slowed down from forty miles an an hour to thirty, lighted a cigarette, swore at the Englishman on the radio talking to the children.

"The English," he thought, "who never know their children, who never meet them, love children most and understand them best. Of all the bores the English are the most delightful. They never blow their noses, the men insist on being untidy, the women look and act like chippies, but both the men and the women have real style."

The Englishman on the radio was speaking to the children in his clear open English voice, and at the same time it was impossible not to hear the man saying to himself, "The little bastards, the silly little bastards, asking for gore and blood all the time, the monstrous little darlings." They *were* people, every one of them, he'd seen them by the hundreds of thousands in London, and every one of them was a character, a man or a woman who stood his own way and talked his own way and thought his own way and smelled his own way, but most of all made jokes and laughed his own way. They were always beefing among themselves and one of them was always saying to another, "Put the box over there? I'll put the box on your *head*, that's where I'll put it." Here was this one now, enchanting the children from a phonograph record over a little station six thousand miles from London where the record was made. There was a special announcer for this half-hour, himself somewhere or other from England, who invariably ended the program saying, as if it were reluctant farewell to joy itself, "Good night, children — every — where." Everywhere? There couldn't be more than a half a dozen children listening to the program, for the station was unknown.

The English, weren't they the best of the lot, though? Weren't they the deadpannest? Didn't they have the most fun on their short change, none of them ever with money enough for anything less than personal brilliance? Weren't they all lords and ladies, and laughing about it because it bloody well didn't mean anything?

The dirty son of a bitch! — another lunatic with his headlights blinding him, hurling his car up and down the hills and around the curves sixty miles an hour, the tires buzzing like a swarm of mad bees. "Get your lights down," he said aloud when the car reached him, but he knew there was no telling them, they were not bad themselves, any of them, they just liked to hurl themselves every weekend, getting into the cars they had polished for hours, hurling the cars through rain and dark as if they had some place to go and something to do there, all of them dull and drab and actually a little foolish, a little ajar where they were supposed to be balanced, most of them out of universities, too, and all alike, all jolly and equal to anything except themselves, all quick to smile, all hearty in friendship.

He'd driven down there to the little town because he'd put up money and put his name on a piece of paper involving a house, and he'd had another look at it. He wouldn't have bothered except that he'd had to drive to the airport post office anyway to get some more stuff off to New York, and the house was only five minutes from there, so he'd given it another look. It was a little house, but it was going to be a new one, at any rate, and they wanted to know what tiles he wanted, what colors he wanted on the walls, what wallpapers, so he'd gone and tried to tell them. "Make it dark gray and chalk white all over," he said, and then they brought out the wallpaper books and he turned the pages and got irritated, but he picked four kinds he thought might do and told the woman they called the decorator where to put them.

It was a forty-five minute drive from his old house in the Sunset in San Francisco to the new house at the bottom of the hills just outside San Mateo — Saint Matthew that would be, most likely, whoever *he* was, however he must have made a fool of himself — and that was where the little radio station was, somewhere in that town, so that the reception improved as he drew nearer, and became perfect when he was there.

Palo Alto (that didn't mean *anything* of course, but then again it meant something to *him* and to his son, the boy in New York now, the boy he hadn't seen in almost two years except a glance a year ago, it didn't mean anything to him and his daughter in New York, but it did to him and his son, but surely by now his son had forgotten, he'd forgotten all about it by now, Palo meant nothing to the boy by now, and neither did Alto, but once, Christ, one night it meant something, it meant the best and most of something anything ever meant) —

Palo Alto was ten or fifteen miles further on down the peninsula, and that was where Stanford was, but he'd never gone to Stanford, he'd tried to get into Cal to study literature when he was twenty but they wanted to know about his high school credits, and that stopped him, that and his slipping on the marble floor of the hall on his way to the place where he was going to try to get them to let him in.

Having slipped, he said, "Ah, let it go, let it go, you can't even stay on your feet in a University, you'll slip every time you try to move, let it go, go on back to Carl Street and *write* the stuff, don't study it, they can't tell you anything you can't find out for yourself, what do you want to go to school for?"

All he'd ever done at Stanford was visit a cousin when his cousin was studying law there, but that wasn't bad at all. His cousin made it, too, got his degree and diploma, opened his office in San Francisco, and went right on being the swift and laughing kid he had always been in Fresno, his eyes swift, his voice swift and laughing, his words always clearly spoken because everybody was misunderstanding everybody. That was the cousin who, when he was bored worst, burst into Kurdish song, wailing and making any Armenian nearby feel better than he'd felt in days, weeks, months, or years.

Stanford meant nothing to him.

His house was being built beside a rainwater ditch just outside San Matthew or Saint Mateo or whatever it was, whoever the poor man was.

They were together in those days, the four of them, in the hopeless hut on Taraval Street, living together in the God-damnedest loneliness anybody ever tried to figure out. It was sundown one evening and the boy wanted to shake the loneliness, the little boy wanted his father to help him shake it, and the father wanted the boy to try to get used to it, wanted him to stand alone in the backyard, or stand there with his sister, and get used to it, because there was always going to be a lot of it, so the Old Boy who'd been fooling around in the backyard   what the hell had he been doing? — taking the weeds out from around the rose bushes or something — got up with the idea in his head to walk four blocks up the street to the saloon and have two or three quick ones. He tried to sneak away, so they wouldn't notice, but they could *smell* when he was going, and the boy caught him at the gate.

"Papa?"

"Papa, Papa," the girl said.

"You kids just play here," he said.

"You stay with us and do your work," the boy said.

"I've got to go somewhere."

"I've got to go, too," the boy said.

He called out to their mother who ought to have been in the kitchen but she didn't hear him or something, so he decided to stay until she showed up and took them upstairs. He went back to the weeds, the boy squatting beside him, helping and wanting to know where it was that he had wanted to go to and then had not gone to. He and the boy had once driven to Palo Alto, and on the way there the boy had kept

asking to see Palo Alto, and then when he saw it, Palo Alto bored him.
He'd thought it was something else. It wasn't, though. Now, he told
the boy he'd thought of going to Palo Alto, but decided it was too far
to bother with. They fooled with the weeds a half-hour longer and
then the boy's mother came out on the first-floor stairs and started chatting with the Old Boy.

"How about calling them up?" he said.

"Why?" the boy said.

"Call them up, will you?"

"All right, children," the mother said, but only the girl was willing.
The boy was not only unwilling, he was angry. He must have been
awfully bored and lonely that evening, for his unwillingness was one of
the most painful things the Old Boy had ever noticed in the boy, but
all the same he wanted the boy to begin getting used to what he was
going to have to learn to get used to.

"Go on upstairs with your sister," he said to the boy, but the boy
looked at him so angry and hurt that he felt there must be something
wrong with the theory that they ought to get used to it as quickly as
possible.

"No," the boy said.

"Come on," the boy's sister said from the stairway. "Be a good boy.
I'm a good girl. *I'm* going in. Come on."

"You shut up," the boy shouted at her.

"You shut up, too, then," the girl said. "You're a bad boy. You're
a very bad boy."

The mother and the daughter went into the house, and the boy began
to strike his father, his small fists as hard as he could make them.

"What's the matter?" the man said.

"You want me to go upstairs," the boy shouted and wept. "You don't
want me to stay with you."

Well, what could he do?

"All right," he said, "let's pull out some more weeds."

"I don't want to pull out any more weeds," the boy shouted, "I want
to go to Palo."

"*Where?*"

"Palo."

"I'm not going to Palo Alto," the man said.

"I want you to take me there," the boy shouted and wept.

"I took you there already once," the man said. "You didn't like it."

"I want to go to Palo."

"Listen," the man said, "I'll tell you the truth. I wanted to go up the street to the saloon and get a couple of drinks. I just *said* I wanted to go to Palo Alto because small boys can't go to saloons."

"Yes, they can," the boy said.

"Well, they're not *supposed* to go in," the man said.

"They can wait outside, can't they?" the boy said. "Are you going to the saloon?"

"Well, I'd like to."

"I want to go, too."

"Well, all right," the man said. "It's not that important, one way or another. I won't keep you waiting long, I'll just have a couple o quick ones."

"What?"

"Whisky."

"I want some whisky, too."

"Well, that's just it, don't you see?" he said. "Four-year-old boys can't have whisky. But we can walk to the saloon together and you can wait outside until I have a couple of quick ones, and then we can walk back together. Do you want a haircut in the barber shop next door while I'm having a couple?"

"Do I need a haircut?"

"Not especially."

"Then I don't want one."

They walked to the saloon, the boy waited out front, and the Old Boy went in and had two double Scotches over ice very quickly, felt better, went out and found the boy talking soberly to an old tramp who might have scared a grown man half to death he was so deteriorated.

"Your boy?" the tramp said.

"Yes."

"He's a good boy."

The tramp moved on up Taraval, and the man and the boy started for home.

"Did you have the quick ones?" the boy said.

"Yes."

"Did you like them?"

"Yes. They were fine."

They walked in silence half a block, and then the boy said, "What *is* Palo? What is *that?*"

"Well," he said, "it's the first half of the name of that town down

there that I took you to that time, Palo Alto, where the university is.
You saw the place yourself."

Palo and Alto meant something to him all right, but it wasn't anything you could pin down.

Another son of a bitch blinded him now, and his neck was hot again,
he was still miles from where Doc had his office, the Englishman on the
radio was still calling them little bastards, and the rain was coming
down heavier than ever, Palo all right, Alto all right, Palo Alto all
right, the boy and the tramp instantaneous friends, standing outside a
saloon, asking and answering questions.

The house was being built for the boy, and for the boy's sister. It
wasn't in Palo Alto but it *was* in that direction. It was being built for
them to visit, to live in with their father a month or two next year when
they were on school vacation — it was being built for them to visit
if it ever worked out that they would be permitted.

He got to town at last, got rid of the car in a garage, walked a block
to the building where Doc had his office on the twenty-first floor, andf
went in, only twenty or twenty-five minutes late.

Doc was sitting there at his desk with two bottles on a tray and two
glasses.

"Sorry to be late," he said. "Got caught in the rain."

"Bourbon or Scotch?" Doc said.

"Either," he said.

"Let's try this bourbon."

Doc dropped two cubes of ice in each glass, then poured bourbon
over the ice, then a little water over the bourbon, and then the Old Boy
took his glass and lifted it and said, "Is that the docks on fire out
there?"

"No, I think it's the baseball stadium."

"It's good seeing you again, Doc."

"I know you're working," Doc said, "but I thought a break like this
would do you good. We'll have a couple here, then go to the bar there
and have some more, then have dinner with them, they're all good
boys, I don't often go, I'm not a club man, but when you came in last
week after fifteen years — your eyes are fine, they're nearsighted instead of far, that's all, they're perfect for your work, and you can put
the glasses on when you want to look at stuff far away, that's all the
glasses are good for — I thought some Thursday night we'd go there
and it would be a break for you."

"I'm glad you did," he said. "I don't like working at all, but let's

face it, what is there any of us can do that's better? The stuff bores
me. It's not bad. None of it's bad, but it bores me."

"Every man's work bores him," Doc said. "Fifteen years ago when
you came here I used to get a kick out of everybody who came here, but
I don't get a kick out of anybody who comes here any more. They're
all alike, and they can't see the way they used to. That bourbon any
good?"

"Fine," he said. "Who set fire to the ball park?"

"Maybe it's the docks or a warehouse," Doc said. "It's been going
on a half-hour or more. Fifteen years ago my prediction, as I told you
at that time, was that your eyes would never go bad. Well, they haven't,
but *something's* happened to them."

"Time," he said. "Whatever it is, it's happened to all of me, not
just my eyes. I *do* get irritated when I drive at night, though, because
I can't see. In the rain at night, I can't see at all. I'm going to have to
eat a lot of carrots."

"Carrots don't do any good," Doc said. "If you like carrots, eat 'em
of course, but carrots don't make you see any better."

"I'm going to exercise the muscles of my eyes, then," he said. "Huxley did that."

"Exercise doesn't do them any good either," Doc said, "unless you
plan to lift things with them. I was on a boat once with Huxley — we
didn't meet or anything — but I knew what the trouble was with his
eyes."

"Thurber's got it bad," he said. "Tarkington had it bad. What
happens to eyes, Doc?"

"We can *name* it after it happens," Doc said. "But who knows why
it happens? How can you know? It happens. Have you tried the
glasses?"

"They're good for looking at clouds," he said.

"You won't be wearing them much."

"I look at clouds once in a while."

"Well, they're the only kind you need," Doc said. "Let's freshen
these a little."

Doc freshened them and the new drink tasted better than the old.

"Fifteen years ago," Doc said, "you were laughing."

"It was a joke, then."

"What did you know?"

"I knew I didn't care. Now I know I do."

"A lot?"

"Too much, most likely."

"That makes it tough."

"That's why working's such a good idea," he said. "Of course it earns a man his living, too, but that's not the reason it's the best thing there is."

"Care for what?" Doc said.

"Everybody," he said. "Everything. Because now my own are out there with them. I don't ever see a boy or a girl that I don't have to look at particularly, and when they're glad their gladness is the most wonderful thing I know in this world, and when they're not glad, when they're something else, anything else, that's the most terrible thing in this world I know. But I care for their mothers and fathers, too, because now I know what they're up against. If they're all right together, I know what they're up against, and if they're not, I know what they're up against, and they're always up against more than the kids ever are. Even so, you've got to care most for the kids because you can't hope for much for anybody else."

They talked a half-hour, then left the office and the building, the stadium still burning, and got in Doc's car and went there, to the bar there, where the boys were, and began to meet and talk and drink with them, a general in a sport coat, a banker rolling dice with a dentist, a lawyer with a red face roaring with laughter at the joke of an insurance broker, the boys all getting along in years and eager to have the Thursday whisky together, see one another again. After half-a-dozen they went upstairs to supper, and then downstairs to the bar again for brandy.

He felt fine, he kept feeling fine, finer and finer, remembering the house by the raindaitch, the radio station down there that played records of good music from half-past six in the morning till midnight, the style of the British, the eyes, the ball park on fire, the boy standing outside the saloon on Taraval, waiting for him, waiting for his damned father inside there having a couple of quick ones, talking with the old tramp, the boy in New York now with his sister and his mother.

"You know, Doc," he said. "You know, I never went to Stanford."

"No?" Doc said.

"No. I went to Palo Alto, though."

"Is that so?"

"Yes. I drove down there."

"You did?"

"Yes," he said. "Palo Alto wasn't Palo Alto, though. It was something else. He didn't care for what it was. I never found out what it was, but I know it was something else."

"Who?" Doc said.

"My son," he said. "Who else?"

It was a good break. It was good being with Doc and the boys. When they were glad, though, that was it. The rest of the time work was it, and then once in a while the saloon.

(*From New-Story*)

I'M REALLY FINE

BY STUART SCHULBERG

THE LETTER from his mother rambled along, asking about his cold, wanting to know if the woolen socks had arrived, describing the new chair she'd bought for his room. It was like all the letters from his mother, somewhat incoherent but full of love and affection and the warm security of his home. Her familiar script covered four small pages and at the top of each page appeared the magic numerals of his home address.

He opened his desk drawer and took out the box of school stationery.

I'll write Mom, he thought. When they come for me I'll be writing a letter and I'll look busy and it'll be better and I won't just be waiting for them here.

Carefully he lifted one sheet out of the box. The sheet was grey with the school's name and crest embossed in scarlet. At first he'd liked to write letters because it gave him a chance to use the school stationery. He'd been infatuated with the school stationery. It had seemed to give him the kind of maturity and independence he wanted. During his first two months at school he'd written everyone he could think of just to impress them with the stationery. It had been a notice to whom it may concern that Donald R. Miller was no longer a child but a young man of the world with a mind and a life of his own. He was fourteen years old.

He laid the sheet down flat on the desk and began his letter.

"Dear Mom," he wrote, "Well, the socks arrived and they're sure swell. Thanks a lot. As for my cold, well it's almost gone but I still have to go to the infirmary twice a day for drops. But don't worry about it because it's really nothing."

He got that far in his letter and then he put his head down on his arm and waited for the tears to come. In his third month at the River

School the tears came often. Not the loud open tears of pain but the small secret tears of frustration. When he wrote the words "don't worry about it" he knew the tears would come. They came because he wanted so much for his mother to worry, to care, to protect. Now he hated his independence. The stationery was no longer a proud boast but a brave front that he put up to cover the tears and the longing for his childhood. In his third month he wrote only to his mother, longingly, as a child holds out its arms for help. But he never asked for help. Inside him a great battle of adolescence had been fought between the instincts of a child and the behavior of a man. Now he was committed to manhood and it was too late to ask for help. He couldn't tell his mother what was happening to him. He could only write the careful letters home, seeking a vicarious security while he waited for them to come.

He heard the loose clatter of boys coming up the stairs in the hall and lifted his head quickly. He knew they couldn't find him like this. He was going to be writing the letter, looking busy, not expecting them. He picked up his pen and began writing again. It would be terrible if they found him waiting.

"Had a lot of fun at soccer yesterday. Our house team beat Hastings and we really razzed them after the game. See, they've been going around saying how they'd beat us so they really deserved it."

The boys' voices in the hall came closer and then were suddenly muffled as a door shut two rooms away. He listened closely trying to pick out the voices and he recognized Haywood's laughter through the walls. The sound of it made him go rigid. He felt blood rushing into his face and a queer tingling in his head. He knew they'd come for him soon now. But he'd be warned by the door opening and have time to go back to the letter. He put the pen down and looked at the large framed pictures of his mother and father on the desk. His mother had written "For my Darling Donald, Always, Mom." His father had said "To a great little guy, Dad." Without quite understanding why, he picked up the pictures and put them in the dresser drawer. He knew they couldn't be on the desk any longer.

He sat down at the desk again after that and read his letter over from the beginning. He thought it struck about the right note. His mother wouldn't guess what was happening to him here. And actually the part about the soccer game was true in a way. His house team had won the game and there had been some razzing though he'd taken no part in it. He'd watched the game silently from the sidelines and then come back to his room. It's hard to cheer alone. You need someone cheering next to you and the other boys had moved away from him as they always did now. Later he'd heard them laughing and shouting to each other as they passed under his window coming up from the field.

He began writing again.

"My room is really fixed up now. I put the banners up over my bed just like they used to be at home. Then I found some swell plane pictures in *Life* and I put them up on the other wall over my desk. I like my room very much."

It was not exactly true that he liked his room. A drowning man doesn't speak of a raft in terms of liking or disliking. Donald Miller clung to his room and in his room he clung to his childhood and to his mother. He escaped to his room whenever he could now. There was nothing else to do. He read in his room or wrote the letters to his mother and waited for the night to come. Night was good because it meant sleep and sleep was the only true escape. Night was eight and a half hours of security, of love, of happiness. At night his mother called him lambkin again and he could smile alone in the dark.

"Classes are going along fine. I got another A in Latin yesterday and the highest mark in the class on the history test. I guess this must sound pretty conceited writing all this to you but I thought you'd like to know. Mr. Peattie says my French accent is good."

Another A in Latin. Sometimes he thought the whole trouble had begun with the first A in Latin. The day Mr. Norris got angry and told the class that Miller was four times brighter than any of the others. "He knuckles down and does the work" had been Mr. Norris' phrase for Miller. And he had noticed the look of hostility that had shot into the other boys' faces. Their eyes told him he was smarter, better, that he had committed the cardinal sin of being different. Maybe that was the beginning of the trouble. "He knuckles down and does the work" had become a battle-cry for the boys who hated him because he was different. Yet he couldn't help it if he found Cicero exciting and his memory for declensions was good.

"By the way, I'm not taking football anymore for recreation. Now I'm taking horseback riding. It's lots of fun and I learned how to saddle my own horse last time. We all go out riding together with Mr. Sage who's chemistry teacher and riding teacher too and I sure like it. Mr. Newman, our housemaster and football coach, said he thought I might like riding more than football and I do too."

He put his pen down, trying to catch a sound from the room two doors down. He knew they were in there. He knew Haywood was in

there, sleek and manly in his expensive sports jacket. Haywood. A
montage of Haywood projected itself in his mind. He saw Haywood
lunging at him with a football hugged to his chest, Haywood twisting a
first former's arm until he'd admit that he'd like to sleep with his mother,
Haywood standing naked in the middle of the shower room exhibiting
his big man's body. And Haywood was always grinning, his hard
mouth opened slightly in an ecstasy of physical achievement, his small
eyes squinting with the delight of his flesh.

He listened carefully. They should be coming by now. He heard
only silence for a moment and then the ting of a bedspring and another
ting and another until they followed in a slow fragile rhythm. He
knew they were doing it again. He covered his letter with his arms and
hid his face in his arms. Oh Mom, he thought, why do they have to
do it? Why can't they be decent and clean and kind? Why can't they
be good? He had been wondering ever since the trouble began. He
didn't know. He knew only that he had become despised because he
couldn't become one of them. The A's in Latin and the failure in football perhaps had begun it. And then they'd noticed that he took no
pleasure in discussing the bodies of men and women and that he carefully avoided the four-letter words. He couldn't be one of them and
slowly they'd drawn away from him until he was left facing them alone.
He was helpless, trapped between his child's innocence and his man's
pride.

"Now what are you crying about?" Haywood was asking.

They'd approached so quietly and opened the door so quickly that
he'd been caught with his head in his arms. They must have tip-toed,
he thought, and he felt his face go red with shame and rage. Five of
them. McCardle, Huss, White, Meyer and Haywood. He got to his
feet, trying to look at them but seeing only Haywood's grin and his
thick hands.

"I'm not crying," he said.

"I'm not crying," McCardle said in a falsetto. .

"Well, what do you call it then if you're not crying?" Haywood asked.

"I'm writing a letter."

"Oh sure, sure, you're writing a letter," McCardle said.

"Who to?" Haywood asked.

"That's none of your business."

"To mommy," Huss said. "He's writing to mommy."

"Please mommy dear, take me away from all the nasty boys,"
McCardle said in his falsetto.

Miller took a step back and managed to get the letter into the desk drawer. Haywood, McCardle, White, Huss and Meyer formed a closer circle around him.

"Secret letter," Huss said. "Special secret mysterious letter."

"Yeah," Haywood said, "he knuckles down and writes secret letters."

"To his own little mommy-wommy," McCardle said.

Haywood stepped closer to Miller and put his arm heavily around his shoulder.

"Say, Donnie," he said, "just between us, what's your mother really like?"

Miller looked down at the floor, waiting for it, knowing it was coming.

"I mean what's she look like naked?"

The punch came automatically, unconscious as the wild kick of a baby in the womb. It was a clumsy hysterical punch that only knocked Haywood a little off balance.

"You dirty guy, you damned dirty guy," he said, knowing he was crying and that he had no chance.

He swung madly again at Haywood's grin which was blurred by his tears. Haywood began to toy with him, ducking the punches or grabbing Miller's arms and pinning them back harmlessly on his chest.

"Saaay," Haywood humored him, "say now . . ." Then Haywood's thick fist sprang into his face.

"Whoever would have thought it of our little mother's boy?" he heard Haywood saying. "Whoever would have thought it?"

He stood leaning against the desk with one hand to his face.

"Please," he said, "please."

McCardle came up and twisted his arm up behind his back and held it there.

"Please, please, please," he said.

"Please, please, please," McCardle mimicked.

"What do you mean 'please'?" Haywood asked. "After what you did, you expect us to be nice to you? Huh?"

"Please let me alone," he said.

"Later," Haywood said. "First a special little treatment for tough guys."

"For mommy's boys," McCardle said.

"A little work to knuckle down to first," Huss said.

McCardle jerked his arm a little higher on his back and marched him out. The others followed. They went down the quiet hallway, turning at the end into the bathroom.

Miller hated the bathroom for its associations of sexual ugliness. It was here the others exhibited themselves, preening their more developed bodies and proudly evaluating their parts. The sterile tile walls made it a cell and everything he hated and feared at the River School was locked inside.

"Well, here we are," Haywood said with his grin.

He went over and took off an "Out of order" sign from one of the stall toilets and pushed open the swinging door.

"Right this way, Master Miller," he said.

McCardle forced Miller into the stall. He looked down into the unflushed bowl. They couldn't do this, he thought, they're dirty rotten guys but they couldn't do this. He heard the others scrambling into the next stall and then he felt their hot faces staring down at him from over the partition.

"Pick it up," Haywood said.

"Oh no, no," he said.

"Pick it up."

He looked down again and felt the sweat forming under his arms and along his spine. He knew he would do it. He knew that he had to do it, that he couldn't scream for Mr. Newman or fight anymore. He knew he couldn't tell his mother, his mother who called him lambkin and wanted to know how his cold was getting along.

"Come on, come on," Haywood was saying.

He dropped to his knees, shuddering and crying and saying "Damn you, damn you, damn you."

He could hear Haywood breathing quickly over him.

"Now squeeze it," Haywood said. "Squeeze it hard."

He knew he was alone.

". . . filthiest thing I ever saw," he could hear Haywood saying. "No kidding, you're filthy, just filthy."

He heard the others climbing down from the partition and racing out, clattering and giggling into the hall.

"Just filthy, that's all, anyone who'd do a thing like that," Haywood said and then he turned and ran out of the bathroom.

When he heard the bathroom door shut, Miller got up on his feet.

"Damn you, damn you . . ." he was saying.

He walked over to the sink and began washing his hands. He moved slowly and jerkily, half paralyzed with revulsion and shame. He washed his hands over and over again, hearing the high-pitched laughter in the hallways and the doors slamming. From far off he could hear an excited voice screaming, "He did it, he did it, my God he did it. . . ."

Then he walked out of the bathroom and down the hall to his room.

He stood for a moment looking around at the banners and the airplane pictures and the desk. He walked over to the desk and sat down and took out the unfinished letter to his mother. He picked up his pen.

"Well," he wrote, "that's about all for now, I guess. Thanks again for the socks and don't worry about the cold. I'm really fine. Your loving son, Donnie."

(*From The New Yorker*)

THE HEALTHIEST GIRL IN TOWN

BY JEAN STAFFORD

*I*N 1924, when I was eight years old, my father died and my mother and I moved from Ohio to a high Western town, which, because of its salubrious sun and its astringent air, was inhabited principally by tuberculars who had come there from the East and the South in the hope of cure, or at least of a little prolongation of their static, cautious lives. And those of the town who were not invalids, or the wives, husbands, or children of invalids, were, even so, involved in this general state of things and conversant with its lore. Some of them ran boarding houses for the ambulatory invalids ("the walkers," as we called them) and many were in the employ of the sanitarium which was the raison d'être of the community, while others were hired privately as cooks, chauffeurs, or secretaries by people who preferred to rent houses rather than submit to the regulations of an institutional life. My mother was a practical nurse and had come there because there were enough people to need her services and therefore to keep a roof over our head and shoes on our feet.

My contemporaries took for granted all the sickness and dying that surrounded us — most of them had had a first-hand acquaintance with it — but I did not get used to these people who carried the badge of their doom in their pink cheeks as a blind man carries his white stick in his hand. I continued to be fearful and fascinated each time I met a walker in the streets or on the mountain trails and each time some friend's father, half gone in the lungs, watched me from where he sat in enforced ease on the veranda as other girls and I played pom-pom-pullaway in his front yard. Once Dotty MacKensie's father, who was soon to die, laughed when I, showing off, turned a cartwheel, and he cried, "Well done, Jessie!" and was taken thereupon with the last awful cough that finally was to undo and kill him. I did not trust their specious look of health and their look of immoderate cleanliness. At the same time, I was unduly drawn to them in the knowledge that a mystery encased them delicately; their death was an interior integument that seemed to lie just under their sun-tanned skin. They spoke softly and their manners were courteous and kind, as if they must live hushed and on tiptoe, lest the bacilli awaken and muster for the kill. Occasionally, my mother was summoned in the middle of the night to attend someone in his final hemorrhage; at times, these climactic spasms were so violent, she had once told me, that blood splattered the ceiling, a hideous thought and one that wickedly beguiled me. I would lie awake in the cold house long after she had left and would try to imagine such an explosion in myself, until finally I could all but see the girandole of my bright blood mount through the air. Alone in the malevolent midnight darkness, I was possessed with the facts of dying and of death, and I would often turn, heartless and bewitched, to the memory of my father, killed by gangrene, who had lain for weeks in his hospital bed, wasted and hot-eyed and delirious, until, one day as I watched, the poisonous tide deluged him and, as limp as a drowned man, he died. The process had been so snail-paced and then the end of it so fleet that in my surprise I had been unable to cry out and had stood for several minutes, blissful with terror, until my mother came back into the room with a doctor and a nurse. I had longed to discuss with her what I had seen, but her grief — she had loved him deeply — inhibited me, and not until we had come West did I ask her any questions about death, and when I did, I appeared to be asking about her patients, although it was really about my father.

The richer of the tuberculars, especially those who had left their families behind, were billeted in the sanitarium, an aggregate of Swiss chalets that crested the western of our twin hills. If they were not bedridden, they lived much as they might have done at a resort, playing a great deal of bridge, mah-jongg, and cowboy pool, learning to typewrite, photographing our declamatory mountain range that stretched, peak and chasm and hummock of purple rock, miles beyond vision. Often in the early evening, from the main lodge there came piano music, neither passionate nor complicated, and once, as I was passing by, I heard a flute, sweet and single in the dusk. On walks, the patients slowly ranged the mesas, gathering pasqueflowers in the spring and Mariposa lilies in the summer, and in the winter, when the snow was on the ground, they brought back kinnikinnick, red-berried and bronze-leaved. These pastimes were a meagre fare and they were bored, but they were sustained by their stubborn conviction that this way of life was only temporary. Faithfully, winter and summer, spring and fall, they went abroad each day at noon to get the high sun, and because the sanitarium was near my school, I used to see them at the lunch recess, whole phalanxes of them, indulging sometimes in temperate horseplay and always in the interchange of cynical witticisms that banded them together in an esoteric fellowship. In the winter — and our winters were so long and cruel that the sick compared this region to Siberia and their residence there to exile — their eyes and noses alone were visible through their caparisons of sweaters, mufflers, greatcoats, but their sanguine, muted voices came out clearly in the thin air. Like all committed people, whether they are committed to school or to jail, to war or to disease, there was amongst them a good-natured camaraderie that arose out of a need to vary the tedium of a life circumscribed by rules. I would hear them maligning and imitating the doctors and the nurses, and laying plans to outwit them in matters to do with rest periods and cigarettes, exactly as my schoolmates and I planned to perpetrate mischief in geography class or study hall. I heard them banteringly compare X-rays and temperatures, speak, in a tone half humorous and half apprehensive, of a confederate who had been suspended temporarily (it was hoped) from the fraternity by a sudden onslaught of fever. They were urbane, resigned, and tart. Once, I recall, I met two chattering walkers on a path in the foothills and I heard one of them say, "All the same, it's not the bore a nervous breakdown is. We're not locked in, at any rate," and his companion amiably answered, "Oh, but we are. They've locked us into these ratty mountains. They've 'arrested' us, as they say."

This colony was tragic, but all the same I found it rather grand, for most of the sanitarium patients had the solaces of money and of education (I was sure they all had degrees from Eastern universities) and could hire cars to go driving in the mountains and could buy books in quantity at Miss Marshall's snobbish shop, the Book End, where they could also drink tea in an Old Englishy atmosphere in the back room. I did not feel sorry for them as I did for the indigent tuberculars, who lived in a settlement of low, mean cottages on the outskirts of the town. Here I saw sputum cups on window sills and here I heard, from every side, the prolonged and patient coughing, its dull tone unvarying except when a little respite came and its servant sighed or groaned or said, "Oh, God Almighty," as if he were unspeakably tired of this and of everything else in the world. There were different textures and velocities to the coughing, but whether it was dry or brassy or bubbling, there was in it always that undertone of monotony.

It was neither the rich nor the poor that my mother nursed but those in between, who rented solid houses and lived — or tried to live — as they had in Virginia or in Connecticut. Whole families had uprooted themselves for the sake of one member; mothers had come out of devotion to a favorite son. There were isolated individuals as well, men with valets and motorcars and dogs (I thought that the bandy-legged basset belonging to the very rich Mr. Woodham, of Baltimore, was named Lousy Cur, because that was how I always heard Mr. Woodham's man address him), and women who were invariably called grass widows whether they were spinsters or divorcées or had left a loving husband and family behind. Grass widows, walkers, lungers — what a calm argot it was! Many of them were not so much ill as bored and restive — lonely and homesick for the friends and relatives and for the landscapes they had left behind. Ma was a valiant, pretty woman and she was engaged more, really, as a companion than as a nurse. She read aloud to her charges or played Russian bank with them or took them for slow walks. Above all, she listened to their jeremiads, half doleful, half ironic, and tried, with kindly derision, to steer them away from their doldrums. It was this attitude of "You're not alone, everyone is in the same boat" that kept them from, as Ma said, "going mental." A few times, solitary gentlemen fell in love with her, and once she accepted a proposal — from a Mr. Millard, a cheerful banker from Providence, but he died a week before they were to be married. I was relieved, for I had not liked to think of living with a stepfather riddled with bugs.

Soon after Mr. Millard died, Ma went to work for a family named Butler, who had come West from Massachusetts, resentfully but in resignation, bringing their lares in crates and barrels, leaving behind only the Reverend Mr. Butler, who, feeling that he could never duplicate his enlightened congregation, remained in Newton to propagate the Low Church faith. Mrs. Butler, a stout, stern woman who had an advanced degree from Radcliffe, had been promised that here her life, threatened twice by hemorrhages, would be extended to its normal span and that the "tendency" demonstrated by all three of her children would perhaps be permanently checked. Beside the mother and the children, there was a grandmother, not tubercular but senile and helplessly arthritic, and it was for her that Ma had been hired. It was the hardest job she had had, because the old woman, in constant pain, was spiteful and peckish, and several times she reduced my intrepid mother to tears. But this was also the best-paid job she had had, and we were better dressed and better fed than we had been since we left Ohio. We ate butter now instead of margarine and there was even money enough for me to take dancing lessons.

Two of the Butler children, Laura and Ada, were in my grade at school. There was a year's difference between them but the elder, Laura, had been retarded by a six-month session in a hospital. They were the same size and they looked almost exactly alike; they dressed alike, in dark-blue serge jumpers and pale-blue flannelette guimpes and low black boots. They were sickly and abnormally small, and their spectacles pinched their Roman noses. All of us pitied them on their first day at school, because they were so frightened that they would not sit in separate seats, and when Miss Farley asked one of them to sing a scale, she laid her head down on her desk and cried. But we did not waste our sympathy on them long, because after their first show of vulnerability we found them to be haughty and acidulous, and they let it be known that they were not accustomed to going to a public school and associating with just anyone. Nancy Hildreth, whose father was a junkman, excited their especial scorn, and though I had always hated Nancy before, I took her side against them and one day helped her write a poison-pen letter full of vituperative fabrication and threats. We promised that if they did not leave town at once, we would burn their house down. In the end, the letter was too dangerous to send, but its composition had given us great pleasure.

After about a month, Laura and Ada, to my bewilderment and discomfort, began to seek me out at recess, acknowledging in their highhanded way that they knew my mother. They did not use the word "servant" in speaking of her but their tone patronized her and their faint smiles put her in her place. At first, I rebuffed them, for they were too timid to play as I played; they would never pump up in the swings but would only sit on the seats, dangling their feet in their *outré* boots; trying to pretend that they were not afraid but were superior to our lively games. They would not go near the parallel bars or the teeter-totter, and when the rest of us played crack-the-whip, they cowered, aghast, against the storm doors of the grammar school. But when I complained to Ma of how they tagged after me and tried to make me play their boring guessing games, she asked me, for her sake, to be nice to them, since our livelihood depended on their mother, a possessive

woman who would ferociously defend her young. It was hardly fair of
Ma to say to me, "Just remember, it's Laura and Ada who give you
your dancing lessons," but all the same, because she looked so worried
and, even more, because I could not bear to think of not going to my
lessons, I obeyed her, and the next day grudgingly agreed to play
twenty questions while, out of the corner of my eye, I enviously watched
the other children organizing a relay race.

Not long after I had made this filial compromise, Laura and Ada began asking me to come home with them after school, and though my
friends glared at me as we left the playground together, I never dared
refuse. Anyhow, the Butlers' house enchanted me.

It smelled of witch hazel. As soon as we entered the cool and formal
vestibule, where a gilded convex mirror hung above a polished console
table on which there stood a silver tray for calling cards, the old-fashioned and vaguely medicinal fragrance came to meet me, and I envis-
aged cut-glass bottles filled with it on the marble tops of bureaus in the
bedrooms I had never seen. It made me think of one particular autumn
afternoon, in the Ohio woods, when my father and I went for a walk
in a clean, soft mist and he cut me a witch-hazel wand, with which I
touched a young orange salamander in the road. As palpable and
constant as the smell in the house was the hush of an impending death;
somewhere, hidden away in such isolation that I could not even guess
where she was, whether upstairs or in a room behind the parlor, lay the
grandmother, gradually growing feebler, slowly petering out as my
mother spooned up medicine for her and rubbed her ancient back with
alcohol. There was hardly a sound in that tomb-still house save for the
girls' voices and mine, or the footsteps of their older brother, Lawrence,
moving about in his chemical laboratory in the basement.

Again, as vivid as the fragrance and the portentous quiet was the
sense of oldness in this house, coming partly from the well-kept antique
furniture, the precious Oriental rugs, the Hitchcock settles that formed
an inglenook beside the hearth, the quaint photographs hung in deep
ovals of rich-brown wood (there was a square piano, and a grandfather
clock that told the time as if it knelled a death), but coming even more
from the Boston accents and the adult vocabularies and the wise, small
eyes of my two playmates. I did not think of them as children my own
age but rather as dwarfed grownups, and when I walked along between
them, towering over their heads, my own stature seemed eccentric, and
in my self-consciousness I would stub my toe or list against one of the
little girls (who did not fail to call me awkward). Probably they had

never been children; if they had, it had only been for a short time and they had long since cast off the customs and the culture of that season of life. They would not stoop to paper dolls, to pig Latin, to riddles, to practical jokes on the telephone, and in their aloofness from all that concerned me and my fellows they made me feel loutish, noisy, and, above all, stupied.

At other houses, visitors were entertained outside in good weather. In the spring and fall, my friends and I rollerskated or stood on our heads and only looked in at the back door to ask for graham crackers or peanut-butter sandwiches; in the winter we coasted down the hills and occasionally made snow ice cream in some tolerant mother's kitchen. If rain or wind quarantined us, we rowdily played jacks with a golf ball or danced to the music of a victrola. Whatever we did, we were abandoned to our present pleasure.

But at the Butlers' house the only divertissements were Authors and I Spy, and it was only once in a blue moon that we played those. Usually we sat primly, Laura and Ada and I, in the parlor in three wing chairs, and conversed — it is essential to use that stilted word — of books and of our teachers. The Butler girls were dauntlessly opinionated and called the tune to me, who supinely took it up; I would not defend a teacher I had theretofore admired if they ridiculed her; I listened meekly when they said that "Rebecca of Sunnybrook Farm" was silly. Sometimes they told me their dreams, every one of which was a nightmare worse than the one before; they dreamed of alligators and gargantuan cats, of snakes, ogres, and quicksand. I would never tell my vague and harmless dreams, feeling that they would arouse the Butlers' disdain, and once, after they had asked me to and I had refused, Ada said, "It's obvious Jessie doesn't have any dreams, Laura. Didn't Father say that people who sleep soundly have inferior intellects?"

Those long words! They angered and they charmed me, and I listened, wide-eyed, trying to remember them to use them myself — "obvious," "intellect," "logical," "literally." On one of my first visits, Ada, picking up a faded daguerreotype of a bearded man, said, "This is my great-grandfather, Mr. Hartford, whom my brother intends to emulate. Great-Grandfather Hartford was a celebrated corporation lawyer." My astonishment at her language must have shown in my face, for she laughed rather unkindly, and, in shocking vernacular, she added, "That is, Larry will be a lawyer *if* he doesn't turn into a lunger first." The Butlers, like the patients at the sanitarium, had their intramural jokes.

Laura and Ada told me anecdotes of Lawrence, who went to high school and was at the head of his class and contributed regularly to the *Scholastic* magazine. They adored him and looked on every word of his as oracular. He was a youth of many parts, dedicated equally to the Muses (he was writing an epic on Governor Bradford, from whom the family was obliquely descended) and to the study of chemistry, and often, commingled with the witch hazel, there was a faint odor of hydrogen sulfide wafted up through the hot-air registers from his basement laboratory. "Lawrence is a genius," said Laura once, stating a fact. "Think of a genius having to live *here* all his life! But, of course, he's stoical."

. They told me, also, of incidents in the brilliant university career of their mother, who wore her Phi Beta Kappa key as a lavaliere. They spoke of her having studied under Professor Kittredge, as if this were equivalent to having been presented at court. The formidable bluestocking, Mrs. Butler, seldom came into the parlor, for usually she was out shopping or doctoring or was upstairs writing a play based on the life of Carlyle. But when she did make one of her rare appearances, she took no cognizance of me, although it seemed to me that her discerning eyes, small, like her daughters', and monkey-brown, like theirs, discovered my innermost and frivolous thoughts and read them all with disapproval. She would come in only to remind the girls that that night they must write their weekly letters to their father or to remark indignantly that it was difficult to shop when one was nudged and elbowed by barbarians. For Mrs. Butler had an orthodox aversion to the West, and although almost no one was native to our town, she looked down her pointed nose at the entire population, as if it consisted of nothing but rubes.

After we had talked for half an hour, Laura would go out of the room and come back after a while with a tole tray on which stood a china cocoa set and a plate of Huntley & Palmers sweet biscuits, ordered from S. S. Pierce. We would drink in sips and eat in nibbles and continue our solemn discourse. Often, during this unsatisfying meal (the cookies were dry and the cocoa was never sweet enough for me), the talk became medical, and these sophisticated valetudinarians, nine and ten years old, informed me of extraordinary facts relating to the ills that beset the human flesh and especially those rare and serious ones that victimized them. They took such pride in being hostesses to infirmity that I was ashamed of never having suffered from anything graver than pinkeye, and so light a case of that that Ma had cured it in a day with boric acid.

The Butlers, besides being prey to every known respiratory disorder, had other troubles: Laura had brittle bones that could be fractured by the slighest blow, and Ada had a rheumatic heart, a cross she would bear, she said, until the day she died.   They had had quinsy, pleurisy, appendicitis; they were anemic, myopic, asthmatic; and they were subject to hives.   They started off the morning by eating yeast cakes, and throughout the day popped pellets and capsules into their mouths; at recess, I would see them at the drinking fountain, gorging on pills. Their brother was a little less frail, but he, too, was often ill.   The atmosphere of the house was that of a nursing home, and Ma told me that the whole family lived on invalid fare, on custards and broths and arrowroot pudding   The medicine chest, she said, looked like a pharmacy.

I never stayed long at the Butlers' house, for Laura and Ada had to go upstairs to rest.   I stayed only until Lawrence came up from the basement, and as I closed the storm door, I saw, through the side lights, the three of them, weak, intellectual, and Lilliputian, carefully climbing the stairs in single file on their way up to their bedrooms, where they would lie motionless until their dinner of soft white food.

I had friends before Laura and Ada whose lives were far more overcast by tuberculosis than theirs — children born in the same month and the same year as myself who had already spat out blood, children whose mothers had died in the dead of night, whose fathers would never rise from their beds again.   But never before had I been made to feel that my health was a disgrace.   Now, under the clever tuition of the Butlers, I began to look upon myself as a pariah and to be ashamed not only of myself but of my mother, who was crassly impervious to disease, although she exposed herself to it constantly.   I felt left out, not only in the Butlers house but in this town of consumptive confederates.   I began to have fantasies in which both Ma and I contracted mortal illnesses; in my daydreams, Laura and Ada ate crow, admitting that they had never had anything half so bad and praising my bravery.   Whenever I sneezed, my heart leapt for joy, and each time my mother told me she was tired or that her head ached, I hoped for her collapse, anxious for even a vicarious distinction.   I stood before the open window after a hot bath in the hope of getting pneumonia.   Whenever I was alone in the house, I looked at the pictures in a book of Ma's called "Diagnostics of Internal Medicine" and studied representations of infantile spinal paralysis, of sporadic cretinism, of unilateral atrophy of the tongue.   Such was my depravity that when I considered the photograph of a naked, obscenely fat woman who was suffering, so the caption

read, from "adiposis dolorosa," I thought I could endure even that dis-
figurement to best the Butlers.

Because my mother valued health above all else (she was not a prig
about it, she was only levelheaded), I knew that these of mine were
vicious thoughts and deeds, but I could not help myself, for while I
hated the sisters deeply and with integrity, I yearned for their approba-
tion. I wanted most desperately to be a part of this ailing citizenry, to
be able casually to say, "I can't come to your house this afternoon. I
have to have an X-ray." If I had known about such things when I was
nine, I might have been able to see the reasons for my misery, but at
nine one has not yet taken in so much as the meaning of the words
"happy" and "unhappy," and I knew only that I was beyond the pale,
bovine in the midst of nymphs. Epidemics of scarlet fever and diph-
theria passed me by. Other children were bitten by rabid dogs and
their names were printed in the paper, but the only dogs I met greeted
me affably and trotted along beside me if the notion took them to. My
classmates broke their collarbones and had their tonsils taken out. But
nothing happened to me that Unguentine or iodine would not cure and
all the while the Butlers' pallor seemed to me to deepen and their
malicious egotism to grow and spread.

I do not think that Laura and Ada despised me less than they did
anyone else, but I was the only one they could force to come home with
them. "Who wants to be healthy if being healthy means being a cow?"
said Ada one day, looking at me as I reached for a third insipid cooky.
I withdrew my hand and blushed so hotly in my humiliation that Laura
screamed with laughter and cried, "The friendly cow all red and white,
we give her biscuits with all our might."

Oh, I hated them! I ground my anklebones together, I clenched my
fists, I set my jaw, but I could not talk back — not here in this elegiac
house where my poor ma was probably simultaneously being insulted
by the querulous octogenarian. I could do no more than change the
subject, and so I did, but my choice was infelicitous, for, without thinking and with a kind of self-defeating desperation which I saw to be
calamitous even before the words were finished, I asked Laura and
Ada if they did not like the tumbling we were having in gym, and Ada,
horrified, appealed to her sister (she rarely spoke directly to me but
through Laura, as if she spoke a separate language that must be translated) — "Oh, tell her that we don't *tumble*" — and her sister went on,
"While the rest of you tumble, we write essays." Who could scale this
Parnassus? On the flatlands of Philistia, I held my tongue, and I en-

dured, for the sake of learning how to execute a *tour jeté* in Miss Jorene Roy's dance salon.

And then, one day, at the height of my tribulation, Ada, quite by accident, provided me with the means to petrify them for an hour with curiosity and awe. It was nearing Christmas, and the parlor was pranked out with holly wreaths in the windows and a tree in the bay window and early greeting cards lined up in military ranks on the mantel. The girls had been uncommonly animated lately, for their father was coming from Boston to spend two weeks with his brood. I would have the privilege, as would everyone else in town, of hearing him deliver a sermon as the guest preacher at St. John's; the girls' implication was that his erudition was so great that not a soul in this benighted place would understand a word he said. That day, in the dark room — a beautiful, obscuring snow was falling and the heavy branches of the cedar trees leaned against the windows — I envied them this tribal holiday, envied them their peopled house, and pitied myself for being a fatherless and only child. I thought I would have given anything at this moment for a brother, even for Lawrence Butler, with his peaked, mean face and the supercilious way he had of greeting me by saying, "How *do* you do?" Ada, as if she had read my melancholy thoughts and wished to twist the knife, said complacently, "What a shame she doesn't have a father, isn't it, Laura? Laura, ask her what her father died of."

My brilliant answer sprang instantly to my lips without rehearsal or embellishment. "Leprosy," I said, and watched the Bostonians freeze in their attitude as if they were playing Statues. I had learned of leprosy some weeks before from the older sister of a friend, who had held me spellbound. The belief that was soon to be current among my friends and me when the movie "Ben Hur" was to enthrall us all was that lepers slowly vanished, through the rotting away of their fingers and toes, and then of their hands and feet, and then of their arms and legs, and that all exterior appointments, as ears and noses, hair and eyes, fell off like decayed vegetables finally falling from the vine. If this had been my first impression of leprosy, I doubt whether I would, even in this emergency, have thus dispatched my father to his grave, but at the time, thanks to the quixotic older sister, who had got her information in some byway trod by no one but herself, I was under the impression that leprosy was a kind of sleeping sickness brought on by the bite of a lion. This intelligence I passed on to Laura and Ada, glib crocodile tears gathering in the corners of my eyes, and never dreamed, as I pursued my monologue, that they had a Biblical acquaintance with leprosy and that what rooted them to the spot was the revelation that I was the daughter of an unclean man.

Before I could finish my story or make the most of its picturesque details, Laura gasped, "He was unclean!"

"Unclean?" I was incensed. "He was *not* unclean! He washed himself exactly like a cat!" I screamed.

"She said he was asleep for thirty months," said Ada. "Ask her how he could wash in his sleep."

"Well, he did, anyway," I said, flummoxed at being caught out. "I don't know how, but he did. He didn't have fleas, if that's what you mean."

"Unclean," repeated Ada, savoring the word. "Tell her to stay where she is until we get out of the room and tell her never to come back to this house again.

"She never will," said Laura. "She'll be sent to the Fiji Islands or someplace. Lepers can't run around loose."

"Oh, Laura, do you think she has it? Do you think we'll get it?" moaned Ada. "Where is Mother? We must tell her *now!*"

"Be careful, Ada," said Laura. "Go out of the room backwards and keep your eye on her, and if she starts to move, scream. We'll be all right as long as she doesn't touch us."

"Poor Grandmother!" wailed Ada. "Did you think of Grandmother being *touched* all this time by that unclean woman? " She backed to the doors, her eyes fixed on me, who could not have moved for anything.

"It's awful!" said Laura, following her sidewise, like a crab. "Of all days for Mother to be at the osteopath! Still, Larry will have an idea."

"Yes," said Ada from the doorway. "Probably Lawrence will send for the Black Maria."

My many selves, all bedlamites, clamored in my faint, sick heart. I wished to tell them on the spot that the whole thing had been a lie. I wished to say it had been a joke. "I was only kidding," I would say. But how heartless that would make me! To jest about my dead father, whom I had loved. Still, I must say something, must in some way exonerate myself and my mother and him. But when I opened my mouth to speak, a throttled sound came out, as surprising to my ears as to theirs, and before I had a chance to find my voice, the girls, appalled, had shut the door. I heard them slowly mount the stairs — even in their alarm they were protective of themselves — and I waited, frozen, for the sound of their avenging brother's footsteps up the stairs from the basement that entered into the front hall. When, at last, mobility returned to me, I slipped out of the parlor and made my way down the corridor to the back of the house, fearful of meeting him in the vestibule. I think I had half expected to encounter my mother in these precincts, but the passage I walked along was doorless until I came to the kitchen, a still, enormous room where there was a soft, sporadic hissing from the banked coal fire in the hooded Glenwood range. Against the varnished wainscoting stood ladder-back chairs, demanding perfect posture of their occupants, and on the trestle table there was a fruit bowl full of wholesome prunes. I knew without looking that there would be nothing good to eat in the cupboards — no brown sugar, no mayonnaise, nothing but those corky cookies. Within the pantry was a deer mouse hunched in death in a trap, and the only ray of light coming through the curtained window made an aura around its freckled fur. I bent to look more closely at the pathetic corpse, and as I did so, I heard, from directly overhead, the sound of Laura and Ada Butler giggling. *At what?* It was a high, aquatic giggle that came in antiphonal wavelets, and then one of the girls began to cough. I fled, mystified, and let myself out into the snow that whirlingly embraced me as I ran blindly home. A block from home, I began wildly to call my cat. "Kitty, kitty, kitty, *kitty!*" I shrieked, to drown out the remembered sound of my terrible lies, and Mr. Woodham's valet, passing me with Lousy Cur on a leash, said, "Whoa, there! Hold on! Where's the fire?" Pretending, with great effort, that I was the same person I had been an hour ago, I stopped and forced myself to grin and to stoop down and lightly pat the sad-eyed dog, and when this amenity was done, I continued on the double-quick.

Mine was a desperate dilemma, for I must either stick to my story and force my mother to confirm it, with the inevitable loss of her job and our probable deportation to the Fiji Islands, or grovel before the girls and admit that I had told a lie. I had told many lies before but I had never told one that involved the far future as well as the near. The consequences of telling my mother that, for example, I had been at the Public Library when in fact I had been prowling on the dump, hunting for colored bottles, were not serious. I might smart under her disapproval and disappointment (I was not forbidden to go to the dump and the needlessness of the lie made her feel, I suppose, that my character, in general, was devious) but I recovered as soon as her reproach was over. But this one, involving everyone — my father, whom I had, it seemed, maligned (although the concept of uncleanness still puzzled me); my mother, whose job and, indeed, whose whole life I had jeopardized; myself, who could never face the world again and must either wear the mark of the beast forever or spend the rest of my days under a banana tree — this lie was calamity. I thought of stowing away on the inter-urban to the city, there to lose myself forever in the dark alleys under the viaducts or in the Palladian comfort stations at the zoo. I thought of setting fire to the Butlers' house, as Nancy Hildreth and I had threatened to do, and burning them all to death. I thought, more immediately, of shaving off my hair by way of expiation.

When I got to the house, I scooped up Bow, the cat, from the rocking chair where she was sleeping, and went to my bedroom. Without taking off my coat, or even my galoshes, I lay down on my bed, my head beneath two pillows, the outraged and struggling cat clutched in my arms. But before I had time to collect my wits to formulate a plan of action (my disappearance in the city had its attractions), the tele-phone screamed its two hysterical notes, one short, one long, and I cata-pulted down the stairs to answer it. Bow trotted after me, resumed her place in the rocking chair, and went instantly to sleep.

It was Laura Butler, who, in a muffled voice, as if she did not want to be overheard by someone nearby, said, "Larry has arranged everything. He knows how we can cure you, and no one will ever know. So you come here tomorrow afternoon on the dot of three o'clock."

The next day was Saturday, and at three o'clock on Saturdays I went to Miss Roy's, and so dear to my heart was dancing class that even in this crisis I protested. "Can't I come at four instead?"

"Why should you come at four?" asked Laura imperiously.

"Because I'm the prince in 'The Cameo Girl.' "

"The *what* in the *what*?"

"I mean I go to dancing class at three," I said. "You know? My fancy-dancing class?"

"Dancing will do you very little good, my dear girl, if your legs fall off," Laura said severely.

"If my legs fall off?" I cried. "What has that got to do with it?"

"Larry says that your legs will undoubtedly fall off if you don't come here at three o'clock tomorrow." There was a slight pause; I felt she was conferring with someone, and she said, "By the bye, your mother doesn't have to have the cure, because she was too old to get leprosy, but of course if you don't have the cure, she'll have to go to the Fiji Islands with you. Larry says that's the law."

"Laura?" My voice explored the tiny tunnel of space between our telephones. Shall I tell her now, I thought. "Laura?" I asked again. "You know it's Laura," she said, so briskly, so contemptuously that on the instant I was stubborn.

"I can't come," I said.

Aside — to Ada or to Lawrence, I presumed — she said, "We may have to take steps after all. Larry says —"

"Wait!" I cried. "Hey, Laura, are you still there? Laura, listen, let me come right now!" For I was thinking of the *entrechat* I had almost perfected, and more than anything else in the world I wanted Miss Roy to tell me, in her jazzy way, that it was "a lulu." But I knew that until my mind lay at rest, I could not dance a single step.

I could hear whispers at the other end, and finally Laura said, "Very well, although it will inconvenience us," and then she warned, "If you are late, my mother will come home, I suppose you don't want *her* to know?"

I sighed deeply into the telephone and heard the other receiver being returned to its hook. Immediately the bell rang again, and Laura said, "Come in ten minutes. We have to get things ready."

The stillness of the house unnerved me as I waited those ten minutes, and, perversely, I frightened myself still more by speaking aloud and hearing my voice come hollowly back to me. "What are they going to do to me, Bow? What *things* have they got to get ready?"

It occurred to me to kill myself. I heard the interurban going out and thought again of skipping town. *Cure* me. What did that mean? I picked up Bow and carried her to the window with me and stood there with her face against mine, watching the storm. She was tense, watching Lousy Cur as he trotted home. "Shall I take the cure, Bow?" I said, and she growled deep in her gentle white belly. "Does that mean yes, Bowcat? Or shall I tell them it was a lie?" She growled again, for Lousy Cur was opposite our house, and, as if he sensed her being there, he paused, one foot uplifted, and gazed with interest at our front door. "Which?" I asked her, and in answer she writhed with a howl from my arms, furious at this double invasion of her privacy. She forgot us both and abruptly took a bath.

My hands were so damp that I could hardly peel my mittens off when I got to the Butlers' front door, and there was a severe pain in my stomach that made me think I had probably got cancer in punishment for my sin (not, as I might have hoped earlier, as a reward for my virtue). Planless still, my parched lips mouthed my alternative opening speeches: "It was a lie" and "I am ready for the cure." The door opened the moment I rang the bell, and Laura and Ada stood waiting for me in the vestibule, ceremonious in odd brown flannel wrappers with peaked hoods attached at the back of the neck. Gnomelike and leering, they ushered me into the parlor, where they had set up a card table and had covered it with a white cloth. On it stood a group of odd-shaped bottles, which, they explained to me, Larry, the chemist, had lent to them. Did they mean to burn me with acids? To sprinkle me with lye? There was also a covered willowware tureen on the table, and an open Bible.

"Ask her if she believes in God," said Ada.

"Yes," I said quickly, although I was by no means sure. "Listen, Laura —" What if I said the joke was on them? What if I said I'd planned this hoodwink for weeks? The worst they could do was get angry. But I knew I could not convince them, and I floundered, stuttering, beginning, stopping dead.

"The prisoner at the dock wishes to speak," said Ada. "Hear ye! Hear ye!"

"Yes?" said Laura, preoccupied. She had lifted the lid of the tureen and to her sister said, "Do you think the insides of one bird will do?"

Ada, looking into the dish, grimaced. "It will simply have to. There's only one to be had. Larry said it would be all right."

"Do you mind asking him again, just to make sure?"

"I wouldn't dream of disturbing him," said Ada. "He's in his laboratory, boiling his spittle. He can make it turn purple and he can make it turn green."

It made me even more uneasy to know that Lawrence was in the house, and again I started to speak. "Laura, listen to me —" But Laura had picked up the Bible now, and she-read, " 'Two birds alive and clean, and cedar wood' " — she held up a beaker half full of cedar berries — " 'and scarlet, and hyssop.' " And her sister pointed to two test tubes, which appeared to be filled, one with red ink and the other with blue.

"Laura —"

"One moment. Be quiet, please." She continued to read, " 'And the priest shall command that one of the birds be killed in an earthern vessel over running water.' " She opened the tureen again and poured out water from a cream pitcher while Ada murmured doubtfully, "Of course, it's already dead."

"A very good thing it is that she believes in God, or the cure would never work," said Laura and went on reading. " 'As for the living bird, he shall take it, and the cedar wood, and the scarlet, and the hyssop, and shall dip them and the living bird in the blood of the bird that was killed over the running water.' " With this, she put into the bowl the picture of an eagle, which she had probably cut out of a magazine, and she poured in the red ink, the blue ink, and the cedar berries. Then, bearing the vessel in both hands, she came to where I stood and allowed me to look into a dreadful mess of ink and feathers and the entrails of the chicken that they were doubtless going to have that night for dinner. She dipped her fingers into the stew, and though she shuddered and made a face, she persevered, and before my nose she dangled a bit of dripping innards.

This was enough for me. I would not be touched by those slithering, opalescent intestines, and I shrank back and I cried out, "Will you listen to me? I told a lie!"

Laura's look roasted and froze me, sent me to jail, to hell; it drew and quartered me. "A lie!" she exclaimed, as if I had confessed to murder. Ada turned to her sister with a pout and said crossly, "I *told* you it would never work."

Laura continued to look hard at me, but at last her face relaxed and, patronizing, like a minister, speciously kind, like a schoolteacher, she said, "Now, what's all this about a lie?"

"He didn't die of leprosy," I said. I looked at my feet and moved them slightly, so that the toes of my shoes pointed to the hearts of two roses in the carpet.

"Why did you say that he did?"

"Because —"

"It's more important, I should think," said Ada sulkily, "to find out what he *did* die of. It's quite possible that he died of something worse."

"Why did you say that he did?" said Laura, ignoring her.

"Because it was a joke."

"A joke? I thought you said you had told a lie. There is a world of difference between the two, Jessie. Well, which was it, a joke or a lie?"

"A joke!" I cried, almost in tears.

"Do you hear that, Laura?" said Ada. "She tells a *joke* about the deceased."

"I mean it was a lie," I said. I was on the verge of a fearful sobbing. "A lie, and I am sorry." The smell of witch hazel was inordinately dense. In the silence, I heard the click of a ball on the Christmas tree. Suddenly, my ignorance of where my mother was in this unhealthy house terrified me, and I loudly said, "How is your grandmother today?"

"Stick to the subject," said Laura.

But Ada was glad to tell me. "Grandmother is not well at all today. She had a bilious attack this morning. So did I."

She smiled smugly at me, and I, magically emboldened by my distaste, moved to the door, and as I went, I said, "*I* am never sick. I have never been sick in my life."

"Lucky you," gloated Ada.

"What did he die of?" persisted Laura.

"He got shot out hunting, if you want to know," I told them. "My father was as tall as this room. The district nurse told Ma that I am the healthiest girl in town. Also I have the best teeth."

Across those small, old faces there flickered a ray of curiosity to know, perhaps, how the other half lived, and for just that split second I pitied them. My mind cleared and I realized that all this torment had been for nothing. If the Butlers had tried to blacken my name for telling a lie, no one would have believed them, for they had no friends, and, by the same token, if they had noised it about that my father had died of leprosy, I could have said *they* were telling lies. Now I was exalted and hungry and clean, and when I had put on my coat and opened the door, I cried exuberantly, "So long, kids, see you in church!" — a flippancy I would not have dared utter in that house two hours before. By way of reply, Ada coughed pitifully, professionally.

Until the grandmother died, in April, and Ma took another job, I went two or three afternoons a week to the Butlers' house, and over our light collation, as Laura and Ada called it, we talked steadily and solely of the girls' grave illnesses. But as I left, I always said, with snide solicitude, "Take care of yourselves." They were unshakable; they had the final word: "We will. We have to, you know." My vanity, however, was now quite equal to theirs. Feeling myself to be immortal and knowing myself to be the healthiest girl in town, I invariably cut an affronting caper on the Butlers' lawn and ran off fast, letting the good mountain air plunge deep into my sterling lungs.

(From Harper's Magazine)

THE TRAVELER

BY WALLACE STEGNER

HE WAS rolling in the first early dark down a snowy road, his headlights pinched between dark walls of trees, when the engine coughed, recovered, coughed again, and died. Down a slight hill he coasted in compression, working the choke, but at the bottom he had to pull over against the three-foot wall of plowed snow. Snow creaked under the tires as the car eased to a stop. The heater fan unwound with a final tinny sigh.

Here in its middle age this hitherto dependable mechanism had betrayed him, but he refused to admit immediately that he was betrayed. Some speck of dirt or bubble of water in the gas line, some momentary short circuit, some splash of snow on distributor points or plug connections — something that would cure itself before long. But turning off the lights and pressing on the starter brought no result; he held the choke out for several seconds, and got only the hopeful stink of gasoline; he waited and let the flooded carburetor rest and tried again, and nothing. Eventually he opened the door and stepped out onto the packed snow of the road.

It was so cold that his first breath turned to iron in his throat, the hairs in his nostrils webbed into instant ice, his eyes stung and watered. In the faint starlight and the bluish luminescence of the snow everything beyond a few yards away swam deceptive and without depth, glimmering with things half seen or imagined. Beside the dead car he stood with his head bent, listening, and there was not a sound. Everything on the planet might have died in the cold.

Indecisively seeking help, he walked to the top of the next rise, but the faintly-darker furrow of the road blurred and disappeared in the murk, the shadows pressed inward, there was no sign of a light. Back at the car he made the efforts that the morality of self-reliance demanded: trying to see by the backward diffusion of the headlamps, he groped over the motor feeling for broken wires or loose connections, until he had satisfied himself that he was helpless. He had known all along that he was.

His hands were already stung with cold, and around his ankles between low shoes and trouser cuffs he felt the chill like leg irons. When he had last stopped, twenty miles back, it had been near zero. It could be ten or fifteen below now. So what did he do, stranded in mid-journey fifty miles or more from his destination? He could hardly go in for help, leaving the sample cases, because the right rear door didn't lock properly. A little jiggling swung it open. And all those drugs, some of them designed to cure anything — wonder drugs, sulphas, streptomycin, aureomycin, penicillin, pills and anti-toxins and unguents — represented not only a value but a danger. They should not be left around loose. Someone might think they really *would* cure anything.

Not quite everything, he told the blue darkness. Not a fouled-up distributor or a cranky oil box. Absurdly, there came into his mind a fragment of an ancient hymn to mechanical transport:

> *If she runs out of dope, just fill her up with soap*
> *And the little Ford will ramble right along.*

He saw himself pouring a bottle of penicillin into the gas tank and driving off with the exhaust blowing happy smoke rings. A mock-heroic montage of scientific discovery unreeled itself — white-coated scientists peering into microscopes, adjusting gauges, pipetting precious liquids, weighing grains of powder on miniscule scales. Messenger boys sped with telegrams to the desks of busy executives. A group of observers stood beside an assembly line while the first tests were made. They broke a car's axle with sledges, gave it a drink of the wonder compound, and drove it off. They demolished the carburetor and cured it with one application. They yanked loose all the wires and watched the same magic set the motor purring.

But here he stood in light overcoat and thin leather gloves, without overshoes, and his car all but blocked the road, and the door could not be locked, and there was not a possibility that he could carry the heavy cases with him to the next farm or village. He switched on the headlights again and studied the roadside they revealed, and saw a rail fence, with cedars and spruces behind it. When more complex gadgets and more complex cures failed, there was always the lucifer match.

Ten minutes later he was sitting with the auto robe over his head and shoulders and his back against the plowed snowbank, digging the half melted snow from inside his shoes and gloating over the growing light and warmth of the fire. He had a supply of fence rails good for an hour. In that time, someone would come along and he could get a push or a tow. In this country, in winter, no one ever passed up a stranded motorist.

In the stillness the flames went straight upward; the heat was wonderfully pleasant on icy hands and numb ankles and stiffened face. He looked across the road, stained by horses, broken by wheel and runner tracks, and saw how the roadside acquired definition and sharp angles and shadows in the firelight. He saw too how he would look to anyone coming along: like a calendar picture.

But no one came along. Fifteen minutes stretched into a half hour, he had only two broken pieces of rail left, the fire sizzled half floating in the puddle of its melting. Restlessly he rose with the blanket around him and walked back up the road a hundred steps. Eastward, above jagged trees, he saw the sky where it lightened to moonrise, but here there was still only the blue glimmer of starlight on the snow. Something long-buried and forgotten tugged in him, and a shiver not entirely from cold prickled his whole body with goose flesh. There had been times in his childhood when he had walked home alone and been temporarily lost in nights like this. In many years he could not remember being out alone under such a sky. He felt spooked, his feet were chilled lumps, his nose leaked. Down the hill car and snow swam deceptively together; the red wink of the fire seemed inexpressibly far off.

Abruptly he did not want to wait in that lonely snow-banked ditch any longer. The sample cases could look after themselves, any motorist who passed could take his own chances. He would walk ahead to the nearest help, and if he found himself getting too cold on the way, he could always build another fire. The thought of action cheered him; he admitted to himself that he was all but terrified at the silence and the iron cold.

Locking the car doors, he dropped his key case in the snow, and panic stopped his pulse as he bent and frantically, with bare hand, brushed away the snow until he found it. The powdery snow ached and burned at his finger tips. He held them a last moment to the fire, and then, bundled like a squaw, with the blanket held across nose and mouth to ease the harshness of the cold in his lungs, he started up the road that looked as smooth as a tablecloth, but was deceptively rough and broken. He thought of what he had had every right to expect for this evening. By now, eight o'clock or so, he should have had a smoking supper, the luxury of a hot bath, the pleasure of a brandy in a comradely bar. By now he should be in pajamas making out sales reports by the bed-light, in a room where steam knocked comfortingly in the radiators and the help of a hundred hands was available to him at a word into the telephone. For all of this to be torn away suddenly, for him to be stumbling up a deserted road in danger of freezing to death, just because some simple mechanical part that had functioned for thirty thousand miles refused to function any longer, this was outrage, and he hated it. He thought of garage men and service station attendants he could blame. Ignoring the evidence of the flooded carburetor, he brooded about watered gas that could make ice in the gas line. A man was de-pendent on too many people; he was at everybody's mercy.

And then, on top of the second long rise, he met the moon.

Instantly the character of the night changed. The uncertain star-light was replaced at a step by an even flood of blue-white radiance. He looked across a snow meadow and saw how a rail fence had every stake and rider doubled in solid shadow, and how the edge of woods beyond was blackest India ink. The road ahead was drawn with a ruler, one bank smoothed by the flood of light, the other deeply shad-owed. As he looked into the eye of the moon he saw the air shiver and glint with falling particles of frost.

In this White Christmas night, this Good-King-Wenceslaus night, he went warily, not to be caught in sentimentality, and to an invisible audience he deprecated it profanely as a night in which no one would believe. Yet here it was, and he in it. With the coming of the moon the night even seemed to warm; he found that he could drop the blanket from across his face and drink the still air.

Along the roadside as he passed the meadow and entered woods again the moon showed him things. In moonlight openings he saw the snow stitched with tiny perfect tracks, mouse or weasel or the three-toed crowding tracks of partridge. These too, an indigenous part of the night, came back to him as things once known and long forgotten. In his boyhood he had trapped and hunted the animals that made such tracks as these; it was as if his mind were a snowfield where the marks of their secret little feet had been printed long ago. With a queer tightening of the throat, with an odd pride, he read the trail of a fox that had wallowed through the soft snow from the woods, angling into the packed road and along it for a little way and out again, still angling, across the plowed bank, and then left a purposeful trail of cleanly punched tracks, the hind feet out of line with the front, across the clean snow and into the opposite woods, from shadow across moonlight and into shadow again, mysterious.

Turning with the road, he passed through the stretch of woods and came into the open to see the moon-white, shadow-black buildings of a farm, and the weak bloom of light in a window.

His feet whined on the snow, dry as metal powder, as he turned in the loop of drive the county plow had cleared. But as he approached the house doubt touched him. In spite of the light, the place looked unused, somehow. No dog welcomed him. The sound of his feet in the snow was alien, the hammer of his knuckles on the door an intrusion. Looking upward for some trace of telephone wires, he saw none, and he could not tell whether the quivering of the air that he thought he saw above the chimney was heat or smoke or the phantasmal falling frost.

"Hello?" he said, and knocked again. "Anybody home?" No sound answered him. He saw the moon glint on the great icicles along the eaves. His numb hand ached with the pain of knocking; he pounded with the soft edge of his fist.

Answer finally came, not from the door before which he stood, but from the barn, down at the end of a staggered string of attached sheds. A door creaked open against a snowbank and a figure with a lantern appeared, stood for a moment, and came running. The traveler wondered at the way it came, lurching and stumbling in the uneven snow, until it arrived at the porch and he saw that it was a boy of eleven or twelve. The boy set his lantern on the porch; between the upturned collar of his mackinaw and the down-pulled stocking cap his face was a pinched whiteness, his eyes enormous. He stared at the traveler until the traveler became aware of the blanket he still held over head and shoulders, and began to laugh.

"My car stopped on me, a mile or so up the road," he said. "I was just hunting a telephone or some place where I could get help."

The boy swallowed, wiped the back of his mitt across his nose. "Grandpa's sick!" he blurted, and opened the door.

Warmth rushed in their faces, cold rushed in at their backs, warm and cold mingled in an eddy of air as the door closed. The traveler saw a cot bed pulled close to the kitchen range, and on the cot an old man covered with a quilt, who breathed heavily and whose closed eyes did not open when the two came near. The gray-whiskered cheeks were sunken, the mouth open to expose toothless gums in a parody look of ancient mischief.

"He must've had a shock," the boy said. "I came in from chores and he was on the floor." He stared at the mummy under the quilt, and he swallowed.

"Has he come to at all?"

"No."

"Only the two of you live here?"

"Yes."

"No telephone?"

"No."

"How long ago did you find him?"

"Chore time. About six."

"Why didn't you go for help?"

The boy looked down, ashamed. "It's near two miles. I was afraid he'd. . . ."

"But you left him. You were out in the barn."

"I was hitching up to go," the boy said. "I'd made up my mind."

The traveler backed away from the stove, his face smarting with the heat, his fingers and feet beginning to ache. He looked at the old man and knew that here, as at the car, he was helpless. The boy's thin anxious face told him how thoroughly his own emergency had been swallowed up in this other one. He had been altered from a man in need of help to one who must give it. Salesman of wonder cures, he must now produce something to calm this over-worried boy, restore a dying man. Rebelliously, victimized by circumstances, he said, "Where were you going for help?"

"The Hill place. They've got a phone."

"How far are they from a town?"

"About five miles."

"Doctor there?"

"Yes."

"If I took your horse and — what is it, sleigh? — could someone at the Hills' bring them back, do you think?"

"Cutter. One of the Hill boys could, I should say."

"Or would you rather go, while I look after your Grandpa?"

"He don't know you," the boy said directly. "If he should wake up he might . . . wonder . . . it might. . . ."

The traveler grudgingly gave up the prospect of staying in the warm kitchen while the boy did the work. And he granted that it was extraordinarily sensitive of the boy to know how it might disturb a man to wake from sickness in his own house and stare into the face of an utter stranger. "Yes," he said. "Well, I could call the doctor from the Hills'. Two miles, did you say?"

"About." The boy had pulled the stocking cap off so that his hair stood on end above his white forehead. He had odd eyes, very large and dark and intelligent, with an expectancy in them.

The traveler, watching him with interest, said, "How long have you lived with your grandfather?"

"Two years."

"Parents living?"

"No sir, that's why."

"Go to school?"

He got a queer sidling look. "Have to till you're sixteen."

"Is that the only reason you go?"

What he was trying to force out of the boy came out indirectly, with a shrugging of the shoulders. "Grandpa would take me out if he could."

"Would you be glad?"

"No sir," the boy said, but would not look at him. "I like school."

The traveler consciously corked his flow of questions. Once he himself had been an orphan living with his grandparents on a back farm; he wondered if this boy went as he had gone, knocking in imagination at all of life's closed doors.

The old man's harsh breathing filled the overwarm room. "Well," the traveler said, "maybe you'd better go finish hitching up. It's been thirty years since I harnessed a horse. I'll keep an eye on your Grandpa."

Pulling the stocking cap over his disheveled hair, the boy slid out the door. The traveler unbuttoned his overcoat and sat down beside the old man, felt the spurting, weak pulse, raised one eyelid with his thumb and looked without comprehension at the uprolled eye. He knew it was like feeling over a chilling motor for loose wires, and after two or three abortive motions he gave it up and sat contemplating the gray, sunken face, the unfamiliar face of an old man who would die, and thinking that the face was the only unfamiliar thing about the whole night. The kitchen smells, coffee and peanut butter and the mouldy, barky smell of wood from the woodbox, and the smell of the hot range and of paint baking in the heat, those were as familiar as light or dark. The spectacular night outside, the snowfields and the moon and the mysterious woods, the tracks venturing out across the snow

from the protective eaves of firs and skunk spruce, the speculative, imagining expression of the boy's eyes, were just as familiar. He sat
bemused, touching some brink as a man will walk along a cutbank
trying to knock loose the crumbling overhang with an outstretched foot.
The ways a man fitted in with himself and with other human beings
were curious and complex.

And when he heard the jingle and creak outside, and buttoned
himself into the overcoat again and wrapped his shoulders in the
blanket and stepped out into the yard, there was a moment when the
boy passed him the lines and they stood facing each other in the broken
snow.

It was a moment like farewell, like a poignant parting. Touched
by his pressing sense of familiarity and by a sort of compassion, the
traveler reached out and laid his hand on the boy's shoulder. "Don't
worry," he said. "I'll have someone back here right away. Your
grandfather will be all right. Just keep him warm and don't worry."

He climbed into the cutter and pulled over his lap the balding buffalo
robe he found there: the scallop of its felt edges was like a key that fitted
a door. The horses breathed jets of steam in the moonlight, restlessly
moving, jingling their harness bells, as the moment lengthened itself.
The traveler saw how the boy, how that his anxiety was somewhat
quieted, now that he had been able to unload part of his burden,
watched him with a thousand questions in his face, and he remembered
how he himself, thirty years ago, had searched the faces of passing
strangers for something he could not name, how he had listened to
their steps and seen their shadows lengthen ahead of them down roads
that led to unimaginable places, and how he had ached with the desire
to know them, who they were. But none of them had looked back at
him as he tried now to look at this boy.

He was glad that no names had been spoken and no personal histories
exchanged to obscure this meeting, for sitting in the sleigh above the
boy's white upturned serious face he felt that some profound contact
had unintentionally, almost casually, been made.

For half a breath he was utterly bewitched, frozen at the heart of
some icy dream. Abruptly he slapped the reins across the backs of the
horses; the cutter jerked and then slid smoothly out toward the road.
The traveler looked back once, to fix forever the picture of himself
standing silently watching himself go. As he slid into the road the
horses broke into a trot. The icy flow of air locked his throat and made
him let go the reins with one hand to pull the hairy, wool-smelling
edge of the blanket all but shut across his face.

Along a road he had never driven he went swiftly toward an unknown farm and an unknown town, to distribute according to some wise law part of the burden of the boy's emergency and his own; but he bore in his mind, bright as moonlight over snow, a vivid wonder, almost an awe. For from the most chronic and incurable of ills, identity, he had looked outward and for one unmistakable instant recognized himself.

(From The Atlantic Monthly)

A RIDE ON THE SHORT DOG

BY JAMES STILL

*W*E FLAGGED the bus on a curve at the mouth of Lairds Creek by jumping and waving in the road and Dee Buck Engle had to tread the brake the instant he saw us. He wouldn't have halted unless compelled. Mal Dowe and I leaped aside finally, but Godey Spurlock held his ground. The bus stopped a yard from Godey and vexed faces pressed the windows and we heard Old Meg Hyden cry, "I'd not haul them jaspers."

Dee Buck opened the door and blared, "You boys trying to get killed?"

We climbed on grinning and shoved fares to Roscoe into his hand and for once we didn't sing out, To Knuckle Junction, and, Pistol City, and, Two Hoots. We even strode the aisle without raising elbows to knock off hats, having agreed among ourselves to sort of behave and make certain of a ride home. Yet Dee Buck was wary. He warned, "Bother my passengers, you fellers, and I'll fix you. I've put up with your mischief till I won't."

That set Godey and Mal laughing for Dee Buck was a bluffer. We took the seat across from Meg Hyden and on wedging into it my bruised arm started aching. Swapping licks was Godey's delight.

The bus wheezed and jolted in moving away, yet we spared Dee Buck our usual advice: Feed her a biscuit and see will she mend, and, Dock her tail and teach her manners. The vehicle was scarcely half the length of regular buses — "The Short Dog" everybody called it. It traveled from Thacker to Roscoe and back twice a day. Enos Webb occupied the seat in front and Godey greeted, "Hey-o, chum. How's your fat?" Enos tucked his head, fearing a rabbit lick, and he changed his seat. He knew how Godey served exposed necks. Godey could cause you to see forked lightning and hear thunder balls. Though others

shunned us, Meg Hyden gazed in our direction. Her eyes were scornful,
her lips pucked sour. She was as old as a hill.

Godey and Mal couldn't sit idle. They rubbed the dusty pane
with their sleeves and looked abroad and everything they saw they
remarked on: hay doodles in Alonzo Tate's pasture, a crazy chimney
leaning away from a house, long-johns on clotheslines. They pointed
toward the mountain ahead, trying to fool, calling, "Gee-o, looky
yonder." But they couldn't trick a soul. My arm throbbed and I had
no notion to prank, and after a while Godey muttered, "I want to know
what's eating you."

"We'd better decide what we can do in town," I grouched. Roscoe
folk looked alive at sight of us. And except for our return fares we
hadn't a dime. The poolroom had us ousted. We'd have to steer clear
of the courthouse where sheriffs were thick. And we dare not rouse the
county prisoners again. On our last trip we'd bellowed before the jail,
"Hey-o, you wife-beaters, how are you standing the times?" We'd
jeered and mocked until they had begged the turnkey to fetch us inside,
they'd notch our ears, they'd trim us. The turnkey had told them to be
patient, we'd get in on our own hook.

Godey said, "We'll break loose in town, no two ways talking."

I gloomed, "The law will pen us the least thing. We'll be thrown
with the meanest fellows that ever breathed."

Godey screwed his eyes narrow. "My opinion, the prisoners scared
you plumb. You're ruint for trick-pulling." He knotted a fist and hit
me squarely on my bruise.

My arm ached the fiercer. My eyes burned and had I not glanced
sideways they'd come to worse. "Now, no," I said; but Godey's charge
was true.

"Well, act like it," he said. "And pay me."

I returned the blow.

Old Meg was watching and she blurted, "I swear to my Gracious.
A human can't see a minute's peace."

Godey chuckled, "What's fretting you, Mam?"

"Beat and battle is all you think on," she snorted. "You're meaner'n
snakes."

"We're not so bad we try to hinder people riding the bus," he coun-
tered. "Aye, we heard you squall back yonder."

Old Meg's lips quivered, her veiny hands trembled. "Did I have
strength to reach," she croaked, "I'd pop your jaws. I'd addle you
totally."

Godey thrust his head across the aisle and turned a cheek. "See your satisfaction," he invited. He didn't mind a slap.

"Out o' my face," she ordered, lifting her voice to alert Dee Buck. She laced her fingers to stay their shaking.

Dee Buck adjusted the rear-view mirror and inquired, "What's the matter, Aunt Meg?"

"It's these boys tormenting me," she complained. "They'd drive a body to raving."

Dee Buck slowed. "I told you fellers ——"

"What've we done?" Godey asked injuredly.

"Didn't I say not bother my passengers?"

"I never tipped the old hen."

"One more antic and off you go."

Godey smirked. "Know what?" he said. "We've been treating you pretty but we've done no good. Suit a grunt-box, you can't."

"You heard me," Dee Buck said.

The twins got on at Lucas. They were about nine years old, as like as two peas, and had not a hair on their heads. Their polls were shaven clean. Godey cherrupted, "Gee-o, look coming," and he beckoned them to the place quitted by Enos Webb. Dee Buck seated the two up front and Godey vowed, "I'll trap the chubs, just you wait," and he made donkey ears with his hands and brayed. The twins stared, their mouths agape.

Mal said, "Whyn't we have our noggins peeled?"

"Say we do," laughed Godey, cocking a teasing eye on me. "They can't jail us for that shorely."

I replied, "We're broke as grasshoppers, keep in head."

It didn't take Godey long to draw the twins. He picked nothings out of the air and chewed them — chewed to match a sheep eating ivy; he feigned to pull teeth, pitch them again into his mouth, to swallow. The twins stole a seat closer, the better to see, and then two more. Godey had them where he wanted. He spoke: "Hey-o, Dirty Ears."

The twins nodded, too shy to answer.

"What's you little men's names?" he asked.

They swallowed timidly, their eyes meeting.

"Ah, tell."

"Woodrow," ventured one; "Jethro," said the other. They were solemn as firepokers.

"Hieing to a store to throw a pocketful of nickels, I bet."

"Sykes," one said. "To Grandpaw's," said his image.

"Well, who skinned you alive, I want to know?"

"Pap," they said.

Godey gazed at their skulls, mischief tingling him. He declared, "Us fellers aim to get cut bald in Roscoe. Too hot to wear hair nowadays."

I slipped a hand over my bruise and crabbed, "I reckon you know haircuts cost money in town." Plaguing Godey humored me.

"Witless," Godey said, annoyed, "we'll climb into the chairs, and when the barbers finish we'll say, 'Charge it on your short list.' "

"They'd summons the law in an eye-bat."

"Idjit," he snapped, "people can't be jailed for a debt." Yet he wouldn't pause to argue. He addressed the twins: "You little gents have me uneasy. There are swellings on your temples and I'm worried on your behalf."

The twins rubbed their crowns. They were smooth as goose eggs.

"Godey's sharp on noggins," said Mal.

"Want me to examine and find your ailment?" asked Godey.

The twins glanced one to the other. "We don't care," said one.

Godey tipped a finger to their polls. He squinted and frowned. And then he drew back and gasped, "Oh-oh." He punched Mal and blabbed, "Do you spy what I spy? Horns, if ever I saw them."

"The tom truth," Mal swore.

"Sprouting horns like bully-cows," Godey said. "Budding under the hide and ready to pip."

"You're in a bad way," Mal moaned.

"In the fix of a boy on Lotts Creek," Godey said. "He growed horns, and he turned into a brute and went hooking folks. Mean? Upon my word and honor, Old Scratch wouldn't claim him."

"A feller at Scuddy had the disease," Mal related. "Kept shut in a barn, he was, and they fed him hay and cornstalks, and he never tasted victuals. I saw him myself, I swear to my thumb. I saw him chewing a cud and heard him bawl a big bawl."

Godey sighed. "The only cure is to deaden the nubs ere they break the skin."

"And, gee-o, you're lucky tads," Mal poured on. "Godey Spurlock's a horn-doctor. Cured a hundred, I reckon."

"Oh, I've treated a few," said Godey.

"Spare the little masters," pled Mal.

Dee Buck was trying to watch both road and mirror, his head bobbing like a chicken supping water. Old Meg's eyes glinted darkly. I poked

Godey, grumbling, "Didn't we promise to mind ourselves?" But he went on: —

"They may enjoy old long hookers, may want to bellow and snort and tear up ground."

"We don't neither," a twin denied.

Godey brightened. "Want me to dehorn you?"

The boys nodded.

Though I prodded Godey's ribs, he ignored me. He told the twins, "The quicker the medicine the better the cure," and he made short work of it. Without more ado he clapped a hand on each of their heads, drew them wide apart, and struck them together. The brakes began to screech and Old Meg to fill the bus with her groans. The twins sat blinking. Dee Buck halted in the middle of the road and commanded: "All right, you scamps, pile off."

We didn't stir.

"You're not deaf. Trot."

"Deef in one ear, can't hear out of the other'n," Godey jested.

Dee Buck slapped his knee with his cap. "I said Go."

Old Meg was in a fidget. "Shut o' them," she rasped, her arms a-jiggle, her fingers dancing. "Make'em foot it."

"Old Mam," Godey chided, "if you don't check you're liable to fly to pieces."

"Rid the rascals," she shrilled to Dee Buck. "Are ye man enough?"

Godey said, "He'll puff and he'll huff — all he ever does. He might's well feed the hound a bit of gas and let's travel."

Dee Buck blustered, "I've got a bait of you fellers. I'm offering you a chance to leave on your own free will."

"Collar and drag'em," Old Meg taunted. "A coward, are ye?"

"Anybody spoiling to tussle," Godey challenged, "well, let him come humping."

Dee Buck flared, "Listen, you devils, I can put a quietus on you and not have to soil my hands. You don't want to be aboard when I pull into town. I can draw up at the courthouse and fetch the law in two minutes."

"Sick a sheriff on us," Godey said, "and you'll wish to your heart you hadn't. We paid to ride."

"Walk off and I'll return your fares."

"Now, no."

"I won't wait all day."

"Dynamite couldn't budge us."

Dee Buck slammed his cap onto his head. He changed gear, readying to leave. "I'm willing to spare you and you won't have it."

"Drive on, Big Buddy."

The bus started and Old Meg flounced angrily in her seat. She turned her back and didn't look round until we got to Roscoe.

We crossed two bridges. We passed Hilton and Pot Tomlinson's sawmill and Kingry and Thorne. Beyond Thorne the highway began to rise. We climbed past the bloom of coal veins and tipples of mines hanging the slope; we mounted until we'd gained the saddle of the gap and could see Roscoe four miles distant. Godey and Mal cut up the whole way, no longer trying to behave. They hailed newcomers with, "Take a seat and sit like you were at home, where you ought to be," and sped the departers, "I'll see you later, when I can talk to you straighter." The twins left at Sykes and Godey shouted, "Good-bye, Dirty Ears. Recollect I done you a favor." We rolled through the high gap and on down the mountain.

I nursed my hurt and sulked, and eventually Godey growled, "I want to know, did you come along just to pout?"

"You've fixed us," I accused bitterly, and I openly covered my crippled arm.

Godey scoffed, "Dee Buck can't panic me. You watch him turn goodfeller by the time we reach town, watch him unload in the square the same as usual. Aye, he knows what suits his hide." He grabbed loose my hand and his fist shot out.

It was too much. My face tore up, my lips quivered and tears smeared my cheeks. Godey stared in wonder. His mouth fell open. Mal took my part, rebuking him, "No use to injure a pal."

"I don't give knocks I can't handle myself," Godey said; and he invited, "Pay me double. Throw a rabbit lick and make me see lightning." He leaned forward and bared his neck.

I wiped the shameful tears, thinking to join no more in Godey's game.

"Whap him and even up," Mal said. "We're nearly to the bottom of the mountain."

"Level with me," said Godey, "or you're no crony of mine. You'll not run with my bunch."

I shook my head.

"Hurry," said Mal. "I see town smoking."

I wouldn't.

Mal advised Godey, "Nettle him. Speak a thing he can't let pass. Make him mad."

Godey said, "Know what I'm in the opinion of? Hadn't it been for Mal and me you'd let Dee Buck bounce you. You'd have turned chicken."

"I'd not," I gulped

"Jolt him," Mal urged.

"You're a chicken leg," Godey said, "and everybody akin to you is a chicken leg, and if you're yellow enough to take that I'll call you 'Chicken Leg' hereinafter."

I couldn't get around Godey. Smite him I must, and I gripped a fist and struck as hard as I could in close quarters, mauling his chest.

"Why, you couldn't punish a flea," he belittled. "Anyhow, didn't I call for a rabbit lick? Throw one and let me feel it; throw one, else you know your name." Again he leaned and exposed his neck.

"He's begging," Mal incited.

I'd satisfy him, I resolved, and I half rose to get elbowroom. I swung mightily, my fist hitting the base of his skull. I made his head pitch upward and thump the seat board; I made his teeth grate. "That ought to do," I blurted.

Godey walled his eyes and clenched his jaws. He began to gasp and strain and flounder. His arms lifted, clawing the air. Tight as we were wedged the seat would hardly hold him. Mal was ready to back a sham and he chortled, "Hark, you folks. See a witty perish." But none bothered to glance.

Then Mal and me noticed the odd twist of Godey's neck. We saw his lips tinge, his ears turn tallow. His tongue waggled to speak and could not. And of a sudden we knew and we sat frozen. We sat like posts while he heaved and pitched and his soles rattled the floor and his knees banged the forward seat. He bucked like a spoiled nag. . . . He quieted presently. His arms fell, his hands crumpled. He slumped and his gullet rattled.

We rode on. The mountain fell aside and the curves straightened. The highway ran a bee line. We crossed the last bridge and drew into Roscoe, halting in the square. Dee Buck stood at the door while the passengers alighted and all hastened except Old Meg and us. Old Meg ordered over her shoulder, "Go on ahead. I'll not trust a bunch o' jaspers coming after me." We didn't move. She whirled and her eyes lit on Godey. She sputtered, "What's the matter with him?"

Mal opened his mouth numbly. "He's doing no good," he said.

(*From The Hudson Review*)

THE LETTERS

BY HARVEY SWADOS

*T*HE FIRST WEEK out of Brisbane was a throbbing nightmare. The tanker rode easily enough in the long slow swells of the South Pacific, but Philip Stolz, the radio operator, was slow in recovering from a prolonged bout of alcohol and sex in which he had indulged at Lennons Hotel.

The ship had sailed somewhat early. They were already casting off, the first mate hanging over the bow and the old man standing on the bridge cursing at him, when Philip arrived at the pier in a taxi. His armpits were not yet dry, his uniform was wrinkled, stained, and ill-smelling, his hair was matted under the no longer clean summer white hat, and his parched lips, on which he could feel some flakes of the girl's cosmetics, still tasted of her sleep- and brandy-swollen kisses. But as soon as he had stripped off his soiled blue jacket and rolled up the grimy cuffs of his white shirt he had to mount to the bridge, sore, damp, and sleepy, and see that the antennas were properly rigged, with the sun beating down mercilessly on his strained eyeballs; and then, covered with grease and his head ringing like a gong, he had to go into the radio shack and test the equipment. When he finally finished he tore off his clothes, fell on his bunk, and slept through dinner and the slow journey out of Brisbane harbor, awaking only in the middle of the night, the ship already at sea, and time for him to go on watch.

It was like that for the first week. The physical effects of the thirty-six hours he had spent locked in the hotel room with the tart wore off after a few cold showers and a few glasses of orange juice, except for a trembling at the knees when he made the long walk aft along the cat-walk to the saloon at mealtime, and a dead sensation in the pit of his stomach when he raised his dark troubled head from his plate and looked

305

at the greasy mouths of the intent diners in the saloon. But the other effects of Philip's private little orgy were far more persistent. Over and over he reviewed the details of the wild hours he had passed with the abandoned girl: at the most inopportune moments — when he was busy trying to raise Honolulu by short wave, when he stood under a cold shower with the tropical sun beating in through the open porthole, when he lay on his bunk slimed with sweat trying to read a paper-bound book of short stories — he smelled the girl's fevered flesh, or recalled her breasts swinging frantically above his face as she crouched over his recumbent torso, or felt the sweat-soaked, wrinkled bed sheets grating under his curled fingertips, or saw the empty brandy bottles rolling about, tangled in her torn stockings, on the speckled carpet.

Probably his most painful memory was the shameful recollection of the way he had whipped up his flagging appetites with the aid of the brandy and the violent and cunning connivance of the fantastically insatiable girl. He had regarded the episode at first as a duty he owed to his body, and then, while the febrile hours slid by in the half-darkened room, as something that had to run its predestined course, like a long and useless life. How his wife (when he wanted to be funny, he occasionally referred to her as "my current wife") would have wrinkled her nose in disgust! It was not the idea that he had been unfaithful to her that galled Phil — he had been going to sea too long for that — but the certainty of the scorn with which she would greet his depraved conduct, seated at her metal desk in the insurance company offices in Hartford. Phil recognized the fact that he was no longer very fond of his wife, and that his prolonged absences had made her less interesting to him, but he was as vulnerable as ever to her intimations of superiority, made on the basis of her regular attendance at concerts, her regular reading of advanced periodicals, and her association with what she liked to call "thoughtful" people. It was difficult to justify his mode of exist ence when his wife asserted that he enjoyed living with seamen because they were his intellectual inferiors, or that he continued to go to sea because it gave him an excuse to keep from "really doing anything." And now this . . .

The sun and the sea did their marvelous recuperative work. Sitting on the boat deck with his desk chair tilted against a bulkhead, full in the sun, Phil gazed through his dark glasses at the dully shining endless water stretching monotonously through space to the horizon. After a few days, he could step from the dark sweaty loneliness of the radio shack directly into the tropical sun, feeling with a hard delight the burning heat of the deck plates on his thin sneakers; easing himself slowly into the chair, his bare flesh crying out against the white sun, he could really open *A Tour to the Hebrides* and give himself over to it and to the sun, without having to stare fixedly, like an angry victim of tuberculosis, at the impersonal spectacle of nature surrounding him on all sides. And eventually, he could even begin to look about the ship itself and note the little changes that had taken place around him.

There were, for example, several men aboard the tanker who had not been there on the trip out from Panama. Two of these passengers who had boarded the ship in Brisbane ate in the saloon, although Phil did not see them there very often, since he usually got there almost at the end of the serving period, ate quickly, and left without stopping for a cigarette. One of them, who was obviously not a seafaring man, was a genuine puzzle: what was this fat middle-aged man, self-consciously dressed in creased khakis, doing on a slow-moving tanker that rarely carried passengers? But when he finally accosted Phil one morning by the Number Two lifeboat, he turned out to be such an uninteresting fat man that Phil could not even bring himself to find out what he was doing aboard ship.

"You're the radio operator, aren't you?"

"That's right."

"How do you keep from going nuts? Always the same, day in and day out, week in and week out. You can't even see a movie. No variety, not a bit of variety."

"I like it." It was of course impossible to explain to the passenger that he had named precisely the things about sailing on the flat Pacific that Phil liked best. He picked up his book and began to read rudely, dismissing the man with the lowering of his eyelids.

The other passenger was something else. The first time that Phil really saw him he was jumping up and down on the catwalk. Phil felt the vibrations, perhaps; at any rate, he looked up, blinking away from Boswell, and saw a tall, excessively thin young man, wearing only (like himself) shorts and sneakers, skipping rope along the catwalk, his thin hairy arms flashing through the sunny air as he vaulted up and down, moving erratically astern along the steel walk like some great eccentric spider. Despite these unusual actions he looked as though he was somehow at home on a ship; but Phil took an immediate dislike to him.

For one thing, this leaping about with a piece of clothesline seemed an excessively familiar action for one who was aboard on sufferance, so to speak, and was not integrally concerned with the movement of the vessel on which he jumped. In addition, the passenger's skin was extraordinarily white, gleaming flatly like the belly of a leaping fish suddenly exposed to the sun; if he was a seafaring man, it was strange that here in the South Seas there should be no trace of sun on his long thin body. What was more annoying was the very idea of the exercise. It always seemed to Philip that there was something infinitely depressing about a grown man indulging in the pastimes of a child; and when the performance went on in public, as it did now, the exhibitionism and the arrogance implicit in such action were an affront.

If there was anything mystical about this swift dislike, it was strengthened early that evening when Henson, the third mate, and the only man aboard ship whose company Phil enjoyed, said to him, "Come into my stable, Phil. Eight days out and you haven't even shown your face yet."

"All right," Phil said. "In a few minutes."

There were three men in Henson's cabin when Phil walked in: Henson himself, Caputo, the Steward, and the tall passenger who had been skipping rope along the catwalk during the afternoon. Although the door was open wide and the porthole glass was hooked back against the overhead, there was little air in the room. All three men were smoking, and each one held a bottle of Panamanian beer; and since Henson slouched in his arm-chair, Caputo lay across the bunk, and the stranger sat on the settee, the room appeared unpleasantly crowded. Phil began to regret the sociable impulse that had drawn him down here, especially when he observed that all of the men were dressed only in shorts and slippers. Their skin was slick with a fine film of tropic sweat, and the cabin seemed to be filled with their heavy naked legs.

Henson handed Phil a bottle of beer and said, "I don't think you've met Bradley Holliday, Phil. Holliday, this is our radio man, Phil Stolz."

They shook hands.

"Holliday's an engineer." Henson's round old face smiled blandly, his eyes roving, joke-making, behind oldfashioned steel-rimmed glasses. "But we let him up forward because he's got some new records. We're a very democratic ship."

Phil sat down on the settee next to Holliday, who smiled pleasantly at him and offered a cigarette. "Smoke, Sparks?"

"Thanks."

Holliday was losing his hair. His face was long, smiling, and polite; the balding skull gave his head just the needed touch of elegance, like a boutonnière. For without the gently receding hairline that made him look properly twenty-eight or thirty, there would have been something vulgar, something falsely genteel and cultivated, in his young American college man's expression. He gets away with it, Phil thought, looking down at the Rachmaninoff album that Holliday held across his bony knees. No doubt he was well liked by his shipmates and by men who met him casually, if they did not notice the self-satisfied glint that played across his otherwise ordinary face: it was the sure, arrogant gleam of a man who has always had his way with women, principally by choosing women who were his inferiors to the extent that they would be taken in by his youth and his looks alone — and now by his urbane, thin-haired maturity alone.

He in his turn glanced down at the bright yellow dustjacket of Phil's book and murmured, "I see you're a lover of fine books."

"I like to read." Philip hated the man, he was sure of it now, but he could not get up and leave, if only because Henson would be embarrassed.

"I don't care much for travel books," Holliday said. "I prefer poetry, like Carl Sandburg." He smiled around the cabin. "I'm a West Coast sailor myself, but Sandburg made me *feel* just what Chicago is like."

One poem, Phil said to himself, one poem in a stray anthology has made him an intellectual. The man's very name was an affront; Bradley Holliday indeed . . . it sounded like the hero in one of the *American Boy* stories that Phil had read every month in an agony of excitement and envy when he was thirteen: Brad Holliday, madcap leader of Dormitory B, Brad Holliday, ace goalie of Percival Prep, Bradley Holliday, bronzed lifeguard at Bide-A-While Summer Camp . . .

Watching Holliday as he slipped the first record out of the album with long graceful fingers and placed it on the hand-winding victrola, Phil realized, in one of those sudden painful bursts of insight that bring one face to face with the condition of one's life, that if the man's name only betrayed a Jewish or a European origin one would feel compelled by one's sense of fairness not to condemn him without searching for the neurotic roots of his slippery and false manner; but a Bradley Holliday had to be held accountable for every overt expression of his essential vulgarity. Philip felt his spirit withdrawing from the room, leaving only his gross body seated next to Holliday, as the passenger tested the needle with his forefinger and said, "I hope you men enjoy this. I prefer Victor Herbert myself, but my girl is very fond of Rachmaninoff, so I bought her this album in Calcutta. After all, if you only have a limited number

of records, this will be a change." He finished his beer and chuckled,
"It's a long voyage home, as Eugene O'Neill once said."

Phil sat quietly through the recording, which happened to be excellent; the beer was not cold but cool, the ship pulsated quietly beneath
the scratching needle, and when a touch of a breeze slipped in through
the open porthole he could smell Holliday's pungent shaving lotion.
At one point — Holliday was changing a record and saying something
about the value of great music as a solace for lonely seamen — Henson's
round and wrinkled eyelid drooped slowly behind the steelrimmed eyeglasses in an exaggerated wink. The gesture was almost enough to
establish a community of dislike, and Phil relaxed a little on the settee.

The final notes of the Rachmaninoff concerto were still floating heed-
lessly out to sea on the tropical evening air as Henson heaved himself
out of his chair and pulled on a pair of khaki trousers. "Almost eight,"
he said. "I'm due on the bridge. But stay," he gestured hospitably,
"stay right where you are. I never lock my valuables."

Philip arose. "I want to get a few hours sleep before I go on watch."

Holliday glanced at him curiously. "Don't you keep a day watch?"

"I prefer to split the hours. I enjoy the quiet at night, and the reception is usually better."

"I wonder . . ." Holliday looked down uncertainly at the book that
Phil held in his hand, apparently unable to formulate a transitional
statement that would smoothly bridge the gap between his feelings and
his expectations. "Do you think it would be all right . . ." Once again
he hesitated, and at that instant, that moment of honest uncertainty,
his real charm, natural and unforced, shone through his false exterior.
It seemed to Philip that whereas all too many people were cloying and
over-confidential when their guard was down, men like Holliday could
only be more likeable in their moments of revelatory weakness. He
smiled encouragingly, and Holliday destroyed everything by saying, "I
don't often get the chance to talk with a man who enjoys good reading.
You're a college graduate, aren't you?"

How false he rang after his little moment of sincerity! Philip replied
coldly, "I had two years at Tufts once."

"Would it be all right if I came up to the shack some time, just to
shoot the breeze for a while?"

"The old man doesn't want visitors in the shack, especially during
watchkeeping hours. The best time to stop in is during my night
watch, when he's asleep." Why didn't he lie? He could have insisted
that no one ever entered the radio shack. Holliday's irresoluteness,
his sudden uncertainty, had wrung from him this grudging invitation.

Holliday was once again in command of the situation. "That's very white of you, Sparks. I'll drop up real soon, and we'll have a good long talk. I'm sure we'll find that we have a lot in common."

Thus dismissed, Phil retreated in some confusion, tripping over the mat in Henson's doorway as he stepped out to the passageway.

Shortly after Philip went on watch that evening the third mate stepped into the shack on his way down from the wheelhouse. "I'm going to examine the night lunch," he said. "Can I bring you a sandwich?"

Phil shook his head. "No. What's the story on the passenger?"

Henson smiled slowly. "Holliday? You don't like him, do you?"

"Not much. He's a phoney, Henson."

"I wouldn't put it that strongly. There's some good in the worst —"

"He skips rope."

Henson laughed. "Christ, Phil, if you're looking for gossip . . . He's been passing himself off on the black gang as a First Assistant Engineer — he even hinted that he sailed Chief during the war. But I've seen his license, you know. The man's only a Third Assistant."

"That's typical." Phil looked up angrily. "Isn't it typical, Henson?"

"You're pretty hard on him. I think Holliday is a very likeable fellow, and a damn sight more intelligent than the average engineer. I've seen more of him than you have this past week, and I find him good company. If I had his trouble, I doubt if I'd be so even-tempered and cheerful."

"What's his trouble?"

"He's got syphilis."

"Are you sure?"

Henson waved his hand tiredly through the hot breathless air. As he reached up to remove his steelrimmed glasses he blinked; without the glasses he looked old and worn. Philip felt ashamed, looking at him like this.

"You know that fat passenger?"

"Yes."

"He's a company doctor going home on leave. He's been treating Holliday, trying to keep things under control until we dump him at Pearl, or Pedro. That's why we couldn't sign Holliday on as a workaway back in Brisbane. He isn't fit to stand watch, so the company decided to give him a break and a free ride home. After all, he's been riding their tankers for a good many years. And Phil . . ."

"Yes?"

"If the company can afford to be charitable, why can't you? Sometimes you tend to judge people as though they were on trial. I'm not complaining about that," he added hastily, warding off Philip's protestations with his outspread hand. "That's your privilege. But can't you take into account the suffering that people have undergone when you pass judgment? Suppose that Holliday talked this way about you — wouldn't you want him to make an effort to understand you before he shot off his mouth?"

"I don't —" Phil checked himself. Suddenly he saw Holliday as he had been that afternoon, his thin, sick body clothed only in khaki shorts, cavorting about on the catwalk, trying to *build himself up*, trying to *soak up sunshine*. "What about his girl? The one he bought the Rackmaninoff records for?"

"Are you being cruel?"

Phil flushed. "No. I'm curious."

"And I'm a cynic." Henson lifted his shoulder wearily. He moved slowly to the door. "For all I know, she gave him the chancre as a going-away present, before he left home . . ."

Phil sat until four o'clock in the morning in his iron and concrete room, listening to the throbbing heartbeat of the ship, choked and muffled as though it were slowly strangling in the warm Pacific, and listening occasionally to the plaintive chirping of other ships far away, which sounded as though they had settled only momentarily, like some strange and frightened birds, on the bosom of the southern sea. Conscientiously he noted what they had to say in his log, but their weak cries were no different on this white and star-filled night from what they had been or would be on any other such night. The peace and terror of the world, a thousand miles from the nearest thrust of rock, were such that it was almost an impiety to listen to other voices when one floated godlike and alone.

But *What do you do with all your time?* his wife had to ask him when they lay in bed. 'Some men paint watercolors of the sea, Joseph Conrad even wrote great novels about it, but you don't even seem to be able to keep up with your reading.' *Keep up*, indeed. How could one possibly explain that he floated alone, like this, in order that it should not be demanded of him that he keep up? If the noblest human achievements could not compete with the annihilating force of the marine sun and moon on one's lowered eyelids, why should one even attempt to struggle against a surrender to the timeless bronze days and the white silent nights?

He no longer maintained the pretense of holding a book before him on the desk while he sat half-listening to the little voices of the distant ships. It was in these hours that he knew his own life and its ugliness as no artist could possibly reveal it to him, simply by extending his palm (which had participated in the countless brutalities he had committed in common with all the rest of humanity) and feeling, along its coarse surface, the velvety breath of this pure and unpeopled night. Shortly before dawn he could rouse himself and type *Off Watch on 500 KC*, leaving the swivel chair and the radio which committed him to the reactionary necessity of facing in the direction from which he had come.

He customarily slept out on deck, on an army cot which he had borrowed from the sick bay. Tonight he lowered himself quietly to the cot, slipped off his sneakers, loosened his shorts, and stretched himself out at full length beneath the white and blue brilliance of the stars. There, on the slowly rocking sliver of cooling metal, his eyes bathed in an effulgence so brilliant that he had finally to blot it from his vision, Phil felt the very essence of his being stirring itself slowly, uncoiling and rising to the very heights for which it had striven unsuccessfully for thirty years . . .

The next day Holliday did not present himself on deck with his skipping rope, and Philip felt obscurely grateful, as though there had been some unspoken understanding between them in the final moments of their meeting in Henson's cabin the night before, as though Holliday had agreed: if you don't hate me any more, Sparks, I won't exercise in public any more.

They did not, in fact, meet at all during the day, and Phil went about his marvelously monotonous routine: breakfast with the captain and his sullen Swedish jokes about things that had probably not happened aboard a windjammer in 1911; shaving before the unrevealing mirror, the disc of the sun once again driving heat before it like a searing knife through the portholes; inspection of the massive batteries oozing sulphuric acid; the specially cold water of the shower stall dripping continuously behind all the other noises on this deck; the colorless hot iron of the ship itself as he made his way aft once again to the saloon where the engineers and deck officers, their chins sweating, fattened themselves on hot food and loud lying memories of their nights in Noumea and Brisbane.

This same, same routine, hour following hour like the endless plash plash of blue water slapping the plates of the ship, was as soothing to Phil as a compress laid across his dry burning eyes. While he sat and baked, Boswell hanging laxly from his sweating hand, he could watch the first mate standing at the clothesline on deck below him, tying up his dripping white socks and shorts; he could watch the arc of the sky, curving like a concave plate-glass window to meet the pale shining body of the sea. The sun, suspended behind the arching sky as though it hung in a clear curved window, sparkled coolly as always on the wetly glistening sea; but against his bare wet brown flesh it felt as though it were being focussed through a burning glass. He squirmed about in a slow agony of pleasure, observing his skin browning through the dark glasses while rancor oozed like sweat out of his pores. Yes, while he broiled in the equatorial blaze, shifting now and again to match the slow swing of the day, he grew certain that every mean deed — the rotten fornications, the small hatreds and puny envies, the inconsequential and fruitless marriages — all were being baked out of his interior being; if he were ever again to touch land, he would return to combat renewed and whole.

By evening the recuperative process had advanced so far that Phil could regard even Bradley Holliday with a kind of benevolent neutrality. He awoke from an evening's slumber in time for a cold shower and a beef sandwich; it was midnight and time for him once again to go on watch.

And once again he sat facing Australia, facing the slate-grey radio panels with their eye-like dials that kept him, literally, in touch with the other little vessels sliding along the surface of the southern sea — an island, two islands, three islands away. *Wiper age 39, cramps lower rt. qdrt., pse adv med.* . . . The plaintive little calls of the distant ships, flutey and disembodied in the rich velvet-black air, served only to lull him further away from the reality of their thread-connected world.

It was with some surprise, therefore, that Phil looked up from the deep green of his desk, and saw Bradley Holliday standing in the doorway. He must have made some slight gesture in order to attract Phil's attention, perhaps he merely coughed; in any event, he was carrying a tall bottle of Bols gin with two glasses, a folded leather case the size of a notebook, and a bulky folder wrapped in manila paper.

"I'm not intruding, am I?" Holliday looked serious, and even — aided by his impressive paraphernalia — purposeful. "You suggested —"

"Come in. Take my sneakers off the chair and sit down."

"Thanks." Holliday did as he was told, then held the gin bottle critically up to the light. "You don't have any scruples about drinking on watch, do you, Sparks?"

"This is a free and easy ship."

"So I've noticed. I go up on the bridge every afternoon to chew the fat with the second mate, and the old man hasn't kicked me down below yet. That's remarkable in itself."

"I suppose so."

"You've got a good feeding ship too — the steward is an all right guy. As a matter of fact, I persuaded him to give me —" he unbuttoned his khaki shirt and drew forth a bottle of Australian lemon juice, "— a quart of this stuff from the freezer. Makes the gin more palatable, you know. Say when."

Phil indicated the correct level with his forefinger as Holliday decanted the bottle, then placed it on the desk before the little set of radio manuals and Penguin books and leaned back gingerly in his chair as though he were still unsure of his welcome.

"But no matter how good . . ." He stopped, moistened his lips, and then said determinedly, "It really doesn't matter whether you're on a happy ship or not if you have a serious problem. There's something about being at sea that cuts you off psychologically from the ordinary solutions. If you come up against something that you can't find an answer for by yourself, then you're stuck. You're really stuck."

Philip looked at him in surprise. Just as he thought he had Holliday properly pigeonholed, the man popped out of place, insisting on his claim to individuality.

"It doesn't make any difference what the size of the crew is either, whether it's forty-five, or fifty, or a hundred and fifty. The point is that although they're your shipmates, they're still not the people you'd voluntarily choose for friends. It's sheer luck if you find just one person you can talk to. That's why I've come up here tonight."

The earphones which Phil wore looped around his throat like a primitive necklace seemed to have grown suddenly both heavy and loud; would Holliday feel that it was rude of him to go on wearing them? He lowered their volume and suspended them from one of the knobs of the short-wave-receiver where they swung like a gift offering, squawking faintly. If Holliday wanted to, he could accept the gesture as an invitation to proceed.

"Frankly," Holliday said warmly, "I felt that you were the kind of person I could talk to. Perhaps it sounds silly, but I believe that college men and people who like good books in general are usually more understanding than uncultured people. I studied engineering at U.C.L.A. for a while, until my dad's money ran out, and I appreciate the difference between people who are *simpatico*, like yourself, from having really made an effort to appreciate the finer things, and people who simply don't care."

This appeal to Philip's superior sensibility was gratifying, even though it drifted off into the No Man's Land between sincerity and insincerity that was seemingly so congenial to the passenger. Phil had raised his hand protestingly during Holliday's short oration; now he dropped it as the statement was brought to a close and Holliday handed him a glass. "Here's looking at you, Sparks."

Phil gulped at the concoction, glancing uneasily over the rim of the glass at his drinking companion. If Holliday wanted to be regarded as an intelligent individual, and not as a clod, he would not hasten to insist upon Phil's listening to his confidences. Or would he begin by being a little reticent, simply because his conception of the cultivated young man included a modicum of reserve as standard equipment? Phil set down his glass as Holliday unwrapped the manila bundle and straightened the leather case.

"I've been having a bit of trouble with my girl," Holliday said, in a more casual tone. "You know how it is when you're out on one of these Pacific runs. There's so much time to think things over that you don't take anything for granted. Are you married, Sparks?"

Phil nodded, but did not volunteer any information. It was one thing for this man to walk into the room with his personal troubles in his pocket, ready to be uncorked and poured like gin; but there was no reason for Phil himself to counter with Natalie, as though the calculated wifely hypocrisy which he suffered from her could somehow cancel out Holliday's difficulties. Holliday however seemed content to accept the nod as Phil's contribution to their mutual understanding.

"Then you'll see my problem that much more clearly." He unfolded the leather case and stood it on end, like an open book, facing Phil. It contained a kodachrome photograph of a girl who smiled directly out of the picture at him. "This is Phyllis. I thought I'd set the scene for you a little, so to speak, if I brought her picture along so you could see what she looks like. Attractive, isn't she?"

The picture, embossed with the label of a prominent Hollywood photographer, was of a girl in her twenties, no longer flushed with youth, but still fresh and piquant. Her Norse cheekbones, slanting tautly towards the little creases of her neat ears, were thrown into relief by the smile, which was not the cajoled grimace of an ordinary portrait. There was a wistfulness in the slight arch of her back-flung neck and in the pouting curve of her full parted lips that was reminiscent of the wholehearted tenderness possessed by a few girls whom Phil had known. Even her oval eyes, slanting upwards and paralleling the line of her cheekbones, looked out at him with a special recognition, as though he were as familiar to her as an old story or a well-remembered piece of music. Only her hair was uninteresting; it was set in conventional curls mounted toward the front of her head, as though she could not — dared not — make the final gesture that would set her apart from all the other girls of her world, as though finally she had to cling, to capitulate in this little way to its demands.

Everything that the photograph revealed about this girl, yes, even her hair, was infinitely touching to Phil: the tender, sensitive countenance was moderately intelligent, but achingly anxious of acquiring, by conquest or by absorption, a greater intelligence, and Phil paid her the tribute of turning to the man who claimed her and saying, "She's really lovely."

"Isn't she?" Bradley Holliday smiled gratefully. "She's just that good in bed too. Sensational." His smile broadened but did not become vulgar. "I know I can speak frankly to you, Sparks. A lot of sailors would blow their corks if I said anything like that to them. Once you sleep with a girl you're not supposed to have any respect for her, unless she's your wife; and then you can't ever mention the fact that you lay her. The whole world is divided into the whores that you bang and the women you love. Some of these smart apples brag to me — they actually brag! — that they've never seen their wives with their clothes off. With people like that it's useless to talk.

"But my problem is a little more complicated than anything those sailors ever encountered. For one thing, Phyllis is after me to marry her and I'm damned if I know what to do. Sometimes I think, go ahead, marry her. One of these days you may hit the beach and find her married to someone else. And then I say to myself, why look for trouble? She's got a nice apartment and a comfortable bed. Everything is fine as long as I come and go when I please. How do I know what will happen after we get married? Supposing I discover that we're not compatible after all?"

It was really absurd. Philip had posed the same unreal questions to himself when he married Grace, and again when he met Natalie, and he had been unable to answer them sensibly. How then could he answer them now, when they were asked by a man who was not even aware of the meaning of the words that he used?

But apparently Holliday did not expect an answer. "I took the liberty —" he said quietly, as he opened the manila folder and drew forth a packet tied with string, "— of bringing along Phyl's letters, the ones she's written me since I left on the last voyage. If I may —"

"Whose letters?"

"Phyl." Holiday inclined his head toward the picture. "My fiancée."

"You startled me. That's my name too, you know."

"Oh, is it? I'm afraid I didn't catch it when we were introduced. What did you say your last name was?"

"Stolz." Phil hesitated for an instant. "That means 'proud' or 'pride' in German," he added, and hated himself as soon as the words were out. What a horror, he thought agitatedly, what a lurking horror to know that the hateful need of "justifying" one's very name lay always hidden in ambush, like an ugly beast, ready to leap forth snarling whenever identification was demanded.

Holliday did not seem to notice Philip's perturbation. He turned over the tied bundle of letters with curious caution, as though he were examining a stack of new banknotes. "Would it be too much of an imposition —" he glanced up warily, as if to say *We* know that I'm not worried about it being an imposition, "— if I were to read some of Phyl's letters to you now?"

But if he had come to the radio room simply to read the letters, why did he bother to ask permission? Was it possible that he was troubled by pangs of conscience, that he desired simple masculine approval for what might otherwise be considered a betrayal of confidence?

Phil said, "I'm perfectly willing to listen. But do you think —"

"Oh, I know!" Holliday cried, almost gaily. "You're afraid that Phyl might be offended. But she's not that type, not at all. In fact, I think she'd be rather pleased about my reading some passages to you. You'll see what I mean; some of her letters sound as though she'd written them for an audience, instead of just for me."

Phil studied the girl's photograph. It was possible, wasn't it, that Holliday was right, that this girl, with her determined brows and her smiling but fervent eyes, was fully capable of a public utterance of her feelings. . . . Or was he being swayed, as Phyllis very likely had been, by Holliday's insolent charm?

Holliday clinched it by saying calmly, "Phyllis works for an advertising agency. Unfortunately, she takes it seriously, so . . ." His shrug was both worldly and cynical.

Phil felt baffled and powerless. Even if he too were to shrug in reply, the graceless motion of his shoulders could hardly compete with Holliday's eloquent gesture. But before the silence could become awkward, Holliday had snapped the string and begun to read the topmost letter.

"*Darling Brad, just a few hours since you've left* —this was last May — *and yet everything seems different. Isn't it odd how you can go on doing the same things, and yet feel that all meaning has been sucked out of them, merely by virtue of one person's departure from your life? The egg that was so juicy and tempting suddenly becomes an Easter egg, gaily colored still, but hollow and empty on the inside . . .*"

So this was the prose that she had polished for Holliday and his chance acquaintances. Phil looked at the girl's picture with compassion and contempt. If she had entrusted her private dreams to Holliday, she had no one to blame but herself for what became of them.

"*. . . of course, I can hear you saying, isn't it foolish of her to sit down and write to me when I've just left, and she hasn't any news for me? But darling, I only want to tell you that suddenly I understand how it is that there won't be any news, not any at all, until you come back. The job isn't going to have any flavor, even the apartment that I've been so proud of because you've been so comfortable here. . . .*"

Phil knew now that he was going to have to listen to the entire series of letters. He reached for the bottle and poured two more drinks. It was the first liquor he had tasted since the final night with the girl at Lennons Hotel, but it aroused only pictorial memories of that scene as it trickled warmly down his throat. This was going to be one of those occasions when he would remain sober, seeing everything with a cold and painful clarity, no matter how much he drank. Holliday, already absorbed in presenting the evidence of his manhood, gulped absently at the gin, drew forth another letter, and cleared his throat.

"*Darling Brad,*" he read, "*here goes another letter off into space. I sometimes think that the worst thing about separation is this hollow routine of sending off a whole series of letters before I can even hope for a single answer. But then that's not your fault, is it? If I had been shrewd and calculating I would have tied in with a junior executive type who would be here for dinner every evening at six thirty sharp, instead of with a seagoing engineer. Perhaps things will be different when you return from this voyage . . .* dot, dot, dot," Holliday said. "She puts three dots here, after voyage. That's a little habit of hers.'

Phil nodded ambiguously. Was it really possible that with hardly anything more to go on than three dots (and God alone knew what they signified to Holliday) he could begin to construct for himself a portrait of the girl, not contradicting, but only paralleling the portrait that stood before him on the desk? Yet it was already apparent to him that she was a proud and spirited person, conforming a little more to the highly developed type of the young American college graduate than she would have liked to admit, deluding herself that she was more flattered when the Hollidays admired her intellect than when they paid homage to her physical attributes.

"*. . . so that by the time I got home I was really too worn out to curl up on the studio couch with a box of stationery and write you all about the concert, as I really wanted to. Anyway, Serkin was simply magnificent, at the top of his form, and I wanted to cry — I would have cried — during that wrenching, indescribable slow movement, if only it had been you sitting next to me instead of Doris.* That's the girl she shares the apartment with. *But I couldn't very well hold Doris's hand, could I, dear? . . . the result is that I'm stealing company time to write to you, and even, as you can see only too plainly, company paper. The folder that I'm supposed to be working up on California lettuce just doesn't seem particularly intriguing to me now, especially when I think of you making for those sloe-eyed Oriental maidens. Tell me, Brad, are they really sloe-eyed?*" Holliday paused and cocked an eye at Phil. "She's being eu-pha-mistic, you know," he explained.

Phil did not answer. The badly pronounced interpolation was doubly offensive; he was just beginning to feel like an omniscient author who is presented the facts of the case by a nervous shipboard acquaint-ance. This pleasurable certainty that he was being given a series of facts, some essential and some peripheral, whose significance as fiction he would determine for himself at his leisure, was badly shaken by the engineer's self-interruption. In a sense it recalled him to a gross reality that had been gratefully diminishing during the reading of the first few letters. He looked up from the scratch pad (on which he had been abstractedly jotting the weather report of a distant freighter as it cheeped from the earphones before him, high above Holliday's voice), intending to say "Please go on reading," or something of the sort, but en route to Holliday his eyes met the girl's, smiling warningly at him from the picture frame, and suddenly he understood that he and Phyllis had become friends. Was she as much of a friend as an author's newly developing character? More, perhaps, for with any luck at all he would now learn from her own pen, aided by his own retrospective surmises those things which an author is never quite able to construct; and as he moved towards an identification so absolute that it emboldened him to forecast the entire course of the correspondence, he was gladdened by a sense of his own power and insight surely surpassing, he thought, even the vision of a skilled and inventive writer. He leaned forward eagerly to hear the ardent beginning of a new series of letters.

Holliday smoothed the sheets over his bare hairy knees. *"My own darling,"* he read, with an odd kind of detached fervor, like an actor reading for an audition, *"it's a week today that you're gone, a week torn out of my life, as useless and meaningless as the seven empty sheets of the calendar that I crumple up and throw away. It's just impossible to write you a chatty letter about Doris or the new slip covers or what the supervisor said to me yesterday or those brutal cramps that started up this morning. I can't Bradley, because I am sick from thinking about you and about how I love your slow, hard smile and the way you smoke in bed with your arms clasped behind your head and the cigarette dangling down towards your chest and the smoke curling over your face . . ."*

Philip felt himself flushing. But Holliday, pausing only to replenish his glass, continued to read in an impersonal monotone, his voice gradually thickening as the gin slurred down his throat.

". . . one thing I can't discuss with Doris, even tho' she sleeps in the next room and is closer to me than anyone in the world but you. Precisely because she's always slept alone, how could she know anything of that sickening loneliness on a Sunday morning in May? No one else could know the way it was when you and I lay here watching the sun sneak through the long window and crawl across the foot of the bed, while E. Power Biggs blasted away majestically at the organ all the way across the country, and we sipped coffee and listened to Bach and got ready to make love . . ." Holliday flipped open his Zippo lighter with a metallic snap and lighted a fresh cigarette, then went on: *". . . that dreadful thrashing about, which is at bottom I suppose the fear that everything is lost and irrevocably in the past. And then. . . la recherche du temps —"* He pronounced the word *temps* as though it were *Thames.*

Philip broke in furiously, "You're pronouncing it wrong!"

"That's possible." Holliday nodded equably. "My French is pretty poor — although I've never had any trouble making myself understood by the babes in Marseilles. It's different with Phyl. She takes it as a personal affront every time I mispronounce a word."

It was fantastic. By admitting his inadequacy, Holliday succeeded in representing himself as a simple, straightforward fellow; while Phyllis became, to just that extent, the snob and the fake. But was that completely false? Didn't Phyllis reveal herself in her letters as a girl driven by anxiety and ambition to the kind of extreme attitudes that would entitle her lover to smile patronizingly, secure in the knowledge that he was by comparison more unassuming and more honest?

Holliday however could not rest content with having planted these seeds of doubt in his listener's mind; he had to add, "Phyl claims that she prefers French movies to Hollywood movies. I think it's just an affectation. We have to sit through all those arty movies instead of being able to see a decent show, in order that she can discuss them afterwards with her intellectual friends. Let me read on a bit — you'll see what I mean."

As Holliday read on, the all too familiar words, *anguish, love, the hideous power of loneliness, the memory of you lying beside me in the dark*, falling dully from his lips like tarnished stones, Phil asked himself: Why did I become angry? Why should I care how he pronounces her words?

The answer lay not so much in Holliday as it did in the girl, and in Philip's own attitude towards her. It was no longer possible for him to maintain the pose of the detached author, to listen to these revelations with the keen hopefulness of one who would hasten to note his impressions in his journal upon the conclusion of the reading. For he knew the girl too well already, and any further display of the literary efforts and the borrowed French phrases with which she exposed herself to this coarse man reflected less on Holliday than it did on her, or even on Phil himself. The truth was — one of the truths was — that the more she was a type and the less an individual the more she resembled the long train of ambitious and intense young women with whom Phil had involved himself in these last ten years.

Something very strange was happening. It wasn't even necessary for him to regard her taut cheekbones, or her serious and sensuous mouth, in order to visualize her in any number of "honest" poses: listening to a Horowitz recording, semi-recumbent on a studio couch in her stockinged feet, her paired shoes standing neatly on the rug; leaning forward in a hard undertaker's chair at a protest meeting for Spain, or Czechoslovakia, or Greece, or Palestine, her chin cupped firmly in her large white hand and her hair tied back behind her ears; lounging in an arm chair with him, running her fingers easily through his hair and teasing him with a little private dirty joke about the similarity of their names, her legs lying fluidly athwart his lap while he plucked at the nylon hose, feeling the close grain of her neatly shaved shins under his thumb, and thinking cloudily of how it would be when he moved his hands upwards under her clothing to undefended smoother places. He shuddered . . .

Meanwhile Holliday was reading: ". . . *as though I could burst when the crescendo swells through the room. Brahms appeals to the adolescent in me, my*

darling, just as Thomas Wolfe would appeal to the adolescent in you." Holliday
flicked at the letter with his long index finger. "Phyl thinks there's
something of me in Wolfe. Or vice versa. She's a great one for literary
allusions — is that the expression? Here, for example, she says: "*I must
quote you a few lines from Jean Stafford's lovely first novel, which I am belatedly
reading. Miss Pride, a crusty old spinster, like me, is . . .*"

Phil looked at him in horror. You son of a bitch, he thought, you're
reading my mail. Who do you think would write you letters like that?
How dare you open my mail? Phyllis is my kind of girl, he wanted to
cry out. He knew it, not only because she was so obviously not Holliday's kind, but also because everything about her was so familiar. These
letters were the sort he had been receiving for years. Why, even Natalie
had written to him like this before the game had palled on her. He
could have predicted, if Holliday had asked him, that presently Phyllis's
pride and frustration would fuse into an irritated analysis of what she
now began to call "our relationship."

"*Our relationship*," Holliday read stolidly (if they only knew, Phil
thought, how I despise those stale words!), "*can only be understood when
we're separated. Because it's true, isn't it, my dear, that our mutual sexual attrac-
tion blurs the edges of all the sharp and strong reasons for our remaining separated?
Any rational attempt to explain what we mean to each other has to start from the
premise that . . .*"

As Holliday droned on, violating every rule of privacy and good taste,
Phil felt himself shrinking down into his chair, embarrassed for Phyl by
what she was saying to him, the way she was saying it, and the inter-
mediary who was intercepting her letters to him. Ah, Phyl, Phyl, he
thought, everything you're going to tell me has been told to me before;
why must you persist in spelling it out, why must you delude yourself
into believing that you are saying something profound, or acute, or
even especially intelligent? He looked at her picture again. She still
looked as bright and as pretty, in her wistful and touching way, as she
had when Bradley Holliday had first placed the photo on the desk;
but now Phil sensed another quality in her taut and sharp-boned face
that he had not seen before when he looked into her full, piquant smile:
it was a special kind of ambition, the ambition to achieve sexual
dominance and psychic mastery peculiar to educated American women.
But your aggressive ambition, my love, he said silently to the photograph, is really nothing more than fear. You can disguise it with tough
second-hand phrases about — he heard Holliday mouthing the words —
personality differences and clashes of interest and *areas of incompatibility*, but

behind this tangled shrubbery of pseudo-technical jargon there lies still the cold sweating body of fear. And that's why, in the end, after you have bravely attempted to talk away the salty terror, the awful certainty that the final decision: to quit or not to quit? lies not in your hands, but in mine, then you will capitulate. Yes, you will capitulate. Because you know what it means, you and all the other girls like you that I have known so well, to be past twenty-five and to feel in the very marrow of your bones that there will no longer be an infinite number of Philip Stolzes, or even Bradley Hollidays, for you to meet, with a shivery foretaste of excitement, at a party, on a bus, or even in your imagination. It is this knowledge that breeds the bitter rebellion, and yet also enforces the ultimate capitulation. I know, Phyl, he told the picture, because it was my profile that graced the other side of the coin in the bedroom in Brisbane; heads or tails, we all proceed, protest though we may, to be melted down together in the same final furnace.

Holliday was drinking from the bottle now. He wiped his lips carefully with a clean white handkerchief and said shrewdly, "You know where she gets this analytical business — it's her job. That advertising agency pays her sixty bucks a week for what they call market research. Women are all the same, aren't they? Instead of forgetting about the job when she gets home, she has to sit down and write up a report on the status of her love-life." He stared cunningly at the photograph. "You don't fool me, baby. I don't impress as easily as you think, not even when I'm all alone in the middle of noplace, and sick, and —" Turning back to Phil, he said lightly, "She doesn't pull any of that stuff when we're alone together. She may indulge herself in public, it's true, but never in the bedroom."

Well, wasn't it true of himself too? There was no reason for him to feel superior, no reason to hate this man who was so like himself, when he too had more than once been rendered cynical by the instantaneous reflection that what caused a girl's eyeballs to roll upwards, her toes to crisp, her fingers to scrape against his flesh, was something other than an intense satisfaction at the discovery of common intellectual interests.

"Watch how her mood changes now," Holliday said confidentially, like a mechanic explaining the workings of an engine. "This one is dated the twelfth of June, before she got my first batch of letters. *My very very dear Brad*, she says, *Still no word from you, and I begin to wonder if I shall ever open another one of your exotic envelopes. I feel obliged to tell you, prompted by the special kind of honesty that we have saved for each other, darling, that it might be better for us both if I were never to receive another letter from you. . .*"

"What a special kind of dishonesty!" Phil murmured aloud.
"What?"

"Nothing." He ducked his head, as if to listen to the earphones, and scrawled a few words on the pad before him. "Go ahead."

"*. . . another letter from you. There are two reasons for this feeling, which strengthens day by day. First is the very strong suspicion that we would both be too cowardly to ever bring things to an end face to face — perhaps if our love must end, it would be better for it to peter out in unwritten letters . . . And I must admit, darling, that the letters I have received from you during your previous absences have not been such to set me aflame with desire for you. . . .*"

"I'm not that kind of a person." Surprisingly, the reading of these words had put Holliday a little on the defensive. He took another drink and coughed quietly, like an after-dinner speaker, preliminary to going on with his explanation. "I could never sit down and say all those things. It's a woman's place . . . Besides, how did I ever know if I'd be writing the truth? If I never really knew how I felt, how could I let go with a lot of romantic . . ."

Philip felt closer to his enemy than he had at any time since their first meeting. If Phyl was going to be "victorious" by capitulating, the temporary dishonesty of her pleading was forcing Holliday into the same kind of virtuous refusal to commit himself that Philip had always prided himself upon. This demonstration of honorable male solidarity was so unexpected that Phil did not know quite how to react.

He listened with dismay as Phyl gave herself away in this series of letters written in the month of June, growing more vituperative as her desperation increased. How terrible that she could not find it in herself to maintain the minimal dignity of silence! But no, here aboard the tanker that slid along the surface of the black warm sea at three o'clock in the morning, Holliday, perceptibly drunk by now, went on relentlessly reading aloud from this serialized chronicle of guilt and shame.

"*Was I a girlish fool to have expected that mere exposure to the books I liked, to the people whom I call my friends, to the music that is so important to me, would alter the ingrained attitude of vulgar mockery and lowbrow disdain that seems more important to you than any affection? . . . Shouldn't I have known, Bradley, from your first stilted, insincere letters, that you would fall asleep at a chamber music recital, and that on the way home you would attempt to justify yourself by impugning the sincerity of my appreciation of the music?*"

Holliday looked up from the letter, his mouth twisted. "She doesn't mention how we made up when we got to her house that night. Funny, isn't it, the way they can forget the things that really count? Then she says, *Shouldn't I have known that you would seize the first opportunity to sneer at my dearest friend, the girl with whom I live, the girl whose hospitality you have accepted on so many occasions?* That's Doris Fleischman, her roommate. She's got a beak sharper than the bow of this ship."

Phil cringed. The hackles of terror rose tremblingly, his fingers suddenly began to drum senselessly against the green table, and he had to blink to clear the film from his eyeballs. All of the old taunting phrases came surging into his gullet like vomit. And Holliday was saying:

"All I said to Phyl was that Doris ought to get her nose bobbed if she really wanted a man. I wouldn't have said it to her face, Phyl knows that, and she didn't hear us, because she was out in the kitchen mixing drinks. Dor isn't a bad sort — for a Jew. She even baked some brownies once and mailed them out to me. But that's no reason to live with one, is it?"

So once again he was accepted into the community of Gentiles. What could be more humiliating than the knowledge that he was too cowardly to become enraged, that secretly he was pleased at what should have disgusted him. . . . Yes, he was pleased that this weak, sick, vulgar man, this personification of everything that he despised, had casually included him in his world; by its very nature, the compliment excluded even the possibility of his protesting. He lowered his head to the table, his forehead resting on his slowly sweating forearm, thinking that perhaps he might cry; but it was too long since he had indulged himself in the feminine pleasure, even the dry sobs of self-pity would not come, and he was forced to sit quietly with his face rubbed in his own sweat while his faithful antagonist read aloud from the pathetic diary of their mutual mistress.

"*. . . seven of them, all at once! I was such a child, darling, I lined them up on the rug and plopped down on my stomach and fondled them, making sure that I would read them in the order in which you had written them. Such wonderful letters!*

"*Have I been terribly foolish, sweetheart? If I could have only one wish granted, I would wish with all my heart that the letters I have written you could disappear before they reached your hand. Did I really say that I couldn't possibly love anyone who didn't care for the Emperor Concerto? You're going to have to try very hard to forgive me for all the snobbish nonsense that I've been inflicting on you in these last few weeks. But pride feeds on loneliness, I guess. All I can promise you is that when you finally return to me I will know how to make you forget the cruel and stupid things I have been writing. I wouldn't care if you never wanted to go to another concert with me again, as long as you still wanted to be with me, Bradley. We have been so happy, and we will be happy again.*

I know it in my bones, just as I know that all of our superficial differences are not central to the one new person that both of us merge into when we are really alone together. . . ."

Above, on the night-wrapped bridge, the ship's bell tinkled seven times. It was half past three. This was the blackest hour of all. In another hour, perhaps two, dawn would come sneaking over the horizon like a sob. Holliday was still reciting the final chapter of the girl's capitulation; the ugly desperate lies knocked against Philip's ear with the flat finality of a radio announcer's description of doom. If only Holliday would accept her, how quickly Phyllis would prove that she meant what she said! How quickly the pot roasts and the babies would replace the anxious insistence upon an immediate acquaintance with the critically certified! You will put them off, Phyl, he thought tiredly, first the concerts, and then the plays, and at last the books. And in a few years you will content yourself with the intellectual luxury of a Saturday matinee while Bradley is out golfing — perhaps you will be able to slip off your shoes midway through the first act, to ease your swelling feet and your shrivelling soul. . . .

He looked up from the green linoleum into Holliday's bleak eyes. The Bols was almost empty; in the sudden silence he could see, he could almost hear the last few ounces of gin stirring gently in the bottom of the bottle, quickened by the soft vibrations of the ship's engines.

Now was the time for confidences and revelations. In this final hour before dawn. Holliday doubtless expected to receive advice and sustenance that would enable him to adopt an unfaltering attitude toward Phyllis. But his hands trembled as he slid her picture carelessly into the manila folder with all of her letters, so that her exquisite face, composite of all the best of Philip's girls, was pressed against her own truths and her own lies. Was there a light fragrance hanging in the air above the manila folder, a mild fresh scent emanating from the lonely letters of May, the bitter letters of June, the tear-drenched letters of July, that had outlasted the briny air in which they must have been handled so much?

Holliday, falsely casual, gathered together his liquor and his letter and rose to his feet. He wavered, belched, smiled an apology behind the back of his hand, but said nothing. Wasn't he going to ask any questions? Could he dare to believe that everything explained itself? You rotten coward, Phil muttered, staring malevolently at Holliday's naked bony feet that jutted from his sandals as they slapped across the room, you dirty rotten coward. Then he noticed that Holliday was still trembling involuntarily, as a tree moves when it is shaken by a slow steady soundless wind. It reminded Philip of something he had quite forgotten: Holliday's terrible sickness. Not even the fat doctor could know what it had already done to him. One thing however was certain; he wanted to be relieved of the moral responsibility of deciding in what way it would affect his future with Phyllis. Go ahead, ask me, Phil said to himself, ask me, you syphilitic bastard, I'll tell you what you ought to do.

But Holliday did not ask. Instead he walked quietly to the door and stopped there for a moment with one foot on the coaming, looking more like a gaunt drunken spider than ever, his lank shadow falling jaggedly across the high metal filing cabinet and the ten-gallon jug of distilled water. He smiled insolently and said, "I'd better hit the sack right away. I like to get up fairly early so that I can skip rope before the sun gets too high."

He was gone before Philip could open his mouth to reply. His conduct was as unexpected as it was unfathomable. Did he really believe that Philip was unaware of his illness, or did he mean to trade on Philip's knowledge of it, as a blind singer on a subway benefits from the guilty superiority of his seated listeners, so that he could wrench the final coins of pity from his own listener? Whatever his belief, whatever his intention, he was tricky, mean, dishonorable, and despicable.

Philip jerked the typewriter towards him and typed out the entries in his log from the sweat-soaked jottings he had made while listening to the letters. When he had finished, bringing himself up to the minute in this impersonal diary that no one would ever read aloud, he leaned back weakly, exhausted by the force of his hatred and the realization of what it meant.

As he sat numbly watching the complex clock, with its slowly swinging silver hand, and its hypnotic double circle of numbers that indicated both Greenwich Mean Time and Ship's Time (neither of which had any meaning for him now), Phil could smell the stale fumes of his visitor's gin. The room was too quiet. The subdued static that had sputtered softly throughout the reading of the letters was dying away to a whisper. One of his batteries had gone dead; he noted the fact in the log and signed his name as self-witness to his exit from this room. Then he dismounted the battery and connected a fresh one.

He stepped warily out on deck, staggering a little under the weight of the dead battery, which he now had to give a decent burial. Moving slowly along the boat deck past the captain's cabin, his eyes gradually strengthening in the pale glow of the masthead lights as the rest of his body weakened, the battery which he carried on his shoulder (like a young father stealthily bearing the coffin of his dead infant to a moonlit cemetery) growing heavier with each step, he came abreast of the chart room at last under the watchful stars and paused to catch his breath. Then he noticed a figure standing on the bitts at the bow of the vessel. He was leaning over the side, apparently watching the phosphorescent fish fleeing in the white spume from the ship's cutting edge. He was not the bow lookout; he was not, in fact, a crew member at all. Who else but myself, thought Philip, would stand nervously peering ahead, towards America, at four o'clock in the morning, on this swaying, laggard vessel? The man straightened, flung something to leeward with the sweeping motion of a baseball pitcher, then bent over the gunwale once again. It was Bradley Holliday.

Rage rose like blood in Philip's throat. He hawked up a mouthful of Holliday's gin and lemon juice — it tasted sweet and thick, like blood — and spat it over the side. Holliday was probably so exultant over his betrayal of Phyllis that he could not go directly to sleep; now he looked forward, no doubt, to leaping up and down on the catwalk once again with a length of rope, exposing his rotting body to the sun and the sea and Philip's loathing gaze.

Philip lowered himself carefully and silently down from the boat deck on the iron-runged ladder. As he approached Holliday from the rear, stepping quietly in his sneakers, he saw the engineer pick up a bottle and stuff it with paper. Holliday was so intent upon his task, twisting sheets of paper and cramming them into the narrow neck of the bottle, that he would have been unaware of anyone's approach even if it had been less stealthy.

When Philip was only a few feet behind his quarry, he stopped and hefted the battery, high in the air. Held over his head in this way, like an offering, it seemed to have grown lighter; and yet, he reflected, how easily it could crush a man's skull! Standing this close, he could see the exact spot where it should land: a little bald area at the crown of Holliday's head, circled like a target by thin wet strands of hair. The blow would send Holliday and his letters to the bottom of the ocean. While Philip stood behind him and a little below him, gathering his moral strength to a focus, Holliday raised the gin bottle which he had stuffed with Phyllis's letters and flung it into the sea. At another time the gesture would have been outrageously melodramatic, but now, in the pearly grey morning just before dawn, alone at the wet clear bow of the tanker, it bore a stern logic of its own, terrible and final. Yet, when Holliday proceeded to tear the girl's picture into long thin fluttering strips that took to the air almost of their own accord, like the colored rag-tails of a kite, Phil was moved to protest this abandoned act. He took a step forward.

Holliday whirled about and revealed his true face to Philip. Everything of the rake, the lady-killer, the poseur, was eaten away. His feet slid from the bitts to the deck. His eyes, spray-flecked and mad in the growing light, glared desolately at the dead battery that was suspended over his head, then moved across Philip's face until they encountered their mirror in Philip's eyes.

As they stood at the bow of the ship that swayed slowly towards their homeland, face to face in this final moment of recognition, they stared silently into each other's eyes, and the sun came slowly and silently crashing over the horizon of the southern sea.

(*From Harper's Magazine*)

NOBODY SAY A WORD

BY MARK VAN DOREN

AFTER THE CHILDREN stopped asking she told them. "I
don't know where your father is," she said quietly during supper on the sixth day. They were all at the table — neither of
the girls had gone to the kitchen for anything, and their small brother
hadn't bolted yet to resume his playing in the yard. They sat, paralyzed, and listened.

"I simply don't know." The strain of saying this was nothing to
what it had been when Madie, the first evening he wasn't there, kept
running to the door and reporting that he hadn't come in sight yet up
the walk; or when Arthur, always a hard one to satisfy, had insisted
every night when he went to bed: "Papa's on a business trip. He'll be
back tomorrow." He would say it the next night as if he had never
said it before, and Margaret learned soon enough to nod and say
nothing, as if of course the child knew.

But the worst thing had been the anticipation of what Madie asked
now. She was the directest of the three, though she wasn't the oldest.
"What did he say, Mother, the last time he — what did he *say?*"

The worst thing was to have to answer, "Nothing," for in a way it
wasn't true. George hadn't ever said: "I'm going, and I'm not coming
back," but she had always known he would leave her, and so he didn't
need to say so. He knew she knew.

But here was Madie looking at her, accusing her of holding something back. And a deep, sudden blush was her way of admitting that
she had; only, what was there to tell, and how could it be told to these
three? To Sarah most of all, who never had really asked. Sarah was
the serious one who didn't like things to go wrong or change. No child
does, said Margaret to herself; but the others had talked and Sarah

331

hadn't — except, of course, with her strange large eyes. They had got larger every day, under the fine hair she insisted on combing straight back from her forehead. Young as she was, she knew the effect of that — knew it gave her authority, as if she weren't young after all; and in a sense she never had been.

"He didn't say anything," said Margaret, "about not — I mean, about not ever —"

"Not ever!" Madie was scowling in the odd way that made everybody love her. She looked near-sighted, though the doctor said she wasn't. She looked fierce; whereas she was the fondest of them all.

The words had given too much away. "Not ever" sounded — well, as fatal as the fact. And Margaret felt that she must have grown all at once very pale, for the children stared at her with a new intentness, and Arthur barely mumbled, "Papa's on a business trip — we know that," as if he had lost his confidence that this was so.

But Sarah's face had altered less, and her eyes not at all. Did Sarah understand that some men did what George had done? Some women, too? But the men. That father of five children, years ago when *she* was a child, that meek neighbor man, she forgot his name, who did so poorly and was so apologetic — "No force," her own father said — who disappeared one day and didn't come home for years. But he came home, and the town never knew how he made it up with his family: what he said to them, or they to him, or whether there was bitterness and quarreling. Not a sound or a sign from the house into which he walked one night and — well, what then? The next day he was in his leather shop as usual, and nobody had the nerve to ask him where he had been. He had so little nerve himself, it would have been torture on both sides.

Sarah had never heard of him, but she looked now as if she might have. Margaret was startled by the suspicion, yet there it was: Sarah's mind was on the same track as her own. She was even thinking —

Then she said it.

"When he does come" — Sarah closed her eyes a moment, imagining — "I know what we should do. Act just the same as if he never went anywhere. No talk, no questions. Not a word. I know."

Madie shook her brown hair out of her eyes. "I couldn't. I'd have to tell him I was glad."

Arthur merely stared down at his napkin.

They were all trying to help, they were all trying to seem undeserted, unafraid.

"You wouldn't have to tell him," Sarah said. "Wouldn't he know? *He'd* be glad. He'd like it best if none of us said a word."

At least, thought Margaret, motionless in her chair, it's confessed now. They realize he *did* desert me — and them. But me first of all. They are sorry for me. They are trying to be good children. And they are, they are.

Madie and Arthur, flying from their places across the table, reached her at the same moment. Neither one of them had ever seen her weep like this.

But Sarah didn't come.

What was she saying? She had been right — she really had, except of course that George would never —

What was she saying? The two others were so close about, it was almost impossible to hear.

"Listen! Mother, Madie, Arthur — listen! Nobody say a word."

For there was George.

Sarah must have seen him out of the back of her head; the hall door was behind her. Margaret, facing him with Madie and Arthur, started to her feet, but the two children clutched her closer and she sat down again, trembling. They hadn't looked up yet. When they did —

"Madie!" she managed to whisper. "You and Arthur — don't say anything. Don't go to him — not yet. Your father's come. He's here."

Now she had to clutch at them, they were so wild in her two arms. They all had to wait till Sarah spoke. Sarah hadn't been wrong about *one* thing. George couldn't stay away. And her heart struggled with itself, not knowing how the whole of her should feel. It was bad, it was good. She was still hurt, yet she was happy — in a strange way, as if she were asleep; in a bitter way, as if this new sweet taste — it might be so, it might — were the taste of poison.

The two children were quieter than she would have believed possible. They were minding her, they were waiting for Sarah. Or was it because George looked so terribly tired? Standing in the door, his shoulders drooping, he must have shocked them too. They seemed to want to look away; to close and stay closed; but they couldn't. They were for Margaret entirely, they saw no children there, no chairs, no table, no dishes, no clock.

"Hello," said Sarah, turning halfway round. "You're late. Was it a hard day at the shop?" It was scarcely her voice they heard. "Was Mr. Meeker mean, and kept you? Did somebody have an accident? You know, I was the one that set the table and I counted wrong. You go wash up, I'll fix a place." It was as if she were reciting from mem-

ory. "All of us helped get supper, even Arthur. He mashed the potatoes — partly."

But her father, if he listened to a single word, gave no sign that he did.
His dark eyes traveled for a moment, impartially, over the three young
faces that separated him from Margaret, then returned to her where
she sat, half guilty because of her silence, in her walnut armchair that
matched his across the room. His stood against the wall, in shadow, as
it had stood all week.

"Arthur," she said, "get Papa's chair for him." She spoke slowly, as
if it were a deep wrong to mention only this. "Go on."

For the boy was staring at the man. A business trip, a business trip
— he must be fighting the temptation to say those words and prove he
had been right. A business trip. But he looked sidewise at Sarah and
said nothing; then, embarrassed, ran to drag the armchair into place.

Madie's face burned with excitement, and her body shook all the
way down; Margaret's arm felt the straight, strong back trembling as
if in terror. But it wasn't terror. It was doubt that she ought to be
where she was. It wasn't like Madie to keep this distance from someone she adored.

She only said: "Hello, Dad. We had a test in history today. I think
I did all right. I'll tell you about it later. Miss Martingale —"

She stopped because he didn't seem to hear. He hadn't shifted a
foot, he hadn't twitched a finger, since he came.

Margaret thought: He's a ghost, he isn't really there. It's like a game
— all of us pretending to see him. It's like children who play family,
and make up uncles and cousins. They're making up a father. That
isn't him, that isn't George.

And suddenly she screamed — not loud, not long, but she knew she
screamed. The sound was worse because it was so weak — she was
ashamed, and reached for Arthur who had jumped away.

But he was already at his father's knees, and Madie, her face streaming tears, had hold of one of George's arms, which she embraced as if it
had once been wounded in a war. It was veritable flesh. She hung
upon it with all her weight.

Sarah came around the table, defeated, and stood while Margaret
kissed her pale forehead. "All right, dear," said her mother. "It was
a good thing to try, even if I broke down. You go over there with
them. Quick, now."

For still George had not said a word. His hands strayed over two
young heads, then three; but even while they did this they seemed to

be thinking of the wife they had not touched. Never had touched, maybe, or else might never touch again. As if *she* were the ghost.

Margaret settled it. "All three of you," she said, standing straight up at last, "go somewhere else now. Outdoors, or anywhere. Don't stay long, I mean, but — oh, I don't need any help with Papa's supper. Madie — really — I don't need help."

"Are you sure?" asked Sarah. She was so responsible

"Yes, dear. You take Arthur."

Sarah led them both out, never looking back, while Margaret waited for him to come close, to touch her flesh with him, to make one sound she could hear.

He didn't, soon enough. He was still all eyes, mournful and ashamed. He was still a man come out of a new grave.

So she went close to him.

EVENSONG

BY DANIEL WALDRON

*A*FTER SCHOOL was out Joel Harris walked swiftly to the drugstore. He peered through the plate-glass window at the wide magazine rack inside. He hoped he wasn't too late. "Excuse me," he murmured, breathless, as he brushed the large woman who was coming out the door.

A pickle-faced man with his name sewn above the pocket of his tan clerk's jacket looked at him. "Want something?" He eyed Joel's washbeaten clothes.

"I —" Joel's voice clogged and broke like phlegm. He started again. "I'd like to see Mr. Bigelow."

Clement Zane slouched against the corner of the counter as though he had been built into it. Joel could see Mr. Bigelow working behind the glass partition at the back of the store. "What for?"

"I've gotta talk to him about something." The blood burned his face.

"Want to buy something?"

"Yes . . . I mean —"

"I can sell you anything in the store." Still he didn't move.

"I — I gotta see *him*."

Clement Zane eased from the counter and strolled slowly through the empty store. Joel followed him.

"Kid here wants to see you," Zane said.

Mr. Bigelow looked up from his prescription and squinted his small eyes at Joel. Then he squinted back at the red fluid he was measuring from a beaker into a clean bottle. He screwed the top on the bottle.

"What can I do for you?"

He took a small typed sticker, slid it over his tongue, and pressed it to the bottle.

"I wanted to see you," Joel said. He could feel Mr. Zane still looking at him. "I wanted to get some . . . work."

Mr. Bigelow poured the remaining fluid into a large bottle and crossed the cubicle to put it high on a shelf. "Your pa out of a job again?"

"No sir," Joel stammered. "I — I just wanted the job for myself — for tonight."

"Yourself? Your pa know about this?"

"No sir. But this is something . . . special."

"How's that?"

"I didn't expect to get paid for it — not money, I mean."

Mr. Bigelow gazed at him a moment. "What *did* you mean?"

The door at the front of the store finally opened, and Joel waited until Mr. Zane went at last to wait on the customer. "I thought you could pay me with a magazine." He felt red and foolish, but he had said it.

Mr. Bigelow ran his tongue around the inside of his mouth. "Now what kind of magazine were you thinking of, Joel?"

"That one in the rack up there. That — *Mode* — Magazine."

"That's an expensive magazine," Mr. Bigelow said. "Fifty cents. You think you can work long enough to get that? Hadn't you ought to be home helping your pa?"

"Yes," Joel said. "But . . ." He paused. "How long do you think it would take?"

"Weeell . . ." Mr. Bigelow ruminated, scratching his purple jowls; "The rest of this afternoon anyhow, and maybe part of tonight."

Joel said anxiously: "I'd work through suppertime if I didn't have to come back after."

"Well, we'll see," Mr. Bigelow said.

Joel rolled up the sleeves of his pink-faded shirt and tried to hold the boxes he carried up and down stairs away from him so he wouldn't dirty the front. He carted dusty cartons to the floor and new merchandise down into the storage room. The shelves of the dingy place were box-lined and labeled in faded brown ink: Father John's, Lyd. Pinkham, Dailey Worm Caps., Pepto-B., and Know-Kare — names that made him feel, as he sorted the boxes by the bilious dark of the lone bulb, that he was working on the inside of a huge distressed stomach. He wished the work had been in the daylight, but down here at least no one would see him.

At the back of the basement a brilliant light sliced under a door. Joel went back cautiously. Inside something was going: slap. slap.

slap. He listened a moment. He tiptoed up. The slapping stopped. He pushed the door open a little. On a low pile of magazines, with her back to him, a girl sat reading something. He pushed the door the rest of the way open and went in. There were magazines all over the floor. He said: "What are you doing?"

She spun around so suddenly the magazines on which she sat squeaked. "Jesus!" she said. "Don't you ever knock before you open the door?" She glared at him with violent, eating eyes. Her puffed, blowzy face looked pebbly as though there were little particles of tapioca beneath the skin. He had seen her up in the store once in a while.

"I'm sorry," he said. He started to back out.

"Naw," she said. "Don't be so touchy! Come on in. I ain't had anybody to talk to all afternoon. Jeez, I hate this job. All these damn magazines. Have a smoke?"

She thrust a package of cigarettes at him. He shook his head.

"'Smatter, don't you smoke? If you hear old man Bigelow coming give me the word. I ain't supposed to smoke in here. Got a match?" Before he could say no she said: "No, I don't suppose you got that either." She turned back around on the pile of magazines, searched about for a match, finally found one, and lit her cigarette. He stepped among the magazines, not knowing which one to look at first.

"What are you doing with the covers?" he asked.

"Aw I have to tear 'em off and send 'em back to the company so we get our money back." The cigarette in her mouth bobbed up and down as she spoke. She snatched it from her lips. "Say, he ain't sent you down here to take my job has he?"

"No," he said, startled. "I'm just working here today, temporary."

"I shoulda known." She sat with her heavy legs wide apart, two piles of coverless magazines between them. She took a long drag. "Jeez, look at this!" she exclaimed, holding up the magazine she's been perusing. "Acres of Flesh," she read, "the girls of France's Frenchiest show — the Follies Ber — Ber . . ." She stopped. "Jeez, I bet they have fun!"

He bent beside her and stared at the grainy photographs: a line of thighs and smeared faces; white flesh, glaring hard in the raw, white glare of the bulb. He felt a swampwind in him. He turned away. Her eyes were grinning directly into his — darting, inflamed, pinched with a wicked, leering mirth. Her teeth seemed monstrous.

"How would you like some of that, eh kid?"

He moved away to the magazines beyond her. Her eyes followed him.

"How old're you, kid?"

"Fourteen."

"I was twenty-one yesterday. Jeez, what a feeling! You look older than fourteen. What grade you in?"

"Ninth grade." He felt as though she were trying to find something to laugh at.

"You on the football team?" she asked.

"I gotta get back to work," Joel said.

"Aw, I won't bite you," she said. "C'mere a minute. Lemme feel your muscle."

Joel felt foolish. He stepped over to her. He flexed his biceps. She squeezed his arm hard a couple of times.

"Kid, you oughta be on the boxing team!" she exclaimed.

"There isn't any boxing team," Joel said. Her grin stuck to him like gum.

"Then you oughta be on the rasslin team!" She snorted suddenly. "Hey, yeah. You ever do any rasslin, kid? What's your name?"

"Joel," he said. He wished he could leave. The place where she had squeezed him crawled.

"Yeah, Joel, you know," she said, her eyes digging into him like little hair-legged bugs scurrying under chips. "I bet you'd make a good rassler. I used to be on the girl's rasslin team —!" She snorted again. Her eyes crackled wildly. "— Till I found out it was more fun to rassle boys! Hey kid?!" She doubled over forward, as if she were broken at the middle, and chortled gleefully.

"I gotta leave," Joel said.

She was on her feet. "Want me to show you a good hold?"

"I gotta carry up some boxes."

"You work too hard," she said. "Here, gimme your arm."

She almost touched him again, but he slid away to the door. He had felt the heat from her body, she had come so close.

"Aw what the hell, can't you take a joke?" she said. She gave him the same look he'd gotten from Mr. Zane upstairs. She started to say something but he didn't listen. He went back down the dark corridor to the storeroom, his mouth coated with tallow, afraid she might follow him. Then he heard someone coming down the stairs and he was glad he'd left when he did.

Mr. Bigelow was carrying a broom. "You can sweep the hall and this room here, and then I guess that will be all."

The cellar-oppression melted. "Is the time up already?"

"The next issue's coming out pretty soon," Mr. Bigelow said, "It's not really worth fifty cents any more."

I know the secret value, Joel thought. He would have worked two afternoons, or a week, if he'd dared, to get it. The song began to surge in him again, the song that had been with him ever since he first saw the magazine.

Helen, thy beauty is to me . . .

The words thrilled him, the same as the image in the magazine. They never really made any sense, but they went with the picture — maybe for that very reason. They were mystical. *Helen, thy beauty is to me . . .* He could never get past the first line though they had studied the poem in last semester's English class. *The agate lamp within thy hand . . .* He remembered that. And *Gently o'er a perfumed sea . . .* But the rest was an immense, over-whelming impression, and he had found a picture of it upstairs.

"My name's Ethel," the voice startled him. The grin-faced girl was leaning against the jamb in the doorway, with a cigarette. "If you ever need any rasslin lessons come to me."

For a moment after Joel left the basement the fear that someone might have bought the magazine while he worked seized him, but when he reached the rack he saw it was still there. Mr. Bigelow took it out for him. "You're sure this is the one you want?"

"Yes," Joel said, reddening. He wondered if Mr. Bigelow knew what was in all the magazines. "Thank you."

He had it at last. For the past week he'd come in to leaf through the magazine again and again. Every afternoon he had gone a block out of his way as he went home, just to see it. Each time he had stopped at that one page and looked at it until he heard someone opening the door, or saw Clement Zane starting over in his direction. Then he had put the magazine back in the rack and picked out another one, glancing through it as casually as he could. A terrible thought struck him. Suppose someone else had discovered the page and had deliberately removed it? He wanted to open it right there on the street. But he couldn't do that. It would be sacrilege to expose that page to the public glare. He thumbed through the corner flaps to make sure no pages were missing. None were. He would open it only in private. He owned it now, and could treat it as it deserved.

In the late sun the spring-budded trees glowed pink. The delicate green of new grass along the sidewalk filled him with joy like the fresh-earth wind. He crossed the river, passed the tanning factory, the paper mill, the hissing creamery. When the sidewalk left off he took the path across a small field towards the tarpaper buildings clustered at the edge of town. His father would probably larrup him for being late from school. He needed him whenever he had a well-drilling job. None of the other kids were old enough to help yet.

Joel hid the magazine in his shirt front and approached cautiously. The old truck was not in the yard. The front door was shut. He crossed the muddy, rusty-can strewn yard. He stepped up on the chunks of railroad tie that formed the steps and tried the door. It was locked. He went around to the back, found a piece of wire, unlocked the back door and went in.

The house was quiet. Joel wiped his feet on the door sill, closed the door, and went through the kerosene-smelling kitchen to the small living room. The horizontal, moted beams of the last sunlight fell through the curtainless windows and drew color from the hueless bulges of the davenport. But it made the wallpaper sickly, especially the ray which fell on a violently colored Sunday School lithograph of Jesus and a flock of kids titled "Suffer the Little Children." Joel picked his way among the pieces of toys and old newspapers to the bedroom he shared with his two brothers and sister. He had slept with his sister until a month ago when his mother decided he should move into the other bed with one of the younger boys.

Joel took out the magazine and put it on a bed. Sliding sideways into the narrow space between the two beds he opened the window. A quarter of a mile away the smoke from the garbage dump curled upward and slanted with the west wind today. Joel took a deep lungful of air. A singing bird was in the deformed crabapple tree, singing the sunset.

Now it was all right. At last, in this hollowed silence, he could perform the ceremonies undisturbed, with adoration and reverie. He sat down on the bed, took up the magazine with deliberation and found page 33. He held it on his lap and looked at it.

It was an advertisement, a full page photograph of a woman wearing a mass of jewels. She was nude.

Motionless, without breath, he gazed at the figure. She had the duskhued body of a native dancer, caught at the height of her dance. One arm was raised, the other, hand downward, manacled with gems, curved across one breast. The sensuous rhythm which began at the tip of her upraised hand flowed down her arm, circled her shoulders, slid down the lowered arm, spun like a carnival car around one updrawn breast, and swept in a dizzy plunge down the swerve of her hips.

Joel's lips dried. He shifted the magazine onto the bed beside him and stared at it, his eyes aching. The rhythm of the body made him

giddy. There must be words to say what he felt, or even to tell him
what he felt — he did not know. He could only stare, and feel a tongue
licking his insides clean, purging him somehow. His throat ached, as
though something were about to give way. And yet the mystery was
still within him, undissolved, a lump, pressing in his stomach and chok-
ing off words or coherent thoughts.

He could only worship. That was it. Worship — with altar, orison,
heavenly choir, procession, votive lights . . .

He cut the picture from the page. He would prop it before him by
the window and light two flames, one on either side. He would gaze
all night with prayer and fasting, all night on his knees.

Helen, thy beauty is to me . . .

He found the book beneath the bed. Might she not move to resolve
his longing, unlock, explain and soothe away the hunger in him? Her
nakedness made him naked, bare to the core. It stripped him to the
very soul! If only he could tear away what was between them, push
beyond, touch, make one!

In the twilight he slipped out of his clothes.

Helen, thy beauty . . . He propped the picture against the pillow on the
opposite bed and lay on his stomach, holding the book in one hand so
he could read by the deep, faint light.

Like those Nicean barks of yore
That gently, o'er a perfumed sea
The weary, wayworn wanderer bore
To his own native shore.

The figure glowed before him, intense, magnified.

On desperate seas long wont to roam
Thy hyacinth hair, thy classic face,
Thy Naiad airs have brought me home . . .

He felt the cool breeze chill hot and cold up his back. His brain blinked
with studded images overflowing. The light was swiftly fading.

Lo, in yon brilliant window-niche
How statue-like I see thee stand
The agate lamp within thy hand,
Ah! Psyche, from the regions which
Are holy land!

Holy land! holy land! holy land!

Too beautiful. He winced. Too pure and beautiful. He pressed
himself hard against the bed until he could feel the springs. He felt he
must cry out. His brain soared. The image pulsed like a motor
pounding, like metal beating against metal, like the tread of feet, like
the writhing waves of night . . .

"*What are you doing in here?*" The light switch clicked like a guillotine. "Joel!"

He jerked upright on the bed. The picture tumbled to the floor.

"What's going on here?" His father came over by the bed, his glance searing the length of him. His mother and the children stood wide-eyed in the doorway. "Where's your clothes?"

Joel's frantic eyes went to his mother, then to his father. He glanced at the floor. "There," he said. His voice sounded as if it were in the cellar.

"Pick 'em up."

Shivering, Joel slid off the bed, glanced up once at his father's grimy, motionless face, and bent to pick up his shirt and trousers.

Before he could touch them, his father's belt had whipped from its loops and blazed across his buttocks. He shrieked as he snapped upright. He backed against the side of the bed, his hands behind him. His lips trembled.

"Now," roared his father. "Where have you been?"

"I — I was downtown," Joel said.

"Ain't you got a home no more?"

"Y-yes sir."

"Why'nt you think of it once in a while?"

"I —"

"I needed you for a job and you run off someplace. Now what were you doing? Don't you lie to me!" Joel opened his mouth but his father cut him off.

"You don't need to tell me. You were working at Bigelow's Drugstore, is that right?"

Joel nodded.

George Harris said: "Yes or no?"

"Yes."

"All right. Now hand it over."

"What?" Joel blinked.

"Don't get sassy with me!" George Harris drew back his hand as if to cuff him. "How much did he pay you?"

Joel looked frantically to his mother. She stood staring, her sick eyes vacant in her pale, blotched face. Joel said finally: "F-fifty cents."

"Give it to me."

Joel tried to speak but he couldn't. His tongue clogged in his throat.

"You didn't spend it already?"

"No sir — I — he didn't pay me in money."

His father craned around at his mother. "Did you hear that?" He turned back to Joel. "What *did* he pay you with?"

Joel's whole body creeped. If only his father would let him put his clothes on. He swallowed hard. "A — magazine."

"Magazine! You worked for that rich sonofabitch Bigelow and you let him pay you with a magazine?"

"I — I wanted it."

"Uh-huh. What did you want it for? Where is it?"

Joel glanced at the window.

"Where's the magazine?" his father said.

Joel stepped around to the other side of the bed, keeping his face to his father. He picked up the magazine where it had fallen onto the floor. The cutout page lay beside it. He tried to shove it farther under the bed.

"Well!" George Harris exclaimed as he took it. "Ain't this nice! Look at this, Myra."

His mother shuffled over beside him. One by one he turned the pages.

"Whaddaya know! Just look here — clothes! Women's clothes! Fancy-pancy. Well well well. You thinking of buying some clothes for somebody? Maybe you've got a girl, huh?"

Joel shook his head. He watched as his father slowly turned the pages.

"I guess the stores in town ain't good enough for Joel, Myra. He's gotta send away to get his clothes — from a woman's magazine!"

He leafed nearer and nearer the center. In the draft from the window Joel began to sweat.

His father looked up. "You let old man Bigelow pass this off onto you as being worth fifty cents?"

His mother fumbled with the cover. "I saw the front, George. See. It says fifty cents on the cover." Her hands fidgeted back together at her waist.

"Well, you can take this back and tell Bigelow you'd rather have the money. Take it back right now —" Joel started to move. "— Soon's I get done looking at it."

Joel took another step, then saw his father's face, and knew that it had happened.

"Jesus Christ!" George Harris cried. He jerked out the strip of paper that Joel had left at the bottom of the picture. "The Earth's Rare Gems" he read. "Somebody's ripped out a page."

His look spitted Joel. "What did you do with this page?"

Goosebumps flowed over Joel, then swept away in a wash of heat, then returned again, as though he were at the gravelly bottom of an ocean. He felt dizzy. He would lie to his father, if he could think of a lie. He would tell him the page was gone when he got it. But the scissors were there on the bed. He would tell him . . . but all he could see was the dark torso and the jewels and the rhythmic swerve of her hips. *Helen* —

"What did you do with it?"

"I can't tell you."

His father loomed before him like an hallucination. "What did you do with it?" he thundered. His belt was coming loose.

"I cut it out."

"Where is it? Get it."

With a swift sob Joel dropped beside the bed and fished it out. His father seized it.

He said nothing. His lips moved but he only expelled a great heave of air. When he finally spoke Joel could barely hear him.

"You cut this out?" he breathed. "You worked all afternoon just for this — naked woman?" His voice raised. "Why you filthy minded little runt. I oughta turn you right outa this house — just like you are now. No wonder your Ma had to move you to another bed. Collecting whore-pictures! By God " His belt slid out.

He grabbed Joel around the waist, bent him over and brought the belt down against the white skin. Joel caught a flash of the picture like the his cut-off breath, as it crumpled. He tried to choke down the pain; but the third lash vomited up the hurt in a white scream that flamed and cut. He saw his sister on the davenport in the other room, her head in her hands, weaving back and forth.

"Maybe you'll think twice before you try another stunt like that," his father bawled above the sound of the strap. "I lost a job today because you wanted that damned dirty picture. Come home and find you doing God knows what on the bed. If you ever want hot pants again, I'll warm 'em for you!"

He struck him twice more. Then, breathing hoarsely, he let him up, snaked the belt back in his trousers and went out of the room. The agony broke into jagged sobs and gasps. Painfully Joel pulled his trousers on and collapsed, shuddering, onto the bed.

Later the light went out, and past his shoulder he could see his mother pulling the curtains shut.

He lay for a long time, the feverish spurs in his brain tapering finally to soft blobs of pain; and the grotesque merrygoround of the night and the room slowly came to a stop and were stable before him. The other rooms were very quiet. Gradually, like half-digested gobbets, images returned and sickened him. Mixed with the paint-scaled walls, the chipped iron bedstead, the smell of kerosene, the sound of dishes in the kitchen, he saw again the cubbyhole in the drugstore basement, Clement Zane, the pages of magazines turning and turning; then a gashed page, and cold sweat and then a lustrous image of dancer hips and breast and curved hands, and then in a sudden wrenching sob, where the head should have been, the gargoyle-grinning, grime-toothed face in the raw light, leering at him.

My name is Ethel. If you ever need any rasslin lessons come to me.

(From Mademoiselle)

LOUD SING CUCKOO

BY CHRISTINE WESTON

*W*ALT lay in bed and watched flies beat against the window on the farther side of the room where the sun struck it hot as molten lead though it was November, and beyond the frost-blackened garden alder berries in the hedge and oak leaves burned against a frieze of pines. The sun beat down on the roof directly over his head and the room was as warm as summertime. He could feel the sun exploring him as he lay naked between the blankets. His body felt smooth as silk between the blankets and he stretched with a sense of luxury, though he knew he ought to be getting up. It was after twelve and he'd been in bed since ten the night before, after walking Elsa home from school and staying at her house till all his own home chores were done and he knew that he had nothing to face except his father's glance as he came in through the kitchen door and asked his mother for a glass of milk, and saw by her face that she had decided not to get after him about the chores, though he saw too by her look that she had meant to and had worn herself out rehearsing what she'd say and saying it to herself and then finally giving up. She and the old man had fetched water and stacked wood against the morning's requirements and had watered the cow and cooped the chickens and done all the rest long before he left Elsa, his lips still warm from kissing, his brain full of how he could escape again tomorrow and meet her when school let out and walk her home.

Lying here watching the flies and conscious of his warm nakedness under the blanket, Walt wished that he had not left school last year but that he had stayed so he could be near Elsa all day and every opportunity outside of school. But he couldn't go back because he was getting too old and people would guess why and laugh, and he couldn't stand for that, not with Elsa round to hear and perhaps be affected by it as girls were apt to be by such things. As it was, he knew he was tall and narrow in the hips, with a handsome mouth and deep eyes and hair tarnished by the sun so that here it looked like gold and there brown as a deer's back, so Elsa had told him. He was very strong for only seventeen and could work all day in the garden or haying and never tire, but what was the use of it? He ought to get up now and go downstairs and help with the cow and feed the pig its slops and carry in more wood, and get after those cornstalks his father had spoken of every day for the past week and burn them against disease in the corn next year. And he ought to harvest the last of the cabbages, all filled as they were with wet green worms and their droppings like balls of chewed spinach — which he'd hated ever since he was little.

His parents would think of other things for him to do, he knew, like going over to Art's to help with the burst tire on Art's truck. Art being his brother-in-law and sickly after being in the war, and to paint the side of Pierce's barn, for which old Pierce had promised to pay him the same as regular painters' wages out of consideration for his parents, whom everyone liked and felt sorry for, they having so little and never having had anything more except kids. Eight kids. Five married, all living, none of them having much except more kids. But it was two miles to walk to Pierce's, and anyway they'd gone away like most the summer folk and he'd have the barn painted long before they got back next summer even if he were to let it go till April, the Pierces living in New York and never getting down to the country before June anyway. Old Pierce used the barn for a garage, not for pigs or cows or hay, and he wanted it painted to keep the weather off through the winter, and the paint was all stored in the barn and ready for Walt, with brushes and even rags for wiping up afterward. The only trouble was the money would go to Walt's parents and not to Walt because that had been the deal, and though it filtered down to Walt in the form of food and maybe a new pair of shoes it was not what he'd have liked to do with it himself.

Flies buzzed against the window and he saw flights of crows fly past and heard them calling and knew that they were going south, which meant cold weather farther north, though here it was so hot and still, like a summer day. Crows and rich people went south winters: the rich because they could afford it and the crows because they didn't have to afford it. Walt could see light glancing off their black wings and fancied he heard the rushing sound of their flight like when duck-hunting the ducks held their wings still and came past with a sound like a scythe, shearing the ripe grasses in August. Then the crows had passed and there were only the flies green and blue against the pane and their frenzied pattering against the window. They always collected up here when the weather changed. Then they'd disappear, no signs of one, and first thing on a spring day he'd see them again hammering against the sun and wanting to be out and to the manure heap and the old chicken bones pushing through the refuse heap back of the barn.

Suddenly he sat straight up in bed remembering. The Jordans had gone away, gone back to Boston yesterday, and there was their house across the next strip of field and the hedge, locked and boarded up and the chimneys capped and the late flowers and vegetables standing in their fullness under the sun, and pretty soon the procession would begin, starting with Elsa's folk down the line with their wheelbarrow, and Nagy, the Finn, on the other side with his basket, and Art and May with their paper bags and their kids with the kiddy cart, all headed toward the Jordans' after the golden dahlias and the late beets and chard, and cucumbers turned fat and soft but still good for boiling if you liked them that way. And this year there'd be roses too because Mrs. Jordan had sent them down last spring and Elsa's dad had set them out and they'd bloomed all summer, being the expensive kind, not the sort you bought at chain stores or dug up out of old cellar holes round about. Last year Walt had been first over to Jordans' after the old magazines they'd left on their back steps and he'd come on another summer neighbor. Mrs. Pierce, who'd stayed over a week and was busy cutting Mrs. Jordan's bittersweet: she had plenty in her own garden but didn't want to pick that if she could have someone else's. He remembered once going over to the Pierce house at this season and then Mrs. Pierce had gone, but Mrs. Jordan had stayed and there was Mrs. Jordan cutting Mrs. Pierce's bittersweet and even carrying a paper bag into which she'd popped the last of Mrs. Pierce's tomatoes.

Walt leaped out of bed and dressed, dragging on his dungarees and plaid shirt. He went downstairs with his shoes unlaced and found the kitchen deserted, that is to say his parents were not in it though otherwise it was full enough with a hamper of washing and the sink piled with dishes and the two cats and their kittens in the chairs and Sam the retriever, given Walt by Mrs. Jordan when it was still a pup brought about by its mother having been a pedigreed dachshund and its father a retriever belonging to Mrs. Pierce. But anyway Sam looked more like a retriever than like a dachshund, though undeniably on the stringy side. Sam took up an awful lot of room in the kitchen but he retrieved ducks all right and that was what mattered.

Walt crossed the peeling green-painted floor with its covering of torn druggets, baskets of muddy carrots, regiments of boots and pans and pails, and went to the stove where the coffee pot had boiled over, spilling on the iron covers and smelling up the room. He poured himself half a cup and filled the rest with milk and sugar and stirred it till it tasted like sirup, and ate a couple of cream-of-tartar biscuits left over from his father's breakfast on the kitchen table, then took his hat from a nail behind the door and let himself out the side entrance away from the garden where he guessed his father and mother were now pulling up the cornstalks, his mother with a brown sweater knotted under her chin and a handkerchief over her head, his father in the brown overcoat, too big for him, that Mr. Jordan had given him last year and that was too small for Walt.

It was no day for overcoats; the sun hit you like a hammer and except for the blaze of leaves and berries and the unnatural depth and green of the grass — it having rained late this year and then making up for the dry summer — you'd have thought it was another time of year altogether and looked to hear the lambs, and the robins and crows headed north this time instead of the other way. He walked quickly down the road and turned up by the hedgerow that separated his father's land from the Jordans' and at once it was like being in a different country — this where his feet sank sole-deep into the Jordans' lawn and even the air felt thick and rich and the wild bushes on their side of the hedge had a cared-for look — whereas on the other side they were all spines and color and roughness what with nobody caring, and who should care about black alder and purple asters and goldenrod all gone to seed and berries, not to say the thorn plums? — which only the partridges liked when they dared show their noses within shotgun range of his window.

The Jordans' place was painted white so clear and hard it blinded you almost, and with green shutters and ornamental urns beside the front steps painted to match the shutters, and a brass knocker shaped like an eagle, sort of, and the shutters were fastened across the windows so no one could get so much as a peek into the rooms, the Jordans being particular about things fading inside, or at any rate that was what they said. It was Elsa's father's job to give the lawn a last going-over with the power mower and to put manure on the flower beds and rake the dead leaves and so on after the Jordans had gone. It had begun by their asking Walt to do it two years ago, but then they'd soured on him for some reason and he'd heard that they thought him shiftless and lazy, which was a lie only they were old themselves and so fat they knew what it felt like to be disinclined for dull things or to have some things so fixed in your mind one just naturally came before another, and what difference did it make so long as you did their job too, only in your own time instead of in theirs? Well, anyway, they'd switched to Elsa's father and that was all right by Walt, who never could look at Mrs. Jordan without laughing; she looked like she'd been squeezed through a pastry bag, built like a pencil, kind of.

He walked over the grass, feeling it give as though there was sponge rubber under it, and round a corner of the house to the back where Mrs. Jordan's rose garden was, and there was Elsa with the sun on her hair, picking Mrs. Jordan's roses and one tucked just above her ear and her blue slacks pressing against her legs in the warm breeze blowing across the fields.

"Caught you!" said Walt, coming up behind her over the grass. "Caught you stealing!"

She turned, reddening up to her hair like one of the roses in her hand, and said: "What you doing sneaking round here anyway, Walt Simmons, is what I'd like to know?"

"And you," he asked, "did Mrs. Jordan say you could have her flowers the minute her back is turned?"

"Father asked me to look in and see did the grass need mowing or did I think it would wait till the end of the week, and anyway I got a better right in Mrs. Jordan's yard than you have, as you well know."

"Not stealing her flowers you haven't, and why aren't you in school? This ain't Sunday, is it, nor any vacation that I've heard of, though I may have missed something not hearing the radio news this morning."

"Morning! You know you weren't up this morning but lying in bed while your pa and ma break their backs in the garden doing your chores for you, you lazy you!"

He put his hand on her arm, feeling her warmth through the cotton-flannel shirt she was wearing, and he thought how she'd let him kiss her yesterday in a way that he guessed showed she was not used to it and that had made him want never to stop. She shrugged his hand off and went back to picking the roses, and he put his arms round her from the back and pulled her against him, burying his face in her hair, which smelled of soap and of Mrs. Jordan's roses, and she twisted free and slapped him so it really hurt, making his eyes water.

"You want to be careful," he told her then, backing away. "I'm dangerous when aroused."

"So's a flea," she said, and went back to her picking Mrs. Jordan's roses, and he watched her till her hands were full and he had gotten over his shock at her slapping him and was back at thinking his usual thoughts about her, then he asked why she was not at school and wouldn't she get in wrong, and she answered kindly, apparently forgetting about the slap, that her father wasn't feeling good and had asked her to stay back this noon and do a few things for him he didn't feel like doing, like coming up here to take a look at the Jordans' place and to go in the house — he'd given her the keys that the Jordans always left with him winters for safekeeping and in case of fire or other emergencies — to go in the house and get something Mrs. Jordan had forgotten when she went away yesterday and had called up all the way from Boston to ask him to get for her and to send on by mail.

"What was it she forgot?" asked Walt, and stooping he picked a rose, a yellow one, and held it under his nose, looking over it at Elsa, not knowing that its color made the skin under his eyes golden, also his lashes like the anthers of the rose itself.

"Her fur neckpiece she left hanging in the front bedroom closet or if it isn't there then I'd find it in the clothes closet off the spare bedroom."

She left off picking the roses, having picked all but a few buds that looked wormy anyway, and Walt said all right, that he'd go in with her and help find Mrs. Jordan's neckpiece, and though he half-expected her to tell him no, he couldn't go in the house with her after that slap, she said nothing, only smiled at him over the roses, and they turned to the side door and Elsa opened it and then the one inside and they walked into almost pitch darkness except for the glow that followed them in from the open door, which Walt closed again at once and slid the inside bolt and felt Elsa laughing beside him in the gloom that smelled like roses against his face.

"I never thought to bring a flashlight," Elsa said, groping for the light switch and then remembering that the power was turned off in the house for the winter. "You got a match, Walt?" she asked, and he felt her hand touch his arm and quickly put his hand on it, sticking it full of thorns from the roses she was carrying. Elsa was still laughing softly as though half-pleased and half-frightened and he thought that perhaps after all she hadn't let him get his hand full of thorns, not on purpose anyway. He had matches in his pocket and struck one on his boot, and as the flame rose between them it was amazing how much light it shed in that darkened place where they stood, a sort of entry between the parlor and the dining-room with everything shrouded and mysterious, with here and there a spark bouncing off a bit of glass or some metal object on the tables and sideboard.

"Here," said Elsa as the match went out. "Take my hand and we'll go upstairs and find the neckpiece. I know the way."

He took her hand and they moved across the floor in the dark again because the match had gone out and he had only a few left and there was no point in wasting them if one could do without. Elsa drew him after her and they found the stairs and went up and when they got to the top she tried to disengage her hand from his but he held it fast and kissed her blindly in the darkness, kissed her nose and her mouth and her hair, and in that darkness the roses she held smelled very strong and their petals brushed the back of his hand, feeling cool and silky and with no thorns this time. "Be careful," Elsa whispered, "you'll knock off all the flowers and stick yourself again. Come on, that's their room through that door. My, how dark! You scared of the dark, Walt?"

"Yes," said Walt, kissing her as they walked, not knowing where the kisses went — on her clothes, her neck, her ear, and then their feet caught in a rug in the darkness and both fell and he gathered her in his arms as they lay on the floor, laughing and groaning from the shock of the fall, which really hurt from that hard maple floor Mrs. Jordan had been so particular about laying down and waxing when she made over the house.

"You're just as clumsy as you're lazy," Elsa told him as she sat up and pushed him away. "I bet every rose is broken. Have you got another match?"

He lighted another match and the whole room took on a faint golden shine, seeming very small and inclosing them like a halo. It was Mrs. Jordan's bedroom, Mr. Jordan's being across the hall and the bathroom in between. Walt saw the mahogany bed with its canopy against the wall between two windows, which he guessed looked over the front lawn, and the other furniture all looking very fine and shining where it wasn't covered with old bed sheets to keep off the dust or whatever it was Mrs. Jordan feared might spoil things with the place shut up tight the way it was.

"So this is where the old biddy keeps herself nights," said Walt, getting up and pulling Elsa to her feet. "That her pup tent, between the windows? Must be awful to be so old and fat you got to put your old man in another room, don't you think so, Elsa?"

"You talk as careless as you act," Elsa said, and the match having gone out again she told him to light another one so she could find the closet. "I only got one more match," said Walt, "if you want to use that now how'll we find our way out of this place in the dark?"

"I'll find it, don't you worry. Come on, let's have a look in the closet. Hurry up, we can't spend all day here, Walt Simmons."

"Who said we can't?" he asked, and finding her near him he put his arms round her and drew her against him and they stood for a long time so clasped with their hearts beating wildly and their eyes tightly closed, though heavens knows it was so dark it didn't matter whether they kept them closed or open. Then Elsa released herself, but gently this time, and as Walt lit another match she went to the closet in a corner of the room and opened it, but it was quite empty and cleaned out the way you might expect Mrs. Jordan would leave a closet.

"Well, we better try the spare-room closet," Elsa said, shutting the door and turning away. "Think you can make that match last, Walt, till we get there?"

"I found another match," Walt said, staring at her hair, which had turned red in the tiny glow of the match, and at her eyes, which had turned very dark and her lips shadowy and soft before the match went out and she said: "Come on, we better hurry."

"But why, you don't have to go to school and I don't have to do anything but tend out on you, so what's the hurry?"

"You told me yesterday you had a job painting Pierce's barn. Don't you ever do the things you're supposed to do, you worthless thing?"

"Sure I do them but in my own time. What's all the hurry about? You don't want to get like old people who always want things done the minute they open their mouths to say so, just because they know they may not live out the night."

"You follow me and see you don't trip again. Gosh, we forgot to pick up the roses!"

Walt said never mind, they'd pick them up after they'd found Mrs. Jordan's neckpiece, and then the two of them left Mrs. Jordan's bedroom and crossed the hall to the spare room off in a corner, and here it smelled of camphor and that kind of stuff because it was where Mrs. Jordan stored the blankets and other things when she didn't have guests, but Walt guessed even in the dark that it was an elegant room, and as he followed Elsa with his hands outstretched to guard against colliding with the furniture he felt the silken texture of a quilt folded at the foot of a bed, the velvet cushion on a chair and the polished surface of a table or two and then they reached the closet and Elsa said: "We better have that other match; this is where she said it'd be if it wasn't in her room."

Walt lit the last match that really was the last one now, and Elsa opened the closet door and the draft blew the match out and there they

were in the almost total darkness again, and first Elsa and then Walt
piece, would you be apt to guess, Walt?"
felt around in the closet but it was empty just like the one in Mrs. Jordan's room, not a thing in it except some hooks and a metal rod hung
with silk-covered coat hangers. "There," said Elsa. "It isn't here.
Now I wonder where she might have left such a thing as a fur neck-
He said nothing but put his hands on her shoulders and brought her
toward him and their lips met and each could feel his own and the
other's heart striking like clocks, and the silent darkness seemed to bind
them around and about and to exclude the world outside, the world
of sun and shining leaf and flying birds and the old people plodding
through the day's chores without a thought maybe of what it might
once have been to be like this, together in a shut-up house that smelled
of solitude and camphor and roses and a girl's hair freshly washed and
feeling stranger against one's mouth than when one saw it in the open
air, feeling potent as gold in one's hand as one touched it, held it in
thick soft handfuls like something very strange and alive by itself.

"Listen," said Elsa, and drew away, her arms still on his shoulders.
"Listen, Walt, did you hear something?"

"Mice," he said, his eyes half-closed, his hand still behind her head
where her hair lay in coils above the collar of her shirt.

"No, it's people — outside." She left him and went to a window,
but it was closed and shuttered and not a chink of light showed through.
Walt heard what she had heard, voices, coming from the road, coming
across the lawn toward the house, and he guessed at once what it was
and said: "I bet it's my sister May and her kids come after Mrs. Jordan's tomatoes, that's all."

"What right's May got to come after them tomatoes?" demanded
Elsa, turning from the window. "She got her own tomatoes or she
can get them from your folks or buy them in the store, can't she?"

"Sh, she'll hear you," whispered Walt. "Let's go up attic and spy
on them from there. There's no shutters on the attic windows."

He took her hand and they went back across the spare room and
across the hall to the end where a door gave on the attic stairs, and
opening it they saw light at once, streaming across the top of the straight,
narrow staircase, coming from both windows of the attic, and Walt
heard at once the hammering of flies against the hot panes just as he
did in his own room when he waked on sunny mornings like this. It
was warm in the Jordans' attic and sort of blinding after the darkness
downstairs and he felt suddenly shy with Elsa as he had not done down-

stairs when they were together in the darkness, and so did she because she would not look at him but went at once to the southeast window and crouched down so she could see outside, and after a slight hesitation he went and crouched beside her and looked out and sure enough there was his sister May in a faded print dress and a red sweater and her head done up in a scarf, leading one of the kids by the hand, followed by the second pulling a kiddy cart with the third kid in it, her youngest, named Walt after him.

"I'd like to know what May thinks she's doing coming over here to help herself like the place belonged to her," Elsa said in a temper, not looking at him. "I've a good mind to go down and ask her at that."

"She's not doing any harm that I can see," said Walt. "Only taking the kids for a bit of a walk and you know how everyone likes to pick other people's stuff this time of year when there's no harm in it, no one wanting it only those that goes to the trouble, like you picking the roses."

"I got a right to pick the roses seeing my dad takes care of the place when the Jordans are away, they trusting him," replied Elsa, and stared at May approaching slowly across the grass, big with another child on the way.

"Then would you say Mrs. Pierce and Mrs. Jordan got a right to pick one another's bittersweet when one or the other's not there to see?" he asked her, and leaned his shoulder against hers, which she had to let him do because the window was small and if she'd moved she'd have missed the view of May and the kids making their way slowly across the grass, May stopping to pick up fallen apples or to wipe one of the kids' nose and walking as women do when they're that way, as though every step had to be slow and considered for fear of slipping or maybe just out of the tiredness of it.

"I don't see what Mrs. Pierce's and Mrs. Jordan's bittersweet's got to do with the case," Elsa said, talking in a whisper though there was hardly a chance of May hearing her at this distance. "May got no right trespassing on this property and you know it."

"Trespassing!" he scoffed. "You sound like summer folk — trespassing!"

"They'd call it trespassing if they was to see it," she returned in an angry whisper, leaning against him hard so as not to overbalance as he pressed against her. And she added in disgust: "I shouldn't think May would want to be seen walking round the way she is just now, anyway."

"She can't help it the way she is. The baby's due in another week."

"And after that there'll be another one and another and another.
It's always the shiftless folks has the most children."

"Yours had nine," he reminded her, smiling, and turned to stare at
her profile, which the light molded to silver with a flush on her cheeks
going back to the curve of the ear nearest to him. "You wish you'd
never been born, Elsa?"

"No, but I bet there's times your sister May does, only twenty-two
and with three kids already and another on the way."

He was silent and they watched May and the kids disappear round
a corner of the house in the direction of the Jordans' vegetable garden
and then Walt said: "Here's more coming — Neddy Pike and his
grandmother with her wheelbarrow. May'd better hurry if she expects
to get any of the tomatoes with old lady Pike on the job."

"I'm going down and tell them they better get right out of here before my dad finds them," Elsa said, starting to her feet, but Walt pulled
her down again. "Look," he said, "there's Nagy with his shopping
bag. I know what he's after — the old cucumbers. He told me once
that where he come from in Finland they takes old cucumbers and boils
them and stuffs them with meat and onions and they tastes good that
way."

Elsa turned very red and gazed into his eyes without a particle of
the love that he'd felt a while ago downstairs in the dark.

"Thieves," she said in a trembling voice. "Nothing but a bunch of
thieves. They won't leave a flower or a carrot behind them, you'll see.
Wait till I tell my dad about it."

"Anyway you got the roses," he said, and caught her round the
shoulders and bent her back over his arm and kissed her with his eyes
closed, and she let him until suddenly a thought occurred to her and
she struggled free, saying: "They could see us if they looked up this
way."

"They won't look up, they're all too busy stealing," he answered and
kissed her again, opening his eyes to find that she had closed hers. Then
suddenly both gave a start and a sort of concerted small scream and
flew apart as something large and soft fell on them from a coat hanger
suspended on a rod over their heads, which they had not noticed when
they came up here blinded by the stream of light after the darkness
downstairs. Elsa went on screaming softly with her hands against her
mouth and her eyes squeezed shut in a paroxysm of fear. "Kill it,
Walt . . . kill it . . . what is it . . . mice or a skunk or what . . . kill it . . ."

Walt, who had bounded half-across the room in his terror, came bounding back and flung himself down beside her again. "Look," he said, and picked up Mrs. Jordan's neckpiece where it had fallen behind them and wrapped it round Elsa's neck while she went on screaming softly and trying to fight him off. "Look, it's a real live fox and just feel its tail." He tickled her neck and face with the blue-fox brush and perhaps the smell of camphor in it and the softness and the feel of something tame and rich reassured her for she opened her eyes at last and looked at him. "She never even mentioned that it might be hanging in the attic, I suppose, the old coot — and we hunting everywhere for it downstairs in the dark where we might have fallen and broken our necks." He gazed at Elsa's face framed in the dark fur and said: "You look like a movie star, only more beautiful."

She stroked the fur with the palm of her hand and then flung the tail nonchalantly over her shoulder with an air of knowing just how and rose to her feet. "Come on, we better be going. Dad said he wanted to get this in the mail before evening and we've taken long enough finding it anyway."

"Wait," said Walt, holding her back with one hand. "We better not go out, had we, with all them people out there in the garden apt to see us?"

"Why not? It isn't their property, is it, and my own dad sent me here to get Mrs. Jordan's neckpiece, didn't he? What's the matter with our going out if we want to?"

Walt felt himself flushing and looked away to the other window where the flies were beating their wings against the strong light. "Nothing," he answered, "only they might think things, you know how people are, the way their minds work, and you and me coming out of the house like this together."

Elsa pulled her hand free and clutched the neckpiece round her neck and stared at him with a white empty look in her eyes.

"All I mean," Walt said, "is that if May was to see us or Neddy and Mrs. Pike they'd maybe make a few jokes, and know how people do, and they'd be sure to mention it around and it might get us in wrong with our folks, especially with yours."

"Yes," Elsa said bitterly. "My dad always did say you were shiftless and no-account like the rest of your family, not willing to do an honest day's work if you could squawk out of it."

"Who's squawking? I come in here with you because you asked me to, scared as you was of mice and rats and ghosts and what not."

"I never asked you nothing of the sort. You come sneaking in the Jordans' yard after whatever you could get away with just like May done and them others that wouldn't dare if the Jordans was here to protect their property, the poor things."

"You didn't think to say any such things as that last night when I took you home and stayed at your house till ten, nor did your folks tell me then that they thought I was shiftless and no-account, did they? But they always was the kind talks about a person behind his back instead of straight to his face . . ."

A sound outdoors arrested them and both rushed back to the window, where they crouched once more, and saw a Packard in two tones of gray, driven by a colored chauffeur, draw up at the entrance of the Jordans' driveway and a lady in a fur cape and carrying a basket emerge from it.

"Mrs. Pierce," whispered Walt as the lady crossed the lawn and disappeared round the same corner of the house as May and the children and Mrs. Pike and Neddy.

"She's come after Mrs. Jordan's bittersweet. She always does though she got plenty of her own only she hates to pick it."

"What we going to do?" asked Elsa and looked as though she was getting ready to cry. "Suppose they take it into their heads to come in the house and find us, what we going to do?"

"They won't," Walt told her soothingly and felt suddenly strong and tender and in command of the situation. "They won't find us because I took the key out the door and put it in the inside and bolted the storm door. You don't have to worry."

"You bolted the door? What put it in your head to do that I'd like to know, Walt Simmons?"

"I didn't think you'd want anyone following after us and perhaps scaring the daylights out of us thinking they was only playing a joke or something. May's kids, for instance, they're always up to tricks."

She was looking at him strangely and said in a changed voice: "You know what would happen, don't you, if you so much as lay a hand on me, Walt Simmons, and all them folks out there in the garden within hearing if I was to scream like I really meant it? If you don't know what would happen then you're just as dumb as you are lazy. . . ."

He said nothing to that, only gazed at her out of his deep eyes, then turned and started for the attic stairs, and she came after him quickly and took his arm and said: "We can't go out like this now, not whiles there's all them people out there to see us — and Mrs. Pierce's colored man in the car out front, he'd see us if we tried to get out that way."

But Walt kept going, finding his way blindly down the steep stairs, and Elsa came after him, clutching Mrs. Jordan's neckpiece, and in the darkness of the downstairs rooms he turned and she went straight into his arms as though he was a magnet, and they clung to each other, kissing wildly, kissing with knowledge and with all the violence of their blood and the thought beating between them like a third heart that they must not stay another moment and that they would never be young again but this once yet staying and staying there in the dark hall and Mrs. Jordan's neckpiece engulfing both their faces in its soft heat like a live animal really, while outside, beyond the shuttered windows, in the great expanse of sunlight which felt more like summer than like fall, the others went self-consciously trying to ignore one another as they picked Mrs. Jordan's flowers and her tomatoes and cumcumbers and the golden dahlias that had blossomed too late this year for Mrs. Jordan to pick before she left.

(*From Furioso*)

YONEKO'S EARTHQUAKE

BY HISAYE YAMAMOTO

YONEKO HOSOUME became a free-thinker on the night of March 10, 1933, only a few months after her first actual recognition of God. Ten years old at the time, of course she had heard rumors about God all along, long before Marpo came. Her cousins who lived in the city were all Christians, living as they did right next door to a Baptist church exclusively for Japanese people. These city cousins, of whom there were several, had been baptized en masse, and were very proud of their condition. Yoneko was impressed when she heard of this and thereafter was given to referring to them as "my cousins, the Christians." She, too, yearned at times after Christianity, but she realized the absurdity of her whim, seeing that there was no Baptist church for Japanese in the rural community she lived in. Such a church would have been impractical, moreover, since Yoneko, her father, her mother, and her little brother Seigo, were the only Japanese thereabouts. They were the only ones, too, whose agriculture was so diverse as to include blackberries, cabbages, rhubarb, potatoes, cucumbers, onions, and canteloupes. The rest of the countryside there was like one vast orange grove.

Yoneko had entered her cousins' church once, but she could not recall the sacred occasion without mortification. It had been one day when the cousins had taken her and Seigo along with them to Sunday school. The church was a narrow, wooden building, mysterious-looking because of its unusual bluish-grey paint and its steeple, but the basement schoolroom inside had been disappointingly ordinary, with desks, a blackboard, and erasers. They had all sung "Let Us Gather at the River" in Japanese. This goes:

Mamonaku kanata no
Nagare no soba de

361

Tanoshiku ai-masho
Mata tomodachi to

Mamonaku ai-masho
Kirei-na, kirei-na kawa de
Tanoshiku ai-masho
Mata tomodachi to.

Yoneko had not known the words at all, but always clever in such situations, she had opened her mouth and grimaced nonchalantly to the rhythm. What with everyone else singing at the top of his lungs, no one had noticed that she was not making a peep. Then everyone had sat down again and the man had suggested, "Let us pray." Her cousins and the rest had promptly curled their arms on the desks to make nests for their heads, and Yoneko had done the same. But not Seigo. Because when the room had become so still that one was aware of the breathing, the creaking, and the chittering in the trees outside, Seigo, sitting with her, had suddenly flung his arm around her neck and said with concern, "Sis, what are you crying for? Don't cry." Even the man had laughed and Yoneko had been terribly ashamed that Seigo should thus disclose them to be interlopers. She had pinched him fiercely and he had begun to cry, so she had had to drag him outside, which was a fortunate move, because he had immediately wet his pants. But he had been only three then, so it was not very fair to expect dignity of him.

So it remained for Marpo to bring the word of God to Yoneko, Marpo with the face like brown leather, the thin moustache like Edmund Lowe's, and the rare, breathtaking smile like white gold. Marpo, who was twenty-seven years old, was a Filipino and his last name was lovely, something like Humming Wing, but no one ever ascertained the spelling of it. He ate principally rice, just as though he were Japanese, but he never sat down to the Hosoume table, because he lived in the bunk-house out by the barn and cooked on his own kerosene stove. Once Yoneko read somewhere that Filipinos trapped wild dogs, starved them for a time, then, feeding them mountains of rice, killed them at the peak of their bloatedness, thus insuring themselves meat ready to roast, stuffing and all, without further ado. This, the book said, was considered a delicacy. Unable to hide her disgust and her fascination, Yoneko went straightway to Marpo and asked, "Marpo, is it true that you eat dogs?", and he, flashing that smile, answered, "Don't be funny, honey!" This caused her no end of amusement, because it was a poem, and she completely forgot about the wild dogs.

Well, there seemed to be nothing Marpo could not do. Mr. Hosoume said Marpo was the best hired man he had ever had, and he said this often, because it was an irrefutable fact among Japanese in general that Filipinos in general were an indolent lot. Mr. Hosoume ascribed Marpo's industry to his having grown up in Hawaii, where there is known to be considerable Japanese influence. Marpo had gone to a missionary school there and he owned a Bible given him by one of his teachers. This had black leather covers that gave as easily as cloth, golden edges, and a slim purple ribbon for a marker. He always kept it on the little table by his bunk, which was not a bed with springs but a low, three-plank shelf with a mattress only. On the first page of the book, which was stiff and black, his teacher had written in large swirls of white ink, "As we draw near to God, He will draw near to us."

What, for instance, could Marpo do? Why, it would take an entire, leisurely evening to go into his accomplishments adequately, because there was not only Marpo the Christian and Marpo the best hired man, but Marpo the athlete, Marpo the musician (both instrumental and vocal), Marpo the artist, and Marpo the radio technician:

(1) As an athlete, Marpo owned a special pair of black shoes, equipped with sharp nails on the soles, which he kept in shape with the regular application of neatsfoot oil. Putting these on, he would dash down the dirt road to the highway, a distance of perhaps half a mile, and back again. When he first came to work for the Hosoumes, he undertook this sprint every evening before he went to get his supper but, as time went on, he referred to these shoes less and less and, in the end, when he left, he had not touched them for months. He also owned a muscle-builder sent him by Charles Atlas which, despite his unassuming size, he could stretch the length of his outspread arms; his teeth gritted then and his whole body became temporarily victim to a jerky vibration. (2) As an artist, Marpo painted larger-than-life water colors of his favorite movie stars, all of whom were women and all of whom were blonde, like Ann Harding and Jean Harlow, and tacked them up on his walls. He also made for Yoneko a folding contraption of wood holding two pencils, one with lead and one without, with which she, too, could obtain double-sized likenesses of any picture she wished. It was a fragile instrument, however, and Seigo splintered it to pieces one day when Yoneko was away at school. He claimed he was only trying to copy Boob McNutt from the funny paper when it

failed. (3) As a musician, Marpo owned a violin for which he had paid over one hundred dollars. He kept this in a case whose lining was red velvet, first wrapping it gently in a brilliant red silk scarf. This scarf, which weighed nothing, he tucked under his chin when he played, gathering it up delicately by the center and flicking it once to unfurl it — a gesture Yoneko prized. In addition to this, Marpo was a singer, with a soft tenor which came out in professional quavers and rolled r's when he applied a slight pressure to his Adam's apple with thumb and forefinger. His violin and vocal repertoire consisted of the same numbers, mostly hymns and Irish folk airs. He was especially addicted to "The Rose of Tralee" and the "Londonderry Air." (4) Finally, as a radio technician who had spent two previous winters at a specialists' school in the city, Marpo had put together a bulky table-size radio which brought in equal proportions of static and entertainment. He never got around to building a cabinet to house it and its innards of metal and glass remained public throughout its lifetime. This was just as well, for not a week passed without Marpo's deciding to solder one bit or another. Yoneko and Seigo became a part of the great listening audience with such fidelity that Mr. Hosoume began remarking the fact that they dwelt more with Marpo than with their own parents. He eventually took a serious view of the matter and bought the naked radio from Marpo, who thereupon put away his radio manuals and his soldering iron in the bottom of his steamer trunk and divided more time among his other interests.

However, Marpo's versatility was not revealed, as it is here, in a lump. Yoneko uncovered it fragment by fragment every day, by dint of unabashed questions, explorations among his possessions, and even silent observation, although this last was rare. In fact, she and Seigo visited with Marpo at least once a day and both of them regularly came away amazed with their findings. The most surprising thing was that Marpo was, after all this, a rather shy young man meek to the point of speechlessness in the presence of Mr. and Mrs. Hosoume. With Yoneko and Seigo, he was somewhat more self-confident and at ease.

It is not remembered now just how Yoneko and Marpo came to open their protracted discussion on religion. It is sufficient here to note that Yoneko was an ideal apostle, adoring Jesus, desiring Heaven, and fearing Hell. Once Marpo had enlightened her on these basics, Yoneko never questioned their truth. The questions she put up to him, therefore, sought neither proof of her exegeses nor balm for her doubts, but simply additional color to round out her mental images. For example, who did Marpo suppose was God's favorite movie star? Or, what sound did Jesus' laughter have (it must be like music, she added, nodding sagely, answering herself to her own satisfaction), and did Marpo suppose that God's sense of humor would have appreciated the delicious chant she had learned from friends at school today:

> There ain't no bugs on us,
> There ain't no bugs on us,
> There may be bugs on the rest of you mugs,
> But there ain't no bugs on us?

Or, did Marpo believe Jesus to have been exempt from stinging eyes when he shampooed that long, naturally wavy hair of his?

To shake such faith, there would have been required a most monstrous upheaval of some sort, and it might be said that this is just what happened. For early on the evening of March 10, 1933, a little after five o'clock this was, as Mrs. Hosoume was getting supper, as Marpo was finishing up in the fields alone because Mr. Hosoume had gone to order some chicken fertilizer, and as Yoneko and Seigo were listening to Skippy, a tremendous roar came out of nowhere and the Hosoume house began shuddering violently as though some giant had seized it in his two hands and was giving it a good shaking. Mrs. Housoume, who remembered similar, although milder experiences, from her childhood in Japan, screamed, "*Jishin, jishin!*" before she ran and grabbed Yoneko and Seigo each by a hand and dragged them outside with her. She took them as far as the middle of the rhubarb patch near the house, and there they all crouched, pressed together, watching the world about them rock and sway. In a few minutes, Marpo, stumbling in from the fields, joined them, saying, "Earthquake, earthquake!", and he gathered them all in his arms, as much to protect them as to support himself.

Mr. Hosoume came home later that evening in a stranger's car, with another stranger driving the family Reo. Pallid, trembling, his eyes wildly staring, he could have been mistaken for a drunkard, except that he was famous as a teetotaler. It seemed that he had been on the way home when the first jolt came, that the old green Reo had been kissed by a broken live wire dangling from a suddenly leaning pole. Mr. Hosoume, knowing that the end had come by electrocution, had begun to writhe and kick and this had been his salvation. His hands had flown from the wheel, the car had swerved into a ditch, freeing itself from the sputtering wire. Later, it was found that he was left per-

manently inhibited about driving automobiles and permanently incapable of considering electricity with calmness. He spent the larger
part of his later life weakly, wandering about the house or fields and
lying down frequently to rest because of splitting headaches and sudden
dizzy spells.

So it was Marpo who went back into the house as Yoneko screamed,
"No, Marpo, no!" and brought out the Hosoumes' kerosene stove, the
food, the blankets, while Mr. Hosoume huddled on the ground near
his family.

The earth trembled for days afterwards. The Hosoumes and Marpo
Humming Wing lived during that time on a natural patch of Bermuda
grass between the house and the rhubarb patch, remembering to take
three meals a day and retire at night. Marpo ventured inside the house
many times despite Yoneko's protests and reported the damage slight:
a few dishes had been broken; a gallon jug of mayonnaise had fallen
from the top pantry shelf and spattered the kitchen floor with yellow
blobs and pieces of glass.

Yoneko was in constant terror during this experience. Immediately
on learning what all the commotion was about, she began praying to
God to end this violence. She entreated God, flattered Him, wheedled
Him, commanded Him, but He did not listen to her at all — inexorably, the earth went on rumbling. After three solid hours of silent, desperate prayer, without any results whatsoever, Yoneko began to suspect
that God was either powerless, callous, downright cruel, or nonexist-
ent. In the murky night, under a strange moon wearing a pale ring
of light, she decided upon the last as the most plausible theory. "Ha,"
was one of the things she said tremulously to Marpo, when she was not
begging him to stay out of the house, "you and your God!"

The others soon oriented themselves to the catastrophe with philosophy, saying how fortunate they were to live in the country where the
peril was less than in the city and going so far as to regard the period
as a sort of vacation from work, with their enforced alfresco existence a
sort of camping trip. They tried to bring Yoneko to partake of this
pleasant outlook, but she, shivering with each new quiver, looked on
them as dreamers who refused to see things as they really were. Indeed, Yoneko's reaction was so notable that the Hosoume household
thereafter spoke of the event as "Yoneko's earthquake."

After the earth subsided and the mayonnaise was mopped off the
kitchen floor, life returned to normal, except that Mr. Hosoume stayed
at home most of the time. Sometimes, if he had a relatively painless

day, he would have supper on the stove when Mrs. Hosoume came in from the fields. Mrs. Hosoume and Marpo did all the field labor now, except on certain overwhelming days when several Mexicans were hired to assist them. Marpo did most of the driving, too, and it was now he and Mrs. Hosoume who went into town on the weekly trip for groceries. In fact, Marpo became indispensable and both Mr. and Mrs. Hosoume often told each other how grateful they were for Marpo.

When summer vacation began and Yoneko stayed at home, too, she found the new arrangement rather inconvenient. Her father's presence cramped her style: for instance, once when her friends came over and it was decided to make fudge, he would not permit them, saying fudge used too much sugar and that sugar was not a plaything; once when they were playing paper dolls, he came along and stuck his finger up his nose and pretended he was going to rub some snot off onto the dolls. Things like that. So, on some days, she was very much annoyed with her father.

Therefore when her mother came home breathless from the fields one day and pushed a ring at her, a gold-colored ring with a tiny glass-like stone in it, saying, "Look, Yoneko, I'm going to give you this ring. If your father asks where you got it, say you found it on the street," Yoneko was perplexed but delighted both by the unexpected gift and the chance to have some secret revenge on her father, and she said, certainly, she was willing to comply with her mother's request. Her mother went back to the fields then and Yoneko put the pretty ring on her middle finger, taking up the loose space with a bit of newspaper. It was similar to the rings found occasionally in boxes of Crackerjack, except that it appeared a bit more substantial.

Mr. Hosoume never asked about the ring; in fact, he never noticed she was wearing one. Yoneko thought he was about to, once, but he only reproved her for the flamingo nail polish she was wearing, which she had applied from a vial brought over by Yvonne Fournier, the French girl two orange groves away. "You look like a Filipino," Mr. Hosoume said sternly, for it was another irrefutable fact among Japanese in general that Filipinos in general were a gaudy lot. Mrs. Hosoume immediately came to her defense, saying that in Japan, if she remembered correctly, young girls did the same thing. In fact, she remembered having gone to elaborate lengths to tint her fingernails: she used to gather, she said, the petals of the red *tsubobana* or the purple *kogane* (which grows on the underside of stones), grind them well, mix them with some alum powder, then cook the mixture and leave it to stand overnight in an envelope of either persimmon or sugar potato leaves (both very strong leaves). The second night, just before going to bed, she used to obtain threads by ripping a palm leaf (because real thread was dear) and tightly bind the paste to her fingernails under shields of persimmon or sugar potato leaves. She would be helpless for the night, the fingertips bound so well that they were alternately numb or aching, but she would grit her teeth and tell herself that the discomfort indicated the success of the operation. In the morning, finally releasing her fingers, she would find the nails shining with a translucent, red-orange color.

Yoneko was fascinated, because she usually thought of her parents as having been adults all their lives. She thought that her mother must have been a beautiful child, with or without bright fingernails, because, though surely past thirty, she was even yet a beautiful person. When she herself was younger, she remembered, she had at times been so struck with her mother's appearance that she had dropped to her knees and mutely clasped her mother's legs in her arms. She had left off this habit as she learned to control her emotions, because at such times her mother had usually walked away, saying, "My, what a clinging child you are. You've got to learn to be a little more independent." She also remembered she had once heard someone comparing her mother to "a dewy, half-opened rosebud."

Mr. Hosoume, however, was irritated. "That's no excuse for Yoneko to begin using paint on her fingernails," he said. "She's only ten."

"Her Japanese age is eleven, and we weren't much older," Mrs. Hosoume said.

"Look," Mr. Hosoume said, "if you're going to contradict every piece of advice I give the children, they'll end up disobeying us both and doing what they very well please. Just because I'm ill just now is no reason for them to start being disrespectful."

"When have I ever contradicted you before?" Mrs. Hosoume said.

"Countless times," Mr. Hosoume said.

"Name one instance," Mrs. Hosoume said.

Certainly there had been times, but Mr. Hosoume could not happen to mention the one requested instance on the spot and he became quite angry. "That's quite enough of your insolence," he said. Since he was speaking in Japanese, his exact accusation was that she was *nama-iki*, which is a shade more revolting than being merely insolent.

"*Nama-iki, nama-iki?*" said Mrs. Hosoume. "How dare you? I'll not have anyone calling me *nama-iki!*"

At that, Mr. Hosoume went up to where his wife was ironing and slapped her smartly on the face. It was the first time he had ever laid hands on her. Mrs. Hosoume was immobile for an instant, but she resumed her ironing as though nothing had happened, although she glanced over at Marpo, who happened to be in the room reading a newspaper. Yoneko and Seigo forgot they were listening to the radio and stared at their parents, thunderstruck.

"Hit me again," said Mrs. Hosoume quietly, as she ironed. "Hit me all you wish."

Mr. Hosoume was apparently about to, but Marpo stepped up and put his hand on Mr. Hosoume's shoulder. "The children are here," said Marpo, "the children."

"Mind your own business," said Mr. Hosoume in broken English. "Get out of here!"

Marpo left, and that was about all. Mrs. Hosoume went on ironing, Yoneko and Seigo turned back to the radio, and Mr. Hosoume muttered that Marpo was beginning to forget his place. Now that he thought of it, he said, Marpo had been increasingly impudent towards him since his illness. He said just because he was temporarily an invalid was no reason for Marpo to start being disrespectful. He added that Marpo had better watch his step or that he might find himself jobless one of these fine days.

And something of the sort must have happened. Marpo was here one day and gone the next, without even saying good-bye to Yoneko and Seigo. That was also the day the Hosoume family went to the city on a weekday afternoon, which was most unusual. Mr. Hosoume, who now avoided driving as much as possible, handled the cumbersome Reo as though it were a nervous stallion, sitting on the edge of the seat and hugging the steering wheel. He drove very fast and about halfway to the city struck a beautiful collie which dashed out barking from someone's yard. The car jerked with the impact, but Mr. Hosoume drove right on and Yoneko, wanting suddenly to vomit, looked back and saw the collie lying very still at the side of the road.

When they arrived at the Japanese hospital, which was their destination, Mr. Hosoume cautioned Yoneko and Seigo to be exemplary children and wait patiently in the car. It seemed hours before he and Mrs. Hosoume returned, she walking with very small, slow steps and he assisting her. When Mrs. Hosoume got in the car, she leaned back and closed her eyes. Yoneko inquired as to the source of her distress, for she was obviously in pain, but she only answered that she was feeling a little under the weather and that the doctor had administered some necessarily astringent treatment. At that, Mr. Hosoume turned around and advised Yoneko and Seigo that they must tell no one of coming to the city on a weekday afternoon, absolutely no one, and Yoneko and Seigo readily assented. On the way home, they passed the place of the encounter with the collie, and Yoneko looked up and down the stretch of road but the dog was nowhere to be seen.

Not long after that, the Hosoumes got a new hired hand, an old Japanese man who wore his grey hair in a military cut and who, unlike Marpo, had no particular interests outside working, eating, sleeping, and playing an occasional game of *goh* with Mr. Hosoume. Before he came Yoneko and Seigo played sometimes in the empty bunkhouse and recalled Marpo's various charms together. Privately, Yoneko was wounded more than she would admit even to herself that Marpo should have subjected her to such an abrupt desertion. Whenever her indignation became too great to endure gracefully, she would console herself by telling Seigo that, after all, Marpo was a mere Filipino, an eater of wild dogs.

Seigo never knew about the disappointing new hired man, because he suddenly died in the night. He and Yoneko had spent the hot morning in the nearest orange grove, she driving him to distraction by repeating certain words he could not bear to hear: she had called him Serge, a name she had read somewhere, instead of Seigo; and she had chanted off the name of the tires they were rolling around like hoops as Goodrich Silver-TO-town, Goodrich Silver-TO-town, instead of Goodrich Silvertown. This had enraged him, and he had chased her around the trees most of the morning. Finally she had taunted him from several trees away by singing "You're a Yellow-streaked Coward," which was one of several small songs she had composed. Seigo had suddenly grinned and shouted, "Sure!", and walked off, leaving her, as he intended, with a sense of emptiness. In the afternoon, they had perspired and followed the potato-digging machine and the Mexican workers, both hired for the day, around the field, delighting in unearthing marble-sized, smooth-skinned potatoes that both the machine and the men had missed. Then, in the middle of the night, Seigo began crying, complaining of a stomach ache. Mrs. Hosoume felt his head and sent her husband for the doctor, who smiled and said Seigo would be fine in the morning. He said it was doubtless the combination of green oranges, raw potatoes, and the July heat. But as soon as the doctor left, Seigo fell into a coma and a drop of red blood stood out on his underlip, where he had evidently bit it. Mr. Hosoume again fetched the doctor, who was this time very grave and wagged his head, saying several times, "It looks very bad." So Seigo died at the age of five.

Mrs. Hosoume was inconsolable and had swollen eyes in the morning for weeks afterwards. She now insisted on visiting the city relatives each Sunday, so that she could attend church services with them. One Sunday, she stood up and accepted Christ. It was through accompanying her mother to many of these services that Yoneko finally learned the Japanese words to "Let Us Gather at the River." Mrs. Hosoume also did not seem interested in discussing anything but God and Seigo. She was especially fond of reminding visitors how adorable Seigo had been as an infant, how she had been unable to refrain from dressing him as a little girl and fixing his hair in bangs until he was two. Mr. Hosoume was very gentle with her and when Yoneko accidentally caused her to giggle once, he nodded and said, "Yes, that's right, Yoneko, we must make your mother laugh and forget about Seigo." Yoneko herself did not think about Seigo at all. Whenever the thought of Seigo crossed her mind, she instantly began composing a new song, and this worked very well.

One evening, when the new hired man had been with them a while, Yoneko was helping her mother with the dishes when she found herself being examined with such peculiarly intent eyes that, with a start of guilt, she began searching in her mind for a possible crime she had lately committed. But Mrs. Hosoume only said, "Never kill a person, Yoneko, because if you do, God will take from you someone you love."

"Oh, that," said Yoneko quickly, "I don't believe in that, I don't believe in God." And her words tumbling pell-mell over one another, she went on eagerly to explain a few of her reasons why. If she neglected to mention the test she had given God during the earthquake, it was probably because she was a little upset. She had believed for a moment that her mother was going to ask about the ring (which, alas, she had lost already, somewhere in the flumes along the canteloupe patch).

BIOGRAPHICAL NOTES

BERGE, BILL. Born twenty-four years ago in Rock Island, Illinois, Mr. Berge received his early education at the public schools there and at sixteen entered the State University of Iowa. After his freshman year, he entered the Army, but returned to college following his discharge, graduating in the spring of 1951. A week later, he wrote "That Lovely Green Boat," included in this volume, and a week after that, got married. He now lives in Iowa City, Iowa, where he is studying for a Master's degree at the State University. "That Lovely Green Boat," his first published short story, was the winner of the Alfred A. Knopf–*Furioso* Fiction Contest for 1951.

BOWEN, ROBERT O. Mr. Bowen is thirty-two years old and was born and raised in Bridgeport, Connecticut. From 1937 to 1945, he served in the Navy as a fireman, spending the last three years of that period in Japanese prisoner-of-war camps in the Philippines. After the war he took a Bachelor's and Master's degree in English from the University of Alabama, studying writing under Hudson Strode. He has published poetry and short stories in *A.D.*, *The Montevallo Review*, *Span*, *Western Review*, and other little magazines, and has stories waiting publication in *Esquire* and in an anthology of war fiction edited by Maxwell Aley. His first novel, *The Weight of the Cross*, was published by Alfred A. Knopf last year. At present, Mr. Bowen teaches fiction writing at the University of Alabama Extension Center in Birmingham, Alabama, and is at work on another novel.

BOYLE, KAY. Miss Boyle was born in St. Paul, Minnesota, in 1903, but has spent most of her life abroad. At present, she lives in the U.S. Zone of Germany with her husband Joseph W. C. Franckenstein who is on civilian duty with the War Department. Widely known as a short story writer and novelist, she is the author of some twenty books, including *Plagued by the Nightingale*, *Year Before Last*, *Gentlemen, I Address You Privately*, *The White Horses of Vienna*, *Monday Night*, *Cray Hunter*, *Primer for Combat*, and *A Frenchman Must Die*. Her stories have been included in many anthologies, and she has twice won first prize in the O. Henry Awards *Prize Stories*. "The Lost," reprinted in this volume, is included in *The Smoking Mountain*, a collection of Miss Boyle's stories recently published by McGraw-Hill.

BRADBURY, RAY. Mr. Bradbury was born in Waukegan, Illinois, in 1920. He sold his first story when he was twenty-one, but had begun writing at the age of twelve. Graduation from Los Angeles High School terminated his formal education, and he sold newspapers on a street corner for the following three years while trying to interest editors in his stories. His first acceptances appeared in *Super-Science*, *Thrilling Wonder Stories*, *Astounding Science-Fiction*, and *Weird Tales*, in the early forties. Since 1945, his stories have appeared in such varied magazines as *The American Mercury*, *Charm*, *Collier's*, *Epoch*, *Harper's Magazine*, *The New Yorker*, *New-Story*, and *The Saturday Evening Post*. He has been represented in *The Best American Short Stories 1946* and *1948*, and has also appeared twice in the O. Henry Awards *Prize Stories*, in 1947 and then as a third prize winner in 1948. In 1947, Arkham House published his first book of short stories, *Dark Carnival;* since then, he has had two more collections published by Doubleday and Company, *The Martian Chronicles* in 1950 and *The Illustrated Man* in 1951. His fourth book, *Summer Morning, Summer Night*, will be brought out by Doubleday late this year. He writes that he believes "science-fiction as a literary form is here to stay, and will increase in quality as well as quantity in the coming decade." He now lives in Los Angeles with his wife Marguerite, and two daughters, Susan and Ramona.

CALISHER, HORTENSE. Born in New York City in 1911, Hortense Calisher attended city schools and graduated from Barnard College in 1932. She held various depression jobs, including head of stock in a hat department, hostess, investigator in a public welfare agency, consultant in an advertising department, and case worker in a family service agency. In 1935, she married H. B. Heffelfinger, an engineer, and spent the next ten years in upstate New York and the Middle West. At present, she and her husband live in Nyack, New York, with their two children, aged fourteen and eight. Her first published story appeared in *The New Yorker* in 1948, and was included in the O. Henry Awards *Prize Stories* of 1949. Since that time, her work has also appeared in *The American Mercury, Harper's Bazaar, Harper's Magazine, Mademoiselle,* and in *The Best American Short Stories 1951.* A collection of her stories, *In the Absence of Angels,* was published last fall by Little, Brown and Company. She writes that she is still doing short fiction, but is "trying to arrange for a more continuous span of working time in which to think over a longer project — either a novel or a play."

CARDOZO, NANCY. A native New Yorker, Nancy Cardozo was born in 1919. Most of her childhood was spent in the city, where she attended the Dalton School. After graduating from Swarthmore College, she travelled in France and Mexico, and later lived and worked at various times in places as remote from each other as San Diego, Terre Haute, and Monhegan Island. She has been writing since the age of twelve — first poetry, which was published in *Scribner's Magazine, The New Yorker, Poetry,* and some of the little magazines. More recently, her short stories have appeared in *Charm, The New Yorker, Redbook,* and *Seventeen.* She is married and has two small sons, Nicholas and Jan. At present, she is living again in New York and is working on a novel.

CHAIKIN, NANCY C. Mrs. Chaikin was born in Brooklyn, New York, in 1923. After graduating from Erasmus Hall High School in that city, she attended the University of Michigan; there she worked in fiction writing with Alan Seager, wrote a column for the *Michigan Daily,* and won two Avery Hopwood awards, the first in 1944 for short stories, the second in 1945 for essays in literary criticism. Following her graduation in 1945, she returned to New York where she did reading for the Book-of-the-Month Club and reviewing for *The Saturday Review of Literature.* In 1946, she was married to Marvin Chaikin, a communications engineer, and continued book reviewing for some time, later studying for a year and a half as a member of Martha Foley's fiction workshop at Columbia University. Dividing her time between housekeeping and writing, Mrs. Chaikin now lives in Great Neck, New York, with her husband and their four year old daughter and one year old son. "The Climate of the Family," originally written while at Columbia, is her first published story.

CHIDESTER, ANN. Miss Chidester was born in Stillwater, Minnesota, which she continues to visit part of every year, and was educated in parochial and public schools, later attending Saint Catherine's College in St. Paul. She has lived in the West, in Mexico, and has travelled and skiied in Alaska. Since 1942, she has had five novels published: *Young Pandora, No Longer Fugitive, The Long Year, Mama Maria's* and *Moon Gap.* Her short stories have appeared in several magazines and she was represented in the O. Henry Awards *Prize Stories* of 1950. At present, she is writing a new novel which she hopes to finish this year.

EATON, CHARLES EDWARD. Mr. Eaton was born in Winston-Salem, North Carolina, in 1916. He graduated from the University of North Carolina in 1936, and studied philosophy at Princeton the following year. During 1937–38, he taught English in Puerto Rico, returning to this country to take a Master's degree in English at Harvard and to study creative writing there with Robert Frost and Robert Hillyer. After leaving Harvard in 1940, he taught creative writing at the University of Missouri for two years. Upon the recommendation of Robert Frost, he was awarded a fellowship to the Bread Loaf Writers' Conference in 1941, and the following summer was awarded a similar fellowship to the Boulder (Colorado) Writers' Conference. For the next four years he was Vice-Consul at the American Embassy in Rio de Janeiro, Brazil, traveling widely throughout South America. Since 1946, he has been teaching creative writing at the University of

North Carolina. His poetry has appeared in numerous magazines, both here and in England, and two volumes of his poems have been published: *The Bright Plain* in 1942 and *The Shadow of the Swimmer* in 1951. The latter book was awarded the Ridgely Torrence Memorial Award for 1951 by the Poetry Society of America. His short stories have been printed in *The Arizona Quarterly*, *Epoch*, *Perspective*, and the *University of Kansas City Review*. "The Motion of Forgetfulness Is Slow," reprinted in this volume, is one of a collection of short stories with a Brazilian background which he is preparing for publication.

ELLIOTT, GEORGE P. Mr. Elliott has lived in California since the age of eleven, but was born in Indiana in 1918. He received his M.A. in English from the University of California, following which he had "the usual variety of jobs for a writer," from surveyor's helper to bureaucrat to union business agent to taxicab driver. He is at present teaching English at St. Mary's College, the occupation he prefers, and living in Berkeley with his wife and daughter. His poems and short stories have appeared in several of the little magazines during the past eight years, and his story, "The NRACP," was reprinted in *The Best American Short Stories 1950*. Last summer, he received an Albert Bender Literary Grant-in-Aid, with which he has completed a novel and written further short stories and poetry.

ENRIGHT, ELIZABETH. Although she was brought up in New York, Elizabeth Enright was born in Oak Park, Illinois. Coming from a family of artists, she went to the Art Students' League in New York and to the School of Applied Art in Paris, and started her career as an illustrator of children's books. She soon turned to the writing of such books, and to date she has published seven juveniles — one of which, *Thimble Summer*, was awarded the Newbery Medal in 1939. In more recent years, Miss Enright has written many short stories which have appeared in *The New Yorker*, *Collier's*, *The Yale Review*, and other magazines. She has been represented in *The Best American Short Stories 1951*, in the O. Henry Awards *Prize Stories* of 1946, 1949, and 1950, and a collection of her short stories, *Borrowed Summer*, was published by Rinehart and Company in 1946. Married to Robert Marty Gillham, she lives in New York City and has three sons, the youngest being three years old.

GARNER, HUGH. Mr. Garner was born in England in 1913, and came to Canada at the age of six. He was educated in the Toronto public schools, and spent three years at a technical high school. During the depression, he worked throughout Canada and the United States in the kind of jobs "that seem to fall to beginning writers," including busboy in New York City cafeterias, Long Island soap salesman, and harvest hand and tomato picker outside Santa Barbara, California. During 1937, he served in the Abraham Lincoln Batallion of the International Brigade in the Spanish Civil War; from 1939 to 1945 he was a member of the Royal Canadian Navy as a Chief Petty Officer. Mr. Garner now lives in Toronto and is a full time free-lance writer. His stories have appeared in many Canadian and English magazines, and he is the author of two novels, *Storm Below* and *Cabbagetown*, published in Canada by William Collins and Sons. A collection of his short stories is scheduled for publication this fall.

GELLHORN, MARTHA. Miss Gellhorn is well-known as both a foreign correspondent and a fiction writer. Born in St. Louis, Missouri, she was educated at the John Burroughs School and at Bryn Mawr College and later studied abroad. She first worked on *The New Republic* and the Albany *Times-Union*. From 1937 to 1941, she covered the war in Spain and the Russian invasion of Finland for *Collier's*, and in 1943, returned to Europe as a correspondent in France, Italy, Germany and England. She has contributed to many magazines, and her books include *The Trouble I've Seen*, *A Stricken Field*, *The Heart of Another*, *Liana*, and *The Wine of Astonishment*. Her short story, "Miami-New York," was included in *The Best American Short Stories 1948*. At present, she is living in Cuernavaca, Mexico, with her Italian son.

GLEN, EMILIE. Born in Syracuse, New York, Miss Glen was educated at Syracuse University and Columbia, and later traveled in England, Greece, and other parts of Europe. She came to New York first as a piano student, but gave up music as a serious career in favor of writing. Her short stories have appeared over a number of years in *The American Mercury*, *The Canadian Forum*, *Decade*, *New Mexico Quarterly*, *Prairie Schooner*, *University of Kansas City Review*, and other magazines. Much of the material for her stories has been drawn from jobs she has held in New York writing for trade publications such as *Women's Wear* and *Stores* magazine. She was also on the staff of *The New Yorker* for two years, and has worked for Crowell-Collier and The Macmillan Company. At present, she is the editor of *Conference Trails*, the Congregational magazine for New York state. She writes that the background for "Always Good For a Belly Laugh," included in this volume, came from "many a skate and a fall at Rockefeller Skating Rink where I met my soldier husband, and now skate with my seven-year-old Glenda and her daddy."

HALE, NANCY. Miss Hale was born in Boston in 1908, the granddaughter of Edward Everett Hale and the daughter of the painters Philip L. Hale and Lilian Westcott Hale. After graduating from the Winsor School in 1926, she attended the School of the Museum of Fine Arts in Boston and studied in her father's studio. In 1928, she married and went to New York where from 1928 to 1934, she was successively a staff writer on *Vogue*, assistant editor of *Vanity Fair*, and the first woman reporter on *The New York Times*. In 1930, she sold her first writing (discounting a story printed in the Boston *Herald* at the age of eleven) to *Scribner's Magazine*, and in 1932, Scribner's published her first novel, *The Young Die Good*. Since then, her books have included three more novels, of which the most widely known is *The Prodigal Women*, and two collections of short stories. Her stories have also appeared in numerous magazines and in over thirty anthologies. In 1936, she went to live in Virginia, and worked in Washington during the war as a writer for the Treasury Department. She was married in 1942 to Fredson Bowers, Professor of English Literature at the University of Virginia, and lives with her husband in Charlottesville. She has two sons, Mark Hardin, twenty-two, and William Wertenbaker, fourteen. At present, she is writing a play to be presented by the University of Virginia Players, and is active in the League of Women Voters and the Unitarian Church.

HORTON, PHILIP. Born in Providence, Rhode Island, Mr. Horton was educated at Mercersburg Academy in Pennsylvania and at Princeton University, where he received a B.A. degree in 1934. He later studied abroad at the University of Berlin and the University of Aix-Marseille, and worked as a journalist for the *Providence Journal* and the North American Newspaper Alliance, with assignments on the Continent and in Russia. Mr. Horton's literary criticism and reviews have appeared in various periodicals, and he is the author of a biography, *Hart Crane, The Life of an American Poet*, published in 1937 by W. W. Norton. From 1939 to 1941, he was an instructor in the Department of English at Harvard University; from 1942 to 1948, he was in government service with the Office of Strategic Services and later with the Central Intelligence Agency, in London, Paris, and Germany. On his return to this country, he worked as an associate editor of *Time* Magazine from 1948 to 1949. Currently, he is the assistant editor of *The Reporter* and lives in New York City.

KUEHN, SUSAN. Miss Kuehn was born, and still lives, in Minneapolis, Minnesota. She attended Wellesley College, and while still an undergraduate became associated with *Mademoiselle* Magazine, first as a college board guest editor in the fiction department. *Mademoiselle* subsequently published her first two stories, which were included in the O. Henry Awards *Prize Stories* of 1947 and 1950. After graduating from college, she joined the staff of the *Minneapolis Star and Tribune*, where she is now a women's feature writer; at the same time, she studied with Saul Bellow and Robert Penn Warren at the University of Minnesota. During 1949–50, she held a Jones creative writing fellowship at Stanford University, and it was in Wallace Stegner's class at Stanford that she wrote "The Searchers," included in this volume. The story underwent some rather strenuous revision and research she writes that "at Stegner's suggestion, I spent an afternoon stalking alone through the woods near his Los Altos, California home — and got thoroughly lost. I immediately tore out my previously written section on the search in the woods and substituted my own plight. I don't believe writers need to live, literally, all things they write about, but in this case such experience was helpful!"

LAURENCE, BETHEL. Miss Laurence was born in the midwest, but came to New York at the age of sixteen to attend a dramatic school where she studied acting and the theatre arts. After graduation, she had a job carrying write-ups from the theatrical magazine, *Billboard*, to producers' offices, "where even secretaries could reduce me to trembling, so my acting jobs were negligible and I was forced to a rather premature retirement at the age of twenty." Following this period, she went into the department store business until the war when she took care of war workers' children. When the emergency was over, she returned to New York to study writing in Martha Foley's fiction workshop at Columbia University. During the last couple of years, her stories have been appearing in *Today's Woman, Redbook, Woman's Home Companion*, and on television.

ROONEY, FRANK. Mr. Rooney was born in Kansas City, Missouri, in 1913; he lived there until he was twelve and then moved to Los Angeles, where he stayed until his entrance into the Army in early 1941. During these years, he first attended Belmont High School, then "washed dishes, sold various articles from house to house, did a little professional cooking . . . and finally ended up on the labor gang at one of the Hollywood studios." After the war, he came to New York where he did some stage and radio work and decided to write. In the summer of 1946, he attended Martha Foley's writing class at Columbia University. His story, "Cyclists' Raid," reprinted in this volume, has also been included in the O. Henry Awards *Prize Stories* of 1951. Mr. Rooney is married and has two sons; at present, he lives in Mount Vernon, New York, and is at work on a novel.

SAROYAN, WILLIAM. Mr. Saroyan was born in Fresno, California, in 1908. He left school at the age of fifteen to go to work, and had a wide variety of jobs until the publication of his first book, *The Daring Young Man on the Flying Trapeze*, in 1934. Since then, he has devoted almost all his time to the writing of fiction and plays. Among his many published novels and short story collections are *Inhale and Exhale, Love, Here Is My Hat, Peace, It's Wonderful, My Name Is Aram, The Human Comedy*, and *The Adventures of Wesley Jackson*. As a playwright, he has been equally prolific. *The Time of Your Life*, produced in 1939, won the Drama Critics Circle Award and was awarded the Pulitzer prize — the latter declined by Mr. Saroyan. His succeeding plays have included *Love's Old Sweet Song, The Beautiful People, Across the Board on Monday Morning, Get Away, Old Man*, and several others. At present, he lives in Beverly Hills and writes that he has several books scheduled for forthcoming publication, "several more unscheduled."

SCHULBERG, STUART. Born in 1922 in Los Angeles, California, Mr. Schulberg was educated at preparatory schools in Colorado, London, and Geneva, and attended the University of Chicago for two years. After a period of free-lance film writing immediately following the war, he created and headed the Documentary Film Unit of the U.S. Military Government in Germany. One of the films he wrote during this time was a feature-length documentary on the rise and fall of the Nazis, entitled "Nuremberg"; produced and distributed under the Military Government's re-orientation program, it received wide attention in Germany. From 1949 to 1951, he was Deputy Chief and later Chief of the ECA Motion Picture Section in Europe, with headquarters in Paris. At the present time, he is vice-president and general manager of Rathvon Overseas, Ltd., a new international film production company having its main offices in France. He lives in Paris with his wife and two small children. "I'm Really Fine," included in this volume, is both his first written and first published story; a second is planned for future publication in *New-Story*. He has also written special motion picture articles for film periodicals.

STAFFORD, JEAN. Born in Covina, California, in 1915, Jean Stafford was educated at the University of California and at Heidelberg, Germany. She later taught school for a year in Missouri, worked for *The Southern Review* in Louisiana, and lived for various periods of time in Massachusetts, New York, Tennessee, Connecticut, and Maine. She is the author of three novels, *Boston Adventure*, *The Mountain Lion*, and *The Catherine Wheel*, the last published earlier this year. Her short stories have appeared in *The Kenyon Review*, *The New Yorker*, *Harper's Magazine*, *Harper's Bazaar*, *Mademoiselle*, and *The Sewanee Review*. In 1945, she received an Academy of Arts and Letters Award, and was granted two Guggenheim Fellowships, in 1945, and 1948. Her work has been represented in *The Best American Short Stories* in 1945, 1947, 1949, 1951, and in other anthologies. She is married to Oliver Jensen, journalist and publisher of *Picture Press*, and lives in Westport, Connecticut.

STEGNER, WALLACE. Mr. Stegner was born in Iowa in 1909, and educated in Canada, Montana, Utah, California, and Iowa, where he received his Ph.D. degree in 1935. For the past few years, he has been Professor of English and director of the creative writing program at Stanford University. His stories and articles have been published in numerous magazines; "The Traveler," included in this collection, is the sixth of Mr. Stegner's stories to appear in *The Best American Short Stories*, and he has also been a three-time winner in the O. Henry Awards *Prize Stories*. His books include *Remembering Laughter* (his first novel which won a Little, Brown and Company prize in 1937), *On a Darkling Plain*, *The Potter's House*, *Fire and Ice*, *Mormon Country*, *The Big Rock Candy Mountain*, *One Nation*, *Second Growth*, and most recently, *The Women on the Wall* (a collection of stories) and *The Preacher and the Slave* (a novel), both published in 1950. Currently, he lives in Los Altos, California, and is using up a postponed Guggenheim fellowship to complete a biography of Major John Wesley Powell, the explorer of the Colorado River. Last year, Mr. Stegner and his wife were sent under the joint sponsorship of Stanford University and the Rockefeller Foundation to make "contacts and conversation and common cause" with writers and writing groups in India, Thailand, the Philippines, and Japan.

STILL, JAMES. Born in Chambers County, Alabama, Mr. Still attended school near Cumberland Gap, Tennessee, and college at Vanderbilt University and the University of Illinois. He taught for six years at Hindman Settlement on Troublesome Creek in the Kentucky hills. During the war, he spent nearly four years in the Army Air Force, serving in Africa and the Middle East. Mr. Still's books include *Hound on the Mountain* (poetry), *River of Earth* (novel), and *On Troublesome Creek* (short stories). He has contributed both poetry and fiction to *The Atlantic Monthly*, *The Virginia Quarterly Review*, *The Yale Review*, and other magazines, and his work was included in *The Best American Short Stories* in 1946 and 1950. In 1946, he was the recipient of an American Academy of Arts and Letters Award. At present, he lives on Wolfpen Creek in Bath, Kentucky.

SWADOS, HARVEY. Born in Buffalo, New York, in 1920, Mr. Swados graduated from the University of Michigan in 1940 and has since earned his living "in most of the improbable ways that are considered standard material for authors' biographical notes." His first short story was included in the late Edward O'Brien's *Best Short Stories of 1938*. Since then he has contributed stories, articles and reviews to *Epoch*, *The Hudson Review*, *The Nation*, *The New Republic*, *The New York Post*, *The Progressive*, and other publications. He has recently completed a play and is now working on a novel. His home is in Valley Cottage, New York.

VAN DOREN, MARK. Mr. Van Doren was born in 1894 on a farm near Hope, Illinois. He was educated at the University of Illinois and Columbia University, and has taught English at Columbia since 1920. From 1924 to 1928, he was literary editor of *The Nation*. Best known as a critic and poet, his *Collected Poems*, published in 1939, was the winner of the 1940 Pulitzer prize. Among his other works are *Spring Thunder* (1924), *Now the Sky* (1928), *Jonathan Gentry* (1931), *Our Lady of Peace* (1942) and *New Poems* (1948), all volumes of poetry, and *The Transients* and *Windless Cabins*, both novels, published in 1935 and 1940 respectively. He is also the author of several critical studies and editor of a number of anthologies. His most recently published book has been *The Short Stories of Mark Van Doren* (1950). A new collection of his stories is scheduled to be published in 1953 by Abelard Press, and William Sloane Associates will bring out his latest poetry, *Spring Birth and Other Poems*, the same year. Mr. Van Doren is a resident of New York City.

WALDRON, DANIEL. Mr. Waldron was born in 1925 in Big Rapids, Michigan, where he lived until his entry into military service in 1943. During the war, he was a member of the Army Medical Corps, serving in the United States and overseas in such varied capacities as file clerk, hospital orderly and litter bearer. After his discharge, he spent the summer of 1947 at the Art Institute of Chicago, and his next four years at the University of Michigan, where he majored in English and received his B.A. degree in 1951. His story, "Evensong," included in this volume, was written for a college writing course and won a prize in the University of Michigan's Avery and Jule Hopwood Contests for 1949; it is his first published story. During his college years, two of his plays were produced, one in Ann Arbor and the other (written in collaboration) at Denison University. In addition, he wrote several radio shows, the libretto for a one-act opera, and helped found a quarterly magazine, *Generation*, on which he was drama editor. He writes that other "occupations along the way . . . included soda jerk, road gang laborer and newspaper editor and writer." Since graduation, Mr. Waldron has been doing office work at the Kaiser-Frazer plant at Willow Run and lives in Ann Arbor. For the future, he hopes to devote full time to the completion of an opera libretto and the writing of a projected novel.

WESTON, CHRISTINE. Although an American citizen since 1928, Mrs. Weston was born in Unao, India, forty-seven years ago. Her father was French, her mother English; both their families had been in India for several generations, her father's as indigo planters, her mother's in the British Army service. Much of the material in Mrs. Weston's widely read novel, *Indigo*, was taken from her family's history in India. Her formal education comprised a couple of years in a Catholic convent in Naini Tal, India, but she writes that she "made up the deficit under my father's tutelage at home, and my own voracious reading." In 1923, she married an American, Robert Weston, and came to the United States where she and her husband lived in Maine for almost twenty eight years. In 1951, she was divorced, and since that time has been living in New York City. Her short stories have appeared in several magazines, and she is the author of five novels and one juvenile. At present, she is writing another novel, after which she hopes "to return to India to collect material for yet another!"

YAMAMOTO, HISAYE. Miss Yamamoto was born in Redondo Beach, California, in 1921, and has spent most of her subsequent years in other small Southern California towns. She studied at Excelsior Union High School and Compton Junior College, majoring in foreign languages. In the spring of 1942, she was among the 110,000 Japanese evacuated to inland "relocation centers;" her family was assigned to the Colorado River Relocation Center in Arizona and she remained there until just before the war's end, except for a brief stay in Massachusetts. Since then she has lived in Los Angeles and has worked, as a rewrite man and columnist, for the *Los Angeles Tribune*, a Negro weekly. Her short stories have been published in *Furioso, Harper's Bazaar, The Kenyon Review, Partisan Review*, and in the Japanese-American publications, *Pacific Citizen, Crossroads*, and the *Rafu Shimpo*. In 1950, she was the recipient of a fellowship from the John Hay Whitney Foundation. At the present time, she is trying to write more short stories and to raise an adopted son, Paul Anthony, age three.

THE YEARBOOK OF THE AMERICAN SHORT STORY

JANUARY 1 TO DECEMBER 31, 1951

ROLL OF HONOR

1951

I. *American Authors*

BABB, SANORA
  Snow Is a Promise. New-Story, July.
BARO, GENE
  Joey the Hero. Georgia Review, Summer.
  Pattern. Prairie Schooner, Summer.
BECKER, STEPHEN
  To Know the Country. Harper's Magazine,
  Aug.
BENNETT, PEGGY
  Snowy Robes. Accent, Spring.
BERGE, BILL
  That Lovely Green Boat. Furioso, Fall.
BONOSKY, PHILIP
  ... And of the Son. Masses & Mainstream,
  May.
BOWEN, ROBERT O.
  The Other River. Western Review, Sum-
  mer.
BOYLE, KAY
  The Lost. Tomorrow, March.
BRADBURY, RAY
  The Other Foot. New-Story, March.
  The Rocket Man. MacLean's, March.
BROWN, NAOMA
  The Pair of White Shoes. Antioch Review,
  Winter.

CALISHER, HORTENSE
  A Wreath For Miss Totten. Mademoiselle,
  July.
  Night Riders of Northville. Harper's
  Magazine, Sept.
CANINE, WILLIAM
  Vinnie. Antioch Review, Spring.
CARDOZO, NANCY
  The Unborn Ghosts. New Yorker, June 30.
CASSILL, R. V.
  The Black Horse. Furioso, Summer.
  The Waiting Room. Perspective, Autumn.
  This Hand, These Talons. Western Re-
  view, Autumn.
CHAIKIN, NANCY G.
  The Climate of the Family. Mademoiselle,
  Jan.
CHEEVER, JOHN
  Clancy in The Tower of Babel. New
  Yorker, March 24.
  Goodbye, My Brother. New Yorker,
  Aug. 25.

CHIDESTER, ANN
  Wood Smoke. Harper's Bazaar, June.
COATES, ROBERT M.
  The Karpies. New Yorker, Oct. 20.
CONNELL, EVAN S.
  The Condor and the Guests. Tomorrow,
  Jan.
COOK, JAMES
  Spring Pastoral. American Mercury, Apr.
CRISWELL, CLOYD
  The Heat In the Far Hills. New-Story,
  June.
CURLEY, DANIEL
  The Man Who Was Drafted. Accent,
  Summer.

DERLETH, AUGUST
  Mr. C. University of Kansas City Review,
  Winter.
DU BOIS, WILLIAM PENE
  Squirrel Hotel. Mademoiselle, May.

EATON, CHARLES EDWARD
  The Motion of Forgetfulness Is Slow
  Death, Summer.
ELLIOTT, GEORGE P.
  Children of Ruth. The Hudson Review,
  Winter.
ENRIGHT, ELIZABETH
  Death of a Doll. McCall's, Apr.
  The First Face. New Yorker, Dec. 15.

GALLANT, MAVIS
  Madeline's Birthday. New Yorker, Sept. 1.
GARNER, HUGH
  The Conversion of Willie Heaps. Northern
  Review, Feb.–March.
GELLHORN, MARTHA
  Weekend At Grimsby. Atlantic, May.
GLEN, EMILIE
  Always Good for a Belly Laugh. Prairie
  Schooner, Summer.
GOLD, HERBERT
  The Heart of the Artichoke. The Hudson
  Review, Autumn.
GOYEN, WILLIAM
  The Ghost of Raymond Emmons. Made-
  moiselle, Feb.

GUTHRIE, A. B., JR.
Ebbie. Southwest Review, Spring.

Hale, Nancy
Brahmin Beachhead. Town and Country, June.
HALEY, GLEN
I'll Call You Eager. Harper's Magazine, Aug.
HORTON, PHILIP
What's in a Corner. New Mexico Quarterly, Spring
HUMPHREY, WILLIAM
The Fauve. Sewanee Review, Summer.
HUNTER, LAURA
The Experiment. Western Review, Summer.

KNIGHT, DAVID
The Fall of Irish Johnston. Hudson Review, Autumn.
KUEHN, SUSAN
The Searchers. Harper's Magazine, March.

LAURENCE, BETHEL
The Call. Today's Woman, March
LEVIN, MEYER
After All I Did For Israel. Commentary, July.
LEVINE, NORMAN
A Sunday Walk. Northern Review, June–July.
LORTZ, RICHARD
The Loon. Virginia Quarterly, Winter.
LOVERIDGE, GEORGE
The Cruise. Yale Review, Autumn.
LOWRY, ROBERT
Passing Star. American Mercury, June.
The Mammoth Tooth. Mademoiselle, Sept.

MALAMUD, BERNARD
The Bill. Commentary, Apr.
MARTIN, PLACIDE
When Only One Is Shining. Sewanee Review, Spring.
MATTHIESSEN, PETER
Sadie. Atlantic Monthly, Jan.
McCARTHY, MARY
The Groves of Academe. New Yorker, Feb. 3.
McCLURE, JANE
The Ivy-Covered Skyscraper. Collier's, Feb. 17.
MILLER, DICK
The Image. Prairie Schooner, Spring.

PARRY, ALBERT
The Sales Manager. Southwest Review, Winter.
PETTY, DENISE
Subway. Kansas City Review, Summer.
PHILLIPS, THOMAS HAL
Lone Bridge. Southwest Review, Spring.
Mostly in the Fields. Virginia Quarterly Review, Autumn.
PIERCE, PHOEBE
Fish in the Air. Mademoiselle, Apr.
The Green Catherine. Mademoiselle, Oct.

ROONEY, FRANK
Cyclists' Raid. Harper's Magazine, Jan.
ROSENFELD, EVA
Pillar of a Cloud. Commentary, Feb.
ROTHBERG, ABRAHAM
The Very Presence of God. New Mexico Quarterly, Winter

SAROYAN, WILLIAM
Palo. Tomorrow, March.
SARVIS, ISABEL
Jack Knife. Quarto, Summer.
SCHENK, LESLIE
Lost in a New Room. New-Story, Apr.
SCHULBERG, STUART
I'm Really Fine. New-Story, Oct.
SINCLAIR, JO
The Angry One. Today's Woman, Oct.
SINGER, HOWARD
The Big Table. Commentary, May.
STAFFORD, JEAN
The Healthiest Girl in Town. New Yorker, Apr. 7.
STEGNER, WALLACE
The Traveler. Harper's Magazine, Feb.
STILL, JAMES
A Ride on the Short Dog. The Atlantic, July.
SWADOS, HARVEY
The Letters. Hudson Review, Spring.

TAYLOR, PETER
Two Ladies in Retirement. New Yorker, March 31.
Bad Dreams. New Yorker, May 19.
THOMPSON, R. E.
It's a Nice Day — Sunday. Tomorrow, Apr.

VAN DOREN, MARK
Nobody Say a Word. Harper's Magazine, July.

WALDRON, DANIEL
   Evensong. New-Story, Oct.
WELTY, EUDORA
   The Bride of the Innisfallen. New Yorker,
   Dec. 1.
WEST, JESSAMYN
   The Lesson. New Yorker, Aug. 11.
WESTON, CHRISTINE
   Loud Sing Cuckoo, Mademoiselle, Nov.
WHEELIS, ALLEN
   Goodbye, Mama. New Yorker, Oct. 13.

WILKES, DAVID
   Recalled to Life. Epoch, Summer.
WIMBERLY, LOWRY CHARLES
   Windfall for Whitford. Harper's Magazine,
   June.
WITT, HAROLD V.
   Death Is a Mexican in a Santana Wind.
   Decade of Short Stories, Spring.

YAMAMOTO, HISAYE
   Yoneko's Earthquake. Furioso, Winter.

II. *Foreign Authors*

GENET, JEAN
   Our Lady of the Flowers. New-Story,
   March, 1951
GODDEN, RUMER
   The Oyster, New Yorker, Jan. 27.
GORDIMER, NADINE
   The Catch. Virginia Quarterly Review,
   Summer.

HIGHET, GILBERT
   Another Solution. Harper's Magazine, Nov.
HOUSEHOLD, GEOFFREY
   The Hut. The Atlantic, Dec.

LANE, MARGARET
   The Festive Amazon. Harper's Bazaar,
   March.
LAVERTY, MAURA
   The Golden Web Parents' Magazine, Oct.

MACKEN, WALTER
   The King. The Atlantic, June.
McCONNELL, WILLIAM
   Raise No Memorial. Northern Review,
   Dec.-Jan., 1950–51.

O'CONNOR, FRANK
   Baptismal. American Mercury, March.

ROE, IVAN
   The Woman of the South. Mademoiselle,
   March.

SHONE, PATRICK
   The Four Winds and the Seven Seas. Virginia Quarterly Review, Winter.

SMITH, EMMA
   Jasper. Harper's Magazine, May.
STERLING, MONICA
   It's Later Than You Think, Atlantic, July.

WARNER, SYLVIA TOWNSEND
   Hee-Haw! New Yorker, May 12
WELCH, DENTON
   The Diamond Badge. Harper's Bazaar,
   Sept.

DISTINCTIVE VOLUMES OF SHORT STORIES

Published in the United States and Canada

1951

BARKER, A. L.
Novelette with Other Stories. Charles Scribner's Sons.

BECK, WARREN
The Far Whistle and Other Stories. The Antioch Press.

BOWEN, ELIZABETH
Early Stories. Alfred A. Knopf.

BOYLE, KAY
The Smoking Mountain: Stories of Post-War Germany. McGraw-Hill Publishing Company.

BRADBURY, RAY
The Illustrated Man. Doubleday and Company.

BRICKELL, HERSCHEL, Editor
Prize Stories of 1951; The O. Henry Awards. Doubleday and Company.

CALDWELL, ERSKINE
Kneel to the Rising Sun and Other Stories. Duell, Sloan and Pearce.

CALISHER, HORTENSE
In the Absence of Angels. Little, Brown and Company.

CAMPBELL, C. G., Editor
Tales from the Arab Tribes. The Macmillan Company.

CHEKHOV, ANTON
Selected Short Stories. Edited by G. A. Brikett and Gleb Struve. Oxford University Press.

COLLIER, JOHN
Fancies and Goodnights. Doubleday and Company.

DAVIES, RHYS
Boy with a Trumpet and Other Selected Stories. Doubleday and Company.

DERLETH, AUGUST W., Editor
Far Boundaries. Pellegrini and Cudahy Company.

FARRELL, JAMES T.
The Short Stories of James T. Farrell. Vanguard Press.

FITZGERALD, F. SCOTT
The Stories of F. Scott Fitzgerald. Charles Scribner's Sons.

FOLEY, MARTHA, Editor
The Best American Short Stories 1951. Houghton Mifflin Company.

HEALY, RAYMOND J., Editor
New Tales of Space and Time. Henry Holt and Company.

LEHMANN, JOHN, Compiler
Best Stories From New Writing. Harcourt, Brace and Company.

LEINSTER, MURRAY, Editor
Great Stories of Science Fiction. Random House.

LINCOLN, VICTORIA
Out from Eden. Rinehart and Company.

NEWHOUSE, EDWARD
Many Are Called. Sloane Associates.

STEGNER, WALLACE EARLE and
SNOWCROFT, RICHARD PINGREE, Editors
Stanford Short Stories, 1951. Stanford University Press.

STERN, JAMES A.
The Man Who Was Loved. Harcourt, Brace and Company.

TCHEKOV, ANTON PAVLOVICH
Selected Tales of Tchekov. Translated by Constance Garnett. The Macmillan Company.

WILSON, ANGUS
Such Darling Dodos and Other Stories. William Morrow and Company.

WOLFE, DON
Which Grain Will Grow. Cambridge Publishing Company.

YAFFE, JAMES
Poor Cousin Evelyn. Little, Brown and Company.

DISTINCTIVE SHORT STORIES IN
AMERICAN MAGAZINES

1951

I. *American Authors*

AGAZARIAN, YVONNE
Final Absolution. Canadian Forum, June.
AIKMAN, ANN
Buck Bascom. Mademoiselle, Feb.
ALDRICH, VIRGIL
The Outsider. Kenyon Review, Spring.
ALDRIDGE, JAMES
Bush Boy, Poor Boy. Harper's Magazine,
May.
ALLEN, MARIE
Night Watch. Decade of Short Stories,
Spring.
ALSAKER, RICHARD
War Surplus. Antioch Review, Spring.
ANDERSON, DILLON
The Weather Prophet. Atlantic Monthly,
Jan.
The Receiver. Atlantic Monthly, March.

BAIR, TOM
The Woman at Saint's Rest. Prairie
Schooner, Summer.
BALDWIN, JAMES
The Outing. New-Story, Apr.
BALLARD, JAMES
The Proud Ones. Hopkins Review, Winter.
BARTLETT, PAUL
Woodcut. New-Story, Oct.
BAUM, MARY
Constant Interval. New Mexico Quarterly,
Autumn.
BELLOW, SAUL
Looking For Mr. Green. Commentary,
March.
By The Rock Wall. Harper's Bazaar, Apr.
The Coblins. Sewanee Review, Autumn.
The Einhorns. Partisan Review, Nov.–
Dec.
BENCHLEY, NATHANIEL
The Squirrel. New Yorker, Sept. 1.
BENNETT, JOSEPH
Armistice Day. Accent, Winter.
The White Whale. Sewanee Review,
Winter.
BENNETT, PEGGY
Snowy Robes. Accent, Spring.

BENSON, EARL M.
The Circus. New Yorker, Nov. 3.
BERGER, T. L.
Marginal Man. New-Story, March.
BERLAND, ALWYN
Get Up and Live. Perspective, Summer.
BERNSTEIN, HELLEL
The Two-Legged Horse. Holiday, Jan.
The Man at the Window. New Yorker,
June 2.
BONOSKY, PHILLIP
. . . And of the Son. Masses & Mainstream,
May.
BOWLES, PAUL
A Gift for Rinza. Esquire, March.
BOYLE, KAY
Home. Harper's Magazine, Jan.
Cabaret. Tomorrow, April.
BRADBURY, RAY
These Things Happen. McCall's, May.
BRADSHAW, STANFORD
Cricket in the House. Quarto, Summer.
BROCK, CONSTANCE
Adsum. Charm, Nov.
BRONSON
Within. Intro, Vol. I, No. 3 & 4.
BROSSARD, CHANDLER
Vacation for Three. American Mercury,
June.
BROTHERTON, JOSEPH
On the U.S. 10. New-Story, Nov.
BROWN, WILLIAM
A Canto of Hours. New-Story, July.
BUECHNER, FREDRICK
Prelude to Morning. Town & Country,
Aug.

CABLE, MARY PRATT
The Old Maid. Harper's Bazaar, Oct.
CALISHER, HORTENSE
In the Absence of Angels. New Yorker,
Apr. 21.
CALLAGHAN, MORLEY
On the Edge of a World. Esquire, Jan.
CAPOTE, TRUMAN
The House of Flowers. Mademoiselle, Apr.

CARDOZO, NANCY
A Hundred Years from Now. Seventeen, Dec.

CARROLL, JOSEPH
April's Amazing Meaning. A.D., Autumn.

CARROLL, SIDNEY
The Three Friends. Cosmopolitan, Aug.

CARROLL, WALTER
River's Boy. Prairie Schooner, Winter.

CASPER, LEONARD
Ruzuki. Southwest Review, Summer.
A Nest of Boxes. New Mexico Quarterly, Winter.

CHAMBERLAIN, ANNE
Marvin. Tomorrow, February.

CHAMBERS, MARIA CHRISTINA
Maria. Tomorrow, July.

CHAY, MARIE
Trees Are Like People. Prairie Schooner, Sept.

CHIDCHESTER, ANN
Arden. New Yorker, May 12.

CIARDI, JOHN
The Burial of the Dead. University of Kansas City Review, Summer.

CLARKE, ROBERT M.
The Hollister. Arizona Quarterly, Autumn.

COATES, ROBERT M.
The Decline and Fall of Perry Whitman. New Yorker, Aug. 18.

COOK, JAMES
Spring Pastoral. American Mercury, Apr.

CORLE, EDWIN
Patron of the Arts. American Mercury, Nov.

COWLEY, JOSEPH G.
Heart's Desire. A.D.
The Thief. New-Story, March.

COXHEAD, NINA
Not Love Itself. Yale Review, March.

CRAWFORD, CONSTANCE
The Boats. Mademoiselle, August.

CRISWELL, CLOYD
The Stirrup Cup. Olivet Quarterly, Summer.

CURLEY, D.
The Bat. New-Story, Sept.

DAHL, ROALD
Taste. New Yorker, Dec. 8.

DANZIS, MORDECAI
The Rabbi and the Jester. American Jewish Times–Outlook, Oct.

DAVIDSON, BETTY SUE
The Rivals. Pacific Spectator, Winter.

DAVIDSON, SUE
The City of the Angels. Antioch Review, Summer.

DAVIS, EILEEN
The Three Men Who Went Away. Prairie Schooner, Spring.

DAVIS, JUDITH
Change of Season. New-Story, June.

DEBELIUS, H. AUGUST
A Rose. Hopkins Review, Spring.

DE FORD, MIRIAM ALLEN
Another Day. Pacific Spectator, Autumn.

DE JONG, DAVID CORNEL
A Braist for a Plug Idler. Southwest Review, Winter.

DEMBY, WILLIAM
The Table of Wishes Come True. New-Story, Apr.

DE MOTT, BENJAMIN
The Dead Writers. Partisan Review, July–Aug.

DEMPSEY, DAVID
Jessica. Mademoiselle, July.

DESSLER, HAROLD
Uncle Ben of Upper Broadway. Commentary, Oct.

DI DONATO, PIETRO
Uncle Barbarosso. American Mercury, Nov.

DOUGHTY, LE GARDE S.
The Spring. Arizona Quarterly, Spring.
Afternoon of a Squid. Arizona Quarterly, Autumn.

ELDER, WALTER
The Divorce. Kenyon Review, Autumn.

ELLIOTT, GEORGE P.
The Well and the Bulldozers. Pacific Spectator, Winter.

EMMETT, MORRIS
Season of Exile. Harper's Bazaar, Aug.

ENGEL, MONROE
Four Hours to Rome. Hudson Review, Summer.

ENRIGHT, ELIZABETH
The Moment before the Rain. Charm, June.

ETNIER, ELIZABETH
Spring Suit. Charm, March.

FAULKNER, WILLIAM
The Jail. Partisan Review, Sept.–Oct.

FAY, SARAH
The Death of Pierce. New Yorker, Sept. 15.

FERRONE, JOHN R.
  About My Sons. Pacific Spectator, Summer.
  The Rise of Lorenzo Villari. Epoch, Fall.
FLOCOS, NICHOLAS G.
  The Spangled Barrette. A.D., Summer.
FOXHALL, BETTY JEAN
  My Sister Callie. Montevallo Review, Summer.
FRANCIS, H. E.
  The Broken Bottle. Prairie Schooner, Fall.
FRENCH, DORIS
  The Spider Spino. Canadian Forum, Apr.

GAER, GAY
  The Sisters. Atlantic Monthly, March.
  The Absent Ones. Atlantic Monthly, June.
GALLAGHER, THOMAS
  The One and the Many. Perspective, Winter.
GARNER, HUGH
  The Yellow Sweater. Chatelaine, March.
  A Couple of Quiet Young Guys. Canadian Forum, July.
  Our Neighbors the Nuns. Northern Review, Aug.–Sept.
GELLHORN, MARTHA
  Paco's Donkey. Good Housekeeping, Apr.
  Darling Believe Me. Esquire, Aug
GIBBON, RICHARD
  To See the Sea. Perspective, Autumn.
GILLIES, ALAN
  A Tamer of Birds. Quarto, Spring.
GLEN, EMILIE
  About Her Being Colored. Decade of Short Stories, Spring.
GOLDKNOPF, DAVID
  The Indian Who Danced in Carnegie Hall. Antioch Review, Summer.
GORDON, ETHEL EDISON
  A Shadow Cast Before. Charm, Jan.
  Leavetaking. Charm, Sept.
  The Climate of Mexico. Charm, Nov.
GOYEN, WILLIAM
  Pore Perrie. Mademoiselle, July.
  Children of Old Somebody. Southwest Review, Summer.
GRAUBART, ROSE
  Sheep in the Meadow. Perspective, Winter.
GREENE, DONALD
  The Adjutant. Atlantic Monthly, Dec.
GREENE, ERNEST S.
  Brother Logan. Intro, Winter.
GROSSMAN, SYLVIA
  The Government's Got a Heart. Antioch Review, Spring.

GUSTAFSON, RALPH
  Helen. New Mexico Quarterly, Winter.
GUTHRIE, A. B., Jr.
  Ebbie. Southwest Review, Spring.

HALE, NANCY
  The Snows of Childhood. New Yorker, March 17.
HALL, JAMES B.
  In The Time of Demonstrations. Western Review, Spring.
  Active Time in Twilight. Furioso, Fall.
HALL, OAKLEY
  The Retaining Wall. Western Review, Autumn.
HALPER, ALBERT
  The Big Slide. Commentary, Dec.
HARNACK, CURT
  Portrait of Sarami. Quarto, Summer.
HARNETT, EDWARD
  Prisoner's Base. Furioso, Summer.
HARRIS, ROSEMARY
  The Storm. Charm, March.
  The Photograph. Charm, Dec.
HARTMAN, CARL
  A Season of Mists. Tomorrow, May.
HAUPT, ZYGMUNT
  La Marseillaise. Perspective, Spring.
HAUSER, MARIANNE
  The Rubber Doll. Mademoiselle, June.
HENDERSON, ROBERT
  The Argonaut. New Yorker, Nov. 3.
HENDERSON, ZENNA
  Come On, Wagon! Fantasy & Science Fiction, Dec.
HENSEL, JAMES
  A Four-Way Love Affair. Today's Woman, Oct.
HERMANN, HELEN MARKEL
  I Gave My Love a Summer. Ladies' Home Journal, Apr.
HIGHET, GILBERT
  Another Solution. Harper's Magazine, Nov.
HONIG, EDWIN
  Report on a Recent Tide. Furioso, Spring.
HORWITZ, JULIUS
  The Generations of Man. Commentary, Sept.
HUBBELL, ALBERT
  The Most Different Summers. Park East, Aug.
HUDSON, THOMAS
  The Hunter. New-Story, Oct.

HUNT, HAMLEN
Now They Bring the Matches. Commentary, Aug.

HUNTER, MICHAEL
We Play the Fool. Atlantic Monthly, Aug.

INGRAM, BOWEN
Tea Dance. Town & Country, Oct.

JACKSON, RALPH H.
Manhood. New-Story, Nov.

JACKSON, SHIRLEY
Mrs. Melville Makes a Purchase. Charm, Oct.

JACOBS, HARV
A Wind Age. Tomorrow, June.

JACOBS, WILLIS D.
Frigolero. Arizona Quarterly, Summer.
King of the Hill. University of Kansas City Review, Summer.

JOHNSON, DUNCAN
Dr. Colley and Dr. Wheeler. Antioch Review, Fall.

JOHNSON, JOSEPHINE W.
The Changeling. Atlantic Monthly, Nov.

JONES, JAMES
Greater Love. Collier's, June 30.
Two Legs for the Two of Us. Esquire, Sept.

JONES, MADISON P., JR.
The Homecoming. Perspective, Autumn.

KAPLAN, H. J.
Anywhere Else. New-Story, July.

KARCHMER, SYLVAN
The Man with Sloping Shoulders. Perspective, Spring.
A Lift to Town. Hopkins Review, Summer.

KASHMANIAN, ARMAND
Withered on the Vine. American Mercury, Aug.

KAYKO, INGEBORG
Floyd. Decade of Short Stories, Summer.

KENNY, HERBERT A.
Thrushagull. A.D., Autumn.

KIKER, DOUGLAS
Somewhere a Little Rain. Yale Review, Winter.

KILCRIN, ISABEL
Katiz and the Cat. Seventeen, Feb.

KLEIN, ALEXANDER
The Pit. New-Story, Sept.

KLEIN, ARTHUR
Like Waves... New-Story, Sept.

KOBER, ARTHUR
Reconciliation in the Bronx. New Yorker, Sept. 1.

KRESH, PAUL
Even in My Lifetime. American Jewish Times-Outlook, Sept.

KRIM, SEYMOUR
Three Pleasures of a Young Chinese. American Mercury, Apr.

KRUGER, FANIA
Sabbath Magic. Southwest Review, Autumn.

LA FARGE, OLIVER
Money To Burn. Argosy, Jan.
The Unbeliever. Town & Country, March.

LAIDLAW, CLARA
The Nest. Prairie Schooner, Winter.

LANE, MARGARET
The Festive Amazon. Harper's Bazaar, March.

LANGFORD, GERALD
Honor Code. Georgia Review, Apr.

LANNING, GEORGE
Aunt Sarna. Northern Review, Aug.–Sept.
News About Miss Painer. Kenyon Review, Autumn.
The Wild Geese. Prairie Schooner, Winter.

LAURILA, S. E.
A Joke on Mr. Scrimpley. Proteus Quarterly, Summer

LEE, LAWRENCE
In the Forests of the Night. Virginia Quarterly Review, Spring.

LINCOLN, VICTORIA
The Snowfield. Harper's Magazine, Oct.

LIVESAY, DOROTHY
The Last Climb. Northern Review, Aug.–Sept.

LORTZ, RICHARD
Logos. New-Story, Oct.

LOVERIDGE, GEORGE
The Cruise. Yale Review, Autumn.

LOWERY, RAYMOND
The Big Back Yard. Phylon, Second Quarter.

LOWREY, H. P.
A Country Life. Accent, Autumn.

LOWRY, ROBERT
It's Dark in Here. Western Review, Autumn.

LURIE, ALISON
Hansel and Gretel. New-Story, Apr.

LYNCH, JOHN A.
The Game. Perspective, Summer.

MacCAULEY, ROBIE
The Thin Voice. Kenyon Review, Winter

MACKEN, WALTER
Parade Day. Collier's, July 14.
MAIN, JONI
Holiday. Prairie Schooner, Fall.
The Front Porch. Husk, Dec.
MALAMUD, BERNARD
The Bill. Commentary, Apr.
An Apology. Commentary, Nov.
MARTIN, PLACIDE
When Only One Is Shining. Sewanee Review, Spring.
MARRIOLT, ANNE
The Ice Forest. The Canadian Forum, March.
MASON, FRANKLIN
When the Horses Came. Hopkins Review, Winter.
MASTERS, CHARLIE
Citizen Martinez. Arizona Quarterly, Autumn.
MASTERS, DEXTER
The Little Visits. New Yorker, Sept. 8.
MAYHALL, JANE
The Miracle. Epoch, Summer.
Leaden Teacups. New-Story, Nov.
The Moment. University of Kansas City Review, Winter.
McCARTHY, MARY
The Groves of Academe. New Yorker, Feb. 3.
McCONNELL, WILLIAM
Raise No Memorial. Northern Review, Dec.–Jan., 1950–1951.
McCOY, ESTHER
Trouble With Philip. Decade of Short Stories, Spring.
McCULLOCH, ELIZABETH
The Kindergarten Chairs. Charm, Sept.
McDONALD, BOYD
Memorium. Southwest Review, Summer.
McDONALD, HELEN F.
Give Us This Day. Pacific Spectator, Spring.
McNULTY, FAITH
Seventeen Storeys Down. Harper's Magazine, Oct.
McNULTY, JOHN
Eleven Dollars a Day. New Yorker, Feb. 3.

MILLER, ARTHUR
Monte Saint Angelo. Harper's Magazine, March.
MILLER, NOLAN
The Only Thing to Do. Antioch Review, Summer.

MOORE, JOHN
Naboth's Vineyard. Charm, Feb.
A Long Day in the Sun. Epoch, Fall.
MORRIS, WRIGHT
The Character of the Lover. American Mercury, Aug.

NEWCOMER, JAMES
The Little People. Southwest Review, Summer.
NEWTON, WESTLY
Rite of Passage. Prairie Schooner, Fall.
NORRIS, HOKE
Chain. Prairie Schooner, Fall.
OGILVIE, ELISABETH
Scobie. Woman's Day, Aug.
OLIVER, CHAD
The Boy Next Door. Fantasy & Science Fiction, June.
OLSON, CHARLES
Stocking Cap. Montevallo Review, Summer.
ORAM, CAROLINE NEILSON
The Cross-Eyed Lady. Town & Country, Nov.
ORLOVITZ, GIL
Tears from a Glass Eye. Intro, Winter.
ORNSTEIN, WILLIAM
Same Line, Old Tune. Wildfire, Jan.–Feb.
Tea on Wednesday. American Jewish Times–Outlook, Jan.
Badge of Honor. American Jewish Times–Outlook, May.
Harold (The Shamus) Klein. American Jewish Times–Outlook, June.
Ocarina Nocturne. American Jewish Times–Outlook, July.
Family Tree. American Hebrew, July 13.
Fun, Feast and Fast. American Jewish Times–Outlook, Sept.
The Apprentice. American Jewish Times–Outlook, Oct.
Eventide Song. American Jewish Times–Outlook, Dec.
The Crime of These Corners. Kansas Magazine, 1951.

PARADISE, JEAN
The Wooden Indian. Epoch, Fall.
PARSONS, ELIZABETH
The Invisible Bridges. Kenyon Review, Summer.
An Empty Box. New Yorker, Dec. 22.
PASCHE, SYLVIE
The Opening Sea. New Yorker, July 21.

PATTON, FRANCES GRAY
Remold It Nearer. New Yorker, March 10.
PERPER, SALLY
The Hands. Decade of Short Stories, Summer.
PEDRICK, JEAN
Never One of Us. Park East, Feb.
PETERS, ASTRID
Honeymoon. New Yorker, July 7.
PETTY, DENISE
The Other Pilgrims. Prairie Schooner, Winter.
PHILLIPS, FREEMAN
Little Nooley's Blues. American Mercury, Apr.
PIERCE, JOHN
The Green Years of Abie Macscale. New-Story, March.
Sam Beasley Won't Come Back No More. New-Story, June.
PIERCE, O. W.
The Shade of the Grave. Southwest Review, Autumn.
POWERS, J. F.
Defection of a Favorite. New Yorker, Nov. 10.
PRESTON, JOHN DUNCAN
A Family Town. Hudson Review, Autumn.
PUTNAM, CLAY
A View of Toledo. Furioso, Fall.

RAYMUND, BERNARD
A Trip to the Corner. Arizona Quarterly, Summer.
REDFORD, GRANT H.
The Day of the Child. Pacific Spectator, Summer.
REINER, MARGRIT
Morning. Masses & Mainstream, March.
RICE, JOHN ANDREW
The Last Maltby. Collier's, August 18.
RICHARDS, CHRIS
The Way I Figure It. Arizona Quarterly Summer.
RISKIN, ROBERT
Tools. Epoch, Fall.
RITER, FAYE
Winter Shadow. University of Kansas City Review, Winter.
ROBERTS, DOROTHY
Hunger. Northern Review, Apr.–May.
ROBERTSON, GEORGE
The Rains That Fall on Gentle Oregon. Tomorrow, Aug.
ROGERS, JEANNE
Melancholy Bait. New-Story, March.

ROSENFELD, EVA
Pillar of a Cloud. Commentary, Feb.
ROSENFELD, ISAAC
In the Monastery. The Kenyon Review, Summer.
ROSOLENKO, HARRY
The Neighbors. New-Story, Apr.
ROTHCHILD, SYLVIA
The Mothers. Commentary, Oct.
RUGEL, MIRIAM
The Medal. Epoch, Summer.

SALINGER, J. D.
Pretty Mouth and Green My Eyes. New Yorker, July 14.
SANKEY, BEN (JR.)
You Lose. The Hopkins Review, Fall.
SARVIS, ISABEL
Jack Knife. Quarto, Summer.
SAUNDERS, JULIET TOUBIN
Stay, Mother. University of Kansas City Review, Spring.
SCHUYLER, JAMES
A Memory Haunts Me. Accent, Summer
SELTZER, CHESTER
Jim Mortimer. Decade of Short Stories, Summer.
SENIOR, EDWARD
Making of the Wine. Prairie Schooner, Winter.
SEWELL, ELIZABETH
The Living Rock. Harper's, July.
SHATRAW, JOANNE
Discipline. Mademoiselle, Aug.
SHEPPERSON, GEORGE
The Obsequies of Lance Corporal Amidu. Phylon, First Quarter.
SHORE, WILMA
The Daring Young Woman, California Quarterly, Autumn.
SINCLAIR, JO
The Angry One. Today's Woman, Oct.
SOBEL, STANFORD
Prognosis Good. Arizona Quarterly, Spring.
SOHMERS, HARRIET
The Nearest Exit. New-Story, Apr.
Snow White. New-Story, Nov.
SOMMERS, DAVID
The Emperor of Ice-Cream. Western Review, Winter.
SPECTOR, HENRY
But After All. Menorah Journal, Spring.
SPETTIGUE, D. O.
Asters for Teddie. Northern Review, June–July.

SPINGARN, LAWRENCE P.
A View of the Harbor. New-Story, Sept.
SPRINGER, NORMAN
A Summer by the Lake. Perspective, Summer.
STACTON, DAVID DEREK
Trip to the Wedding. Decade of Short Stories, Spring.
STEINER, HARRY
Rice. Antioch Review, Fall.
STERLING, PAN
Horses on Far Hills. Woman's Day, Oct.
STOCKWELL, JOSEPH
Beyond Recall. Harper's Magazine, May.
Snake at Noon, Evening's Sorrow.
STONE, LOUISE
Emma and the Sabbath Day. Canadian Forum, May.
STOUTENBERG, ADRIEN
Because You're You. Seventeen, Jan.
STRICKLAND, JACK
Pooch-Old-Boy. Accent, Spring.
STRONG, JOAN
The Big Sea Wall. New Mexico Quarterly, Autumn.
STUART, JESSE
The Devil and Television. American Mercury, Oct.
SULLIVAN, WALTER
Fowling Piece. Georgia Review, Summer.
SWALLOW, ALAN
Golden Girl. New Mexico Quarterly, Summer.

TABAK, MAY NATALIE
Party. Commentary, Jan.
TALMADGE, JOHN E.
The Emancipation of Rufus. Prairie Schooner, Fall.
TARCOV, OSCAR
Multiple Double. Antioch Review, Summer.
TAYLOR, ELIZABETH
Oasis of Gaiety. New Yorker, Aug. 18.
TAYLOR, PETER
What You Hear from 'Em? New Yorker, Feb. 10.
THOMPSON, ROBERT E.
Like a Mountain. Prairie Schooner, Spring.
TRAGER, BRAHNA
Sunday Drive. Pacific SPECTATOR, Autumn.

UHLARIK, CARL
The Myth of Wild Bill Hickok. Prairie Schooner, Summer.

VAN DOREN, MARK
The Quarry. Olivet Quarterly, Summer.
VAN GHENT, DOROTHY
The Bridal. Western Review, Spring.

WAGNER, ELIOT L.
The Straw Hat. Commentary, June.
WALLER, LESLIE
The Last Fix. Cosmopolitan, Nov.
WANKLYN, CHRISTOPHER
The Flight of the Swan. New-Story, Nov.
WEAVER, WILLIAM FENSE
The Omen. New-Story, June.
WEIS, MARTIN L.
The Heart Is a Desert. Arizona Quarterly, Spring.
WEISBERG, BRENDA
Run No More. Collier's, Jan. 27.
WELD, ART
The Cell. New-Story, June.
WELTY, EUDORA
The Burning. Harper's Bazaar, March
WEST, JESSAMYN
Love, Death and the Ladies' Drill Team. New Yorker, Sept. 22.
WESTON, CHRISTINE
A Day in Spring. New Yorker, May 5.
WILLEN, GERALD
English Is a Culture Course. Perspective, Summer.
WILLINGHAM, CALDER
Graveyard in Brooklyn. American Mercury, Dec.
WILSON, ETHEL
The Funeral Home. Northern Review, Apr.–May.
WILSON, SLOAN
The Alarm Clock. New Yorker, Feb. 24.
The Powder Keg. New Yorker, Oct. 27.
The Black Mollies. Harper's Magazine, Dec.
WIMBERLY, LOWRY C.
The Catch. American Mercury, May.
WINSLOW, ANNE GOODWIN
Her Place. Virginia Quarterly Review, Spring.
Highborn Kinsmen. Harper's Magazine, Nov.
WITT, HAROLD V.
Love Among the Ruins, Arizona Quarterly, Spring.
Francis. Prairie Schooner, Spring.
Walnuts. Quarto, Summer.
WOHL, SAM
The Dream Lover. The Hopkins Review, Summer.

WOLFE, BERNARD
Jose Schenck, Reverse the Charges. American Mercury, July.
WOOLF, DOUGLAS,
The Imaginative Present. New Mexico Quarterly. Spring.
The Cure. Perspective, Winter.

WRIGHT, THOMAS
The Blue Shawl. The Hopkins Review, Fall.
YAMAMOTO, HISAYE
The Brown House. Harper's Bazaar, Oct.
YOUNG, NARCELLA
The Home Place. Canadian Forum, Nov.

II. Foreign Authors

BOWEN, ELIZABETH
So Much Depends. Woman's Day, Sept.

CLARKE, DESMOND
The Drunkards. Prairie Schooner, Winter.
CLOETE, STUART
The Writing on the Wall. Town and Country, May.
COLLIER, JOHN
Are You Too Late or Was I Too Early? New Yorker, Apr. 14.
Interpretation of a Dream. New Yorker, May 5.
The Lady on the Gray. New Yorker, June 16.

DAHL, ROALD
Taste. New Yorker, Dec. 8.
DE POLNAY, PETER
The Horseman and the Red Brick House. Tomorrow, July.
DINESEN, ISAK
The Ghost Horses. Ladies' Home Journal, Oct.

FORD, DONALD
Idyll. New-Story, June.

GONZALEZ, N. V. M.
Where's My Baby Now? The Hopkins Review, Spring.
GORDIMER, NADINE
A Watcher of the Dead. New Yorker, June 9.
The Hour and the Years. Yale Review, Winter
GROSSMAN, VASILI
Triumph of Life. Masses & Mainstream, June.

HOPKINSON, TOM
The Man Who Crossed Gaps. Harper's Bazaar, Nov.
HUGHES, RICHARD
Justice. New Yorker, Sept. 29.

HUXLEY, ALDOUS
Time's Revenges. Esquire, Oct.

KOVAL, ALEXANDER (Trans. by Edouard Roditi.)
The Letters of Sebastian Schirkmaker. University of Kansas City Review, Summer.

LUCEY, MICHAIL
Magic Glassy Alleys Should Not Be Buried. New-Story, Apr.

MACKEN, WALTER
Parade Day. Collier's, July 14.
MACMAHON, BRIAN
The Pyrrhic Victory. Town & Country, Dec.
MARCUS, DAVID
Symphony No. 1. New-Story, July.
MOORE, JOHN
Naboth's Vineyard. Charm, Feb.

NORTON, MARY
The Girl in the Corner. Woman's Day, July.

O'BRIEN, TERENCE
Fingle Bears Like Very Soft Things. American Mercury, Feb.
O'CONNOR, FRANK
What Girls Are For. Collier's, March 17.

PEARSON, BILL
Babes in the Bush. New-Story, May.
Indemnity. New-Story, July.

RAMA RAU, SANTHA
By Any Other Name. New Yorker, March 17.
ROE, IVAN
The Woman of the South. Mademoiselle, March.

SANCHEZ, JOSE M. (Trans. by Genevieve Stenger)
A Necessary Explanation. Western Review, Winter.

SEWELL, ELIZABETH
The Living Rock. Harper's Magazine, July.

STIRLING, MONICA
The Village Schoolmistress. New-Story, May.
It's Later Than You Think. Atlantic Monthly, July.
Adventurers Please Abstain. New-Story, Oct.

STIVENS, DAL
The Pepper Tree. Masses & Mainstream, Nov.

SYMONDS, JOHN
A Woman's Love. New-Story, May.

TABORI, GEORGE
D. P. California Quarterly, Autumn

THOMAS, GWYN
Where My Dark Lover Lies. California Quarterly, Autumn.

WARNER, SYLVIA TOWNSEND
Hee-Haw! New Yorker, May.

WILLIAMS, WINIFRED
Ward Number Seven. Jan.
Visiting Day. New Yorker, Apr. 14.

ADDRESSES OF AMERICAN AND CANADIAN
MAGAZINES PUBLISHING SHORT STORIES

Accent, Box 102, University Station, Urbana, Illinois
A. D., 109 Greenwich Avenue, New York City
Adventure, 205 East 42nd Street, New York City
American Hebrew, 48 West 48th Street, New York City
American-Jewish Times Outlook, 603–4 Southeastern Bldg., Greensboro, North Carolina
American Magazine, 250 Park Avenue, New York City
American Mercury, 251 West 42nd Street, New York City
Antioch Review, 212 Xenia Avenue, Yellow Springs, Ohio
Argosy, 205 East 42nd Street, New York City
Arizona Quarterly, University of Arizona, Tucson, Arizona
Atlantic Monthly, 8 Arlington Street, Boston, Massachusetts
Blue Book, 444 Madison Avenue, New York City
California Quarterly, 7070 Hollywood Boulevard, Los Angeles, California
Canadian Forum, 16 Huntley Street, Toronto, Ontario, Canada
Canadian Home Journal, Richmond and Sheppard Streets, Toronto Ontario, Canada
Carolina Quarterly, Box 1117, Chapel Hill, North Carolina
Catholic World, 411 West 59th Street, New York City
Charm, 575 Madison Avenue, New York City
Chatelaine, 481 University Avenue, Toronto, Ontario, Canada
Chicago Review, Reynolds Club, University of Chicago, Chicago, Illinois
Collier's, 250 Park Avenue, New York City
Commentary, 34 West 33rd Street, New York City
Commonweal, 386 Fourth Avenue, New York City
Compact, 52 Vanderbilt Avenue, New York City
Comprehension, 1010 Bush Street, San Francisco, California
Cosmopolitan, 57th Street and Eighth Avenue, New York City
Country Gentleman, Independence Square, Philadelphia, Pennsylvania
Decade of Short Stories, 20915 Vanowen Street, Canoga Park, California
Elks Magazine, 50 East 42nd Street, New York City
Ellery Queen's Mystery Magazine, 570 Lexington Avenue, New York City
Epoch, 252 Goldwin Smith Hall, Cornell University, Ithaca, New York
Esquire, 366 Madison Avenue, New York City
Everywoman's, 31 West 47th Street, New York City
Family Circle, 25 West 45th Street, New York City
Fantasy and Science Fiction, 570 Lexington Avenue, New York City
Four Quarters, La Salle College, Philadelphia, Pennsylvania
Furioso, Carleton College, Northfield, Minnesota
Georgia Review, University of Georgia, Athens, Georgia
Good Housekeeping, 57th Street and Eighth Avenue, New York City
Hairenik Weekly, 212 Stuart Street, Boston, Massachusetts
Harper's Bazaar, 572 Madison Avenue, New York City
Harper's Magazine, 49 East 33rd Street, New York City
Holiday, Independence Square, Philadelphia, Pennsylvania
Holland's Magazine, 3306 Main Street, Dallas, Texas
Hopkins Review, Box 1227, Johns Hopkins University, Baltimore, Maryland
Household, Topeka, Kansas
Hudson Review, 439 West Street, New York City
Husk, Cornell College, Mount Vernon, Iowa
Interim, Box 24, Parrington Hall, University of Washington, Seattle, Washington
Intro, Box 860, Grand Central Station, New York City

Jewish Forum, 305 Broadway, New York City
Jewish Life, 35 East 12th Street, New York City
Kansas Magazine, Box 237, Kansas State College, Manhattan, Kansas
Kenyon Review, Kenyon College, Gambier, Ohio
Ladies' Home Journal, Independence Square, Philadelphia, Pennsylvania
MacLean's, 481 University Avenue, Toronto, Ontario, Canada
Mademoiselle, 575 Madison Avenue, New York City
Masses & Mainstream, 832 Broadway, New York City
Matrix, Box 757, Pleasanton, California
McCall's, 230 Park Avenue, New York City
Minorah Journal, 20 East 69th Street, New York City
Montevallo Review, Alabama College, Montevallo, Alabama
Neurotica, 143 West 53rd Street, New York City
New Mexico Quarterly, Box 85, University of New Mexico, Albuquerque, New Mexico
New-Story, 6 Boulevard Poissonnière, Paris, France
New Yorker, 25 West 43rd Street, New York City
Northern Review, 2475 Van Horne Avenue, Montreal, Quebec, Canada
Olivet Quarterly, Olivet College, Olivet, Michigan
Pacific Spectator, Box 1948, Stanford, California
Park East, 220 East 42nd Street, New York City
Partisan Review, 30 West 12th Street, New York City
Perspective, Washington University Post Office, St. Louis, Missouri
Phylon, Atlanta University, Atlanta, Georgia
Prairie Schooner, 12th and R Streets, Lincoln, Nebraska
Protocol, 134 Campbell Avenue, St. John's, Newfoundland, Canada
Quarterly Review of Literature, Box 287, Bard College, Annandale-on-Hudson, New York
Quarto, 801 Business, Columbia University, New York City
Queen's Quarterly, Queen's University, Kingston, Ontario, Canada
Redbook, 230 Park Avenue, New York City
Saturday Evening Post, Independence Square, Philadelphia, Pennsylvania
Seventeen, 488 Madison Avenue, New York City
Sewanee Review, The University of the South, Sewanee, Tennessee
Short Stories, 9 Rockefeller Plaza, New York City
Southwest Review, Southern Methodist University, Dallas, Texas
This Week, 420 Lexington Avenue, New York City
Today's Woman, 67 West 44th Street, New York City
Town and Country, 572 Madison Avenue, New York City
University of Kansas City Review, University of Kansas City, Kansas City, Missouri
Virginia Quarterly Review, One West Range, Charlottesville, Virginia
Wake, 18 East 198th Street, New York City
Weird Tales, 9 Rockefeller Plaza, New York City
Western Review, State University of Iowa, Iowa City, Iowa
Woman's Day, 19 West 44th Street, New York City
Woman's Home Companion, 250 Park Avenue, New York City
Yale Review, Box 1729, New Haven, Connecticut
Yankee, Dublin, New Hampshire